I0608594

Forged in Fire

Heir to the Firstborn, Volume 2

Elizabeth Schechter

Published by Elizabeth Schechter, 2020.

Forged in Fire

Published by Raven's Wing Books

Previously published as **Forged in Fire** (Elizabeth Schechter, 2020)

Editor: Michael Schechter
Cover design by GetCovers

Raven's Wing Books

ravens-wing-books.com
ISBN:9781393542841

Table of Contents

CHAPTER ONE

THERE WERE A LOT OF things Aven didn't know about living on land. He knew that. He accepted that, just as he accepted the fact that he knew so little about living on land that what he did know was dwarfed by the many, many things that he didn't know. Not to mention the things that he didn't know that he didn't know. Ignorance was annoying.

There was, however, one thing that he could have done without learning.

Falling off a horse *hurts*!

He sprawled in the dusty road, glaring up at the horse that seemed to be studying him with placid confusion. The horse was a mare, Memfis had told him, and docile enough for a novice rider. Her name was Cloud, and she stood over Aven, as if to ask, "What are you doing down there? I thought we were past that."

"Aven?" Owyn had turned his horse and came back down the road. "Are you all right? What happened?"

Aven slowly got to his feet, grumbling. "I'm fine. Just bruised, I think." He caught Cloud's dangling reins. She snorted and rubbed her nose against his sleeve, and he scratched the star on her forehead. "I'll be sore later, but it's not the first time."

Owyn didn't look convinced. "You haven't fallen off in days. Are you sure you're all right?"

Memfis joined them, leading Aria's horse and their packhorse. He drew his big horse up next to Cloud, studied Aven, then said, "You fell asleep, didn't you?"

Aven looked down as his face warmed. That was exactly what had happened. "I think so," he answered.

Memfis nodded. "You've been looking a little drawn since we moved out of the trees and we had to put the hammock away. Still having trouble sleeping on the ground?"

"It was fine the first two nights," Aven said. "Last night, though?" He shrugged. "Not sure why—" His voice trailed off as Aria circled low and landed on the road nearby.

"Why did you stop?" she asked as she joined them, tossing her dark braids back over her shoulder. "Is something wrong?"

"Aven just learned it takes skill to sleep on a horse," Memfis answered. "He's not broken." He looked around. "Did you see anything?"

Aria shook her head. "We're still not being followed. Nor do I see any structure that's not a ruin."

Memfis swore softly. They'd been on the road ten days, and their supplies were starting to run low. "I had no idea things were this bad outside Forge," he said. He gestured widely, taking in the brown and barren fields around them. "The last time I rode this way at this time of year, this was farmland. These fields were ready for the harvest."

"When was that?" Owyn asked. "Because there have been food shortages in Forge since I was still on the streets."

Memfis grumbled, then nodded. "Point made. It's been too long. But you'd think that this sort of thing would be more widely known—"

"It is," Owyn interrupted. "When you have to make the choice about paying for a roof over your head, or paying for a meal? It's known. Food prices have been going up and up for a long time now.

Best meal I ever had was the first one under your roof, Mem. When you've always had coin, you don't notice as much how expensive things are getting. Especially when it creeps up a little at a time."

Memfis' frown deepened. "I thought I was paying better attention than that. I thought I was keeping an eye on things."

"In Forge, you were," Aria said. "But if, as you said, all of the news wasn't getting to Forge? What would you have done differently?"

Memfis nodded. "That doesn't change the fact that I should have paid better attention." He looked around. "I've been keeping my head down, waiting for you all. But that means I haven't seen what's been happening outside my own walls."

"We'll be all right, Mem," Owyn said. "How much further to the healing center?"

Memfis looked up at the sky, then down the road. He shook his head. "Three, maybe four days. But we're low on supplies. That dead village we rode through two days ago was supposed to be where we resupplied."

"Can we hunt?" Aven asked. "Aria, have you seen any game at all?"

"I've seen very little game from up high, but I was paying more attention to looking for hunters," Aria answered. "Regardless, if there's nothing for game to eat, there's no game for us to eat."

Memfis frowned. He looked around. Then he nodded. "Aven, mount up. I know where we'll spend the night tonight. It's a bit out of the way, but it'll be safe and we'll be able to hunt."

"It's still early, though," Owyn protested. "We got a lot of ground to cover."

"We're stopping early," Memfis said, in a voice that brooked no argument. "And we need to figure out what our next step will be. I've been running on faulty information. We need to rethink. I need to rethink. No. No, I need to think, and properly plan, and that was never something I was any good at. Aria, ride with us a little."

Aria nodded. She went to Aven's side and slipped her arm around his waist. "Are you sure you're all right?" she asked.

"I'm fine," Aven answered, putting his arm around her and pulling her close. "Just tired. And now a little sore."

"We need to get you used to sleeping on the ground," Owyn said. "We can't always use the hammock. You want to ride with me a bit? You can nap, and I can keep you from falling again."

"I appreciate it, but I'm awake now," Aven answered. He sighed and shook his head, reaching for his water skin. The warm, salty water tasted good, and he drank deeply before sealing the bottle and slinging it from his saddle. "All right. Let's go."

Aria kissed his cheek, then went and mounted her own horse. Aven smothered a yawn and hauled himself back into Cloud's saddle.

"Where are we going?" he called.

"Someplace where you might just be able to get a full night's sleep," Memfis answered. He led them down the road, then onto what looked to be a rarely used trail that branched off from the northern road, veering west. Owyn guided his horse alongside Cloud, riding knee to knee with Aven.

"You're sure—"

"I'm fine, Mouse," Aven said with a laugh. "A little bruised is all."

"You can fix that, though," Owyn said. "Right?"

"No," Aven answered. "Have to let it heal on its own."

"What?" Aria brought her horse up on his other side. "Why? Why should you be uncomfortable?"

"Because healers can't work on themselves," Aven answered. "I'm not entirely sure what would happen. I asked my father once, and all he said was 'Don't even think of it.' He called it Healer Rule One. So I'm guessing it's bad."

Owyn grimaced. "That could get ugly, couldn't it?" he asked. "Healing power gone very, very wrong?"

"What was it you said, back in Forge? Six heads and no ears?" Aven grinned. "I don't think it would be that bad, but I'm guessing that the wounds wouldn't heal right. So I'll be purple from my hip to my shoulder for a few days. I've had worse."

"I like purple," Aria said, softly enough that Aven wasn't sure anyone but him heard it.

Until Owyn snorted and added, "Me, too."

Aven looked at Aria, at her small smile and high color. Then he glanced at Owyn, who was grinning. No, no, the other man wasn't grinning. He was leering.

Well, they had been on the road for ten days, traveling constantly, and had no privacy to speak of. Aven snickered and shook his head.

"You both can take a nice, close look later," he said. Aria giggled, which started Aven and Owyn both laughing. Memfis glanced back at them, shook his head, and kept riding.

THE TRAIL LED NORTH and west, and gradually down, and long before they could see it, Aven could smell salt water.

"Memfis, are we camping tonight near the sea?" he called.

"You'll see," Memfis called back. "The trail is going to get steep. Go slow, and single file, and let your horse pick her footing."

Aven frowned, looking at Owyn. "Do you know where we're going?"

"Not a clue," Owyn answered. "I've never been more than a mile outside Forge before. This is all new to me, too. When we get onto the trail, lean back. It'll help. And let the reins go loose. Cloud and Star will follow Memfis and Dasher."

It did help, but Aven still felt as if his horse was going to slip and tumble all the way down the steep high-walled trail. It turned sharply, then turned again. "Owyn?"

"It's all right," Owyn called from behind and above him. He was at the rear of the line, following Aria. "It's a switchback. Keeps it from being too steep. The trail to the coal yards is like this. Worse, because you have to do that one with a cart."

"I do not want to do something like this in a cart," Aria called out. "Or on a horse. There is a reason I have wings."

"It's not bad," Owyn said. "Just let Star and Cloud do the work."

Aven clung to his saddle-horn and tried to trust that Cloud wasn't going to fall, but it was hard. He thought about closing his eyes and waiting for it to be over, but decided that, if he was going to fall to a certain death, he wanted to be able to see it. Another sharp turn led to another trail that seemed to turn almost immediately, as Memfis vanished from view. Then Cloud took the turn, and Aven saw the sea for the first time since he and Aria arrived in Forge.

The trail opened out into a cove — seaside plants gave way to a white sand beach. Small waves kissed the shore with the crash and hiss that was almost as welcome to Aven as his parents' voices would have been. He tore his gaze from the water to see that Memfis had dismounted, and was leading Dasher over. He took hold of Cloud's bridle and grinned up at Aven.

"Were you waiting for an invitation?" he asked. Aven gaped at him, then looked back at the water.

"I can swim?" he asked. "I can change?"

"Go on. Just bring something up to eat."

Aven swung down from his saddle and started toward the water. It felt strange to be walking on sand and not feeling it, so he stopped and tugged his boots off, leaving them where they fell. He stopped at the high water line in the sand, and started to unbuckle the harness that held his swords.

"Are you not going to wait for us?" Aria called. Aven turned and saw her and Owyn coming toward him.

"Are you going to swim?" Aven asked. He laid his swords down on the sand, then took off his carry-bag and his vest. "Owyn, do you want me to teach you?"

"Nah, you go ahead and hunt. I'll watch," Owyn said. "Memfis is going to take care of the horses, so someone has to stay on watch. That'll be me."

Aria laughed. "But what will you be watching? The trail, or us?"

"I never said I was going to watch the trail," Owyn answered, and Aven laughed.

"Aven, go on," Aria said. "Go be in the deep."

"Don't leave the cove!" Memfis shouted. "Not unless you have to in order to hunt!"

"I'll need something to hunt with," Aven said, stopping as he was about to strip off his trousers. "Aria, may I borrow one of your javelins? It's close enough to my fishing spear."

"Of course!" Aria ran up the beach to where Memfis was taking the tack off their horses. She came back carrying one of the short javelins that Memfis had given her. They were one of the weapons of choice of the Air tribe, and Aria had shown herself to be skilled with them when there was still game that they could hunt. Aven folded his trousers and laid them aside, then accepted both the javelin and a kiss from Aria.

"Do I get one, too?" Owyn asked. Aven grinned. He leaned down and kissed Owyn, then turned and headed out into the water.

OWYN WATCHED AS AVEN dove in and vanished. The sight made him slightly nauseous, but he wasn't going to show it. Not in front of Aria. He turned back to her and blinked — she had reached up to unfasten the buttons across her shoulders.

"Want help?" he offered. "And you're going into the water?"

"It's the closest thing to a bath we have," she answered. She knelt in the sand so that he could more easily reach; once the panel was unfastened, she took off the wrapped jacket and bent to take off her boots. "And to tell the truth, I miss swimming with him. He's beautiful in his sea form, Owyn."

"Will I be able to see it?" Owyn asked. "From here?"

"You could come closer to the water," Aria said. "Or... those rocks, over there? Let's go there. You can stay on the rocks and watch from there. You'll be able to see more. I will swim, then I will join you on the rocks. And when he comes up, it will be a good place for Aven to change."

Owyn looked where she was pointing. The rocks looked as if they'd tumbled from the top of the high cliffs that curved around one side of the cove, and formed a jagged platform that extended out into the water. It looked solid enough. He didn't need to go far. And the water certainly couldn't be that deep — the end of the rockfall wasn't that far from shore....

"All right," he said slowly. "That doesn't look too bad."

Aria kissed his cheek and waded out into the water. Once she was facing away from him, Owyn took a deep breath and rubbed his hands on his thighs — his palms were sweat-sodden. He swallowed, then headed for the rocks.

It wasn't as bad as he'd feared. The rocks were close enough to the shore that walking on them wasn't much different from walking on some of the areas of cracked and broken pavement in the poorer areas of Forge. As he got farther out, he could almost imagine he was climbing over rocks at the coal fields. Almost. There wasn't a cold water spray from waves crashing on the rocks at the coal fields. He tried not to think about it, looking at where Aria was splashing in the water. She'd combed out her long braids, and her wet hair clung to her skin. There was water dripping from her feathers.

"Can you fly with wet wings?" he called.

"Not well, but I should not need to," she called back. "And I will come up there and sun them dry." She smiled up at him. "I will not stay in the water too long. It's cold. You can tell that it's late in the year and winter is coming. In the mountains, it would be snowing already. Does it snow here?"

"Snow? Only once in a while. Not often. Mostly it rains here in the winter. It doesn't get cold enough to snow. What we do get probably isn't anything like what you get in the mountains." Owyn said. He moved to the center of one of the large rocks and crouched on his heels. "It's nice and warm up here on the rocks. Shouldn't take you long to get warm and dry. How long will he be out there, do you think?"

Aria dunked herself under the water, then swam toward the rocks and climbed up onto them. "As long as it takes for him to catch something," she offered. "Although I think we may have a hard time getting him to come out of the water. I can fly whenever I wish. He can only be his true self in the deep." She stretched out on her stomach next to Owyn, spreading her wings wide and pillowing her head on her arms. "The days we were out on the canoe, between when we left the island and when we first saw Mannon's ships, those were good days. He taught me to swim, and we played in the water. Aven taught me to clean fish, and to eat oysters from the shell. His family treated me as if I were one of their own, and we were happy. Since we reached Forge, there's been a tension to him, like a bowstring pulled too tight. I worry that he might snap. This will help." She looked up at him and smiled. "You help."

"Do I?" Owyn murmured.

"You share the weight. It will be easier, when we find the others, I think." Aria closed her eyes and sighed. "The sun feels good."

Owyn looked at her, admiring the lines of her, the curve of her back down to her waist, and the sweet, soft flare of her hips to her arse. She'd told both Aven and him that she wouldn't have sex with either of them until she was sure that she would not come away pregnant. He admired her restraint — he didn't think he'd have been able to say no. Not when faced with two people who both adored him and who were willing to do whatever it took to make him happy. He closed his eyes, remembering the big bed back in Meris' house, being in Aven's arms, with Aria touching them both. He'd stopped them then, before they'd gone too far, because he wasn't sure that his need was his own, or the remnants of the drugs he'd been fed. Now he regretted it.

He heard Aria gasp, and looked up in time to see the long, sinuous form arch out of the water. Aven's tail gleamed in the sun, looking like molten silver as he dove back down into the water. Aria burst out laughing.

"Did you see him?" she asked. "Isn't he beautiful?"

"Yeah," Owyn breathed, and shifted, trying to ease the ache in his groin.

He was definitely regretting stopping now.

CHAPTER TWO

AVEN REAPPEARED, AND swam toward the shore. Owyn hadn't noticed Memfis standing near the edge, not until his adopted father waded into the water and took a long string of fish and the javelin from Aven. He waved one hand toward the rocks; Aven smiled. He waved, then disappeared. Owyn leaned forward, seeing a flash of silver in the water. Then Aven surfaced at the base of the rocks. He pulled himself up out of the water, onto the lowest of the tumbled rocks. Then he made a face.

"Oh," Aria laughed. "He can't get up here. We should go down."

"Down?" Owyn echoed. "Down, closer to the water, down?" He swallowed. "I..."

"Owyn, what's wrong?" Aria rested her hand on his shoulder. "You've gone pale."

"I... don't like the water, is all," he said, trying to control the shaking in his voice. "I'll wait here."

Aria touched his cheek and looked into his eyes. Without turning, she raised her voice, "We'll wait for you here, Aven."

Owyn looked away, and saw Aven's eyes had widened. "You've gone and worried him," he said softly.

"That's only fair," Aria answered. "You've worried me."

Owyn looked back at her. "Because I don't like water?"

"You were fine in the baths," Aria said. "But you do not swim, and you will not go near the sea. You're frightened, and we can both see it."

"It's... it's nothing," Owyn stammered. He shook his head, pulling away from Aria and getting up. "It's really nothing. I'm going back to shore—"

"Stay."

The word was croaked, the voice unrecognizable. Owyn saw Aven frowning at him. He pointed at Owyn, then at the rock. Then he raised his brows. The message was clear; Owyn stuck his tongue out at Aven and sat down, then laughed when Aven nodded.

"He can't talk yet, right?" he asked Aria. When she nodded, he frowned, thinking about his reading. "The Waterborn, they can't talk when they're changed. That's the trade-off, the books say. They go underwater, they give up their voices. So how do they communicate underwater? What do they do?"

"You'll have to ask him," Aria said. "I never asked." She pressed against his side, sliding one arm around his back. "It will be a few minutes before he has changed enough to climb up. Relax. No one is asking you to go into the water. You're safe here with me." She rested her head on his shoulder, her wet hair making his shirt damp. He hesitated for a moment, then put his arm around her and pulled her closer.

"You're cold," he said. "You should put something on."

"This isn't cold to me," Aria replied. "And if I went to put something on, then I would leave you alone. That is something I am not willing to do. I can wait."

Owyn smiled, looking over at Aven. The silver and pearl scales were fading back to olive skin, but his legs hadn't separated yet. All at once, Owyn understood Aven's discomfort about wearing trousers.

"We need to get him back into a kilt as soon as we can," he said softly. "Trousers aren't fair to him."

"Once we reach the healing center, perhaps he will be able to wear what he wishes," Aria murmured. "It should be safe enough. Do you smell something?"

Owyn nodded, looking back toward shore. There was a fire burning, and Memfis was doing... something. "Looks like Mem is cook tonight."

"Memfis is a good cook," Aria said. "Aven, can you speak yet?'

"Almost," Aven answered, his voice sounding almost normal. "I'll climb up in a minute."

"What did you bring up?"

"I'm not sure," Aven admitted. "They're not fish I'm familiar with. They look like moon-fish, but they're not the same color."

"They smell good, whatever they are," Owyn said. He looked down at Aven, cocking his head to the side. "What does it feel like?"

Aven looked puzzled. He looked down at his legs, then back up at Owyn. "Normal?"

Owyn grinned. "Right. Stupid question."

"Not a stupid question, Mouse," Aven corrected. "I just can't answer it. I don't have anything to compare it to." He said up and ran his hands down his legs, rotating his ankles. "I have feet again," he said, and got up. He climbed up the rocks and sat down on Owyn's other side, pressing against him. He leaned down and kissed Owyn, then stretched across and kissed Aria. "Now, explain. You looked a lot like you did in your grandmother's garden, when Fandor showed up."

"I wasn't that bad!" Owyn protested. He scowled down at his hands, then sighed. "What do you know about being a Smoke Dancer?"

"Nothing," Aven replied immediately. "You don't talk about it. None of you talk about it. All I really know is you do something with smoke blades."

Owyn snorted. "I'll show you. Later. And... Aria, did Mem tell you about the waking vision yet?"

Aria nodded, her expression somber. "He explained."

Owyn looked back out at the water. "The waking vision... I had mine about a month after Mem took me in. Woke up screaming, which was impressive, because I was convinced I couldn't breathe." He forced his gaze from the sea and turned to look at Aven. There was deep concern in the Waterborn's hazel eyes. "The first vision that a Smoke Dancer has is how they are going to die."

Aven blinked, and his jaw dropped. He looked horrified. "You... that's horrible!"

"It's the trade-off," Owyn said. "You trade your voice for your tail, and you can heal anyone but yourself. That's the price of the gift. The price of visions is knowing when your end is coming." He nodded toward the sea. "That's my end. I drown. Someday. Dunno when. There wasn't much in the way of time hints. Just... water. Lots and lots of salt water. I mean, I could taste it." He closed his eyes, remembering being unable to move, the weight on his chest, struggling to breathe...

Abruptly, he was being lifted to his feet. He jerked, staring at Aven. He hadn't felt Aven move.

"What?"

"We're going to shore," Aven said. "And I won't ask you again about teaching you to swim." He looked past Owyn. "Take his other arm?"

Owyn snorted, trying to pull his arm away from Aven. "I don't need to be carried. I can walk!" he protested. Aven ignored him. So did Aria, taking his other arm, and they escorted him off the rocks and away from the water. Memfis stood by the fire, watching them.

"Something I should know about?" he asked as they came closer.

Owyn finally managed to pull his arms free. He glared up at Aven, who just grinned at him. Then he turned back to Memfis. "I told them about my waking vision."

"Oh," Memfis breathed. "I see. You know, it might not be a bad idea to let Aven teach you to swim. I'd like to put that particular vision off as long as possible."

Owyn looked back at Aven, who shook his head. "I said I wasn't going to ask you again," he said. "And I'm not. If you ask me, though, I won't say no."

"I'm not going to ask," Owyn said. He shuddered. "I'm just not going anywhere near the water. It's not like I have to go out on a boat or anything, right?" Aven nodded and walked away, heading down the beach toward the pile of his clothes. Owyn frowned. "He's not angry at me, is he?"

"No," Aria answered. "I think he's more worried for you. I think Memfis is right. But it has to be your decision." She sighed and rested her cheek on his shoulder. "He is a good teacher."

"I said no," Owyn answered. For a long moment, the only sounds were the waves and the crackling of the fire. Then Aven came back up the beach. He had put on his trousers, but was carrying everything else.

"Owyn, I was curious," he said. "When you used the whip chain to fight Fandor, some of the movements looked very similar to how I use my hook swords."

Owyn blinked. "Really?"

Aven nodded. "Would you show me? And your smoke blades? My mother told me that she was learning to dance with the smoke blades, and she was teaching Milon to use hook swords."

Owyn nodded, started to turn to where their packs were stacked, then turned back. "Mem, is that all right? I can show him?"

"There are no rules against it," Memfis answered. "And he's right. Milon was teaching Aleia. So go ahead." He looked around. "Aria, put some clothes on and help me? Or do you want to see more about the smoke blades?"

"I should learn more about Smoke Dancing," Aria said.

"But you should still put some clothes on," Owyn called as he went to the packs and picked up his blades. When he turned back, Aria was looking quizzically at him. He grinned. "You're distracting."

She laughed, and went to collect her clothes. As she dressed, Aven looked around.

"The sand between the tide line and the water will probably be the best place to do this," he suggested. "The wet sand is more compact, better for your footing."

Owyn looked down the beach and nodded. The space of dark, wet sand was wide, and fairly level. And at worst, he'd get his ankles wet. "All right," he agreed. "I'll show you. Then you can show me."

To his surprise, Aven snickered. "I thought we already did 'I'll show you mine if you show me yours,'" he said, and Aria giggled.

"That's later," Owyn answered. Aven grinned.

"You said you can fight with these?" Aria said as they walked down to the darker sands.

"I haven't yet, but yeah," Owyn answered. "They're deceptive. By the time your brain registers where the blade is, it's not there anymore. I'll show you. Aven, take Trinket?"

Aven took the fire mouse from Owyn, and he and Aria both sat on the soft, dry sand on the far side of the border of dried seaweed that marked the tide line. Owyn tugged off his boots and walked further down to the wet sand, feeling the cold water between his toes. As Aven had said, it was better footing than the dry sand and he nodded slowly to himself as he started to spin his left-hand blade. He was far enough from the water's edge that he could ignore it.

"Will it be anything like the whip chain?" Aven asked. "Will they disappear as you move?"

"No," Owyn answered. "Just watch." He took a deep breath through his nose, blowing it out his mouth. He did it again. Then he started to move, flowing into the smoke dance. The slow, graceful movements always reminded him of molten rock, or liquid metal as it was poured into a mold, and they did something for Owyn that nothing else ever could. They quieted his ever-racing thoughts, until all that was left in his mind was stillness. Nothing else that he'd ever tried had ever done that. Not strong alcohol, or narcotics, or sleep, or even sex. It was only when he was dancing, either in practice or seeking visions in the vents, that his mind quieted, that the constant chatter of his thoughts finally ceased. The better, Memfis had told him, for the visions to flow.

But the visions had never taken him outside the vents. So when one washed over him, he was completely unprepared, and fell into it completely.

AVEN WAS WATCHING CLOSELY, comparing Owyn's movements to his own when he danced the hook blades. Admiring the play of muscles in Owyn's back and chest and arms, and the simple, fluid grace with which he moved. So he saw the moment where Owyn stopped dancing and started falling, and scrambled to his feet.

"Memfis!" he shouted, and dashed to where Owyn had landed. He had dropped like a discarded doll, and lay sprawled on the wet sand, his smoke blades lying on either side of him. Aven reached for him, only to jump at Memfis' shout.

"Don't touch him!" Memfis ran up to them. "He's caught a vision. He'll come out of it in a minute. Just leave him."

"Caught a vision?" Aven repeated. "Don't you need smoke for that?"

Memfis took a deep breath and picked up the smoke blades. "Not always. Being in the vents helps — the smoke makes the visions stronger. But stronger Smoke Dancers just need the dance. I don't need to be in the vents. Neither did Milon. And Aria's never been in the vents, either."

"Then why did Owyn offer to dance for us," Aria asked. "If it would take him like this?" She knelt in the sand next to Owyn, her hands clasped in her lap. To keep herself from touching him, Aven realized.

"Owyn's never had a vision outside the vents before," Memfis answered. "He may not have realized that he was strong enough to do it. I certainly didn't realize it, and he's danced outside the vents for me ever since he started learning." He frowned. "Something has changed."

"What?" Aven asked. He looked up at Memfis, then back down at Owyn. "No, I know."

"Us?" Aria asked. Aven nodded.

"He changed because of us," Aven agreed. "Because of you." He smiled. "We both did."

"You pushed him to be the man he needed to be, back in the Heart of the Tribe," Memfis said. He crouched down to sit on his heels. "He'd never have faced down Fandor before. This is one serious vision. They're not usually this long. Aria, Owyn should have packed a bag. Did you see it? Blue, with a book and a box in it?"

"I think so, yes," Aria answered. "Is it important?"

"He'll want it when he wakes up," Memfis said. As if on cue, Owyn groaned and shifted. Then gasped and scrambled up to his hands and knees.

"It's all right, Mouse," Memfis said softly. "You're safe."

"And wet," Owyn sputtered. "Safe and wet!" He looked around. "My book. I need my book—"

"I'll go and get it—" Aria started. Owyn shook his head.

"No. It'll get wet." He staggered to his feet and stumbled up the beach, seeming to ignore all of them.

"He's fine," Memfis said softly. "He needs to get the vision down before he loses it. That's what the book is." He gestured, and they followed Owyn back up the beach to the fire. Owyn had dug out his book and the box, and hunched over the book, doing something that Aven couldn't see. Aven glanced at Memfis, who shook his head and gestured toward the fire.

"Check me on this fish," he said. "You're probably better at cooking fish than I am."

"What did you do?" Aven asked. He handed Trinket to Aria, and crouched next to the cooking pot. "It smells good."

"Just a basic stew. We don't have much. I threw the last of the root vegetables, and some of the barley."

"It should be fine," Aven said. He picked up a cloth and tugged the pot away from the fire. "Fish doesn't need much cooking, though. So we can just keep it warm until we're ready to eat." He turned so that he could watch Owyn, who was still hunched over his book. Aria sat next to him, cradling Trinket in her hands and watching Owyn work. No one said anything until Owyn raised his head, setting down what turned out to be a stick of charcoal and shaking his hand.

"You're all staring," he said. "I... how badly did I scare you all?"

"About twice as badly as you scared yourself?" Memfis suggested. Owyn grimaced.

"I'm sorry," he said. "I didn't know that would happen. It's never happened before." He looked up at Memfis. "Guess that means I'm a real Smoke Dancer now?"

"You were a real Smoke Dancer before," Memfis corrected. "Now, what did you see?"

Owyn sat up and handed the book to Memfis. "I don't know. I have no idea who this is, but he's important. Really important."

Memfis frowned slightly as he studied the book. Aria passed Trinket to Owyn, then got up and moved to Memfis' side.

"He's very beautiful," she murmured. "And you don't know who this is?"

"Never seen him before," Owyn answered. "Trust me, I'd remember him."

Aven licked his lips, suddenly certain that he knew who Owyn had seen. He got up and moved to stand with Memfis, looking at the book.

"That's Del," he said. "I thought it might be, when Aria said he was beautiful."

"Del?" Memfis repeated. "Mannon's Del?"

"The one who freed you?" Aria added. Aven nodded.

"That's him." He studied the sketch. "Owyn, you're very good."

"Thank you. And what do you mean, Mannon's Del? Who is he?" Owyn got up. "Can we eat, and you'll explain? I'm hungry."

"You need to eat, to get yourself all the way back in this world. Aven, would you serve?" Memfis asked. Aven nodded and went back to the cooking pot.

"What does that mean?" Aria asked. "Eating to get himself back?"

"After being caught in a vision, a seer needs something to help them settle back into their skin. To bring their minds back to the here and now, as opposed to being off someplace else." Memfis took a bowl from Aven and passed it to Owyn. "Eating, and focusing on eating, brings their attention to the food and the taste, and brings them out of the dreamspace. So after a Smoke Dancer comes down from a vision, it's important for them to eat something. And they're usually ravenous. After that, they'll usually sleep."

"So it acts as an anchor?" Aven asked.

"Exactly," Memfis agreed.

"What happens if they don't eat?" Aria asked, taking her bowl from Aven.

Memfis frowned. "This is advanced for you, Aria. But the meat of the matter is that a seer needs that anchor, or they'll get lost in the dreams. Start seeing things that aren't there. Smoke Dancers are very careful about that, because it's happened. There are warning stories about Smoke Dancers who lost their way back to the waking world. They don't tend to survive long after."

Memfis' explanation was met with silence. Aven served Memfis, then himself. He sat with the bowl in his lap, collecting his thoughts so he could answer Owyn's question.

"Remember I told you that they took me to Fandor's house, to give to Mannon?" he asked finally.

Owyn nodded, swallowing a mouthful. "Yeah. You said you got away. You never said how."

"How was Del," Aven answered. "Del is Mannon's slave. He freed me and helped me to escape. He wouldn't come with me, though. I don't understand why."

"Because he knows better," Owyn said, and took another bite "Runaway slaves don't end up with happy endings."

"It's one of the reasons I made sure that Owyn's adoption and manumission papers were filed before we left Forge," Memfis added.

Aven picked up a stick and poked an ember back into the fire. "He's one of us. I'm pretty sure of that. I knew him the same way I knew you and Aria. And he's mute."

"A Companion?" Owyn asked. When Aven nodded, he whistled. "That's going to be interesting. And not in a fun way."

"We'll find him," Aria said. "And once I see him, I'll know if you are right. Then we'll do what we must."

CHAPTER THREE

THEY FINISHED EATING, and sat around the fire. Owyn set Trinket down so that she could play in the embers, and had picked his book and charcoal back up. He seemed very focused on what he was doing, but kept glancing up. At Aria, Aven realized, and wondered if Owyn was sketching her, and if he'd share the drawing when he was finished.

"Memfis, you said we needed to discuss our plans," Aria said. "We need supplies?"

"I can bring up more fish," Aven offered. "It's not hard to dry it."

"It's not just food," Memfis said. "Aven, how are you doing on salt?"

Aven frowned and reached over to pick up his carry-bag. He pulled out the jar of salt that Memfis had given to him back in Forge, pulling out the cork. There wasn't much left. "I'll need to refill it," he said. "I can refill my waterskin here, though."

"And have it last the three days it will take for us to get to the healing center?" Memfis shook his head. "We're almost out of food. But we *are* out of salt. We need to change plans. The only problem is, I'm not sure what we need to change them to." He sighed. "Planning was never something I was good at. That was your mother's role, Aven. I never needed to plan. I'm a Smoke Dancer. We see what we need to know."

"And if you don't see it, you don't know." Owyn pointed his charcoal at Memfis. "And look at how that's turned out."

"You sound like Meris," Memfis grumbled. "She always told me I was being arrogant, and that it would come around and burn me. She was right."

"Didn't you tell me once that Granna is always right? And didn't she give you a map?" Owyn asked. "I thought she said there was one, right before we left. Isn't it in the packs?"

"A map?" Memfis looked startled. "I never looked. I used to know this road like the back of my hand." He sighed. "There's no fool like an old fool, hm? Go look, Mouse."

Owyn closed his book and put it down, getting up and going to the pile of packs. He started rooting through them, and Memfis sighed again.

"We used to ride this way, Milon and I. He didn't like traveling between Forge and the palace by ship. He wanted to be on the road, so we'd ride. That's how I knew this cove was here. We used to camp here." He gestured off toward the curve of the cove. "There's a little tidal pool, over that way, just around those rocks. Or there was. If it's still there, it'll be a place where you can sleep, Aven."

Aven nodded. "I'll go take a look when we're done here. It sounds like we need to find someone to trade with?"

"We need a town, or a village. Even a farmhouse might have something we can use," Memfis picked up a piece of driftwood and started breaking it into pieces. "Did you find a map, Owyn?"

"Yeah," Owyn answered. He came back and sat down, spreading the scroll out on the sand. Curious, Aven moved over to sit with him, watching as Owyn traced a line on the map with one finger. "That village you said we were going to stop and resupply? It hasn't been gone long. It's still on this map."

"Is there another off the main road?" Memfis asked. Owyn frowned. He ran his finger away from the line — Aven assumed that had been the road — and tapped a spot near the coast.

"We're here, I think," he said. "Which means... yeah. There's something here. Off a side branch, and if you stayed to the main road, you'd never know it was there. If it's still there, we can reach it tomorrow. Maybe... late afternoon?" He looked up at Aven. "What do you think?"

"I think I don't know maps like this," Aven admitted. "This sort of chart isn't anything I've learned about. A static map like this wouldn't mean much out on the deep. Aria? Do you know maps?"

Aria came over and sat down on Owyn's other side. "Yes and no," she said, tucking her hair back and leaning over the map. "We use maps like this, but they're also different, because we travel by air."

Owyn nodded slowly. "Right. What do you need with roads? Mem, it looks like the village is most of a day's ride, if I'm reading this right. And it's well out of the way."

"But we'll be able to resupply," Memfis said. "All right. We'll set out in the morning. Aven, you'll fill your waterskin here?"

"And bring up some more fish," Aven added. "I can set it up to cook in the coals overnight. Then we can eat well before we leave."

Memfis nodded. "Then we have a plan. Or something very similar to one. Aria, let's start your lessons."

"If you're going to teach, then we'll only be a distraction," Owyn said. He rolled up the map and got to his feet. "Aven, want to go take a look at that pool?"

Aven got up. "If it won't bother you."

"It's not the deep water, so I should be good," Owyn said. He glanced down the beach at the shoreline. "And you can tell me how you navigate, if you don't have a map."

———— ❦ ————

ARIA WATCHED AS OWYN and Aven walked away from the fire.

"We need to be sure that Aven understands what Smoke Dancing is about," she said. "He didn't know about the waking dream."

"Which isn't surprising," Memfis said. "It's part of the arcana of the Smoke Dancer, and not something we talk about to people who aren't in training. Aven's father is half-Fire, and he never knew. Not until we told him. It's not something that Smoke Dancers want known."

"But if I cannot trust my Companions, there is no one I can trust in the world," Aria countered. Memfis smiled.

"Truth. All right. You can explain whatever you like to him, and I'll answer his questions. Just be sure that he understands that this knowledge is not to be shared outside your circle. Now, let's start with teaching you how to clear your mind. Find a comfortable spot to sit." He shifted, folding his legs in front of him, and waited until Aria was settled. "Clearing your mind is harder than it sounds. There's almost always something, some distraction, that keeps your mind from ever being truly still. The sound of the water, perhaps. Or an itch where you can't scratch it. But the mind must be clear in order for you to catch visions."

"You make visions sound as if they're butterflies," Aria said.

Memfis grinned. "That's actually very close to what I was taught, back when I was younger than you. My first teacher taught me that visions are always there. We just can't see them because we're too distracted. But if we quiet the mind, we become the net. He called it the web, though. I think he was thinking more of spiders than of butterflies."

"I'd rather think of butterflies," Aria said. "I don't care for spiders."

"You're not supposed to be thinking," Memfis said. "Close your eyes. You're seeking stillness."

Aria frowned. "How will I know when I find it?"

"You'll know." Memfis closed his eyes for a moment, settling himself more comfortably. Then he opened his eyes again. Aria's eyes were closed, but she was frowning slightly. She tipped her head to one side, then to the other. Her frown deepened. Her fingers flexed where they rested on her legs, and her foot twitched. Her wings flared, then folded against her back again. The frown changed to a scowl, and her chin tucked down to her chest as her shoulders crept up toward her ears.

"If you keep on like that, you'll end up with a headache," Memfis said mildly. Aria's eyes opened.

"It's harder than I thought it would be."

"It's the hardest part. But once you master it, everything else falls into place." Memfis shifted, rolling his shoulders and hearing them pop. "Some people have their waking vision and never manage stillness. They go their whole lives only seeing the first vision."

"I didn't think it would be so hard," Aria grumbled. "But everything was so loud and distracting! The water, the wind, and the fire. I couldn't not hear them! And everything itched, all at once. Even my own heartbeat was annoying!"

"What about your breathing?" Memfis asked.

"My... my breathing?" Aria repeated. "I... I don't know. Why?"

"Because breathing is the key. Did you notice, just before Owyn started to dance, he took three deep breaths?"

Aria frowned again, looking thoughtful. "I believe I did. Is that important?"

"It's the key," Memfis answered. He shifted, flowed up onto his feet, and held his hand out to Aria. "Stand up. It's easier to show you when you're standing."

Aria took his hand and got to her feet. He nodded and moved to her side, looking her up and down.

"You have good posture," he said. "Take a deep breath." When she did, he nodded again. "All right. Close your eyes. I want you to take another deep breath, but through your nose. I want you to picture the air filling your whole body, out to your fingertips and down to your toes."

She looked sidelong at him. "That's silly."

"That's the first step," Memfis corrected. "Learning to breathe. Once you learn this, we move on to the next step."

"And what is that?"

"Learning to listen, and not to hear." Memfis grinned at the look on her face, mingled shock and exasperation. "It'll make sense later. Now, breathe!"

"WHAT DO YOU WANT TO know about navigation?" Aven asked as he and Owyn reached the edge of the cove. "Because I'm not sure how much I'm supposed to share outside the tribe."

"How do you do it out in the water, without a map?" Owyn asked.

"I look up," Aven answered. He tipped his head back. "The stars show me. In the Water tribe, every star has a name, and it has a place. The stars move, but in regular cycles. Once you know the cycles, you can tell what time it is by how far a certain star is from the horizon. And you know where in the sky that star is supposed to be. That gives you a direction."

"And the angle changes depending on where you're located?" Owyn asked slowly. "We did stars, Mem and me. He showed me, taught me some names. Told me some stories that went with the patterns. Bedtime stories."

Aven chuckled. "I'd like to hear them. I wonder if they're the same stories we tell?"

"We'll compare them," Owyn said. He looked up. "How does it work in the daytime? No stars."

"Winds," Aven answered. "And swell. And the angle of the sun, depending on the time of year."

"Wait, back up. Swell?"

Aven considered, trying to think of how to explain it to someone who'd never been on the deep water. "The waves. They change depending on how close to land you are, and how strong the wind."

Owyn frowned, turning to look out at the sea. After a moment, his eyes widened. "They're constant, aren't they? The waves out in the deep water? There's nothing to block the wind, so the waves are the same."

"And the wind blows in a straight line," Aven added. "So if you follow the swell, you know you're going straight."

"So when you combine the swell and the angles of the sun or the stars, you know exactly where you are," Owyn said. He shook his head and laughed. "That's fantastic!"

"It's not quite that simple. There's more to it than that, more things you need to be able to recognize. And none of that matters if you don't know how to control a canoe." Aven held his hand out. "My mother is a navigator. She was tested by the mothers of our tribe when she was younger than me. She proved she knew how to find her way, so she has tattoos on the back of her hand." He traced where they would be on his own hand. "They mark star positions at the solstices, primary winds, and the major current that our family canoes sail. It's a high honor to wear them."

Owyn's eyes were wide as saucers. "Tattoos? And... wait, you don't have any. I know. I've seen every bit of you."

Aven grinned. "If I ever go back, we'll see if my grandmother bends enough. I should have at least two by now. My family mark and my hunter mark. And, if I passed the tests, my navigator marks."

Owyn stepped back, cocking his head to the side. He looked Aven up and down, then shook his head. "Nope. I can't see it. I can't see you with ink in your skin. And what do you mean, if? Once we're done here, we're all supposed to go back to our tribes, one per season. So you'll go out on the deep—"

"And then the question rises — will my grandmother finally accept the Mudborn?" Aven asked. He shrugged. "I'll never have so much as a line on my skin until she recognizes me as family. Which she's said she'll never do." He started walking again, passing around the rocks. "When I told Aria, I thought she was going to take off and fly right to my grandmother's canoe and challenge her."

"She'd do it, too," Owyn said as he caught up with Aven. "For you, she'd challenge the Mother Her own self."

Aven glanced sidelong at Owyn. "She'd do it for you, too."

Owyn nodded. He fell quiet as they moved out of sight of the fire. "I can do it," he finally said.

Aven stopped and looked at him. "Do... what? Challenge my grandmother?"

"Not that, no," Owyn laughed. "Not unless she comes to me. No, I could tattoo you. I know how."

Aven's jaw dropped. He stared at Owyn for a moment. "I... no. No, I can't let you do that. But I thank you for making the offer. It wouldn't be the same." He swallowed, remembering something. "Aria made the same offer, you know."

"For probably the same reason," Owyn said. "Because this is something that is important to you. It would make you really happy to be really part of your family, and the tattoos would show it. And... well, we can still do it."

"How?"

Owyn smiled and took Aven's hand. "We can have our own tattoo. We could make it a new tradition for the Heir and the Companions from here on out."

"That's very sweet of you, Mouse, but it's not the same." Aven squeezed his fingers, kicking flotsam out from under his feet. Driftwood, seaweed, and broken shells littered the sand, far more than he'd seen on the beach. He looked around, then searched the rock walls. There was seaweed lodged in the rocks near shoulder-height. He let go of Owyn's hand and went to pull it down. "Look at this. This cavern flooded. Probably with that last big storm."

"The one about two months ago?" Owyn whistled. "And it still looks like this? The beach didn't look like this."

"It's rained since. So it all washed back off the beach, or was collected by anyone else who came through here. This spot is sheltered and high," Aven said. "It would be a safe place to weather a regular storm. Not that last one."

"Yeah," Owyn agreed. "That was really bad." He crouched. "The driftwood is dry. We can bring it out for the fire."

Aven nodded. He could see the pool Memfis had mentioned, the rocks around the edges littered with more driftwood and dried seaweed. The water in here must have been very high, to push trash that far back. He could see now that Memfis had been wrong. This wasn't a tidal pool. Not this far away from the water's edge, and with no channel to the sea. There was a crevice, he assumed. Something that would have caught the water and held it between storms, and kept level with runoff from rain. The air back here smelled sour, and the water in the pool here was probably foul — not good for sleeping at all. He stooped, picked up a piece of dry driftwood, moving closer to the edge of the pool. Something white gleamed in a pile of seaweed. A shell, he assumed, until he took another step and the shape of the pile resolved itself into a configuration that he recognized. He stopped and dropped the driftwood.

"Aven?" Owyn joined him. "What is it? Wait. Is that—?"

"Go get Memfis," Aven said softly.

MEMFIS SIGHED AND RUBBED his forehead. Aria was trying. He could tell that she was trying. But she wasn't making the connection between her breathing and the flow that was necessary to reach stillness. Or maybe he was just not explaining it properly.

"You had all your visions on the wing?" he asked as he sat back down in the sand, facing a very tired and very frustrated Aria. "When you fly, what do you think of?"

Aria closed her eyes. She'd have frowned, but she was already frowning. "Flying," she answered, her voice curt. "You do not think of anything else when you fly."

"Really?" Memfis smiled. "So, you focus on... what? I don't have wings. Explain to me what goes into flying?"

Aria licked her lips and the frown faded from her face. "I... I don't know if I can," she said slowly. "It is just as Aven said to us. Owyn asked him what the change felt like. He said it was normal. Flying is normal. It is... flying. When I am in the air, there is the wind, and my wings. And I do think, but not really, if that makes sense. There is only the wind and the wings. I..." Her expression brightened. "That's what you're trying to get me to do now!" she laughed. "You're trying to get me to fly without flying!"

Memfis grinned. "Looks like it. I knew it would be interesting teaching you. I didn't realize how interesting it would be. All right—" He stopped, lurching to his feet as he saw Owyn running toward them across the sand. Aria turned, and scrambled up, wings flared.

"What is it?" she called. "What's wrong? Where is Aven?"

Owyn skidded to a stop, spraying sand over Memfis' feet. "He's by the pool," he gasped, panting. "He said you need to come. There's a body in there."

CHAPTER FOUR

AVEN CROUCHED NEXT to the body, using a long stick as a probe. He could hear the others coming up behind him, but didn't turn.

"He's been dead quite a while," he said. "He was dead before he hit the water, though. He must have washed up when this cove flooded in the last big storm, and he's been here ever since."

"So, at least two months dead?" Memfis said, his voice coming from directly over Aven's head. "How can you tell he was dead before he was in the water?"

"He's Water. He has gills. And he has legs," Aven answered. He turned his head and looked up. "He didn't change. Which meant that he couldn't change when he was in the water. His legs, though. I've never seen damage like that. I don't know what would cause it." He looked past Memfis to Aria and Owyn. "The visible bone is because of the state of decay, and because the birds and crabs have been picking at him."

"You know, I enjoyed dinner the first time around," Owyn said. "I'd like to not have a second go at it. Could you not go any further with that?"

"Do you know him?" Aria asked, resting her hand on Owyn's shoulder. Aven shook his head.

"There's enough of his family tattoo that I can tell which canoe he's from, but..." he glanced at Owyn. "But there's not enough of his face left for me to tell if I knew him. Sorry, Owyn," he added as Owyn turned a distinct shade of green. "Whoever he was," Aven continued. "He was from Tersera's canoe." He pointed with his stick. "That's their family tattoo. That canoe stayed a lot closer to land than my grandmother liked. We didn't have much contact with them outside of the annual celebrations."

Memfis crouched next to Aven, his head cocked to the side as he studied the body. "I see what you meant about the bone. What was different about the leg damage?"

"The skin isn't broken, but his bones... they're broken in ways I've never seen before. His hips are completely torn apart. If he'd lived, he'd never have walked again." *Or changed.* He didn't say it. Couldn't say it. Just thinking it made him want to scream.

"What do we do with him?" Owyn asked. "Do we have enough wood for a pyre?"

"No," Aven said. He stood up and dusted his hands off on his trousers, turned to face them. "I'll take him out deep, anchor the body to the bottom. That's our way. We came from the deep, we go back to the deep."

Aria nodded. "What can we do to help you? Do we have time to do what needs to be done, and do it properly?"

Aven bit his lip and looked back. "I... there are songs, an honor chant... but I can't do them. I don't have the status to do them. I imagine his canoe did them already, though. If someone doesn't come back, after a few weeks, they're called missing. After a few months, you know they've gone back to the deep."

"So if the rites haven't been done yet, they'll be done soon?" Owyn asked. "Good. That's good. He shouldn't go nameless back to the Mother."

Aven frowned. "Go... what?"

"Fire traditions," Memfis said. "We can discuss it later. For now, it's getting late, and we have work to do. Aven, what do you need?"

Aven folded his arms over his chest, tucking his chin down as he thought. "Rope," he said slowly. "If we have it. The seaweed on the shore is too dry to use, and we don't have time for me to dive for fresh. And... I don't think we have a blanket we can spare, do we?"

"How about an old cloak?" Memfis asked. "Mine is threadbare. I'm always meaning to replace it, and never getting to it."

"It'll be cold soon," Owyn protested.

"And we'll be at the healing center in a few days. I can replace it there." Memfis looked at Aven. "Well?"

Aven nodded. "It should work. I'll need it, so I can get him ready." He looked back over his shoulder at the body. Getting it out of the spot where it was wedged wasn't a job he could do alone. "I hate to ask—"

"I... I'll help," Owyn stammered. He stepped forward. "I—"

"Go fetch the cloak and the rope," Memfis interrupted, his voice gentle. "Then you and Aria go back to the fire. Mouse, you can explain a bit of your training to Aria while I help Aven."

To Aven's eyes, Owyn looked torn. On the one hand, he did seem to want to help. On the other, he looked almost ridiculously relieved that he wouldn't have to; he nodded and took Aria's arm, then practically sprinted away, disappearing behind the rocks. Aven grinned and shook his head, then turned back to the body.

"Memfis, I really don't know what could do that," he said. "Whatever it is, it scares the piss out of me."

Memfis moved past Aven, going closer to the body, studying it for a long moment. "Whatever happened, if he'd survived it would have crippled him in both forms, wouldn't it?"

Aven swallowed around a boulder in his throat. "I think so, yes."

"Poor bastard was lucky to die, then," Memfis murmured. "All right. How do we do this?"

Aven took a long breath. "We put the cloak down. We get him out of there, which will be the hard part. We bundle him up in the cloak, tie it closed, and tie a tow-rope to it. Then we take it to the water and I take it from there. I'll probably be a few hours, at least, to get him out to the deep water and do what needs to be done."

Memfis nodded. "You do what's needful for him, and don't worry about the rest. We'll take care of what needs to be done above the waves."

ARIA BROUGHT THE ROPE and the cloak, claiming a kiss from Aven before leaving him and Memfis to their grisly work. The body was badly decomposed, and Aven was certain that by the time it was secured, hidden away in the folds of Memfis' old cloak, that both he and Memfis were as green as Owyn had been.

"That was... something I never want to do again," Memfis murmured. "To the water's edge?"

Aven nodded, not trusting his voice. He moved around to one end of the bundle and crouched, looking up at Memfis. The older man went to the other end of the bundle and stooped. Together, they lifted the heavy, ungainly package of rope-tied red wool, and slowly carried it out of the cavern and down to the water's edge. They set it down, and Aven stepped back onto dry sand to take off his trousers.

"I'll take them."

Aven jumped, turning to see Owyn had come up behind him. "You didn't need—"

"I need to not be so squeamish," Owyn interrupted. "Barring that, I can at least keep your clothes dry until you get back." He nodded toward the bundle. "Is there anything you need to say, while you've still got a voice to say it?"

"His canoe will have said it already," Aven answered. "Or they will soon. All that I can really do now is give him back to the deep." He stripped and handed his clothes to Owyn. "And it's all right that you're squeamish. If my father hadn't trained me not to be, I'd have been racing you out of there." He sighed. "I'll be gone most of the night, I think."

Owyn grimaced. "Will you be able to sleep underwater when you get back?"

Aven shook his head. "Not safely, no. There's no shelter down there, no place where I'd be able to keep out of the way of predators. If Melody was here, it would be different. But here... no. I'll sleep on the beach when I get back."

Owyn nodded slowly. "I'll see if I can't figure a way to hang the hammock. That way, you'll be able to get some real sleep and you won't fall off your horse tomorrow." He looked at Aven and snorted. "Not really that purple yet. Tomorrow, it'll probably be all kinds of colors."

"You can look real close tomorrow," Aven said. He leaned in and kissed Owyn, then kissed him again. "That one is for Aria. Where is she?"

Owyn pointed up. "We were talking about breathing and flying, and how what she needs to do for visions isn't what I do for visions. She's trying to figure out how to explain to me what flying is like, what's going on in her head when she does it. Which might be a bit like asking a crawliebug how it decides which foot to put first." He grinned. "They've got a hundred legs. Since I'm guessing you've never seen a crawliebug."

"I haven't, and I was going to ask." Aven looked out at the water. "I'll be back. Keep watch, all right?" He started toward the water, only to be stopped by Memfis' raised voice.

"Wait, you should take a weapon. A knife, at least." Memfis turned and headed back to the fire, going through the packs before coming back. He handed a sheathed knife to Aven. "Here. I should have given this to you days ago."

"I haven't needed more than the little one you already gave me," Aven said. He took the knife and drew it — the blade was as long as his forearm, and razor sharp. He handed the scabbard back to Memfis. "It'll get ruined," he explained. "Leather and salt water isn't a good mix."

"How will you carry it, then?" Owyn asked. Aven stooped, picking up the end of the tow rope. He measured off a long length and cut it, then tied it around the hilt of the knife. He tied the ends together and hung the loop around his neck.

"I'll figure out something better later. For now, let me get going. I've got a long swim out, and a long swim back." Aven looked up at the sky, seeing Aria circling overhead. "She should come down. She might be seen."

"I'll signal her," Owyn said. "Go on. Be safe."

Aven nodded. He waded out into the water, then dove under the surface and let the water welcome him home. When he surfaced again, Memfis had waded out to meet him. He handed Aven the knotted end of the tow rope.

"I agree with Owyn. Be safe," he said. Aven nodded. He waved, then dove underwater, tugging the pathetic bundle of body after him.

IT WAS ODD, HOW THE waters here tasted different than the ones that he was used to. He'd first noticed it when he'd changed earlier, but thought it was his imagination. Now, as he swam out of the cove and into the deeper water, he was certain. It wasn't the same. Maybe it was that they were closer to shore. Or maybe it was that there were more people here, more effluvia. He wasn't sure, but it gave him an idea of how he would know when he was far enough out to finish his task. He'd be deep enough when the water tasted right.

As he swam, he watched the light that flickered on the surface above him turn ruddy, then fade to silver. He once saw the underside of a ship, and dove deeper to stay out of sight, tugging the ungainly bundle after him. It didn't want to stay deep, and he realized too late that he should have put rocks into the bundle with the body. Getting it deep enough to secure was going to be a fight, and he was tired already. But he had to do this right.

He wasn't sure how long he'd been swimming before the waters finally tasted right. Long enough that his arms were tired, and his back and hips ached. Long enough that he was hungry, and desperately wanted to sleep. He floated, letting himself rise toward the surface, watching the red-wrapped bundle rising alongside him. No, if the bundle surfaced, it would be that much more work to get it to the deep where it needed to be. He blew a stream of bubbles and dove, dragging the bundle down with him, into the darker waters. His eyes adjusted slowly, revealing fish and tendrils of seaweed, and as he went deeper, stark cliffs and ledges. He started looking there for the right place. Part of him wanted to rush, wanted to pick any spot where he could tie off the rope and be done. But he knew what he needed to do — he needed to find a place where the body could be claimed by the sea, and return to it. Not in a cave, where it would be forgotten. Nor any place where it would break free and return to shore. He needed a good place, the right place.

A long, sinuous form flashed past him, and he jerked in shock. Melody? No, it couldn't be. It was another water-cat, a young male, from the looks of it. It circled him, clearly curious. He clicked at the water-cat, and it squealed in response. It dove, circled again in front of him, then dove once more. When it swam back to him, Aven realized that the water-cat wanted him to follow, so when it dove once more, Aven trailed after it, pulling the bundle along with him. The water-cat flowed through the water, passing through a low arch in the rock that Aven would never have seen from above. He swam down to it, then looked up to see that the water-cat had swum away. Aven gnawed on his lip, then shook his head and started securing the bundle to the top of the arch, using the ropes around the bundle and the tow rope to anchor it in place. Once he was certain that the bundle wasn't going to break free, he swam down and through the arch, examining the underside of the rocks. What he found there somehow didn't surprise him — there were grooves worn in the stones, runes carved by countless generations of Water tribe who had left their dead here. Aven studied them, then swam back up and looked around. There was no sign of the water-cat anywhere. A messenger? Or a coincidence? He wasn't sure, and he was too tired to debate it with himself. He went back to the bundle to finish, tugging the cloak free so that the ruined face was visible. Aven might not know his name, might never know his name, but the Mother knew Her children. With his face bare, the dead man would be recognized by the Mother and welcomed back to the waters that birthed him.

His job done, Aven took one more look around for the water-cat. Seeing nothing, he turned back and started the long swim back to shore.

THE MOON WAS SETTING when Aven surfaced inside the cove. He rolled onto his back and closed his eyes, floating. He couldn't remember ever being this tired before. In Forge, he'd been tired and sick, first from bad food and from the after-effects of dreamflower. Now, though, he was just... tired. He felt as if he could sleep for days. He hoped Owyn had figured out a way to hang the hammock, so that he'd be able to sleep. He rolled and dove, swimming closer to shore, surfacing again to see the figure sitting on the beach. Aria. He slapped the water, and she rose and waded into the water. Once it was over her hips, she swam out to meet him. He pulled her close, sliding his arms around her as she twined her arms around his neck.

"We took turns waiting for you to come back," she said, her voice low. "It's my turn now. Everyone else is asleep. I was worried you weren't coming back, you've been gone so long."

Aven smiled at her. He couldn't tell her that he'd always come back to her, couldn't say anything to reassure her. So he did what he could — he kissed her. She moved closer to him, winding her legs around his tail and kissing him back with a hunger that he could feel. It was more intense than what they'd shared at the pearl fields... and they were alone. He ran one hand down her back, over her hip, and felt her moan against his mouth. He wanted this, wanted her...

But he couldn't. He drew back and shook his head. She looked at him, clearly confused.

"Aven?" she whispered. "What is it?"

He leaned back slightly, creating space between them. He slipped one hand between their bodies and rested his palm against her stomach. He met her eyes, raising his brows, silently asking, *"Do you understand?"*

She looked puzzled. Then she looked down. "Oh," she breathed. "Oh. Aven, I... it's just once." She pouted slightly. "I want this. I want you. I want you like this, now. When you're yourself, when you're free. I love seeing you like this."

She pressed against him again, and for a moment, need almost overrode reason. Almost. One of them had to think, had to be careful. He shook his head again, and her pout grew. Then she sighed.

"You're right," she murmured. "I know you're right. But... you do still want me, don't you?" She didn't raise her eyes, and he wondered what she was thinking. He sighed and tucked his finger under her chin so he could kiss her gently on the lips. He met her eyes, and kissed her again. She smiled.

"Aven, I'm being a trial to you again, aren't I?" He shrugged and smiled, and she laughed. "All right. I do love you. And I do want you. But you're right. I can't risk pregnancy, no matter how much I want you." She looked over her shoulder, then let him go. "We should go in. Owyn found a place to hang the hammock. You can sleep."

Aven swam up to the beach after her, and dragged himself up onto the sand to change. He rolled onto his back, closing his eyes. Only to jerk up in shock as Aria straddled his hips and pressed him down onto the sand. She rested her hands on his chest, then stretched out over him.

"It's maddening, you know," she said. "Knowing you can have Owyn whenever you like, but I have to wait until it's safe. I want you both." She kissed his chin, then straightened, her hands running down his chest. "It's *frustrating*."

Pinned underneath her, excruciatingly aware of her, the only thing Aven could do was nod in agreement.

CHAPTER FIVE

ARIA PEEKED INTO THE hammock and smiled. Aven was still deeply asleep, his hair trailing across his face. She gently brushed the hair back, then left him alone.

"He's still out?" Owyn asked. He was sitting on the sand between the remains of their fire and the rock enclosure where he'd hung the hammock. Memfis was repacking their supplies and making a list of what they'd need when they reached the village.

"He was exhausted by the time he got back," Aria answered. She sat down next to Owyn, leaning into his arm, reaching out and petting Trinket on Owyn's knee. "He was asleep almost before he was in the hammock." She stared out at the water, not mentioning the way she'd welcomed him back. She wasn't sure why she was keeping it to herself. Owyn wouldn't mind, surely. If anything had happened, he'd probably have been more annoyed that they hadn't woken him so that he could watch! "He'll be starving when he wakes up," she added. "I'm not sure what we left for him will be enough."

"It'll have to be," Owyn answered. "We won't have anything else until we get to that village. Unless we hunt..." He frowned. "Or fish. You lived on the canoe with him. Do you know how to fish?"

"Not the way they do it," Aria answered. "They used nets and spears underwater. I'm not sure about how to do it from land. I know how to open oysters. But I don't know how to tell where to find them."

Owyn nodded slowly. Then he perked up. "How about crabs? Aven said there were crabs in... in where we found that poor bastard. You can eat crabs, can't you?"

"Me?" Aria asked. "Or us?"

"Us." Owyn moved Trinket to his shirt pocket. Then he got to his feet and brushed the sand off his trousers. "I'm pretty sure we can eat them. Come on. Let's go see if we can find some."

Aria got up and followed him down the beach and around the rocks. It seemed like a good idea. She just hoped that Memfis knew what to do to prepare crabs — it didn't seem fair to make Aven prepare his own meal, even if he didn't have to catch it. By the time she caught up with Owyn, they were around the rocks and into the sheltered cavern where Owyn and Aven had found the body. Owyn was standing near the edge of the pool of water, frowning.

"Now what?" he asked as she came closer.

"It was your idea," she pointed out. "Do you not know how to do it?"

Owyn grimaced. "I was kinda hoping you did. You hunt. Aven hunts. I've never hunted before, and where I'm from, catching crabs has a whole 'nother meaning."

Aria blinked. "What does it mean?"

He blinked. "You don't know? Right...well, it's not a good thing. That's all I'm going to say. So what do we do?"

Aria frowned, seeing movement around the edge of the pool. "Do we have a net? Or a bag? Something to catch them in?"

Owyn snorted. "It can't be that hard," he answered. "I mean, they're little." He walked closer to the edge of the pool, stooped, and grabbed. "Got one!" he crowed as he started to stand up. Then he howled, shaking his hand wildly. Aria saw something go flying, then Owyn was somehow behind her.

"It *bit* me!" He held his hand out, showing that it was streaked in blood. "Look at this?"

"What are you two doing?"

Aria turned, seeing Aven behind them. He was shirtless, barefoot, still looking half-asleep. He was frowning, but his eyes widened when he saw the blood on Owyn's hand.

"It bit me!" Owyn repeated. "We were trying to catch crabs, and one bit me!"

"It didn't bite," Aven said as he came closer. "It pinched you. The claws are much stronger than you'd think for their size. Why were you hunting crabs?" He took Owyn's hand and examined it. "It's not bad. So, why crabs?"

"In case you were still hungry when you finished the last of the stew from last night," Aria said. "We didn't think what was left would be enough."

Aven's jaw dropped. "You were hunting crabs for me?" he asked. "I... you didn't have to do that! The stew was fine."

Aria blinked. "You've been awake long enough to eat?"

"I woke up when you brushed my hair back," Aven answered. He smiled slightly, met her eyes, then looked down. "You both went off by the time I was awake enough to get out of the hammock. You were right about how hungry I'd be. I ate fast enough that I don't think I tasted it." He looked at Owyn's hand in his, raised it to his lips and kissed the wound. When he lowered Owyn's hand, the cut was closed.

"Oh, now you're just showing off!" Owyn teased. Aven laughed.

"A little. Thank you. That was really sweet. And you need a crab trap if you want to do it right."

Aria sniffed. "We do not have crabs in the mountains. I've never done this before. And crabs in Forge are not something you want to catch."

Aven blinked, then looked at Owyn. "There are crabs in Forge?"

To Aria's surprise, Owyn turned bright red. He tugged his hand out of Aven's and stepped away. "I... ah... never mind. Just... never mind. Let's go see if Mem needs us or something." Stammering, Owyn hurried away.

"I said something wrong," Aven murmured as he watched Owyn go. "I'm not sure what I said, but I said something wrong. What was that about crabs in Forge? I wouldn't have thought that crabs would live in the city. There's no water." He looked at Aria. "Should we ask Memfis?"

"Unless we want to be confused the rest of the day," Aria answered. She took Aven's hand and led him out of the cavern. They could see Memfis loading the packhorse, and beyond him, Owyn was currying his horse, Freckles.

Memfis looked up as they came closer. "What's happening? I thought I heard Owyn shout?"

"He was pinched by a crab," Aven answered. "Memfis, are there crabs in Forge?"

"Crabs? In Forge?" Memfis stopped and looked at them both. "Aven, you should know this better than anyone. There aren't any crabs in Forge. Now what's this about? From the beginning."

Aria frowned. "Owyn and I were trying to catch crabs, so we could have something else for Aven to eat if he was still hungry. Neither of us knew what we were doing. There are no crabs in the mountains, and Owyn said that the crabs in Forge are different."

Memfis looked over his shoulder at Owyn. Then he looked back at Aria. "What did he say, exactly?"

Aria thought about it. "He said that crabs in Forge are not something that you would want to catch."

To Aria's shock, Memfis burst out laughing. He got himself under control quickly, but had to wipe his eyes. "Oh! Oh, I... Aria, he meant lice!"

"Lice?" Aria looked at Aven, then at Owyn. Even from here, she could see that his skin was bright red. "Then why didn't he say so?"

"He may not have known there's another name for them," Memfis said, his voice sounding oddly strangled. "It's a... specific kind of lice. They're something you can get when you're not careful about who you lie down with." He shook his head. "Given what he was doing to survive? He probably had them at least once, although he never mentioned it to me. I don't think it would be something he'd be comfortable talking about."

Aria's insides twisted. "And I embarrassed him."

"I think we both did," Aven said. "Come on. Let's go talk to him."

Owyn didn't turn away from his work as they walked up the beach toward him, brushing Freckles with what seemed to be single-minded intensity. "Owyn?" Aria said softly. "I'm sorry. I didn't know."

"I figured that out," Owyn grumbled. "Fishie, how come you didn't know?"

"I did, once Memfis told us what you were talking about," Aven admitted. "I just didn't know that name for it. And I've never seen it — I just learned about it as part of my training."

Owyn nodded. He didn't turn. "I... you know, it's not fair."

"What's not fair?" Aven asked. "And how's your hand?"

"Fine. It's fine. And... look, I have to say this to the horse, cause I can't say it to your faces. Either of you. But it's not fair. I've know you both... what? Not even fifteen days? It's not supposed to be like this!"

Aria looked up at Aven, who nodded. "You mean about how close we are already?" he asked.

"Yeah," Owyn breathed. He rested the curry comb on Freckles' neck. "I mean, I don't trust nobody. Not anybody. Cause I learned early I can't."

"Not even Memfis?" Aria asked. Owyn sighed, then shook his head.

"Not really. Not completely. Too many times I did, and I got hurt. You know?" He paused. "No. Of course you don't know. But anyhow, that's me. I don't... except for you two. You both... it's like you're inside of me. I don't know how to feel about that. Except that it's not fair. I didn't get to decide I wanted to trust you." He turned around and looked at them, and Aria saw for the first time that his eyes were red. "I just do. And I keep opening my mouth and saying things I shouldn't say, then part of me is waiting to get thrown out because of it, and part of me is ashamed of thinking like that, because you'd never do that to me." He wrapped his arms around his chest, then reached up and touched the fire gem that sat in the hollow of his throat. "I mean, I know you won't. This means I'm part of something. Part of something good. I know you won't tell me you don't want me anymore. But I don't believe it, you understand? Because I just... I don't know how to be part of something real."

Aria stepped closer. She kept her hands clasped in front of her, suddenly afraid that if she reached for Owyn, he'd run. "Owyn, none of us know how this is done," she said. "None of us have ever been part of something like this."

"We can't even compare to the other Companions," Aven added. "My father told me that when he and Ama were Milon's Companions, it was the better part of a year before anyone but Milon and Memfis were sharing beds. We don't have the time to grow together the way they did. So the Mother... she's forcing it. And yes, it's uncomfortable."

Aria turned to look at him. "You think so, too?"

Aven shrugged. "You hear songs about fated love, old stories about it. And you think, that's not real. No one does that. No one looks at someone and says 'that's my forever.'" He grinned. "And then we did. So it's strange. But the idea of turning away from it, that's worse. I couldn't give you two up, any more than I could give up breathing."

Owyn snorted. "Yeah. That's... that's about right."

"And it's going to be like this with the others, too," Aven added. "So once we find our Earth and our Air, we'll be four times as uncomfortable." He frowned. "Five times?"

"A shitload," Owyn offered. "We'll be a shitload more uncomfortable. For a little while. I just... I have to get my head around it." He looked down at the currycomb in his hand. "I'm the odd tooth in the gear right now. But I'll figure it out."

"We all will," Aria told him. "Together." She reached out and touched his arm, and when he didn't move, slipped her arm into his. He shifted, tugging his arm free, then putting it around her waist. He held his other arm out to Aven.

"C'mere, Fishie," he called.

Aven joined them, wrapping his long arms around them both. Aria closed her eyes, enjoying their warmth. But curiosity got the better of her.

"Owyn, may I ask two questions?" she asked. He stiffened.

"If the first one is did I have them? Yes. Twice. It's miserable."

Aven grimaced. "There's a special soap for that. I know how to make it. It won't happen again."

"Since neither of you have them, we don't have to worry about it until we find the other two. And hopefully, we won't have to worry about it then," Owyn said. "What's the other question, Aria?"

"Exactly how big is a shitload?" she asked. The question did exactly what she'd hoped it would — Owyn's eyes widened, and he burst into wild peals of giggles that knocked him off his feet. The laughter was contagious, and before too long, the three of them were all laughing in the sand. Memfis came over, looked at them, then shook his head and walked away.

THERE WERE STILL RANDOM giggles as they worked together to saddle the horses. Aven went down to the water's edge and refilled his water skin, coming back and hanging it from his saddle before sitting down in the sand. He picked up one boot, then looked out over the water.

"Fishie?" Owyn asked. He stood behind Aven, his shins pressed against Aven's back. "You'll get back out there."

"I know," Aven said. He tipped his head back to look up. "Wishing I had time for one more swim. But we don't. We're late getting on the road already. How long will it take us to get to this village?"

Owyn looked up at the sun, judging angles and thinking about the map. "We'll have... maybe an hour or two of daylight once we get there?" he guessed. "We might have to camp and go into the village tomorrow." He frowned and turned, seeing Memfis cinching the last pack onto the packhorse. Aria's horse was already on a leading rein, attached to Memfis' Dasher. "Mem, how are we doing that, anyway? We can't all go in to market."

"I'll think about it, and let you know," Memfis answered. "Are we ready?"

Aven tugged on his second boot, then got to his feet. "I'm ready. Is Aria on sentry?"

Memfis nodded and gestured to the sky. "There's nothing there, or she'd have come and told us by now."

Aven looked up and saw Aria circling. "That's a problem, isn't it?" he asked.

Owyn stopped in the middle of turning toward Freckles and Cloud. "Why would it be a problem that no one is behind us?" he asked. He paused. "Which... that don't make sense. You're right. It's wrong. They want us. Why aren't they chasing us?"

"That's another question we'll think about as we ride," Memfis said. "For now, I want more distance between us and Forge. Let's go." He swung himself up onto Dasher and turned toward the switchback trail.

"Oh," Aven murmured. "We have to go back up that trail."

"Just take it slow, and lean forward," Owyn said. "Hold on to the saddle horn, and let Cloud do the work. She knows what she's doing."

"I don't know what she's doing," Aven grumbled. He went and mounted his horse, turning her head toward the trail. "Are you in front of me, or behind?"

"I'll take the tail end," Owyn said. "Go on. And just take it slow."

CHAPTER SIX

THE SHADOWS WERE GETTING longer and Aven's stomach was getting louder when Owyn drew his horse up alongside Aven's. "So how do you do it?" he asked.

"Do what?" Aven asked in response, after it was clear that Owyn wasn't going to add anything else to his question. On his other side, Aria laughed.

"He wasn't there for our conversation, Owyn," she said. "He doesn't know what you're talking about."

"Oh. Right," Own chuckled. "I asked Aria, and she said she didn't know. How do you communicate when you've got your tail on?"

Aven laughed and watched as Cloud's ears flicked back toward him. "When I have my tail on?" he repeated. "I like that." He grinned. "Well, there are two ways. The first is sounds that you don't need a voice to make. Clicks and whistles, that sort of thing." He trilled at them, then same way he'd have done to Melody, and watched Owyn's eyes widen.

"That works?" he asked. "What does it mean?"

"We use the vocalizations mostly for simple alerts. Warnings. We'll use drums the same way. Now, with water-cats, that trill is a sort of family identification. Each pod has a slightly different one. Different in pitch, or in length, or in modulation." He shrugged. "I'm not sure, but I think they actually do talk to each other."

"Do they really?" Aria asked. "How intelligent are they?"

"Very," Aven answered. "We just haven't learned their language yet. And they're still learning ours." He looked down at the reins in his hands. "If I drop these, will Cloud run away with me? I need both hands to show you the other way."

"Wrap them around your saddle horn," Owyn said. "Besides, it's late, and she's tired. She won't run."

Aven did as Owyn instructed, then flexed his fingers and started moving, using the gestural language that the Water tribes used underwater. He wasn't used to signing to more than one person — how did you use the proper facial expressions when the person you were signing to couldn't see your face? But he did the best he could, and dropped his hands at the end.

"That... that meant something? All that waving around meant something?" Owyn gasped. "What did that mean?"

"That meant that it's been a long day of travel." He repeated one gesture, a graceful motion that mimicked swimming. "And that I'm hungry."

"You're showing them water signs?" Memfis called. "Your mother would never teach us!"

"Fa knows them. At least, he knows them now." Aven frowned. "Did she say why she wouldn't teach you then?"

"She said that her mother would use her guts for bait if she taught drylanders water signs," Memfis answered.

"Well, my grandmother already wants to use my guts as bait. So I'll do what I want." He grinned at Owyn. "Does that answer the question?"

"And leads to one," Owyn answered. "Can you teach me?"

"Teach us both," Aria added. "I want to learn. It's like dancing with your hands."

Aven nodded. "I'll teach you what I can. There are parts you can't learn."

Owyn looked thoughtful. Then he coughed. "You use your tail as part of the signs?"

"Body language is part of it," Aven said with a nod. "What I can teach you are the facial expressions and the body grammar that doesn't involve a tail. Because there's a difference between this—" He made a series of gestures. "And this." He made the same gestures, but finished with his head cocked to one side. "The first was a statement. The second was a question."

"Oh. Oh, that's fantastic," Owyn breathed.

"Mouse, before you get too excited over water signs, you have the map," Memfis called. "I'm thinking we need to make camp near here?"

"Right. Right, let me check," Owyn said. He dug into his saddlebag and pulled out the map, unrolling it between his hands. He studied it for a moment, then looked around. "We should be coming up on a fork. If we take the left fork, we'll hit that village."

"Then we'll go to the fork and find a place to camp off the road," Memfis said. "Aria, are you too tired to go scouting?"

"I'm fine," Aria said. She reined in her horse and dismounted, handing the reins to Memfis before taking to the sky. Aven tipped his head back and watched her as she circled overhead.

"Had a thought," Owyn called. "You're not going to like it."

"I already don't like it," Aven answered immediately. Owyn gaped at him, and he grinned. "Well, whenever you or Memfis say that I'm not going to like something, it ends up being something bad."

Memfis chuckled. "What is it, Mouse?"

"Well, the question was why aren't they chasing us, right?" Owyn asked. He reached up and scratched the back of his neck, then patted the shirt pocket where Trinket rode. "The only reason I can think that they wouldn't be chasing us is that they don't have to. They already know where we're going."

Memfis blinked, his face going slack. Aven swallowed and forced a laugh. "I told you. You say that I'm not going to like what you have to say, and it always ends up being something bad."

"Yeah, I'm pretty sure bad sums it up," Owyn agreed. "If they're waiting for us at the healing center, we're walking right into a trap."

"So what do we do?" Aven asked. "We can't not go there, can we?"

Memfis growled softly, then shook his head. "Right now? We're reprovisioning. We can't do anything until we do that. Then... we'll figure it out." He looked up. "Aria's waving. I think she found a place for us. Let's go."

AVEN LOOKED UP, STUDYING the sky. "She's not up there. Where is she?"

"She landed, somewhere up there," Owyn said. He pointed. "Over that way. I saw her."

Memfis said nothing, leading them in the same direction that Owyn had pointed. He was scowling, and his entire demeanor reminded Aven of heavy storm clouds on the horizon. He glanced at Owyn, then urged Cloud forward until she was walking alongside Memfis' horse.

"What's wrong?" he asked. Memfis shook his head.

"Trying to think of what we do next," Memfis answered. "Because Owyn is right. If they're waiting for us at the healing center, we're walking into a trap."

"Where else can we go?" Aven looked for Aria again, then back at Memfis. "My parents said there were villages on the coast that were part Earth, part Water. Maybe we can get to one of those?"

Memfis sighed. "We'll look at the map. That might be a better choice, at least until we know more." He frowned. "Where is she?"

Aven studied the landscape, then pointed. "There. By those rocks. See her?"

"She found a good place, if it's that hard for us to find her," Owyn said, riding up next to Aven. "Mem, we can't all go into the village. We'll stand out. Who's going in?"

Memfis glanced at him. "I was thinking that you and I would go, Mouse."

Aven coughed. "And leave the two people who don't know anything about living in this part of the world alone? What if you don't come back?"

"He's got a good point, Mem," Owyn said. "Let's get to where we're going to camp, then go over what we're going to do."

Memfis scowled again, and this time, Aven saw lightning in the storm clouds. He knew what it meant now — Memfis was worried. Worried and angry. At himself, Aven guessed, but any of them might bear the brunt of that storm when it broke. He just wasn't sure what shelter they might find before that happened. He looked ahead, saw Aria wave.

"I did not think you would see this from the road," she called as they came closer. "I almost missed it from the air."

"What did you find?" Memfis asked. She smiled and led them around the rocks, making a sharp turn into what turned out to be a large grassy semi-circle, hidden from view by tumbled rocks and a fallen tree. Memfis nodded slowly.

"This is good," he said. "This is very good."

"This is better," Aria added. She gestured, and Aven saw two small, furry bodies on the ground. It took him a moment to remember what they were called. Rabbits. Owyn had told him what they were when they'd seen some in the forest.

"You hunted?" Memfis asked. "Where? I didn't think there was any game."

"I was lucky," Aria answered. "When I found this place, I landed up there—" She pointed at a high ridge of rock. "There is a colony of rabbits on the far side. They did not see my shadow, so I caught two before they hid. If we stay here overnight, I will lay snares. For now, this is half a rabbit for each of us."

"And there's grazing for the horses," Owyn added. "We're camping here?"

"We're camping here," Memfis confirmed. "If you'll start unloading the horses, I want to walk around. I need to see where we are."

He walked away, and Owyn called after him, "We have a map for that!" Memfis just waved, and Owyn shook his head. "He's in a better mood, at least," he said, his voice lower. "I haven't seen him this tangled up... well, the week before you showed up, he was bad. Not this bad, though."

"He's worried," Aria said. She crouched and drew her knife. "If one of you will build a fire, I will clean these and get them ready to cook."

"Owyn, you're better at that than I am," Aven said. "I'll take care of the horses."

"They like you," Owyn said. He started walking around their campsite, looking for wood. "They behave better for you than for anyone."

"Except you," Aven pointed out.

Owyn laughed. "Except me. I'm going to have to go hunting for wood. Back in a few minutes." He walked off in the same direction that Memfis had gone.

Aven busied himself with the horses. He'd taken over most of these chores early, when he'd realized that he wasn't much help with setting up the camp. And the horses did seem to behave better for him than for anyone else, excepting only Owyn. He hobbled the horses, then took off saddles, replaced bridles with softer halters, and unloaded the packhorse. He poured a measure of grain into each of the feedbags, then carried them to each of the horses, laughing as they nudged and pushed, trying to get at what they could smell. Once that was done, he started grooming Anvil, the big packhorse. He glanced up between strokes, watching Owyn as he came back with an armload of wood. By the time he was finished with Anvil, Owyn had a fire burning, and the rabbits were cleaned and spitted, waiting for the flames to die down. Owyn saw him looking and got up, wiping his hands on his trousers as he came over.

"What still needs to be done?" he asked.

"I've only gotten Anvil, and I haven't checked his feet. You know he won't let me do that," Aven asked, moving on to start grooming Cloud. "And they need water. Did you see any place where we can take them to drink?"

"Yeah, there's a stream," Owyn answered. He went to Anvil and rested one hand on the horse's shoulder. "All right, old man. Let's check for rocks," he said as he ran his hand down Anvil's leg. Anvil obligingly picked his foot up, letting Owyn examine his hoof. "Good man," Owyn crooned. "Good Anvil. Yeah, you've got one. That can't feel good, can it? You should let Aven do this, then you wouldn't have to wait for me." He put down Anvil's foot and went to the packs, rummaging through until he found something he'd identified to Aven as a hoof pick. He went back to Anvil and started working, keeping up a steady patter of what seemed to be complete nonsense, until he'd finished checking all four feet. Without asking, he moved on to Memfis' horse, Dasher, keeping up the same constant nonsensical one-sided conversation. The horses seemed to appreciate it, letting him work on their feet while Aven brushed them down. By the time they were done, Aven could smell the rabbits cooking, and Memfis had wandered back from wherever he'd gone.

"I have something to show you, Aven," he said as he came closer. "You and Aria. I hadn't realized that we were at the right place on the coast."

"For what?" Aria asked. "I need to wash, and I want to bury the offal away from the fire. We have no way to tan these skins, I'm afraid. A waste."

"Save them. We can use them for trade. And I'll show you now," Memfis said. "Owyn, will you stay here?"

"Sure," Owyn answered. He looked puzzled, but settled down next to the fire. "I'll go wash when you get back. I'm all over dirt."

Memfis led them out of the campsite, and down an incline toward the stream that Owyn mentioned. Aria went off a little ways, then flew down to meet them at the stream, washing her hands clean. Aven splashed water on his face, then followed Memfis across the stream and toward the edge of what turned out to be a fairly steep cliff.

"Careful," Memfis warned. He pointed. "It's a long way off, but we can see it from here."

Aven blinked, squinting into the distance. The coast curved around, far to the north, and he saw something gleaming in the late afternoon sun. A building? No...

"Is that the Palace?" Aria asked.

"That's the Palace," Memfis confirmed. "I wasn't sure we were far enough north to see it. But that's the Palace. That's the place that should have been your home, the both of you. You were both supposed to have been born there."

"How far is it?" Aven asked. "By horse, I mean. That's maybe a day's sailing, in a good wind."

"We're four or five days from the Palace by horse," Memfis said.

"The healing center is three to four days, you said. It's that close to the Palace?" Aven looked back out over the water. "Owyn was right. Mannon didn't have to chase us. He's already there. He got on his ship and he's been waiting for us to come to him. And probably sleeping in his own bed while doing it." Aria moved to his side, slid her arm around his back. He draped his arm over her shoulders and hugged her to his side.

"What do we do now?" she asked. "If he is waiting for us, where can we go?"

"For right now, we're going back to camp and we're going to eat," Memfis answered. "Then we're going to sit down with the map and make some plans. Real ones, not the dreams of an arrogant old fool who should have known better, and who should have listened to the people telling him not to rely on visions."

"Memfis, it's not your fault," Aria said gently.

"It is. Meris told me more than once I couldn't just live my life from vision to vision. That I had to plan, and look at the real world. If I'd been paying attention, or even actually looked at that map, we'd be in a better state now than we are," Memfis replied. "So now, I'm listening. Once we have real plans, and have an idea of how long we'll be on the road, then we'll reprovision."

They walked back to the campsite, where Owyn was waiting for them. He'd pulled the leather buckets out of the packs, and announced as they came closer, "I need to wash. The horses need water. We do, too."

"Are the rabbits finished?" Aria asked.

"I'm not sure," Owyn answered. "Almost, I think, but I've never cooked rabbit over an open fire before. It's different."

"I'll check," Aria said. She stretched to kiss Aven, then kissed Owyn in passing.

Aven went over and picked up one of the buckets. "I'll help you with the water. Horses or people first?"

"People first," Owyn said. "Then we can take the horses down to drink."

"Mouse, where's the map?" Memfis asked.

"My saddlebag," Owyn answered. "You want it? I'll get it for you."

"Please. I want to study it. The way I should have from the start," Memfis said. He sat down near the fire, rested his elbows on his knees, and stared into the fire. Owyn frowned. He went and got the map, handed it to Memfis, then grabbed the other bucket.

"What happened while you were out?" Owyn whispered as he and Aven headed for the stream.

"I think it really settled in him that he didn't think things through all the way," Aven answered. "He didn't know how things were out here. He didn't look at the map. And he didn't realize that Mannon had to have known where we'd be going, and is probably waiting for us there." He took a deep breath. "He needs to think. We all do, before Mannon draws us in like a hunterfish."

"A what?"

"Hunterfish?" Aven grinned. "It's something from down deep. It's got a... well, a growth, on the top of its skull. And the end glows."

Owyn narrowed his eyes. "You know, I can tell when you're screwing with me."

"I am not!" Aven protested, laughing. "It lives down deep enough that not a lot of light gets there. So when there is light, fish are attracted to it. The glowing draws the prey in."

"And Mannon is drawing us in, just like that?" Owyn nodded. "On land, we'd say moths to a flame. At night, did you notice? Little flying things?"

"There are a lot of little flying things at night here, Mouse," Aven said. They reached the banks of the stream, and he lowered his bucket into the water upstream from where Owyn went to wash off the dirt. "Some of them make me itch."

"Those are bloodflies. No one likes bloodflies," Owyn said, shaking water off his hands. "Moths are like butterflies. It's hard to tell them apart, actually. But moths like bright light, so if there's a torch, or a fire, they'll fly right in."

Aven frowned. "Why?"

"Why do the fish go to the light?" Owyn asked in response. "Because it's probably the same reason."

"I don't know," Aven admitted. He shifted his full bucket to his other hand and sighed. "Mouse, I'm sorry about pushing you about learning to swim."

"That's all right," Owyn said. He filled his bucket and looked up to smile at Aven. "You didn't know. No way you could have known. Only person who knew was Mem. Nah, I'm just... not ever going out into the ocean, is all." His smile faded. "Sorry. I mean... that means I'm never going to see where you're from."

"I'd rather have you alive than out on my canoe," Aven said. He held his hand out. "Come on. Let's go back. We have to bring the horses down."

They started back up the slight slope. Owyn tipped his head back to look up. "The sky is huge. I never realized it until we got out from under the trees."

Aven looked at him. "You can see the sky from Forge."

"Not this much of it. There are buildings in the way. Makes it look smaller. And when you're in the vents, you can't see the sky at all." He snorted. "I never saw so many stars, either. Not in all my life." He squeezed Aven's hand. "I understand a little, I think. What it's like for you. Out here, I don't have any idea of what I'm doing. I'm just doing the best I can."

Aven nodded. "That's all we can do. That, and learn as much as we can, as fast as we can."

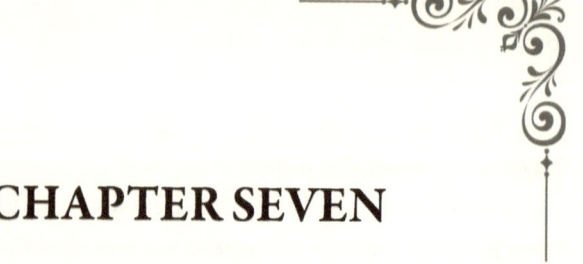

CHAPTER SEVEN

AVEN AND OWYN MADE several trips back and forth, taking the horses to the stream for water, then went back down one last time to wash. When they returned to the fire, they found Aria unpacking the wooden bowls and cups that they used for meals. Memfis sat away from the fire, hunched over the map that he'd spread on the ground. Owyn looked at him, wondering if he should go and help, or at least offer a sounding board. Then Memfis scowled, and Owyn decided that elsewhere was a better place to be.

"Is it time to eat, or can I take Aven for a walk?" he asked. Aven looked startled, but said nothing.

"You have time," Aria answered. "The rabbits are done, but they will need time to cool."

Owyn glanced back at Memfis, then lowered his voice so he could feed his curiosity without getting his head handed to him by a certain moody smith. "Can you tell me what it was that he wanted you for?" he asked Aven.

Aven answered in the same low tones, "He wanted us to see the Palace. We can just see it from the cliffs. It's a good day's sailing away, but we can still see it."

Owyn looked up at him. "You know I have no idea how far a good day's sailing is?" he asked. Aven grinned.

"Memfis said four or five days by horse," he added.

"And we can see it?" Owyn asked, and whistled, impressed. "That's a long way to be able to see."

"The coast curves. And a straight line is shorter than a winding one," Aria said. "Sailing, or flying, is a straight line. We do not need to worry about roads that may not be straight, or land that may not be passable."

"Well, that's all fine and good if you have wings or a canoe," Owyn said. "But some of us have to use roads. Speaking of which, walk with me, Fishie."

Aria giggled. "Go. I'll cut the rabbits and have them ready when you get back."

Owyn took Aven's hand, leading him out of the clearing. Behind them, he heard Memfis' raised voice. "Don't be long!"

Owyn waved to show that he'd heard, and led Aven down the slope to the stream. They followed it for a while, until they got closer to the cliffs.

"Do you want to see the Palace?" Aven asked. "Mother willing, we'll all end up there eventually."

Owyn shrugged. "I'll see it when we get there," he answered. "I just... when Memfis is in a mood, I like being elsewhere. He makes me nervous when he gets like this. Closing me out, and then getting all twisted up because he's gone off in the wrong direction? It's... I don't like it. And since I can't close myself in my room with a book, I'm being elsewhere with you."

"He gets this way often?" Aven asked. He looked back. "He isn't a danger to Aria, is he?"

"No!" Owyn gasped. He laughed. "No. If we had anything to drink right now, he'd be more of a danger to himself, really. Since we don't, he'll grumble and stew for a while, and then he'll figure out what he really needs to do. And he'll do it." He turned and looked back up the slope. "He'd get like this every so often. And the first time, I thought he was going to hurt me. He wasn't," he hastened to add. "He never would. I know that now. But back then, I was still fresh off the streets, still so new in the house that the stripes hadn't really healed yet. So he got dark, and I got scared... and I tried to crawl into his bed."

Aven stopped. "You... what?"

"Remember, I hadn't learned yet that I was anything other than a whore. I had one trick. I thought if I could get him off, he'd be nicer to me." Owyn swallowed, suddenly cold. "Shit," he breathed. "This is another one of those things that I never tell anyone, and here I go, running my mouth."

Aven stepped in behind him, pressing against Owyn's back and wrapping his arms around Owyn's shoulders. "I won't tell anyone. Not even Aria, if you don't want me to."

"I'll tell her, when I'm ready." Owyn leaned back against Aven. He rested his head against Aven's shoulder and closed his eyes. "Not really enough time to do anything."

"This is something," Aven answered. "I like holding you. Just being with you is something." He paused, then let out a short breath that ruffled the hair over Owyn's ear. "Did Aria talk to you at all?"

"No," Owyn answered. "About what?"

"She was waiting for me when I got back last night. She came swimming with me," Aven said. "And she wanted me to have sex with her."

Owyn coughed, and turned around to face Aven. "She did?" he stammered. "And... you did?"

Aven shook his head. "No. I told her no." He frowned. "Well, I didn't tell her. But you get the idea. She was right that we need to wait. But she's frustrated that we get to have what she can't have yet."

Owyn shifted from one foot to the other, wondering about the weird feeling in his belly, like a corkscrew digging away at his entrails. "It's only a couple of days more," he said slowly, feeling sweat prickling along his spine. Where was Aven going with this?

Aven nodded. He rested his forearms on Owyn's shoulders, linking his fingers behind Owyn's neck. "When we next have the time and place, I think she'd appreciate it if we invited her to watch," he said.

Owyn closed his eyes and nodded quickly. "That's fine."

"What?" Aven asked. "What's wrong?"

"I... I thought you might be saying you didn't want me anymore, because she was upset that she couldn't have you yet and I could." The words fell over themselves to get out as Owyn opened his mouth, and he swallowed and shivered, afraid to look any further up than the blue and white stone that sat in the hollow of Aven's collarbone.

"Owyn," Aven murmured. Warm fingers cupped Owyn's face, raising his head, and he met Aven's hazel eyes — warm brown and gold, with a bare hint of green, like new leaves in spring. Aven studied him. then leaned down and kissed him, his lips warm and tasting of salt. Owyn shivered again, and Aven pulled him close.

"I'm not telling you that I don't want you," Aven said, his voice rumbling in Owyn's ear. "And I didn't tell you that to hurt you." He chuckled. "If we had the time right now, there's a sheltered spot near the stream—"

"I saw it," Owyn murmured. "When we were watering the horses. In the trees."

"If I didn't think they'd come looking for us, I'd be pulling you off there right now," Aven rumbled. "I do want you. I love you, Mouse."

"And you love her," Owyn added, and mentally kicked himself. But Aven laughed.

"Yes, I do love her. And so do you. And she loves us both. She wants us to be happy."

Owyn nodded, his cheek scraping on the front of Aven's shirt. "You know, there are things that you can do, that we can do with her that won't get her pregnant."

A long pause, then... "Oh?"

"Yeah." Owyn tipped his head back. "I can teach you. Teach you both."

Aven smiled. "Once we have the time, and a place, you can teach us. Master Owyn, our expert."

Owyn laughed, and the tension drained out of him like water from a sieve. "Do you want to tell her that, or should I?"

"We'll both tell her," Aven answered. "We should go back. I'm hungry."

THERE WAS NO TIME TO tell Aria anything. Once they'd finished eating, Memfis picked up the map.

"I have two ideas," he said, unrolling the map. He stopped, and didn't continue until Aven, Aria, and Owyn had moved around to sit around the map. Then Memfis pointed. "We're here," he said. "The village where we'll resupply is here. And the healing center is there. Now, if you all are right, we can't go anywhere near the healing center. At least, not this healing center." He pointed to another spot, farther east, closer to the mountains. "There's another center here. Another ten to twelve days on the road, depending on weather. But there's a good-sized town here." He tapped his finger on a spot marked with a figure of a house and a well, located about halfway between the healing centers. "We resupply at the village here, and head inland. Resupply again when we hit that town, and go to the healing center in the foothills."

"What is the other idea?" Aria asked.

Memfis pointed to a spot farther north on the coast. "This is a Water and Earth fishing village. Aven suggested it, and it's a good idea. I know this village, and I'm almost certain that we'll find allies here. But to get there..."

"We have to pass the healing center," Owyn finished, and shook his head. "And risk being seen. We can't do that." He looked at the map. "Looks like we pass two other villages to get there. What about those?"

Memfis shook his head. "I don't know them. I've already put us at enough risk with unknowns."

"So we go inland?" Aven asked. "And then what?"

"We go north," Aria answered. "We go to the Solstice village, and I fly up to the mountains to my flock, and to raise the Air tribe. And possibly to find my Air." She cocked her head to the side, studying the map. Then she touched it. "This is the Solstice village, isn't it?"

"That's it," Memfis confirmed. "But I don't think we'd get there before the first snow, and if we don't, then we won't get there at all until spring." He sighed and shook his head, then rolled the map up. He handed it to Owyn. "Put this away, Mouse?"

Owyn took the map and held it. "What about going back to Forge?" he asked. "They know we're gone, so they won't look for us there. We can winter there and set out again in the spring?"

"That's the 'everything else has failed' plan," Memfis said slowly. "I hate to do it, because if we go back with nothing, there's no way the Council will support us. Not again."

"So we will not fail," Aria said, her voice firm. "We will go on, and we will do what we intended to do. But first, we need to resupply. Who is going with you?"

Memfis blinked. Then he smiled. "I thought about taking Owyn, but Aven was right about that, too. Mouse, you stay here with Aria. Aven, you come with me." He looked at Aven. "Change your shirt. That one is all over dirt. Leave your vest, and get your scarf."

Aven nodded and got to his feet. "My vest is packed. I didn't want it to get ruined. What else do I need?"

"Leave your swords here, and take off your gem," Memfis answered. "And when we get to the village, you're Este again. Just in case the name Aven is being bandied around."

Aven stopped in the middle of taking his shirt off. "Do I have to leave my gem?"

"It's safer," Memfis answered. "We don't want someone to recognize it. Oh, and try not to talk once we're in the village."

Aven's jaw dropped, and he sputtered for a moment before demanding, "Why?"

Owyn turned. "You didn't know? No one told you?" he glanced at Aria. "You didn't tell him?"

She shook her head. "I thought it was me. I didn't realize until we got to Forge. It didn't occur to me to say anything."

"About what?" Aven asked, laughing. "What is it?"

"Water folk talk differently," Memfis answered. "Differences in inflection, in vowel sounds. You've got a distinct Water accent."

Aven frowned. Then he looked thoughtful. "I do?" he said slowly. Then he grinned. "And here I thought it was all of you that sounded funny."

Aria squeaked. "I do not sound funny!"

"A little, love," Aven said as he went to his pack and took out a fresh shirt. He put it on and tucked it in, recinching his trousers. Then he took off the Water gem. He closed his hand around it, then held it out to Aria. "Will you hold this for me?"

She took the gem from Aven's hand. "Until you return," she said. Then she glared at him. "And I do not sound funny."

Aven laughed. He leaned down and kissed her, then wound the scarf around his neck. He held his arms out. "Am I ready?"

Owyn got up and joined Aria, studying Aven. He stepped forward, adjusting the scarf, then stepped back. Frowned.

"No, you're missing something," he said slowly. Aven looked down, then up.

"What?" he asked.

Owyn grinned. "Couple of solid kisses from each of us," he answered, and moved closer. "Definitely need those before you go."

"YOU'RE GOOD FOR HIM," Memfis said. They'd opted to ride into the village, and had brought Anvil to carry back their supplies. Memfis brought Dasher alongside Cloud so that he could talk to Aven without raising his voice. "You and Aria both. You're good for him."

Aven nodded, then stole a sideways look at Memfis. The older man seemed more relaxed now that they had a plan. Which was, he realized, just as Owyn had said. Grumble and stew, then figure out what needed to be done and do it. "He's good for me," he said. "I'd be lost without him. Without them." He looked forward again. "What do I do, once we're in the village? Besides not talk?"

"We'll find a place to tether the horses," Memfis answered. "Then just follow me."

Aven smiled. "Sounds like I'll be bored," he said.

"You won't be bored," Memfis answered.

And he wasn't. From the moment they rode into the village, Aven had to fight not to stare. He was expecting something like Forge, but smaller. He'd been wrong. There was a central well, surrounded by a rough square of buildings. In front of most of the buildings were small structures that reminded him of the deck shelters on canoes. Each one had a table of wares, or baskets, or things hanging.

"There's luck. Market day," Memfis murmured. He led the way to the well, and dismounted, tethering Dasher to a post that seemed to be there just for that reason. Aven did the same, and followed Memfis from structure to structure, listening to the conversations, and taking packages as Memfis made purchases. They weren't the only ones, for all that it was late in the day. Aven saw others doing the same thing. One of them was a young woman with the brightest hair that Aven had ever seen. It was like fire, like Trinket's fur. He didn't know human hair came in that color. He watched her as she moved around from merchant to merchant, until her arms were filled with bundles that she carried to a cart near the well. She loaded her bundles in the back of the cart, then went and continued her shopping. It seemed like a good idea, so Aven carried his own bundles to Anvil, and stowed them in the horse's packs. As he walked back toward Memfis, the woman was coming toward him. She was shorter than he was, shorter even than Owyn. She was plumper and more generously curved than Aria, and her pale skin had an array of golden spots that reminded him of seeing the sun dappling the surface of water when he was submerged. He'd have to ask Memfis what they were called. Then she smiled at him as she passed, and he felt the same bolt of recognition he'd felt when he'd first seen Aria, or Owyn.

Companion. She was a Companion.

Memfis arched a brow at Aven as he rejoined the smith. He glanced over his shoulder, then murmured, "See something you like?"

Aven kept his voice low. "I think I see our Earth."

Memfis' eyes widened, and he started to turn. Then he stopped, and walked over to another booth. "I'm needing salt. Two bags, if you have it."

Aven followed, but kept watching the girl. Another armload of bundles, and she was off to the cart again. As she walked, a small bundle slipped out of her arms and fell to the ground. She didn't appear to see it. Aven touched Memfis' arm, then trotted across the square and scooped up the bundle. He followed the girl, who turned to look up at him with eyes as green as vivid coral. He bowed, offered her the bundle, and smiled.

"Oh!" she gasped. "Did I drop that?" He nodded, and she smiled, revealing dimples. "Thank you!" She took the bundle, then took his hand and tugged him closer. Her eyes met his, darted down, then back up, and with her other hand, she grabbed the ends of his scarf and tugged his head down. She moved in closer still, kissed his cheek, then whispered, "If your name is Aven, Waterborn, then you're in danger. There are uniformed men on the far side of town looking for you." Then she let him go, stepped back and smiled. He nodded, smiled his thanks, and went back to Memfis, who handed him two bags of salt.

"So, did she thank you nicely?" Memfis asked. "We're done. Let's go."

Aven followed, and pitched his voice low to keep it for Memfis' ears alone. "She knows who I am," he said softly. "And she says there are people looking for me on the far side of town."

Memfis swore softly, then jumped. Aven looked past him, and saw the girl had come up on Memfis' other side.

"Uncle, I'm ready," she said sweetly. "Let's go."

CHAPTER EIGHT

MEMFIS HESITATED, JUST long enough that Aven noticed. Then he smiled. "Of course. I'm done. Este, let's go."

"Mama said I was to bring you right home," the woman continued. She tucked her hand into the crook of Memfis' elbow and led him toward the cart. "She says that you're not allowed to be late for dinner again."

Memfis laughed. "She knows me too well."

"If you're late, Mama says that you eat with the pigs," she finished, and giggled.

Aven trailed behind them, listening to them banter. It was definitely good camouflage, but he couldn't stop feeling as if he was being watched. He let one of the bags of salt slip from his hand, and as he bent to pick it up, took a look behind him.

There were men and women in matching uniforms entering the village from the far side, fanning out and going to the different merchants. Somehow, Aven didn't think they were in town to buy supplies. Aven hefted his bundle and trotted after Memfis and the woman. Memfis had tethered Anvil to the back of the cart, and was untying Dasher. Aven put the bundles of salt into Anvil's packs, then went to untie Cloud, brushing against Memfis as he passed. Memfis looked at him, and Aven made the smallest gesture with his head, barely a nod toward the crowd of guards. Memfis looked, and his eyes widened.

"Let's get moving," he said, and helped the woman up into her cart. He mounted Dasher, and Aven pulled himself up onto Cloud's back as the woman whistled to her donkey and started forward, driving the cart away from the guard, going out of the village in the direction that Memfis and Aven had come. None of them spoke until they were well out of earshot of the village, and then not until the woman stopped her cart and took a long look behind them.

"I don't think we're being followed," she said. "Do you see anyone?"

"No," Memfis answered. "Thank you."

She smiled. "Anything to spite Mannon and his flea-ridden dogs," she proclaimed brightly. "I'm just glad I saw you first. The scarf does hide a lot, until you get up close. And I imagine a lot of girls want to get up close." She grinned and winked at Aven, who smiled in return.

"Won't they know he's not your uncle?" he asked. "The people in the village, I mean. We don't want you to be in trouble."

"Oh, I'm not from that village," she answered. "They don't know me, and the next time we need supplies, someone else can come. Now, where are you camped? I'll take you—"

"No, you should go home," Memfis interrupted. "It'll be dark soon, and we've disrupted your life enough."

She turned in her seat and looked at Memfis. "I know who you are. I came in from the north, and those guards searched my cart on the way in. I heard them talking. I know that Aven Waterborn is one of the Heir's Companions. Do you really think I'm not going to do everything I can to help you? To help her? Now where's your campsite?"

"Let her be, Uncle," Aven murmured. "It's her choice." He raised a brow, and hoped that Memfis remembered what he'd said in the village. "What's your name?"

She turned back to him and smiled. "I'm Treesi. And I know you're Aven." She frowned. "He's not really your uncle, is he?"

"Memfis, and no," Memfis answered. "Although... by courtesy, perhaps."

Treesi's eyes widened. "Memfis?" she squeaked. "Memfis Fireborn, the Companion?"

Memfis looked startled, then slowly smiled. "That would be me, yes. Now, Treesi, we're heading that way." He pointed.

"And then what?" she asked as they started moving again.

"We're heading east," Aven answered, ignoring Memfis' glare. "There's a healing center near the mountains—"

"Not anymore there isn't," Treesi interrupted. "Mannon burned out all the healing centers, once he found out that the healers were working against him. The last one fell... four years ago, I think? Yes, that's about right. Right after I came west to continue my training."

"You're a healer?" Aven asked.

"Almost," Treesi answered. "There's one healing center left, and Mannon doesn't know where it is." She looked at Memfis, then back at Aven. "I can take you there. You'll be safe, once we get past the guards."

"Which begs the question – how will we get past the guards?" Memfis said. He snorted. "We'll look at the map in camp."

OWYN TOSSED ANOTHER piece of wood onto the fire, then sat back and looked around the campsite. He and Aria had tidied up, putting things back into packs, setting up bedrolls, even hanging Aven's hammock. He'd fed the horses and taken them one at the time down to the stream for more water, then set up the picket line for them for the night. Now Aria perched on the high point of the rock, keeping watch for Memfis and Aven's return.

"See anything?" he called. He wasn't sure how much she could see in the growing shadows. Even now, after so many days on the road, it still surprised him how quickly darkness fell out here. It seemed to go from purple dusk to the dead of night in a heartbeat. And there were so many stars! He'd never seen so many, and Aven was teaching him the names of all of the ones he didn't know. "Aria?"

"I see... yes, I see them!" she called, and flew down to the fireside. "They are not alone. Get your blades or your chain. Something."

Owyn jerked to his feet. "Who's with them?"

"I cannot tell, but they're in a cart." Aria touched the bracer on her left wrist, letting the arms of the miniature crossbow engage. She loaded a dart to the string, then glanced at Owyn. "Are you waiting for them to get here?"

Owyn grimaced and ran for the packs, picking up his smoke blades. Once he had them, Aria returned to the high rocks. He moved to the shadows, waiting.

It was, he thought, the longest ten minutes of his life. The shadows grew longer, grew darker, and he had to force himself not to look at the fire so that he wouldn't be blinded. He felt Trinket shifting in his shirt pocket, and planted one blade in the dirt so that he could pat her through the cloth.

"You should have stayed with Granna," he murmured to the fire-mouse. Then he picked his blade up again, hearing a whistle from outside the walls. One long whistle, two short whistles, then another long whistle; he relaxed.

"It's all right," he called up to Aria. "That's Mem."

"It will not be all right until we know who is with them," Aria called back.

A few minutes later, Memfis rode into the campsite. He was on one side of the cart, and Aven was on the other. And the driver of the cart...

Owyn's breath caught. He had no idea who this girl was, but he *knew* her. He knew her, the same way that he'd known Aria and Aven.

"Aria," he called. "You might want to come down here."

He heard the rush of her wings, then she was on the ground next to him. "What?" she asked. Then she saw the girl, and Owyn heard her swallow. "Oh," she breathed, then stepped forward, her left arm held out and to the side. "Who is this you've brought me, my Water?" she asked. Aven grinned down from Cloud's back.

"My Heir, may I present Healer-in-training Treesi Earthborn?" he said formally. He dismounted, then went to the cart and held his hand out. Treesi laughed and took his hand, letting him help her down, even though Owyn was fairly certain that she didn't need anyone's help. When Aven brought Treesi over to Aria, Treesi looked Aria up and down. Then she giggled.

"Mother of us all. I knew I'd be meeting the Heir, but I didn't know you'd be beautiful," she said. Then her face turned almost as red as her hair. "Oh. I shouldn't have said that. Am I supposed to bow? Or kneel? Or... or something?" She bit her lip, then asked, "Is it permitted to hug the Heir?"

Aria blinked several times, then smiled, clearly amused. "Once the Heir disarms herself," she said, and looked down at her wrist. Treesi gasped.

"Is that a crossbow? A tiny crossbow?" she demanded. "May I see? I've never seen one so small!"

Aria nodded, and Treesi moved closer. Owyn watched them for a moment, then went to stand with Aven.

"Is that who I think it is?" he whispered. Aven nodded.

"I think so. But it's for Aria to say. I'm going to go water Cloud. Come with me?" He glanced at Aria and Treesi, then looked at Memfis. "We'll be back in a bit."

"Don't take too long," Memfis said. "I'll start repacking our supplies."

"I'll take Dasher, if you want," Owyn offered.

"I'll take him and Anvil down later," Memfis answered. "Go on."

Owyn nodded and followed Aven out of the campsite, heading down the slope to the stream. "So how was it?" he asked.

"There were guards," Aven answered. "Treesi helped us get out without being noticed. And we're in more trouble than we thought. Treesi says that Mannon knew the healing centers were working against him. So they're gone. All of them, except one that Treesi says he can't find."

"Oh, fuck," Owyn breathed. "So... we need a new plan."

"She says she'll take us there," Aven added. "That we'll be safe there."

"And... we trust her?" Owyn asked. He frowned. "She's our Earth, isn't she? That means we have to trust her."

"That's for Aria to say," Aven repeated. He took a deep breath. "It was like nothing I've ever seen before, Mouse. I thought it would be like Forge, just smaller. It wasn't."

"There's no place like Forge," Owyn said. Then he bit down on a laugh.

"What?" Aven asked.

"Do you know what the phrase is for feeling like you're out of place?" Owyn asked. When Aven shook his head, he grinned. "You were a fish out of water."

Aven snickered. "I am that, truly." He reached with his free hand for Owyn's. "But I have you, Aria, and Memfis. You're my place now."

Owyn laced his fingers into Aven's, stepping closer so that their arms touched. "She's cute," he murmured as they reached the stream.

"Treesi?" Aven chuckled, letting Cloud move into the stream to drink. "She is. I didn't know hair came in that color."

"What, red?"

Aven snorted. "That's not red."

"For hair? That's red," Owyn said. "What color are her eyes?"

"Green. And she has spots. Gold spots on her skin. Owyn, what do you call spots on the skin?"

"Spots? Oh, you mean freckles," Owyn answered. "She has freckles."

"You mean like your horse?" Aven asked. "Well, he does have a lot of little spots."

"Which is why he's named Freckles." Owyn let go of Aven's hand and stretched. "So, not that I'm complaining, but why did you want me to come down here with you?" Aven looked down, and even in the shadowy remains of sunset, Owyn could see the high color in his face. "Oh. You want to check out that spot in the trees?"

Aven smiled and looked up. "I was hoping we might—" His voice trailed off, and he looked past Owyn. "Did you hear something?"

Owyn turned and looked up the slope. He closed his eyes and listened... and heard a distant sneeze.

"Oh, fuck!"

"We *were* followed," Aven gasped. He tugged Cloud's reins and pushed them into Owyn's hands. "Take Cloud. You're smaller and lighter, she'll go faster. Get back to the fire, tell them we need to move."

"What about you?"

"I'll catch up," Aven said. He reached over his shoulder for a sword that wasn't there. "Go!"

Owyn scrambled onto Cloud's back and kicked her into a run. Glancing back showed Aven running behind him, and quickly losing ground. But Aven would get to the fire long before the guards. Owyn hoped. It only took him a few minutes to cover the distance between the stream and the campsite, and he jumped down from Cloud's back as he cleared the rocks.

"Guards!" he called, seeing Aria and Treesi sitting near the fire, still studying Aria's wrist crossbow. Memfis sat on the other side of the fire from them, and jumped to his feet at Owyn's warning. "We heard them. Don't know how far they are. But we need to move. Now."

"Load your packs into the cart," Treesi said. "Bunny can haul them."

"Or we can harness Anvil," Memfis said. "Where's Aven?"

"Behind me, at a run," Owyn answered. He tugged Cloud's reins over her head and let them dangle, knowing she wouldn't run off. "He'll be here in a minute." He swallowed, closed his eyes. He needed to think... but sheer panic was closing in. They were trapped. They were going to be caught. They'd failed—

"Mouse, saddle Star, Freckles and Dasher," Memfis' calm voice cut through the fog. "I'll be there to help in a minute. Aria, go up high. Try not to be seen, and see how close they are. Treesi, help me?"

Saddle the horses. He could do that. Owyn headed for the picket line, grabbing the closest saddle. It was warm, still damp. Dasher's saddle. The horse seemed to sense Owyn's fear and shied away from him.

"Oh, no," Owyn breathed. "Not now, Dasher. We don't have time for this now." He swallowed, tried to force the panic back, to think. To calm himself down.

It didn't work, and Dasher moved to the end of his tether and snorted, his eyes white-ringed.

"Let me help?"

Owyn turned to see Treesi standing behind him. She moved past him toward Dasher, clicking her tongue gently over and over, moving slowly until she was touching the horse, holding his face between her hands and breathing into his nose. Dasher didn't move when Owyn put the saddle onto him and cinched it tight.

"I'll get his bridle," Treesi said, her voice low. "Get the other horses."

"What about the packs?" Owyn asked, picking up Star's saddle.

"Aven is back," Treesi answered. "He can carry more than I can."

Owyn looked over his shoulder and saw Aven carrying one of the packs and tossing it into the back of Treesi's cart. He turned, saw Owyn looking, and smiled. Owyn tried to smile back, but he couldn't manage it. He turned back to the horses and headed for Star.

"I don't think your Anvil will fit into Bunny's harness," Treesi called. "And Bunny isn't very fast. He's old, and lazy."

"We'll make it work," Memfis called back. "How are the horses?"

"Dasher and Star are done," Owyn answered, checking to be sure his work had been done properly. There was no time for him to do it over if he fucked up this time. He went for his saddle, only to find that Treesi already had it and was hauling it toward Freckles. "I can get that."

"Help me lift it," she said. He nodded and moved in next to her, helping her to hoist the saddle up over Freckles' back. She nodded and went for the bridle while Owyn got to work on the front cinch.

"Aria, how close?" he heard Memfis yell.

Aria swooped down and landed. "We need to leave. Now."

"Right. Everyone mount up. Aria, stay with us now. It'll be too dark for you to fly soon. Treesi, you know your donkey best. You drive," Memfis turned. "Is everyone armed?"

Owyn headed for the packs, digging around until he found the pouch with his whip chain. He slung that from his belt, and picked up his smoke blades. Aven was already there. He held up one of his swords; the other was already on his back. "I'm not sure what good these will do if they start shooting arrows at us."

"They won't," Aria said. "Mannon wants you alive, and he wants me alive. His men won't risk hurting us."

"Maybe, but there's a long road between hurt and dead, and there's no saying what will happen to the rest of us," Owyn grumbled. "Mem, I've got my chain, but I can't carry my blades and ride."

"Put them in the cart where you can reach them," Memfis answered. "That's what I'm doing with mine. Then get on your horse."

Owyn nodded. He laid his smoke blades in the back of the cart alongside Memfis', then ran and mounted Freckles. Aria mounted Star, and Aven guided Cloud up to them.

"How close are they?" he asked. Aria frowned.

"We'll be hard pressed to get away from them," she said slowly.

Aven nodded. Then he turned in his saddle. "Memfis, are you taking them straight due east?"

"Yes, why?" Memfis answered. Then he coughed and sputtered, "What do you mean, me taking *them*?"

"I mean we need a diversion," Aven answered. "Or we won't get away." He looked at Aria. "You need to get away, to be safe. And there are a lot of other canoes out there."

"Aven!" Aria gasped, her face ghostly in the firelight. She closed her eyes and shook her head. "No. You can't—"

"I'm going," he said gently. He reached out and took her hand, kissing her fingers. Then he took his carry bag off over his head and handed it to her. Inside, Owyn knew, were Aven's water gem, the other two gems, the Diadem, and a single, gray pearl. She took the bag and slipped the strap over her head. Aven nodded. "I'll catch up to you. Look for me tomorrow—" he hesitated, then swallowed hard enough that Owyn heard him. "Or not at all."

"Aven—"

"I'm going with you," Owyn blurted. Then he blinked, his head spinning slightly. "I... I did just say that, right?"

Aven met his eyes. "You said you were coming with me."

"Right. I said it. I meant it. Two against however the fuck many? It's more of a chance. Isn't it?" He straightened, and repeated himself, "I'm going with you."

Aven's smile was brilliant. Then he looked at Memfis. "Take care of them, Memfis. We'll meet you when we can. And if we can't... take care of them."

Memfis nodded, his face a study in stone. He took Owyn's smoke blades from the cart and brought them over to Owyn. "You'll need these," he said. He rested one hand on Owyn's thigh. "I'm proud of you, my son. My Mouse. Try not to die, the both of you. Mother watch over you. Aria, Treesi, let's go."

Aria nodded, but she guided Star to stand next to Freckles. She looked as if she was about to cry as she leaned over and kissed Owyn. He closed his eyes and breathed her in, wishing they had more time. Wishing he hadn't wasted time. Wishing...

She broke the kiss, and he saw tears glittering on her lashes. She kissed Aven, then followed Memfis and the cart out of the campsite.

Aven moved Cloud in next to Freckles. "I wish you'd gone with them," he said softly. "But I'm glad you're here."

Owyn looked at him and realized something. "This isn't my place to die," he said, suddenly calm. "And I'm going to make damn sure it isn't yours, either."

CHAPTER NINE

THEY MOVED QUICKLY. Aven dismounted and went through things that had been left behind, lacing together cords so that Owyn could lash his smoke blades to the high cantle of his saddle. Once he was done, he remounted Cloud and they rode out of the campsite.

"We're a diversion," Owyn said. "Do we have a plan?"

Aven nodded slowly. "I think so. They went east. We need to lead the guards off. So we'll head north, and toward the coast. And be loud."

Owyn nodded. "Nice and simple. I like it. All right." He closed his eyes and listened. "Shouldn't they be here by now?"

"Let's go find out," Aven said. He looked up at the stars glowing above, then pointed. "That way." He started forward, and Owyn urged Freckles to follow. He glanced up, saw the north star, then looked back down to try and see through the shadows.

He heard the harnesses creaking before he saw the guards. They'd stopped for some reason, and he heard muffled talking. Someone swearing, followed by laughter.

"Just your luck," someone hooted. "You would throw a shoe!"

"Never mind," someone else answered. "Go on and find them. I'll start walking back and you can catch me up. Remember, the Airborn and the Waterborn are to be taken alive. Anyone else is up to you."

Aven glanced back at Owyn. "Ready?" he asked softly.

"Oh, fuck, no!" Owyn answered. "Straight at them?"

"Start shouting, like we're running scared. Head at them, then bank to the west. We don't want them to see that we're only two until we're too far for them to go after the others." Aven looked forward, then raised his voice, managing to sound as panicked as Owyn felt, "Guards! Run!"

Owyn grinned and shouted, "Head for the coast! We can lose them in the dark!" He kicked Freckles into a gallop, heard Aven whoop from behind him, and they took off into the night. He could hear the guards shouting behind them, and risked a glance backwards. It was too dark for him to see very far past Aven, and he wondered if this was even going to work. But if it was too dark for him to see them, then it was too dark for them to see him. They were following him and Aven by sound.

Aven urged Cloud to give a burst of speed, moving up next to Owyn and Freckles. "We'll need to lose them before the moon rises," Aven called. "We need to go to ground."

"Where?" Own demanded.

"You had the map," Aven pointed out. "You tell me where."

Owyn blinked, thinking fast. The map. The village. The campsite. Where were they going? North and west and...

"Dead village, near the cliffs," he said. "Not far."

"Lead the way."

They pulled ahead of the guards. At least, Owyn thought they pulled ahead. He couldn't hear them anymore by the time that they reached the ruins. He guided them into a meager shelter formed by what remained of two walls. There, he dismounted, moving to stand by Freckles' head, listening with his eyes half closed. Aven joined him, leaning one shoulder against the rough wall as he stroked Cloud's sweat-damp neck. After what felt like ages, they heard riders. Owyn recognized some of the guards' voices as they called to each other. They didn't stop, riding past the ruin. Aven frowned. He leaned closer to Owyn and whispered, "They didn't stop?"

Owyn shook his head. "Dunno. Keep quiet."

Aven nodded and went back to leaning against the wall, his eyes closed. Owyn wondered if he could sleep standing up. He'd tried it once, and had nearly broken his nose. But maybe Aven could? Owyn shook his head to clear the random thoughts. Was that leather creaking, or the wind in the trees? From the frown on Aven's face, it must have been leather. But would Aven know the difference?

The sounds faded away, and Aven relaxed. He looked up, studying the sky. Then he leaned close to Owyn.

"We need to get out of here before they come back, and before the moon rises," he whispered.

Owyn nodded. "If we walk the horses, we might be able to get out quietly," he whispered back. Aven stepped back, and his meaning was clear — lead the way.

Owyn peered out from behind the way, and saw nothing. Not that he expected to see much, given how dark it had gotten. But nothing jumped out at him, or shouted, or even moved in an overly aggressive manner, so he judged it safe enough. He led Freckles out of their shelter, and Aven followed. Owyn had to fight the urge to bolt at every sound, and was soaked in sweat by the time they had cleared the ruins. He kept going until they reached a stand of trees, where he stopped. Aven came up next to him and rested a hand on his shoulder.

"What do you think?" he whispered, his voice barely audible. Owyn shrugged.

"I think we need to put some distance between us and this place," he whispered back. "Let's move. How long before the moon rises?"

Aven looked up again, then looked east. "Not long. Less than an hour."

"Then let's move," Owyn said. He turned back to Freckles, and heard movement behind them. "Oh, shit," he breathed. "They're coming back." He scrambled up into Freckles' saddle.

"Stay calm," Aven hissed. "Go slow. They might not see us."

"They will once the moon is up!" Owyn whispered back. "Which way? We can't go east!"

"South. Stay on the coast," Aven answered. He turned his horse, heading south at a slow walk. Owyn followed, even though every instinct was screaming at him to run. He caught up to Aven without even trying, and they rode side by side for a moment before Aven reached out one hand, touching Owyn's arm.

"We'll be all right," Aven whispered. "We're almost away. We'll head south a while, then east."

Owyn nodded, taking his reins in one hand so that he could cover Aven's hand with his own. He shivered, hard, his entire body almost vibrating with the force of it. Then he turned in the saddle, searching behind them. There. Barely visible, but there.

Movement, evenly spaced behind them.

"Oh, shit," he whispered. "They're following us."

Aven turned, his hand falling from Owyn's arm and leaving a cold spot behind. He breathed out, long and low. "How well do horses see in the dark?" he asked softly.

"Better than we do," Owyn answered. "Run?"

"Run."

OWYN CROUCHED OVER Freckle's neck, feeling the horse's mane whipping at his face. He could hear Cloud, see Aven just behind him and to the right. And behind them, the guards were following, close enough that Owyn could see them clearly, even though the moon was still behind the mountains. Close, but not close enough to catch their quarry. Which didn't make sense — didn't the guards want to catch them?

Unless...

"Aven, they're herding us!" he shouted over his shoulder. "We're heading into a trap!"

He heard Aven swear, and fought the urge to giggle — had Aven even known those words before, or was Owyn a bad influence?

"The trap is south," Aven shouted back. "Possibly east, too. We can't go west. How many are behind us?"

Owyn glanced back, counting fast. "Six," he called. "I think six. They're spread out."

Aven responded by slowing Cloud to a walk. Owyn reined in Freckles, stopping as Aven did, watching as Aven turned to count, then looked at the sky. Suddenly, Owyn knew what Aven was going to propose. What they were going to do.

"You're going to get us both killed," he warned.

"This isn't your place to die," Aven reminded him without looking at him. "They've stopped. Probably wondering what we're up to."

"Oh, you mean like I'm wondering what we're up to? Aven, this is insane!" Owyn protested. "And... and I don't have any other ideas."

This time, Aven grinned. "Here's to insanity," he said. "There's nothing like an insane idea. No one ever expects them." Without another word, he turned Cloud toward the north and charged at their pursuers.

"Aven!" Owyn yelped, and chased after him.

This was clearly the last thing that the guards had expected them to do — they had spaced themselves wide as they were ranging behind Aven and Owyn, and were caught off guard by the sudden charge. It made them slow to close ranks, and Aven passed through the gap between two guards as if he were riding through a gate. The guards were closer, shouting and scrambling as Owyn passed between them, but they were still too far apart to stop him. Owyn caught up to Aven. Passed him. Had it worked? Had Aven's mad idea actually worked?

He heard the thunder of horses behind them. Glancing back, he could see the guards following, really racing this time. One of them was ahead of the others, with his arm raised. No, he was swinging something...

The tangle ropes were in flight before Owyn could open his mouth to shout a warning. He turned Freckles hard enough that the horse nearly fell, but it was too late — the tangle ropes caught Cloud's legs, and the mare screamed and fell. Aven flew over her head, hitting the ground with the sickening sound of breaking bone. He lay very still, and the world seemed to stop.

"No," Owyn breathed. "Nonononono!" He drove his heels into Freckles' flank, and the horse shot forward like an arrow. He held the reins in one hand, and reached into the pouch at his belt with the other, pulling out his whip chain. The familiar whistle cut through the air just as he reached the guard who had murdered Aven. Blood sprayed through the air, painting Freckles' flanks as the guard fell. But he died too quickly, too easily, and Owyn wheeled his horse around, circling back toward where Aven lay. He slowed and jumped to the ground, pulling his smoke blades free from his saddle and dropping them to the ground. Then he stood between the rest of the guards and Aven.

"Stand down," one of the guards called. "And you can live."

"Fuck you," Owyn spat back, and the whip chain began to sing once more.

———— ⟡ ————

OWYN HAD NEVER BEFORE gone into trance while using the whip chain. He didn't think you could. Memfis had never mentioned it, and it had never happened in any of his practicing, nor in his fight with Fandor. But there was no other explanation — one breath, he was staring down the five remaining guards as they rode toward him, and then next...

The next had him standing still, panting as if he'd run for miles. His clothes and his skin were painted with blood, and the whip chain was clotted with gore. And the moon had risen, so he could clearly see that he was surrounded by bodies, the bodies of the five guards, and amazingly, two of their horses. How had he managed to kill a horse with a whip chain? He didn't know. He swallowed, tasting blood, wondering if it was his own, or if it was something that had splashed on his face. His stomach churned, and he whimpered and turned around. Aven... Aven was there. Owyn stumbled through the grass and blood, dropping to his knees next to Aven's body, letting the whip chain fall from his limp hand. He reached to touch Aven's cheek, brushing hair back from Aven's face and running his fingers over skin that was still warm. Gently, he rolled the body over. There was blood on Aven's face, and bone sticking out of a tear in his shirt, in the middle of a bloodstain. His collarbone, maybe? Owyn wasn't sure. And it didn't matter.

"I shouldn't have waited," he whispered. "Now it's too late. I'm sorry." He closed his eyes, wanting to scream.

How was he going to face Aria? Or Memfis?

He shifted, sitting down, moving his hand to Aven's arm, and a little voice inside started whispering. He didn't have to go east. He didn't have to go find them. He could go back. Go back to Forge. Go back to the streets, and to being the animal he had been. That he should always have been. Memfis never should have taken him in. He'd only ever fucked things up.

Or... or he could go west. To the cliffs. To the sea. To his end. He'd never hurt anyone again, if he went west. He looked down at Aven again, at the silver light turning the blood on his shirt the color of jet. There were guards, other guards. Whoever was waiting for them in the south. If he went west, he could take Aven with him. Give him back to the deep.

That made up Owyn's mind, and he moved, putting his weight on the hand resting on Aven's arm as he started to get back to his knees...

And Aven moaned.

Owyn sat back down, almost biting his tongue as his teeth clacked together. "Aven?" he gasped, and fumbled at Aven's throat. It took him two tries to find it, because of how hard his hands were shaking, but it was there. A pulse.

"All right," Owyn breathed. "All right. You're alive. But if we get found here, neither of us will stay that way. So... I need to get you someplace safe." He looked around. "I need a horse. And... and I need a way to keep you on a horse."

The second part was easier than the first — he scavenged belts from the bodies of the guards, and harnesses from the dead horses. He found Cloud, who must have broken her neck when she fell. He took Aven's saddlebags, and his waterskin, and salvaged her harness. He hunted around until he found where Aven's swords had fallen, and picked them up. Then he went back to Aven and took a deep breath, dropping the pile of belts and straps to the ground, then laying the swords down with his smoke blades. He fished two belts out of the pile and used them to bind Aven's broken arm to his body. Had to keep it still, until they reached a healer. He knew that much. He used another strap to fasten makeshift bandaging over the wound. Then he sat back on his heels and tried to think of what the next step might be.

"You know, I don't know a fucking thing about healing," he said to Aven. "So this is the best you get, at least until you wake up and tell me what I need to do. Now, I need to find Freckles." Getting an unconscious Aven up onto the back of a horse was his next problem, but he wasn't ready to attack that one yet. First, he needed a horse. If he didn't have a horse, then getting Aven onto one wouldn't be a problem. And this would all have been for nothing. So he needed to find a horse. His horse. He stood up and turned around, and saw Freckles grazing in the distance. He whistled, and the horse raised his head.

"Freckles, come here!" Owyn called. It felt foolish. Horses didn't come when they were called. Not like dogs. But Freckles shook his head, then slowly walked back toward Owyn, not stopping until he was close enough for Owyn to catch his reins. Owyn ran one hand over the horse's sweaty neck.

"I'm going to need your help," he said, his voice low. It couldn't hurt, he reasoned. And talking things out sometimes helped him keep on track. "I need to get Aven somewhere safe. So I need you to stay still while I get him on your back and secure." He let the reins fall, and went back to Aven, checking the bandaging before turning his mind to his next problem. He had a horse. Now, he just needed to get Aven on to the horse. And he had no idea how — Aven was both taller and broader than he, and much heavier. Owyn could lift quite a bit, but he didn't think he could get Aven up and over the saddle.

"I don't suppose you have any ideas?" he asked. He wasn't sure if he was talking to Aven, to Freckles, or to the moon. Regardless, he wasn't expecting an answer from any of them, so when Freckles sneezed, he jumped. Then he laughed. "I don't speak horse, Freckles," he said, turning around. His jaw dropped.

Freckles was on the ground. Owyn went cold.

"Freckles?" he gasped. "No, you can't be hurt. I *need* you."

Freckles looked at him, and Owyn knew that look. He'd been on the receiving end of it before, from humans. It was a look of complete and utter disgust. He had no idea that horses could even *do* that.

"Hey!" he said weakly, but stopped when Freckles shook his head and lurched back to his feet. He walked over to Owyn, sneezed all over his shirt, then lay back down.

"You... you did that... to help me," Owyn stammered. "I... right. Right." He turned and looked at Aven. "Right. Next step. Aven on the horse." He closed his eyes, tried to think how to do this without hurting Aven. After a moment, he opened his eyes and went to the pile of belts, picking out a long, wide one that he threaded between Aven's injured-and-bound arm and his body, then under his other arm. He buckled the belt, and used it to drag Aven over to Freckles, until he was propped against Freckles' side. Owyn straightened, feeling aches in his hips and his back. So far, so good. But he couldn't have much time left. Someone was going to come looking for the dead guards soon, and Owyn needed to have Aven out of here before they showed up. He moved around to Freckles' far side, picked up the loop of belt, and dragged Aven up into the saddle, swinging his leg over so that he was seated in the saddle. Owyn leaned against him, holding him still while he caught his breath, then used the wide belt to bind Aven to the cantle of the saddle. He moved away slowly, not going too far until he was certain that Aven wasn't going to fall. Then he went for the other straps, wrapping them around Aven's thighs and knees, until he didn't think Aven would be able to fall out of the saddle if he tried. He straightened, studied his work for a moment, then turned to Freckles.

"Think this will work?" he asked. Freckles snorted, and Owyn snorted back at him. "Still don't speak horse, Freckles. But I'll take that as a vote of confidence." He went back to the pile, picking up his smoke blades and Aven's water skin. He slung the strap of the water skin over his shoulder and went back to Freckles. Squeezing into the saddle with Aven was tight, but manageable. They'd done it before, when Aven was first learning to ride. It had been fun then. Now...

Now there was no time for fun. He picked up the reins, balancing the swords and smoke blades across his thighs.

"All right, Freckles. Let's go."

CHAPTER TEN

HAVING AVEN AGAINST his back should have been comfortable. Comforting. Aven took care of them all, protected them all, and Owyn was slowly growing accustomed to having someone other than Memfis caring for him. But Aven was limp and silent, his weight heavy against Owyn. They needed to get someplace safe.

Where was safe? Now that they were moving, that was the next problem to solve. Where to go? Aven had been certain that there were traps waiting for them to the south and to the east. So he had to go north. He couldn't go any other direction. Not yet. Not until he was sure that the guards had given up and gone away.

Wait. Owyn shuddered as the thought occurred to him.

Aria, Mem and Treesi had gone east.

Had they run into a trap? Or had they gone through before the guards had gotten there. Had they been captured?

Was he alone out here?

"No," he said aloud, and watched Freckles' ears flick back toward him. "No, I can't worry about them. I have to worry about us. I have to stay on task. One thing at a time. Mem's only been trying to get me to remember that for years now. Now I need to do it right." He took a deep breath, feeling Aven's breath warm the back of his neck. "We need someplace safe. That ruin, maybe. Or..." He frowned. Would the campsite be safe to go back to? It was hidden, sort of. Near water. And there was still firewood there. It might be safe. Safer than hunting around in the dark trying to find another place. "We're going back to the campsite, Freckles," he said. Now he just needed to find it again. He growled softly. He couldn't use the stars the way Aven did. And it was dark. How was he going to find his way?

The stream. If he found the stream and followed it, he'd find that spot in the trees. Then he'd be able to find the camp. He turned Freckles to the west, and started to listen for running water. And, to his complete shock, found the stream after only a few minutes. He let Freckles drink for a moment, then pointed the horse upstream.

"Aven?" he whispered over his shoulder as they rode. "I don't know if you can hear me, but I'm going to take care of you. We'll be all right." He looked forward, seeing trees. But were they the right trees? Should Aven still be unconscious? The thought rose out of the churning mess that was his mind, and wouldn't sink back down to where he could ignore it. He glanced back over his shoulder, then reached down with one hand and pinched Aven's thigh. And felt Aven wince.

"Sorry," he murmured. He patted Aven's thigh and studied the trees that were growing closer. Not the right trees. Not yet. But they'd ridden for a while before he'd realized they were being herded. It would take him a while before he found the right place. And with Freckles having to carry the both of them, he couldn't ask the horse to go faster. They'd get there when they got there.

He yawned, blinked rapidly. Mother, he was tired! The long day, the fear, and the fight were all catching up to him. He'd need to sleep.

He couldn't sleep. Not until they were safe. And not even then — he needed to keep watch over Aven while he figured out the next step.

What was the next step? He scanned the far side of the stream for a familiar stand of trees. They were going to have to stop until dawn. He only knew which way east was because the moon was still in the east. Once it was overhead, he'd get lost. So they'd stop until the sun rose, and then head for the mountains. Surely by then the guards would give up and go away. And when the sun came up, Aria would be able to fly back and find them. She'd do that, he was certain. She'd find them... and Aven had said that Treesi was a healer! Excitement surged as he remembered that. He'd find them, and Treesi would save Aven, and everything would be all right.

"So here's the plan," he said to Freckles. "We're going back to camp. We're going to get Aven off of your back and we're going to rest. Then we'll ride out at dawn and catch up with the others. Sound good?"

There was, of course, no answer.

THE MOON WAS NEARLY overhead before Owyn saw the trees near the stream. Aven's shy invitation to visit those trees had seemed to come a lifetime ago. Owyn let Freckles drink again, then turned his head to the east, to the campsite. Riding into the hidden area behind the rockfall was like coming home, and Owyn nearly cried from relief when he saw the place was empty. There were no guards waiting for them to return. Nothing looked disturbed — everything was as he and Aven had left it.

Without being told, Freckles stood still as a statue while Owyn figured out how to get out of the saddle without kicking Aven. He dropped the smoke blades and the swords, but he managed to get himself down to the ground with the only damage being to the knee of his trousers. He picked himself up, dusted his hand off, then took a deep breath.

"All right. Let's get him down," he said to Freckles. "Then you can have a rest. I can't brush you. The brushes are with Mem. But

I can take your saddle off and make you comfortable. And you can graze."

Freckles lowered himself slowly down to the ground again. Because he was tired, or because he was being careful of Aven? At this point, Owyn was willing to believe either. He wasn't going to spend time debating it, though — he untied straps and unfastened belts, then dragged Aven out of the saddle and up against the rock wall. Then he took the saddle off Freckles' back and set it aside.

"All right. No getting into trouble," he warned as he took off Freckles' bridle. Freckles snorted at him, then wandered off to the far side of camp, where the picket line had been set up earlier. Owyn closed his eyes, gathered his next thought, then turned to the remains of their fire, and the pile of wood that remained. The fire he started was small, sheltered, and would hopefully be enough to keep them warm without giving away their presence. And, more importantly, it gave him light enough to really get a better look at Aven.

There was dried blood all down the front of Aven's shirt, and on his face, and a horrific bruise discoloring his right temple. The rest of him looked unharmed, although Owyn was sure that the bruises he'd gotten from falling off his horse on the road would be nothing compared to the ones he'd gotten tonight.

"We're safe," Owyn said softly. "For now. Tomorrow, we'll get back on the road, and we'll find them. And Treesi will take care of you until we get... where ever it is that we're going. I don't know. I don't think you know, either. You'd have told me otherwise." He sighed, looked at the fire, then laced his fingers into Aven's and squeezed gently. "I wish we'd had more time," he murmured. "To go off into the trees." He closed his eyes, just for a minute. "Mother, I'm tired. I need to stay awake. I need to keep an eye on you, Fishie, and make sure that Freckles doesn't wander off. Not that he will, I don't think. He's awfully smart." He snorted. "And

I'm rambling. Which will keep me awake, I guess." There was a scratching at his shirt, and looked down to see that Trinket was climbing his chest. He smiled and scooped her up, depositing her on Aven's leg. "You help me keep an eye on him, Trinket," he told the fire mouse. "I want to see if we left anything useful behind. A blanket, maybe. Or a bucket. We'll need water. Well, I'll need water. Which means I need something to carry water in." He got up and walked across the camp to where they had piled the packs. Things had been left behind in the hurry to get away, but nothing really useful. Something moved in the darkness, and he jumped. Then he realized it was the hammock — there had been no time to take it down before they ran.

"Close enough to a blanket," he muttered, and unfastened the hooks at the end of the canvas sling. He pulled it back to the fireside and drew his knife — the dowels holding the ends of the sling open had been sewn into the canvas, and would need to come out for it to be used as a blanket. If he opened the seams, he should be able to slide them out without damaging the hammock, in case they needed it later. He started to hum as he worked, and before too long, the humming turned to singing.

"*The sun is sinking in the west, the moon will soon be high. The stars have come to dance, the midnight festival is nigh.*" He had no idea where he'd learned the lullaby, a silly song about dancing stars entertaining the Mother with their festival. He'd just known it forever. What he could remember of it, at least. He was sure that there was more, that there had to be more than the partial verse he knew, the words he'd had to guess at over the years. But he'd never met anyone else who knew it. The first time Memfis had heard him singing it, he'd asked about it, writing down the lyrics. Memfis had taken those copied lyrics to the musician's guild in Forge, only to find what Owyn had already known — no one else knew it. Not even Meris knew it, and Owyn had been convinced for a long time that she knew everything.

It was another mystery of his past, another bit that never really fit anywhere. He glanced up at Aven, who hadn't moved. Aria sang. She'd said so. Aven sang, and drummed. Maybe one of them knew it? He slipped the dowel out of the end of the hammock, and decided that it was enough; he drew the canvas up over Aven, leaving the intact dowel at Aven's feet, making sure not to trap Trinket in the canvas folds. He settled down next to Aven and tipped his head back, closing his eyes. When Aven was awake, he'd ask. And when they were with Aria again, he'd ask her, too.

And if they didn't know it, he'd teach them. Once he got them all back together.

He needed to get up. Build up the fire. Go find something that would hold water. He needed to secure Freckles.

He needed...

OWYN WOKE UP IN FULL daylight with a dull pain in his neck, a sharp pain in his hand, and fingers in his hair. The dull pain was because his neck was crooked — he'd slumped to the side in his sleep, and was draped over Aven's legs. The sharp pain came from where Trinket had bitten him, probably to wake him up. She'd done it before, and knew it was effective. But it was the fingers that made Owyn jerk up in surprise.

"Aven?" he croaked, and saw Aven looking at him out of one eye. The other was swollen shut, the entire side of his face mottled with dried blood and bruising.

"'Wyn," Aven's voice sounded as broken as the rest of him. "...water."

Owyn blinked rapidly, trying to clear his head. "Water. Yes. I have water." He looked around, spied the water skin, and opened it.

"Small sips. It has to last, and you're in no shape to be throwing it back up." He fed the water to Aven slowly, then resealed the skin and laid it aside. "You scared the piss out of me, Fishie. Thought you were dead."

Aven closed his eye. "Hurts... hurts too much."

"Not surprised," Owyn agreed. "You're lucky. You're broken, but lucky. Cloud... wasn't lucky. She broke her neck. I got you back to the campsite. I'm going to get you back on a horse, and we're going to go find the others." He looked up at the bright blue sky. "It's a lot later than I wanted us to be moving. I fell asleep. But we'll be all right. You stay still. I'll go get Freckles and get him saddled." He leaned in and kissed Aven gently. "I'm going to take care of you," he said softly. "I promise."

The corner of Aven's mouth quirked, as if he was trying to smile, but was too tired. Or hurt too much. Owyn kissed him again, then got up, trying to stretch the aches and kinks out of his neck and back as he walked toward the other side of camp, where Freckles was grazing. "Freckles, it's time to go," he called. The horse raised his head and started walking toward Owyn, then shied away, running to the far side of the camp. "Freckles, what—?" Owyn turned, and his mouth dried.

Guards — a half dozen at least, filing into the camp through the gap in the rocks. Owyn froze, until one of them pointed at Aven.

"There he is," he said. Two guards moved past him, headed toward Aven. But Owyn got there first, tugging his whip chain free from the pouch at his belt as he ran to put himself between the guards and Aven.

"You can't have him," he said, his voice low. He shook the chain out, ran it through his hands, felt the clotted-on gore from the fight the previous night. There'd been no time to clean the chain. Hopefully, the links wouldn't stick together. He shook the chain once more, then draped it across his shoulders. "Leave. You never saw us."

"Be reasonable, boy," the first guard said. He had more braid on his coat, and appeared to be in charge of the others. "He's hurt. We have healers—"

"You can't have him," Owyn repeated. He watched as the guards ranged themselves around him. Six...eight...ten... his stomach clenched as the total climbed to fourteen. A squadron. An entire fucking squadron. "Just... just go," he finished, amazed that his voice didn't shake. "You never saw us."

"We have orders to bring him back. Let us help him. Help you both. He's hurt badly. He'll die without a healer." The guard captain, who Owyn mentally tagged as Braid, spoke gently, but the hand on his sword showed that he meant business. Owyn snapped the chain and started it singing. The tone was off — two of the links must have been stuck together. Fuck.

Braid shook his head and sighed. "So be it. Take him down. I want him alive."

The guards moved, and so did Owyn. He had the advantage — they wanted him alive. Whereas he wanted them dead. He snapped the chain around, and the closest guard fell. The others jumped back, and watched him with wary fascination.

"Watch his arm, you idiots!" Braid snapped. "Have none of you ever faced a Fire whip chain before?" He grabbed a pole-arm from one of the other guards and stalked toward Owyn, moving past the guards who were keeping a safe distance back. He leveled the pole-arm, bouncing in place as he watched Owyn. "Four, Seven, Nine, take him!"

The three guards rushed at Owyn, all from one side. He turned and swung the chain wide, seeing Braid dart forward from his other side. Too late, Owyn realized he'd been tricked, and he felt the shock run up his arm to his shoulder as the end of the chain wrapped around the pole-arm. Braid jerked the weapon back, and the handle of the whip chain flew out of Owyn's hand. Owyn stumbled back, shaking his arm. His blades. He needed his blades. He turned to run—

And sprawled under the weight of two guards, who tackled him to the ground. The wrestling match was short, the results inevitable. One of the guards pinned Owyn down while the other wrestled his arms back, shackling his wrists behind him

"And that is how you take down a man with a whip chain," Braid announced. "Remember it. Five, go take a look at the other one. How badly is he hurt?" He nodded toward Owyn. "Let him up."

The guards got off Owyn, and he rolled onto his knees, spitting grass and dust out of his mouth, tugging against the chains. His shirt hung off his shoulder, torn in the fight. One of the guards came up behind him; Owyn felt a hand on his shoulder, heard cloth tearing.

"Captain, take a look at this," the guard called.

Braid turned and came around Owyn. "A branded slave?"

"Freed," Owyn spat. "Freed and adopted."

"Someone regards you highly, then," Braid said. "Five?"

"He's hurt badly, Captain," the guard called from next to Aven. "His collarbone is broken. And the head wound... his skull might be cracked. Can't say without the healer to look him over."

"Then we'll take him to the healer," Braid called. "Bring the wagon." He came around Owyn and went to one knee in front of him. "We will take care of him. And as for you... what's your name, boy?"

"Owyn."

"Owyn," Braid answered. "Good. I can see you care about him a great deal. So I give you my word that he will be in the best of hands. My orders are to bring him in alive, and that's what I intend to do." He rose and looked past Owyn. Immediately, two guards grabbed Owyn, forcing him to fold forward.

"You, on the other hand," Braid continued. "Have killed one of my men. The penalty for that is death."

CHAPTER ELEVEN

OWYN HOWLED AND STRUGGLED, but it was no good. One of the guards put his knee right between Owyn's shoulder blades, keeping him folded, while the other seemed to be lying over Owyn's bound hands and lower back. He was going nowhere.

But... but this was wrong. This wasn't his place to die!

And yet, he heard the scrape of metal on metal. A sword being drawn, and he tried to throw himself to the side, to get away from the blade. The pressure on his back increased, and he heard one of the guards swear.

"He's feisty for a little guy!" One of them laughed. "Maybe we should keep him."

Owyn's mind raced. "Yeah, yeah, keep me!" he shouted. "I... I'll take his place!"

Pressure eased up for a moment, and the one who'd laughed called, "Captain?"

"Take his place and murder us all in our sleep, hm?" Braid asked. "No, I don't think so. Now hold him still!"

The guards pressed down again, hard enough that Owyn couldn't move, could barely breathe. He heard something. A snap. Another snap. Shouting. What sounded like the rush of wind through feathered wings....

The pressure on him was suddenly halved, as one of the guards fell to the side. There was a javelin embedded in his chest, and a shocked look on his face. The other guard moved, and Owyn was free. He scrambled to his feet and ran toward the rock wall where the guards had Aven — he lay flat on his back, on top of the hammock canvas. They must have been using it as a litter. Owyn crouched next to Aven, looking around wildly. There were archers up on the rocks, picking the guards off from above. One of them had bright red hair — wait, was that Treesi? That meant that... his thought trailed off as Aria landed in front of him. She stood with her back to him, straddling Aven's feet, her wings spread wide, her left arm raised to shoot any guard who made the mistake of threatening her men. Over her shoulder, she asked, "Are you hurt?"

"I'm not. Aven is hurt. Hurt bad." Owyn answered, relaxing as everything that was wrong in his world vanished. His Heir had come. They would be all right. He would be all right. He'd trusted her... and she hadn't failed him. "Mother of us all, you're beautiful," he breathed, and saw the muscles in her back twitch. Had she heard him?

"Not now, Owyn," she whispered, and turned her head just enough that he saw the color in her cheeks. "But thank you."

Relieved, and almost giddy from it, Owyn watched as the guards fell before the archers. "Who are your new friends?"

"Friends of Treesi," Aria answered.

"They're *healers*?"

"Not all of them, but they are from the healing center. Memfis is waiting for us there." Aria looked up and called, "Treesi?"

"There's no one else that we can see," Treesi called. "I think we've dealt with them all. I'll be right there."

Aria lowered her arm, and looked around. "Someone find the keys to the chains," she called.

"The one with all the braid, he'll have them," Owyn added. "He was in charge."

Aria nodded as she secured her crossbow, then turned to face him. She came and knelt down, and Owyn shifted, giving her room so that she could better reach Aven. But Aven wasn't her focus — Owyn was, as she grabbed him and kissed him, more deeply than she had ever kissed him before. He squeaked in surprise, then whimpered, closing his eyes and pulling futilely against the chains. He trusted her, and she'd proved to be worthy of that trust. She'd never hurt him, and while he'd known it before, he truly believed it now. Now, he knew it in his bones. So she could do anything she wanted to him right now, and he'd thank her for it. And he was pretty sure she knew it, as she moved slowly away. Her breathing was quick, her color very high.

He cleared his throat. "Not...not that I'm complaining, but what was that for?"

She smiled. "You had better not be complaining," she murmured, running her fingers over the line of his jaw. "I flew south, to see if I could find you. I didn't think you'd be back here, or we'd have been here before the guards. But I found the others, the ones you killed. Owyn, how can I possibly deserve you?"

Her words sank into his skin like water into dry ground, feeding something he hadn't known was there. "I... I think it goes the other way," he stammered. "I don't deserve you." He swallowed. "You're going to have to kiss me again like that later," he said, his voice low and husky. "Just like that. Once we're safe."

She nodded and smiled, her cheeks going even more red. "I'd like that." She kissed the tip of his nose before she turned. "Treesi!"

"Here I am!" Treesi called. She dropped down next to them, small puffs of dust rising around her knees and staining her skirts. She rested her hand on Aven's chest, then blinked and looked at Owyn and Aria. "Why does he have two hearts? Since when do Waterborn have two hearts?"

"He... what?" Owyn sputtered. Then he laughed. "Trinket, it's safe to come out."

Aven's shirt moved, and Trinket poked her nose out, looking around. Aria laughed and picked up the fire mouse, cuddling her as Treesi giggled. The healer turned her attention back to Aven, and her expression immediately went serious.

"He needs to be back at the healing center," she said, all levity gone from her voice. "His skull is broken, and it's pressing on his brain." She turned and raised her voice. "Marik! I need the wagon now!"

A young man came trotting over. "I found the keys, my Heir," he said.

Aria put Trinket down on Owyn's leg and took the offered keys, using them to unlock the shackles binding Owyn's wrists. She tossed the chains away, then touched his bare shoulder. She adjusted the gem at his throat, then got to her feet and walked away, moving through the others, talking softly with some, giving instructions to others. Owyn stretched his aching shoulders, watching her. Her confidence. Her poise. She was going to kiss him again, just like that, she'd said. Which meant—

"Not keeping the chains?" Treesi murmured, distracting Owyn from Aria. And from the fact that he was indeed thinking of going and picking the chains and keys up so he could save them for later. He turned to stare at her, and she winked. "You liked it. I think we all noticed you liking it."

"You need to stop noticing." Owyn coughed. "You need to pay attention to what you're doing," he continued in a lower voice. "And not me."

"He's in a healing trance, so there's not much else I can do here," she said. "So I'm doing you next." Owyn's face must have shown his shock, because she laughed. "Not like that! Goodness, if you go any more red, you'll burst a blood vessel! Now, are you hurt?"

"Bumps and bruises. Stiff shoulders. I'll ache tomorrow, I think. Nothing really of note," Owyn said with a shrug. He picked up Trinket, then looked down at himself and grimaced, putting the fire mouse back down and stripping his ruined shirt off. "Will Trinket interfere with the healing trance?" he asked as he dropped the rags next to Aven's leg.

"No," Treesi answered. "I just didn't know she was there, so I didn't know to block her. What is she? Besides adorable?"

"A fire mouse," Owyn answered. He put her down on Aven's chest, and she darted back under the folds of his shirt. Owyn smiled and slowly got to his feet, He stretched, looking around. There were two men trying to corner Freckles, who was having none of it, shying away and snapping at them when they got too close. Owyn rolled his eyes and whistled, high and shrill. "Freckles, let them saddle you!" he shouted. "It's all right. They won't hurt you!" The horse didn't seem to hear him, so he headed across the camp, brushed past the two men, and held his hands out. "Freckles, it's all right. It's over. We're all right, and no one is going to hurt you." The horse snorted at him, backing away, his eyes white-ringed with fear. Owyn stepped closer, keeping his voice low. "Really. It's safe. Come on, I'm going to need you. Then you can rest and eat." Freckles' ears perked, and Owyn laughed. "Yes, eat. And more than just grass, too. I know you're hungry. Come on."

Freckles lowered his head, and slowly walked over to Owyn, rubbing his nose against Owyn's bare chest. "Hey, that tickles!" Owyn laughed, and scratched Freckles' forehead. "All right. You're going to let them saddle you, right?" He looked over his shoulder, saying, "He'll be all right now. He was just scared." That was when he realized that everyone within earshot was staring at him.

"You're Earthborn?" one of the two men nearest to him asked. He was looking at Owyn with something very close to awe.

"Me? I... no, I don't think so," Owyn answered. "He's smart, is all. He understands a lot."

The man shook his head. "That was more than a smart horse. You've got the animal sense, and that's something that only an Earthborn would have."

Owyn shook his head. "No, I... look, I was born in Forge, but I really don't know. Orphan."

"Ah." The man nodded. "Well, I'd say you've got a bit of Earth in your past, then. Come on, then... what's his name?"

"Freckles," Owyn answered. "Go on with him, Freckles."

"I might even have an apple for him, if he behaves." The man grinned. "I'm Teva, by the by. Treesi said your name is Owyn?"

"Yeah. Nice to meet you. I think," Owyn said. He looked around. "Could have been under better conditions, but thanks for saving my arse."

Teva laughed. "It's a nice one. Completely worth saving. You're welcome, and maybe we can get friendly once we get back? I'll look you up." He walked away with Freckles, leaving Owyn sputtering behind him. Aria passed Teva, looked at Owyn, then arched a brow.

"You've a strange look on your face," she said. "Are you all right?"

"He just told me I have a nice arse," Owyn said, keeping his voice pitched for her ears alone. "He wants to get friendly when we get where we're going."

She smiled. "Well, he's right. You do have a nice arse."

"Aria!" Owyn stared at her until she giggled. Then he let out a long breath and tried to explain, "Look, I was a street whore for a long time. I'm not shy about sex. But I don't think I've ever been propositioned that openly before when there wasn't money involved. It's... it's—"

"Unnerving?" Aria asked. She nodded. "Jehan warned me, weeks ago. We spoke privately one night, when I couldn't sleep. He told me that I shouldn't be surprised by my Earth and their views on sex, because in the Earth tribes, sex is not considered something about which to be shy. They are more open in their relationships, especially among the healers, he said. He said that he used to shock my mother regularly, when they were Companions to my father."

"Jehan. That's Aven's father," Owyn said. He took Aria's hand as they started to walk. "Aven's not that forward."

"Aven was raised Water," Aria said. "They've moved him into the wagon, so we're ready to go. Owyn, will you ride in the wagon with him?"

Owyn looked at her. "I'm fine—" he started to say. Then he stopped. "But you want me to keep an eye on him."

She smiled. "Treesi says that she's not a full healer yet, and she says that when she was last tested, she was a level two healer. A low two. She is not as strong a healer as Aven is, and she's not sure that her healing trance will keep him asleep until we get there. If he wakes, he will stay quiet if you're with him. He won't fuss."

"Much. He won't fuss much," Owyn corrected, and she laughed.

"He won't fuss much," she agreed. He squeezed her hand and nodded.

"I'll ride in the wagon with him," he said. "Will you take Freckles? He knows you. Assuming you didn't bring Star. Did you fly the whole way from wherever?"

"I flew. So I will take Freckles."

Owyn nodded, and let her hand fall as they reached the wagon. He climbed up into the back, sitting down with his back against the side. Aven lay silent and still next to him, partially covered by a rough, wool blanket. Next to him were his swords and Owyn's smoke blades. Owyn rested his hand on Aven's uninjured shoulder. They were all right. He could relax now.

"Did you bind his arm?" Treesi asked, climbing up into the driver's seat.

"Yeah," Owyn answered. "It was the only thing I could think of to do."

"It was a good idea," she said. "Has he woken up at all?"

"He woke up... not long before the guards found us. I gave him something to drink, and he talked to me a little."

"He was coherent?" Treesi nodded. "That's a good sign. All right." She looked around, then picked up the reins. "You're missing your shirt. If you're cold, there's another blanket back there, if you want it. There's a bit of a nip in the air this morning. It's early for it, too. It'll be a cold winter."

Owyn found the blanket, rolled up against the side of the wagon. He shook it out and wrapped it around his shoulders. As he did, he heard something shift and clink. A bundle. A bundle that he recognized. At least, he recognized the cloth. It was the tattered remains of his shirt. He reached over, unwrapped the bundle, then coughed and wrapped it up again.

"I thought you might want them," Treesi murmured. "So I saved them. And if you don't want them, then someone else will. They're good quality."

"Treesi—"

She turned in her seat, her eyes wide. "Owyn, am I making you uncomfortable?"

"Yeah," he answered. "Yeah, a bit. It's a bit much."

"I should have remembered that. Alanar is always telling me I need to be careful around people who aren't Earth, and who aren't healers. That you're not like us. That you're not as open about loving."

"It's just new, is all," Owyn hurried to say. "I'm not used to it. Well, not anymore. And who?"

"What? Oh, Alanar? He's my training partner." She turned around again, and snapped the reins. "He keeps reminding me that people who weren't brought up in a healing center won't see things the way I do."

The wagon started to move, and Owyn shifted so that he could sit and look up at her profile as she drove. Her freckles were interesting — scattered across her cheeks, and all up and down her arms. He wondered if there were any anywhere else. Trey had freckles, Owyn remembered. All over his back. Owyn used to play connect-the-dots with them. He nodded, and yawned, then looked around and saw Aria riding on the other side of the wagon, where she could watch him and Aven, and see the road. She smiled at him.

"You can sleep, if you want to," Treesi added. "It'll take us a while to get where we're going."

"And we won't be bothered?" Owyn asked. "By guards?"

"They've all been dealt with," Treesi said. "There were only two squads outside the village yesterday, and that's who followed us. Aria thinks they sent one squad on ahead and around to lay the trap, and you got almost half of that one. We picked up the rest of that squad, and did for the others."

"They won't send out anymore?" Owyn yawned again, hearing his jaw crackle.

"Not for hours," Treesi said. "Not until they realize that this lot is long overdue. And by then, we'll be safe." She reached back with one hand and smoothed his hair. "Go to sleep, Owyn."

Owyn smiled. He shifted around until he could stretch out next to Aven. He rested his hand on Aven's stomach, pillowed his head on his other arm, and closed his eyes, letting the swaying of the wagon rock him to sleep. By the time he woke up, they'd be safe.

He wasn't expecting to be woken by Aven screaming.

CHAPTER TWELVE

OWYN BOLTED UPRIGHT when Aven started screaming, looking for whoever was attacking them. But the only person he saw was Treesi, who was swearing as she tried to control the startled donkey. It was dark, the space dimly lit by widely spaced torches that smoked and sputtered. Aven's screams echoed off the stone walls that were close enough for him to reach out and touch. A tunnel? Were they in a tunnel? Or a... oh, *fuck*!

"Oh, no," he gasped, understanding. He rolled onto his knees, catching Aven's flailing arm just before Aven connected, and got down next to him, pinning him down gently. Aven's eye was open, but Owyn didn't think Aven was seeing him at all. No, he was twenty years ago, and underwater.

"Aven!" he shouted. "Aven, listen to me!" He shifted until he was kneeling over Aven, almost nose-to-nose. "Aven, it's Owyn! It's Mouse! Come on, it's all right. I'm here. You're not alone."

"Owyn!"

He hear Aria's voice, but didn't look up. "Aven, you're not alone," he repeated. "You're safe."

Aven's breath hitched. There were no words in his voice, only sounds, "..c-c-c-c-c-c!"

"I know," Owyn said, trying to be gentle. "I know, we're in a cave."

"It's not," Treesi called. "We're in a tunnel. We're almost through. What's happening?"

"You hear that?" Owyn demanded. "Aven, it's not a cave. It's a tunnel. A tunnel! We're almost out. We're almost through. You're not trapped. You're not alone. Aven, can you hear me?"

Aven's breath hitched again, and when he breathed out, it was like a low whistle that ended with: "M—mouse?"

"Yeah," Owyn gasped. "Yeah, Fishie. It's me. You're all right." He paused. "Well, you're not entirely all right. But you're not trapped. We're not in a cave, and I'm here. Aria is here. Somewhere. Treesi is here. We've got you."

Treesi climbed down into the back of the wagon, kneeling next to Owyn. He looked past her to see Teva had taken the reins. "What happened?" she asked

"I'll explain later," Owyn whispered. "Can you put him out again?"

"Move over a little," she said. He shifted, and she moved into his place. "Aven, do you know me?"

Aven frowned slightly. Then he smiled. "Treesi."

"Good. I'm going to put you back into a healing trance." She rested her hand on his chest. "When you wake up again, we'll be out of the tunnel."

"... understand."

"Good," Treesi murmured. She closed her eyes, and Owyn watched as Aven's body softened and relaxed, as his breathing slowed. He sat back and let out a breath, closing his eyes. He was, he realized, shaking. Where was Aria?

"What was that?" Treesi demanded.

"He was trapped in a cave when he was little," Owyn answered. "He told us he doesn't know how long he was trapped before his mother got him out. And he doesn't do well with caves now. I wasn't expecting this, though. When we went into the caves in Forge, he wasn't nearly like this."

"Doesn't do well... that's an understatement! And no one thought to tell me this?" she asked. "I could have reinforced the trance before we got here!"

"And when exactly was I supposed to do that?" Owyn asked in response. "When I was snoring? In case you forgot, I had no fucking idea where we were going, and you told me to go to sleep! Where's Aria? She'd have told you, if you'd asked her."

As if on cue, he heard Aria's raised voice, "Treesi? Owyn?" She sounded shrill. "One of you needs to answer me!"

"He's all right, Aria!" Owyn called back. "You can smooth your feathers!"

"Be gentle! There's no room for her to ride next to us," Treesi said softly. "This tunnel is barely wider than the wagon. But it's a smoother road than the wider tunnel. She's riding near the front, with Marik. We wanted to make sure she had room. Teva, get us moving again. I'm staying back here."

"Yes, Treesi," Teva said, and the wagon lurched. She leaned over Aven, resting her hand on the skin of his chest where his shirt hung open. Then she sat back.

"We'll have the Senior Healer see to him once we get into the center," she said. "I have him stable, but I'm not a strong enough healer yet to do more than that."

"You're doing a lot more than I can," Owyn said.

"I don't think I would have been able to calm him down," Treesi pointed out. "I'm sorry I snapped at you. Do you want to go back to sleep? We're not there yet, but it won't be very long."

"Nah, I'm awake now," Owyn said with a shake of his head. He rolled his shoulders, then looked down at himself and held the blanket open. "Want to share? It's cold."

Treesi smiled and moved to sit next to him, close enough that he could close the blanket around them. It was only once she was pressed against his side that he realized what he'd done — he was half-naked, with a beautiful woman cuddled up against his side.

"You're very tense," she murmured. "Are you all right?"

"I..." Owyn started. He cleared his throat. "This... isn't an invitation. And I don't mean to be insulting, or rude, or... or anything. I just..." He stopped, closed his eyes, took a deep breath, then let it out. "It's been a long day, Treesi."

"And it's not even midday yet," she said with a giggle. "But I understand. You were being sweet and protective, and wanted to keep me warm. Thank you." She rested her head on his shoulder. Her hair smelled like lavender and sunlight. "Don't worry. I'll behave myself. I'll wait until you're more used to me before I ask you for sex."

"Excuse me?" Owyn yelped. She giggled again.

"Did you think I wouldn't?" she asked. "You're awfully cute. I like how intense you get, when you're concentrating. I like your muscles. You're a smith, Aria said. That means you're strong. And we're almost the same height. It isn't often I meet someone who isn't miles taller than me." She snuggled closer still, and Owyn was suddenly much warmer under the blanket than he had been before.

"I..."

"Am I making you uncomfortable again?" she asked.

Owyn opened his mouth, and the truth fell out. "Only because my trousers are getting tight."

Treesi giggled, and Teva laughed merrily. Owyn had forgotten the man was in earshot. He swallowed, and tried to focus on Aven. Tried to think of something dull. Bloodlines. That was it. Aria was the daughter of Milon, who was the son of Varia, who was the daughter of Meris. Meris was the daughter of Armiona, daughter of— A hand on his thigh drove all thoughts of lineages and bloodlines out of his mind. He turned toward Treesi to find her looking at him, close enough that he could feel her breath on his face. In the shadows, he couldn't see the color of her eyes, and at the moment, he really needed to know if they were as green as Aven had said they were.

Then the wagon rolled out into the sunlight, and Teva laughed and called out, "We're here! Welcome to Terraces!"

Owyn looked around, trying to see everything all at once. There was a lot to see — they had come out of the tunnel into what looked like a park in a city that was cut into the cliffside. The city was terraced, with levels rising above the park, and, he assumed, below. He could smell salt water, and wondered if they overlooked the sea. The idea made him queasy.

Teva drew the wagon to a stop near a ramp that led to a lower terrace, and which was crowded with people. Owyn saw a familiar face in the group — Memfis!

"Got a wounded man here!" Teva shouted. "Need a litter! He needs to get to the Senior Healer now!"

From where he sat, Owyn saw Memfis' face go ashen, saw his father start to push through the crowd. Owyn cursed softly and swarmed out of the blanket, jumping down from the wagon as Memfis came running up.

"Mouse!" Memfis gasped. He grabbed Owyn by the shoulders and looked him up and down. "You're not hurt."

"No, it's Aven," Owyn said. "They took down Cloud with a tangle rope. He was thrown—" All at once he was engulfed in a tight embrace, his face pressed against Memfis' chest. He awkwardly hugged Memfis back — the smith had never been demonstrative before, and Owyn wasn't sure how to respond. Memfis let him go, looked him up and down once more, then frowned.

"Where's your shirt? And Trinket?"

"My shirt got torn up," Owyn answered. "Trinket is with Aven. At least, she was the last time I looked. And Aria... where's Aria?"

"Behind you."

Owyn turned and saw Aria a few steps away, leading Freckles. She nodded over her shoulder. "They are taking Aven to the Senior Healer. I am going to go with them."

Owyn nodded. "Go. We'll catch up with you. Having all of us underfoot won't be good for him."

"What happened in there?" she asked. "He was screaming—"

"What?" Memfis gasped. "What happened?"

Owyn sighed. "He woke up, and we were in the tunnel," he said. "He panicked. He thought he was trapped in a cave again. And I didn't see it happening until he was screaming because I was asleep."

Aria nodded. "They asked me if I wanted a smoother road, or to be able to ride with you. I thought the smoother road was the better option." She gnawed her lip, then shook her head. "I will apologize to him when he wakes. Where is Trinket?"

"In his shirt, I think. Unless Treesi has her."

"I'll find her, and hold her for you." She kissed Owyn on the cheek, then on the lips. Then she hurried after the group of people carrying Aven away.

Owyn took a deep breath, let it out, then rubbed his hand over his face. "Mem, where are we?"

"Terraces. Apparently, the last healing center in the Earth tribe lands," Memfis answered. He put his arm around Owyn's shoulder and led him back toward the ramp.

"Owyn! Wait for me!"

Owyn saw Treesi running toward them. "Treesi? Shouldn't you be with the other healers?" he asked.

She shook her head. "I've been told to take a break. Holding the healing trance as long as I did is past where my teacher thinks I should push. Memfis, sir? Where have they put you?"

Memfis smiled. "You don't need to call me sir, Treesi. And Rhexa said it was house Fourteen Southwest."

Treesi nodded. "I'll have the weapons and your funny stick things brought there, and take you on to the main healing complex. That's where they've taken Aven."

Owyn blinked in confusion. "What? Funny stick... you mean my smoke blades?"

"Smoke blades?" Treesi's eyes widened. "Those are smoke blades? That means you're a Smoke Dancer, too?" She grinned. "Will you show me? I want to see you dance!"

Owyn resisted the urge to fidget as his ears started to burn. "I... yeah, sure," he stammered. "I... once we're settled, all right?"

"Oh, definitely!" Treesi agreed. She ran her hand down his arm, smiled, then turned back to the wagon. Memfis tugged Owyn down the ramp.

"She's interested?" Memfis murmured as they walked.

"Because, among other things, I'm short," Owyn answered. "I'm not miles taller than she is."

Memfis chuckled. "Aria told me that she'd approach Treesi with the Earth gem once you and Aven were with us, so you could do it together. Now, I imagine she'll wait until Aven is healed."

Owyn nodded. He looked around, saw no one in earshot then lowered his voice. "Mem, you know I'm not shy about sex—"

"I'd be frankly shocked if you were, given your history," Memfis said dryly. "And, given your history, I'm sometimes a little shocked you're not now. Once burned, after all."

"Really? I just... I'm just... Look, I've been propositioned more blatantly in the past few hours then I would have been in an entire night working the Tannery Row drinking houses after payday!" Owyn ran one hand over his short hair. "I just... they're more bold here than some of the whores I knew, and that's saying a lot." He licked his lips and looked up at Memfis. "I know I don't know a lot about how... regular people handle sex. I never learned that. Is this it?"

"If by regular people, you mean Fire tribe, then no. This is Earth tribe, and these are healers. They're a breed unto themselves, and all the rules are different." Memfis smiled. "We're late having this conversation, Mouse. I was expecting something like it over a year ago. When you didn't ask, I thought I'd gotten off lucky."

Owyn shrugged, shaking off Memfis' arm. "It was easier to not think about it when I was a slave. I mean, who was going to look at me? Except Fandor, and he didn't want me for sex. He wanted me dead." He turned and spat into the grass, then wiped his mouth and looked at Memfis. "Now, I'm free. I'm a Companion. And... I've got people who aren't Aven and Aria looking at me. Wanting to do more than look. And I don't know what to do about that."

Memfis nodded slowly. Then he let out a deep breath. "Well, this is going to be an interesting conversation."

"Mem—"

"No, it's all right. It's just... I know I adopted you, and I know that makes me your father. But I never thought of myself as being a father, so I somehow never expected to have a 'where do babies come from' discussion. Ever. That was always supposed to be Jehan's job. We decided it when Liara told us she was pregnant." Memfis laughed. "You know, I think I might have given up drinking at the wrong time."

It was a joke. Owyn knew it was a joke. But he flinched anyway. He swallowed and looked away. "We don't have to—"

"No, we do. And thank you, for trusting me enough to come to me with your questions. Let me think on how best to answer them." He rested his hand on Owyn's shoulder. "Just remember, they will all always take no for an answer. If you tell them you're not ready, they'll honor that."

Owyn nodded slowly. Then he frowned. "And what if they don't?"

Memfis smiled. "Then you're permitted to beat the shit out of them."

Owyn coughed. "Mem!"

"I'll show you the law that says so," Memfis said with a laugh. "Not in so many words, but it's part of the Earth tribal laws. We learned that years ago, as part of our training." He frowned. "I'll need to get a copy of that. And the other tribal laws. You all need to know them forward and backward."

"Why?" Owyn asked. Memfis turned a corner, leading them away from the park. The area they were entering was laid out more like Forge, but still managed to look entirely different. Owyn looked around curiously at the houses — the doors and windows were wider than he was used to seeing, and he wasn't sure why. They walked for a while before he turned his attention back to Memfis. "We have one Companion from each tribe. Why not just have them know their laws?"

"Because then you only have one person's interpretation of the law," Memfis answered. "That's Fourteen, over there. The one on the end." He led Owyn to the house, opening the door and taking him inside a large front room that spanned the width of the house. Owyn nodded and looked around. To his left was what looked like a dining area, furnished with low backed chairs around a large table. To his right, cushioned benches hugged the walls, and a fireplace faced the front windows. There was a wide corridor across from him, and their bundles were against that wall, next to the fireplace.

"There are three bedrooms down the hall. There's a kitchen, too," Memfis added.

"Three bedrooms?" Owyn asked. "Is Aven sharing with me?"

"You'll have the larger room, the one with two beds. You don't have to use both of them, but you have them." Memfis went over to the pile. "Let's sort this out."

They started moving things, carrying bundles down the corridor, but had made no real dent in the pile before Treesi arrived, carrying a bundle of blanket that contained Aven's swords and Owyn's smoke blades. She smiled merrily as she entered. "Where should I put these?" she asked.

"I'll take them," Owyn replied. He took the bundle and carried it down to the large, airy room at the back of the house. He set the bundle down on one of the two beds, the one where Aven's carry bag already rested. Then he went back to the front room, where Memfis was talking with Treesi.

"Have you seen him?"

"Not yet," Treesi answered. "I came right here from the stables. But if anything had gone wrong, they'd have come and gotten you."

"Wait," Owyn said. "What could go wrong?"

She turned and smiled at him. It wasn't the smile she'd shown him before, the one that showed her teeth and lit her eyes. This was a quiet smile, but it looked as if it had been drawn on her face. It was all closed lips, projected serenity, and absolutely no expression in her eyes.

"Why are you smiling like that?" he blurted before he could stop himself.

"Like what?" Treesi asked. Then she laughed and smiled her open, honest smile. "Sorry. That was me being Healer Treesi. Not plain Treesi."

"All right, Healer Treesi," Owyn said. "Answer the question?"

She sighed. "As Healer Treesi? I can't. I'm not supposed to — I'm not a full healer yet, and he's not my patient. But speaking as plain Treesi? Any kind of injury as serious as the head wound he took could turn sour quickly. Brain bleeding is very bad." She looked around. "Do you want help moving things, or do you want to go to the healing complex?"

Owyn didn't even look at Memfis. "The healing complex. Please."

Treesi nodded. "This way."

CHAPTER THIRTEEN

ONCE OWYN WAS DRESSED, they left number Fourteen, and turned left, walking down the wide street.

"Treesi, this place isn't like any Earth town I've ever been in," Memfis said. "It's laid out more like a Fire city, but the architecture isn't Fire. And it's not entirely what I remember from Earth. And the furnishings in our house? Those look like they're made for Air."

"I know," Treesi agreed. "It's strange. This place was unique. Alanar was born here, and he says that there were all four tribes living here in Terraces when he was small. I was born a long way east of here. Days and days by cart. I'd never seen anything like this before I came here. They kept having to send me out with guides, or send people to look for me. I was always getting lost!"

Memfis nodded. "That explains the Fire streets, and the Air houses. And the Earth healing complex. There was Water here, too?"

"So Alanar says," Treesi answered. "And he knows most things."

"But... how come you got lost? I mean, it's all rings and spokes, isn't it?" Owyn asked. "If it's like Forge?"

"I've never been to Forge, so I'll take your word for it," Treesi answered. "And, well... I have trouble with places. I'm not good with rights and lefts, or compass directions, and I don't navigate really well." She wrinkled her nose. "So unless I know where I am by landmarks, I don't really know where I am. It takes me a while to learn, so when I first came here, I was lost. A lot."

Memfis nodded. "Do you reverse your letters?"

She smiled. "How did you know?"

Memfis laughed. "Because I know someone who is the same way. Owyn, you know who I mean."

Owyn chuckled. "Master Smith Ivo? Yeah, I remember him."

"I trained with him," Memfis said. "He's a wizard in the forge, but he gets lost walking out his own front door. He wears a bracelet on his left wrist, so that when he needs to go somewhere, he knows which way is left. And he has to have everything written down, because he can't remember directions to save his life. We used to go out in pairs, when we were apprentices together. Back before I became a Companion." He frowned. "And they sent you out for supplies alone?"

Treesi snorted. "I know the landmarks to get to the road, and then there's only one road, and it runs straight to the village." She giggled. "And I still turn the wrong way about half the time when I get to the road. A bracelet is a good idea. I'll have to get one." She paused at an intersection, looked around, then pointed. "There. That's where we're going. That's the healing complex."

Their destination appeared to be at the center of the city. In Forge, the center of the city was a central marketplace. There were shops there, and booths that would open once a month for the Full Moon markets. It was also where the slave markets were located, so Owyn tended to avoid the area if he could. Here, though, the heart of the city was a low building that sprawled over a large area. Each section seemed to be made of a different color of stone, and Owyn wondered if the changes marked a place where another wing had been tacked on to the original building. It seemed so — there was no real sense of cohesion to the place, and the additions seemed to change angle in response to the terrain.

"Now, the rules inside are keep your voices down, and keep your hands clean," Treesi told them. "There is a basin just inside. We wash before we go any further. And any time you pass another basin, you wash."

Owyn nodded. "All right." He followed Treesi into the healing complex, blinking a little until his eyes adjusted to the low lights. The basin she'd mentioned was a small fountain in the middle of the room, the water spilling and splashing down into the basin where they all washed their hands. An attendant came and offered them squares of linen that she collected in a basket when they were done.

"Telia, where is Senior Healer Risha?"

"In nineteen," Telia answered. She pointed down a hall. "That way."

They started walking, and Owyn nudged Treesi with his elbow. "They know you here, hm?"

"I've been training since I was fourteen," Treesi answered. "First in the healing center in the mountains, then here when the purges started. The other healers, they know me."

"Training since you were fourteen?" Memfis repeated. "Treesi, how old are you?"

"I'll be twenty at the winter solstice. Five years in training isn't that abnormal. I go a little slower, because it takes me more time to read my lessons," Treesi answered. She rolled her eyes. "I know. Sometimes I think I've been training forever."

"You'll get there," Owyn assured her. "You're very good. And... I dunno. Aven's been training his entire life, so he might have you beat—"

"Aven? Is a healer?" Treesi asked. Her eyes widened. "Is his father's name Jhansri? Companion Jhansri?"

Owyn glanced at Memfis, who nodded. "He goes by Jehan, but yes."

To Owyn's shock, Treesi actually squeaked in her excitement. "And... is he coming *here*? Will I get to meet him?"

Memfis took a deep breath. "We don't know where he is, Treesi. Or if he's alive. So... ah, do I have to say that you shouldn't fawn over Aven about his father? He's already torn up losing about his parents."

Treesi stopped walking. "Oh. Oh, no. Both of them?"

"At the same time. Mannon took them, and we don't know if they're alive."

Treesi's eyes were wide as she nodded. "I'll be good. I won't... should I hide his books?"

"His... Jehan wrote books?"

"His treatise on mountain fever is required reading," Treesi answered. "And he wrote on anatomical differences between the human tribes and the subhuman ones."

"Subhuman?" Owyn gasped. "What does that mean?"

"Air and Water," Treesi answered. "Those tribes are part animal, so they're subhuman. And subhuman means..."

"Not all human," Owyn finished. His skin ran cold, then hot. He'd heard that before. Some of the elite in Forge said that about street boys like him. "Oh, no. No, you're not going to call them that. Aven and Aria are two of the best people I have ever met," he said, his voice almost a growl. "They are loving, and wonderful, and funny, and protective, and they're more fucking *human* than some of the Fire tribe I used to deal with back in Forge. And I don't care who you are, you will not insult them like that—"

"Mouse!" Memfis snapped, and Owyn realized that Memfis had already said his name at least twice. He blanched, and stepped back, seeing the look of shock on Treesi's face, her red face. He swallowed, tucking his hands behind his back and looking down. He had a lot more to say, but none of it was an apology.

"Treesi," Memfis said, his voice low. "I lived in very close proximity to Jehan for five years. I have never heard the term subhuman used for the other tribes before now. The term he used, and the term that was in the books he let me read, was extrahuman."

She stammered a moment before she could speak. "I... I've seen that word, in the older books. Alanar showed me, in his father's books. But in the more recent ones, the books I've been using for my training since I got here, they say subhuman. So does my teacher."

"Really? Is Pirit still around?" Memfis asked.

Treesi shook her head. "Senior Healer Pirit died in the purge. That's when Senior Healer Risha took over, and Chieftess Rhexa."

Memfis blinked and sputtered, "Senior Healer *and* Chieftess?"

"Yes, sir," Treesi answered. "Senior Healer Risha is the one who will be taking care of Aven. You can speak to her when we get to..." She closed her eyes.

"Nineteen," Owyn supplied.

"Thank you," she answered, opening her eyes. She turned away without looking at him, and led the way down the hall.

"I'm not apologizing," he whispered to Memfis as they followed her.

"I'm not asking you to," Memfis answered. "I don't like this, Mouse."

"What?" Owyn asked.

"Remember how I said that the Companions all needed to know the laws? This is a good example. Senior Healer and Chieftess? That's wrong. The Senior Healer is Chief or Chieftess, and the leader of the Earth tribe. Or at least, they're supposed to be. Pirit was the Senior Healer the last I heard. I don't know what it means that the position is split now." He scowled. "I don't like this,

Mouse. And I really don't like that they're teaching the new healers that Water and Air aren't human."

Owyn nodded. "That... I thought hearing that Aven's folks call him Mudborn was bad. This is worse. This is so much worse." He looked at Memfis. "And... she thinks like that. How can she be... one of us, if she thinks that Aven isn't human? If she thinks *Aria* isn't human? How can the Mother choose her? Right now, I don't want to be near her!"

Memfis sighed. "I don't know, Mouse. I think... I don't know. Let's go see how Aven is. She turned left up there."

THEY CAUGHT UP WITH Treesi easily. She acknowledged them with a nod, but said nothing as they walked the rest of the way down the corridor, stopping at a room labeled with the number nineteen. She knocked, and they heard a woman call from inside, "Come in!"

Treesi opened the door, then stepped back and gestured for them to enter. Memfis went first, and Owyn followed him. He heard Treesi behind him, heard the door close, but ignored it because Aven was in front of him. He was lying in a narrow bed, a blanket pulled up to his waist. His face and chest were clean of blood and dirt. The bruise on his right temple had faded to pale purples and yellows, and the swelling had gone down. His right shoulder was bandaged and his arm folded across his chest and secured there to keep him from moving it. And he was still asleep. Owyn stepped closer, then jumped when someone touched his back; he looked over his shoulder to see Aria.

"He'll be fine," she murmured. "And there should be no lasting damage."

"This is the young man who field-set the arm?" a woman asked. She was older, but not quite as old as Memfis, he thought. Her hair was pulled back tightly, making her narrow, serious face look as if the skin had been stretched. She was taller than he was, but that wasn't unusual. She was dressed in a white tunic and trousers, and Owyn wondered at that. Wouldn't white show dirt and blood? How did she keep them clean?

"This is, Senior Healer," Aria answered.

"You did a good job with his arm," she said. "Strapping it down to keep it from moving probably saved him from losing mobility."

Owyn nodded. He hadn't thought of that. All he'd been worried about was keeping Aven from hurting, and keeping him alive. "And his head?" he asked.

The Senior Healer walked around the bed. "We'll see how he is when he wakes. If he's coherent. It's hard to say, with a head wound."

"He woke up," Owyn offered. "Twice. Once before we were found, and once in the tunnels. He seemed to be himself both times."

Her brows rose. "That's a good sign. As I said, we'll see how he is when he wakes. Now, will you wish to stay?"

"How long will he sleep, Senior Healer?" Memfis asked.

"A few hours more, I think," she answered. She turned away, picking up a book and what looked like a stylus. "Now, Aria has told me some of his background. Could you tell me the rest?"

"What do you need to know?" Memfis asked. "And why, Senior Healer?"

"Call me Risha. And because family medical histories are kept in the archives," the Senior Healer said. She opened the book. "Now, Aria has told us that his mother's name is Aleia, and his father is Jehan—"

"If it's for the archives, then you want his full name. Jhansri."

Risha froze. "Healer Jhansri? Son of Senior Healer Pirit?" she asked. She glanced at the bed. "Is Aven a healer as well?"

"Yes," Memfis answered. "Aria, you didn't say?"

Aria shook her head. "It didn't seem to be important at the time, when he can't work on himself," she answered. "Now that he is doing better, yes. He is a healer."

"I'll have to speak to him when he wakes, then." Risha made a note in her book. "What can you tell me about his mother's family? I can have Jhansri's records pulled—"

"How?" Owyn blurted out. Risha looked at him, and he swallowed. "This... this wasn't the main healing center. Not before what Treesi called the purge. Right? Archives are big, heavy things. Hard to move. How'd you get them here?"

Risha chuckled. "You think. I like that. My predecessor was very astute. She could see that there might be trouble, so she had the archives moved here, a little at a time, so that it wasn't obvious what she was doing. When the purge came, we lost very little of the old knowledge." She looked down at her book. "What do I need to know, for his care?"

"No cheese," Owyn answered immediately. "And salt water."

"The Water strain is that strong?" Risha asked. "Interesting." She made some notes, then closed the book. "I think we'll finish this once he wakes. I have questions about his training and his upbringing. Where is Healer Jhansri?"

Memfis grimaced. "We don't know." He glanced at the bed. "Risha, the only ones who know the whole of it are Aven and Aria. But for now, Aven can't answer, and Aria and Owyn have had a long night. Let's leave them to rest, hm? You said that Aven would sleep a few more hours?"

"Yes," Risha answered. "And I'll want to evaluate him as a healer. Who trained him? His father?"

"Yes," Aria answered. "And he told the Dark Council in Forge that Jehan said he was perhaps a second level healer. Owyn, am I remembering that correctly?"

"Yes," Owyn answered. "And when he told them that he beat Rut, they laughed at that. Said a second level healer wouldn't have been able to do that."

Risha's jaw dropped. "Aven? As a second level healer, healed someone from Rut poisoning?"

Owyn held his hand up. "Me. He said he filtered it out of my blood."

"And you're certain that it was Rut?" she demanded. When Owyn nodded, she stared at Aven.

"I will definitely need to evaluate him," she murmured. "No second level healer would have the skill or the power to filter blood that way. All right. Once he is awake, and you're all rested, I'll get the rest of the story. In the meantime, I know the Chieftess wanted to speak with you. Since we have a few hours, would you meet with her now? Her offices adjoin mine, and are on the other side of the building."

Memfis looked at Aria, who turned and walked toward the bed. She reached out and touched Aven's cheek, then looked at Treesi. "Would you stay with him?"

Treesi's eyes widened. She glanced at Owyn, then looked back at Aria. "You... you want me to?"

Aria blinked. She looked at Owyn, and her eyes narrowed. "I've missed something?"

"I..." Owyn started. He frowned. "Yes. We'll talk later. For now, please, Treesi?"

She didn't even look at him. She went to a chair near the bed and sat down. "I'll ring if anything," she said. She looked troubled, and Owyn wondered why.

"Then if you'll come this way?" Risha gestured to the door. They followed her out into the corridor and down the hall. Memfis walked with Risha, and Owyn and Aria followed behind.

"What happened?" Aria whispered.

"She's got some really fucked up ideas about you and Aven. Not specifically you and Aven, but Air and Water," Owyn whispered back. "And she says that she was taught them by her teacher here."

"What ideas?"

Owyn glanced ahead. Hadn't Treesi said that Risha was her teacher? Now he wasn't sure. "She says that you're not human. That you're part animal. Aria, how can she be... one of us, if she thinks like that?"

Aria looked startled. "Not human? An animal? That... that's absurd! We're all children of the Mother's dreams!"

"I know that, and you know that," Owyn said. "But Treesi... Aria, can the choice be wrong?"

"I don't know," Aria whispered. "Thank you. I'll have to speak to her on my own. See if I can understand this." She took his hand, and said nothing more as they walked through convoluted corridors, past closed doors and long hallways, until they reached the end of one corridor where two doors faced each other. Risha knocked on one, and they heard a woman's voice from inside, "Come in!"

Risha opened the door and entered, with Memfis two paces behind her. Owyn stepped out of the way, letting Aria proceed him. Then he stepped into the room, closing the door behind him. He couldn't see the speaker at first, but her voice was clear and melodic.

"Thank you, Risha," she said. "And thank you, for coming to see me. My Heir, you honor me."

Aria smiled. "Thank you for taking us in," she answered.

"How could we not?" the woman said. "Now, I am Rhexa, and I do the administrative work of the tribal government. It's a bit unusual, but I'm not a healer—"

"And I don't have the time for administration," Risha added. "Not and teach. We have to replace our numbers. So Rhexa and I share the load."

"That makes a great deal of sense," Aria said. "I am Aria, daughter of Milon and Liara. I'll present my Water to you once he is hale. This is Owyn, my Fire." She turned and gestured for Owyn to join her. As he reached her side, he saw Rhexa for the first time. She was seated behind a desk, and looked to be a little older than Memfis, her hair gone mostly silver, but with the tarnished gold tints that showed it might have once been red or auburn. Her skin was the same warm shade as Aven's, but she turned pale when she saw him.

"Oh, it can't be. Your name... it's *Owyn*?" She looked at Aria, then back at Owyn. "If you please, Owyn, son of whom?"

Owyn frowned. "Owyn, son of Memfis," he answered. He jerked a thumb at Memfis. "He's my father. Well, adoptive. I don't know my birth parents. Why?"

"Rhexa, you're not thinking—" Risha started.

"You knew her, Risha! Tell me he's not the image of Dyneh!" She rose and came around the desk. She wasn't much taller than Owyn was. "How old are you, Owyn? Do you know?"

Owyn blinked. "I'm not really sure," he answered. "Maybe twenty-two?"

"We've never been sure," Memfis added. "Owyn was a street child, raised by other street children. The best we can figure is that he was orphaned young, in one of the uprisings in Forge. Which makes him twenty-two or twenty-three. Who's Dyneh?"

"My younger sister," Rhexa answered. "She was a healer, and she married a young Fire man. His name was Huris, and he was a Smoke Dancer. She was chosen for the healing center in Forge. The last time I saw them, it was three months after their son was born.

His name was Jaxis." She looked at Owyn. "Unless I am very wrong, your real name is Jaxis."

CHAPTER FOURTEEN

OWYN STARED AT RHEXA. It was all he could do — he was as frozen as a mouse faced with a cat, and with nowhere to run. He couldn't think, couldn't figure out what to say. What to do. His mind went completely blank. Jaxis. Dyneh. Huris. They were all just names to Owyn. They had no meaning. They didn't bring up any memories. Just... people he didn't know.

People that he should have known?

A heavy hand settled on his shoulder as Memfis came up behind him. The weight of it, the solidity, grounded him. He focused on that hand, on his *father's* hand, and cleared his throat.

"My name is Owyn," he said, his voice surprisingly level. "Owyn, son of Memfis, of the line of Nerris." He swallowed, looked over his shoulder at Memfis, then back at Rhexa. "I don't know those names. I don't know those people. I'm not who you think I am." He swallowed again, trying to make sure his stomach stayed where he'd left it. "I... if you have things to talk about, would it be all right if I went back and waited with Aven?"

Memfis glanced at Aria. "My Heir?"

Aria stepped in front of Owyn, facing him, and spread her wings so that they were blocking the view of the women at the desk. "Owyn, are you all right?" she asked softly.

"I... maybe?" he forced a laugh. "No. No, I'm not. I'll stay if you need me—"

143

She shook her head and leaned forward to kiss his cheek. "Go wait with Aven," she said. "Can you find the room again?"

"Number nineteen," he answered. "If the rooms are all numbered, I can find it. You do... whatever it is that you need to do. I'll be all right. I just... I need some space to think." He looked over his shoulder at Memfis. "Mem?"

"If you get lost, ask for help," Memfis said. "Go on."

Owyn nodded and slipped around Memfis. He was out the door as he heard a voice calling his name. Rhexa, he thought. He didn't stop. He couldn't stop. He needed to be away, until he had a chance to think. He turned and walked quickly down the hall, heading back the way they'd come.

ARIA TURNED BACK TO the desk as Rhexa called Owyn's name. The older woman looked upset, but at the moment, Aria didn't care. Owyn being upset worried her far more.

"Let him be," Aria said. "To burden him with that, when he'd barely had time to breathe or rest after the fighting? That was unkind."

"Oh," Rhexa breathed. She pressed one hand to her chest. "Oh, I didn't... I didn't think. I was...he looks so much like Dyneh! And I thought, after all these years, to have found him... well, I got carried away." She shook her head and sat down, gesturing to a low-backed chair near the desk. "If you'll have a seat, my Heir? We'll discuss Owyn later, and what I might do to make amends."

Aria sat down and smiled. "Please, call me by name?"

"Oh, I couldn't! It seems improper," Rhexa protested.

"Please?" Aria repeated. "In private? You can be as proper as you like in public, but we can be informal here."

Rhexa laughed and nodded. "In private, then. Aria, now that everyone is here and safe, what can we do to help you?"

Aria tried not to frown as she thought. There were so many things she wanted to ask and that she needed to do. That she wanted. But first, she needed information. "First, will you tell us what happened here?"

Rhexa sighed and rubbed her forehead. "Do you want me to explain, or do you want to?"

"Go ahead," Risha answered. "I need to go make my rounds with my students. Well, my other student. Treesi is attending Aven; it'll be good practice for her, to work on a Waterborn. There aren't many physiological differences, but the ones that do exist are significant." She grinned. "It'll be interesting to see if she remembers that Waterborn have a different metabolism and greater percent of body fat than Earthborn. Although he is small for a Waterborn. I'll have to remember to ask him if he has issues with cold—"

"Risha, you're rambling," Rhexa interrupted. Risha laughed and nodded.

"True. All right. I'm off." She nodded to Aria and Memfis, then left the room. Once the door closed, Rhexa sighed.

"Now, where to start?" she asked. "What do you know already? So I don't cover ground you've already traveled?"

Aria looked at Memfis, who shrugged and sat down on a low couch near the wall. "To be honest, we don't know much. Part of which was because of my having to keep my head down in Forge, so that they didn't look too closely and notice that Fisher was really Memfis, former Fire Companion. And the rest was me. I spent a good number of years wallowing in grief at the bottom of a bottle, and the past three or four with my head in a bag, living in visions and not willing to see what was happening outside my forge walls."

Aria turned toward Memfis, but before he could say anything, Rhexa sniffed. "You'd lost the focal point of your life, Memfis. I don't think anyone could suffer that great a loss and not try to retreat from the pain. It's understandable." She smiled. "And you brought yourself out of it. That's a hard thing to do. I'm not a healer, but I live with them, and I see how many patients never have that strength."

Memfis shook his head. "The Mother wasn't done with me yet. I still have a job to do. But... I wasn't prepared to do it. I wasn't willing to look outside my visions for answers, so I didn't have the right information. I still don't. So really, we know nothing except for what we've been told over the past day."

Rhexa nodded slowly. "What information did you have?"

"The last I knew, the heart of the rebellion was the main healing center, the one closest to the Palace. That's where we were heading. I didn't know how bad the famines were until we were out here — Owyn pointed out to me that I was a bit insulated from that truth. And I didn't know about the purges at all."

"The famines have been growing gradually worse ever since the Firstborn fell," Rhexa said. "Adavar is out of balance. But you know that. Famine... crop failures were the first sign of the Mother's displeasure, I think. And the easiest to deny. It's far too easy to blame crop failures and blight on weather, or something in the soil. Never mind that we've had the same weather and the same soil for generations. The purges though... that's only been serious over the past four years. And the main healing center was the first to fall. Senior Healer Pirit suspected that it was coming, and made plans, but when it happened, it was a full year ahead of her projections. She thought she'd have the time to get everyone to safety." She shook her head. "It's the only time I ever knew her to be wrong."

"You knew her?" Memfis asked.

She smiled. "I was her administrative assistant. And Risha was her last healing student. Neither of us could do the job that she could on own, so we work together, and we each do what we can." She shook her head. "The purges took all of the healing centers, and a majority of the strongest healers in the tribes. The gift has never been common, and the leaders and the teachers were the first targeted. We aren't entirely certain that the purges of the past four years were the beginning, or the end. There have been other attacks on healer villages over the past ten years. One of Risha's students was the only survivor of one of those."

Memfis looked stunned. "We had no idea. None at all. Rhexa, define majority?" he asked slowly.

"The usual meaning of majority," Rhexa answered. "Almost all, to be completely honest. The few we have left are here, one full healer and a handful of students. We're not going to be much help to you, I'm afraid."

"Right now, all the help we need is here," Aria said. "Healing my Water, and giving us the information that we lack. And a place where we are safe, so that we can plan." She frowned slightly. "Although... Rhexa, are we safe here?"

Rhexa looked startled. "What? Of course you're safe!"

"I mean myself, and my Water. I've heard that there are some here who do not consider Air or Water to be human."

"What?" Memfis gasped. "Aria—"

Rhexa groaned, resting her forehead on her hand. "Again?" she grumbled. "I thought I'd pulled that weed. Who?" She frowned, then sighed. "Treesi? Given the reports I've had, it would have to be Treesi. That girl—"

"Are her views common here?" Aria asked.

Rhexa grimaced. "As I said, it's a weed," she said. "One that we try to pull, but it keeps coming back. I've no idea where it started, but it's been growing stronger the longer we're cut off from the other tribes." She gave Aria a long look. "I wonder... having you here might be to our benefit."

"Because I am Air?"

"And quite obviously Air. Not like some of our Earth and Air children. None of them have wings, so it's easier to ignore that they're not entirely Earth. They pass. You're here, you're clearly not Earth, and you're the Heir. They'll have to confront their views, won't they? Surely the Mother wouldn't choose someone who wasn't human to wear the Diadem, after all." She smiled. "We'll help you, and in return, you can help me to dig this out, once and for all. Let them see you. Let them get to know you. Let them put a face to the other tribes. Do you think your Water would do the same? Aven, you said his name was?"

"Aven, son of Jhansri," Memfis answered. Rhexa's eyes widened.

"Jhansri? Pirit's Jhansri? Tell me he's a healer of his father's caliber?" she said in a low voice. "And he's Water? He changes?"

"Yes, to both," Aria said. "At least, I think he's a healer of Jehan's caliber."

Rhexa laughed and clapped her hands. "Perfect! The lunkheads who claim that Water and Air are less than human hold that healing is the mark of the Mother's favor on us as Earthborn. If he's Water, and he's a healer? He's living proof they're wrong." She nodded, looking thoughtful. "What would you think of working with me while you were here?"

Aria smiled. "I think I'd like that. And it would help me to learn what I'll need to know once we're ready to move forward."

Rhexa got up. "We'll work out a schedule. You're in house Fourteen Southwest, so I'll come see you there tomorrow. Ah... you'll need supplies. I know Fourteen has a kitchen. I'll send a runner down to the dispensary to let them know you'll be drawing from stores."

"You'll have to explain to me how that works here," Memfis said.

"Of course. Let me walk you back." She came around the desk and joined them. "I want to apologize to your Owyn, also."

She led them back down the halls, and gently tapped on the door to room number nineteen. The door opened, and Treesi looked out. She smiled when she saw them.

"I was starting to wonder when someone was coming back," she said. "He'll be waking up soon, I think."

It took a moment for what she'd said to make sense to Aria. "Where's Owyn?" she asked. "He came back before us."

Treesi shook her head. "He's not here. I've been alone since you left."

OWYN SCOWLED AT THE doors on either side of him. These didn't have numbers. They had letters. He'd been distracted, had made a wrong turn somewhere, and now he needed to backtrack. He turned around and started walking back the way he'd come.

"You know, signs might be useful," he muttered as he walked. "This way to room nineteen. And why the fuck are there rooms with letters?"

"Because these are the student residential quarters?"

The voice was deep, and whoever it was sounded amused, but Owyn was already dancing on the edge of his patience, and he hadn't noticed anyone coming up behind him. He screeched and spun, grabbing for a weapon he didn't have as he stumbled backward and fell onto his arse. He landed hard on a bruise, and yelped.

"What happened? Are you all right?"

The man was older than Owyn, and a lot taller. Taller than Aven, Owyn thought. It was hard to tell from the floor. Dressed in a gray tunic and trousers, he was as pale as a ghost — white blond hair that he wore long enough that it almost reached the backs of his knees, gray eyes like storm clouds, and a close trimmed mustache and beard. He seemed worried. He also wasn't looking at

Owyn at all. Instead, he had his head cocked to the side, like he was listening.

"I'm fine," Owyn answered. "Lost my balance. Landed hard. Don't sneak up on people."

The tall man chuckled. "You were outside my door. It wasn't sneaking up, it was sneaking out. Sort of. Are you lost?"

"Yeah," Owyn answered. He got to his feet. Yes, the man was taller than Aven, and much thinner. He looked frail, as if a strong wind would blow him away, and there were shiny burn scars on his arms and the visible skin of his throat. He was barefoot, but still towered over Owyn. "I was supposed to be going to room nineteen, but I made a wrong turn somewhere."

"If you came through the wheel, then you probably turned into the first left instead of the third." The tall man held his hand out. "That's a confusing spot for most people. You'll get used to it if you're here long enough, and you can join us in cursing the memory of whoever decided that was a good idea. Now, I don't know your voice. You're new here?"

"Don't know my voice?" Owyn repeated. He took the offered hand, then realized what the man meant. "You're blind?"

"You really are new here, if no one has told you about me. Yes, I'm Alanar, the blind healer-in-training."

"Well, it's nice to meet you, even if I did have to fall on my arse to do it," Owyn answered, and Alanar laughed. "I'm Owyn. And I've heard your name. Treesi mentioned you. You're her training partner."

Alanar smiled. "Yes. And I was going to meet her and our teacher. Do you know where she is?"

"Well, then, you can show me where room nineteen is," Owyn said. "That's where Treesi is supposed to be right now."

"Fair enough," Alanar said. "May I put my hand on your shoulder?"

"Which shoulder do you want?" Owyn asked.

"The right one is fine," Alanar said. His hand was warm on Owyn's shoulder, and he chuckled. "You have broad shoulders. Strong. You do something physical?"

"I'm a smith," Owyn said. "Well, an apprentice smith."

"Ah. Are you part Fire?" Alanar asked. "Most of the smiths in the Earth tribe land are some part Fire. It seems to just work that way."

"All Fire, as far as I know. From Forge."

Alanar arched a brow. "You're a long way from home. What brings you here? At the first turning, we're going right."

Owyn turned with Alanar. "I'm here with the Heir to the Firstborn. I'm her Fire."

Alanar stopped. "You didn't strike me as being a madman," he said. "Do I need to check that?"

Owyn burst out laughing. "I'm serious," he protested. "Her name is Aria. And you'll meet her, once we get to where we're going."

"Why is she in the healing complex?" Alanar asked as he started walking again. "If the next door is marked no entry, then we'll be turning left into the wheel."

"Me and Aven, we had a run-in with Mannon's guards," Owyn answered. They turned left and entered a round room with corridors branching off in all directions. He stopped. "I don't remember coming through here before."

"You may not have," Alanar answered. "There are two ways to get to the residential wing. This is just the most direct way between them. Also the way that people hate the most, because it's confusing."

"I can see that. It must give Treesi fits."

"She told you about her trouble with directions?" Alanar asked. "She must like you. Who's Aven?"

"Our Water. They used a tangle rope, and he was thrown from his horse."

Alanar shuddered. "He was lucky he wasn't killed!"

"I know," Owyn agreed. "I thought he had been." He looked around. "Alanar, how do you know where you're going here?"

Alanar grinned. "Perfect memory. And I always know where I am. So if you read something to me, I remember it. And if I've been somewhere, I can find it again. We need the third corridor. There'll be blue tiles on the floor."

Owyn nodded, then laughed. "Right, blue tiles. Let's go." As they walked, he realized something. "You weren't born blind, then? You know from colors."

Alanar squeezed Owyn's shoulder. "You listen. I like that. I was blinded in an accident when I was a boy."

Owyn winced. "I'm sorry," he said. Alanar squeezed his shoulder again.

"Don't be," he said. "I made my peace with it a long time ago. Now, we should be in the numbered corridor?"

"If I haven't been distracting you?" Owyn teased. Alanar seemed entirely too easy to talk to. Like Aven, he realized. "And yeah, we are. Number twenty-eight is on your right."

"So nineteen is farther down on your left."

They reached the door, and Owyn tapped on it. It swung open almost immediately, revealing Memfis. He saw Owyn, let out a relieved sounding sigh, and said, "It's him. And a friend?"

Alanar laughed. "I hope so."

"Alanar?" Treesi joined Memfis at the door. "Risha's looking for you."

"She'll have to keep looking," Alanar replied. "I'm not likely to find her first."

Treesi giggled, then stepped out of the way. "Come in. We've been worried about you, Owyn."

"I took a wrong turn, and ended up... where was I?" He looked up at Alanar, and suddenly what Treesi was talking about with men being miles taller than her made sense.

Alanar smiled. "In the residential hall, just outside our suite, Treesi."

They entered the room, and Owyn was almost immediately grabbed and hugged by Aria. He closed his eyes and breathed in the scent of her hair — Aven was right. She did smell like the wind.

"Are you all right?" she whispered in his ear. He nodded.

"Just needed... space," he answered.

"She wants to apologize," Aria said. 'Rhexa. She was here, and she says she'll come back."

Owyn looked at her. "Aria—"

She smiled and kissed him. "If you wish to speak to her. It's up to you. I won't ask it of you. I will say it will make things easier while we're here, if you'll at least tolerate her." She sighed. "She's offered to let me learn from her."

"Learn... what?" Owyn asked.

"About governing," Aria answered. "And I think that perhaps Aven will want to further his training. So we may be here for a while."

Owyn looked over at the bed, where Aven was still sleeping peacefully. "Define a while?"

"It may not be the worst idea to winter here," Aria answered. "Memfis?"

"I'll think on it and let you know when we go back to the house," Memfis answered. Too quickly, and Owyn glanced at him. Memfis nodded at him, and Owyn knew. He had something to say, but he wasn't going to say it in front of Treesi and Alanar.

"Aria," Owyn stammered. "This is Alanar."

Aria turned toward Alanar. "It's nice to meet you," she said. Then her eyes widened as Alanar gave an odd, formal bow — he crossed his arms over his chest, his fingers touching his collar bone, and bowed from the waist, deeply enough that his hair fell forward over his shoulders, and Owyn caught a glimpse of the burn scar on the back of his neck.

"You're Air," Aria gasped. Alanar straightened.

"Half," he replied. "My mother was Air. My father was Earth. I inherited his healing abilities. But I also spent time with my mother's flock, and learned Air manners."

Owyn watched as Aria's gaze shifted from Alanar's face to his shoulders, then back. She didn't say anything. Instead, she smiled. "It's very nice to meet you, cousin."

His brows rose. "Owyn, you didn't tell me she was Air!"

Aria looked at Owyn, then over her shoulder at Treesi, confusion written all over her face.

"Aria," Owyn said in a low voice. "Alanar is blind."

Alanar nodded. "I should have said. I apologize. Everyone here knows. I lost my sight and my wings in a fire when I was ten."

CHAPTER FIFTEEN

OWYN WATCHED AS THE color drained from Aria's face. Her wings twitched, moving in closer to her body. "Lost... your *wings*?" she gasped. "Oh..."

Alanar took a deep breath. "You thought I was wingless, didn't you?"

"I did, and it confused me that you said you spent time with your flock," Aria admitted. "I... I'm sorry."

"It's been a long time," Alanar said gently. "I've grown accustomed to it." He cocked his head to the side. "Treesi, he feels like he's waking. Should he be?"

Owyn turned toward the bed, where Aven had shifted in his sleep. "You can tell that?" he asked. "From across the room?"

"Alanar is a strong healer," Treesi said. She knelt next to the bed, resting one hand on Aven's forehead. After a moment, she nodded. "It's safe for him to wake up now. The bones are still knitting, but that will take a few days. The internal damage is healed." She got up and turned to look at them. "Before he wakes up, may I say something?"

Owyn looked at Aria, who nodded. "Go ahead."

"I... did some thinking while you were with Rhexa," Treesi said slowly. "About what you said, Owyn. And about what I said. About... well, everything."

"Treesi," Alanar said, his tone one that Owyn knew. Memfis had the same way of saying Owyn's name when Owyn screwed up. "What did you do?"

Treesi tucked her hands behind her back. "I said that Water and Air were subhuman."

Alanar's jaw dropped. "Treesi! We've *talked* about that!"

"I know! But the books—"

"Are you going to believe the books over me? Still?" Alanar demanded. "Over the older books, that told the truth? I've told you, the new books push Rhexa's lies!"

"Excuse me?" Memfis said. "Repeat that, and explain it?"

Alanar turned toward him. "I... I've said too much."

"No, you haven't said nearly enough," Memfis countered. "Now say the rest."

Alanar stepped back, his already pale face gone even more pale. "I... spoke out of turn."

"Alanar."

At the sound of Aria's voice, Alanar closed his eyes. "Yes, my Heir," he said softly. "I... it's been since the purge, I think. Since we came here from the main healing center. I... I pass as Earth, for all that I'm more sand colored—"

"Sand colored?" Owyn asked.

"Well, that's what Treesi calls it. I thought it was funny. I'm not dark enough to be Earth, so I'm sand," Alanar answered. "But when I was a boy, we lived here until my mother died. We had more mixed tribe healers. More Earth and Air, more Earth and Water. More of the extrahuman. It's been growing more and more rare. We left Terraces after Mother died – my father took a position as a village healer. It was all Earth there, and they didn't know what to do with me. But it wasn't so bad, until the fire. After the fire, they took me to the main healing center, and I lived there, with Pirit as my guardian. I started training, and there were still some mixed blood healers, but not as many. There were starting to be whispers. Then the purge came, and I came back here. That's when we got the new healing texts that teach that Air and Water aren't human."

"And you think it's Rhexa's doing? Interesting," Memfis said. "Because she told us that she had no idea where it started, except that it's been getting worse the longer that Earth is cut off from the other tribes."

"You told her?" Treesi moaned. "I'm going to get in trouble again!"

"Treesi, no one is getting in trouble," Aria said. She went to the healer and put her hands on Treesi's shoulders. "I needed to be sure that we would be safe here. That my Aven would be safe until he healed. I asked just that — would we be safe? She guessed. So I think you've been told this before?"

"About half a dozen times," Alanar answered. "Tree, why now? What convinced you that you were wrong, when you wouldn't listen to me?"

Treesi looked at him. Then she looked at Owyn and bit her lip. "Part of it was Owyn yelling at me," she admitted. "He had no way of knowing we've had the same discussions, but he used almost the same words that you did. And the rest... the Mother can't make mistakes. And She chose Aria as Heir. I've seen the Diadem. It's real. She's real. And she's Heir. I've known it since I saw her out at their camp last night. And someone who isn't human can't be Heir. So... since the Mother can't be wrong, that means that I am." She looked around, shifting to clasp her hands in front of her. "And I'm sorry. I'm really sorry. I'll try to do better."

Her apology was met with silence, until Alanar barked with laughter. "Really? Living with me, riding my cock for how long hasn't convinced you that I'm human, but a shiny piece of jewelry and a new cock does it that easy?" He sniffed and folded his arms over his chest. "It's been a few hours since you left the suite. Have you had one of them already? I know you're fast, but that's faster than you usually bed someone new. Who was it? Owyn, I bet. Is he that good? He'd have to be, if that's why you're so quick to change your mind."

"Hey!" Owyn gasped.

"It's all right, Owyn," Treesi said. "He's mad, and he has every right to be mad. He shouldn't be lashing at you, though. This is all me."

"I don't care what he thinks of me," Owyn snapped. "He doesn't get to call you a whore."

Silence, and Owyn realized that Treesi was staring at him. Alanar just had a puzzled look on his face.

"I—" Alanar started to say. Treesi interrupted.

"He's Fire, Allie. He doesn't understand." She came over and rested her hand on Owyn's arm. "Owyn, by your tribe's laws, we *are* whores."

"You are not," Owyn protested. "You're healers. I know the difference."

She smiled at him. "I know you know. I know you have every reason to know. Owyn, I saw your shoulder."

He blinked, caught off guard for a moment. Then he realized what she was talking about. "You know..."

"I know."

"I don't," Alanar called. "What are you talking about?"

Treesi laughed. "Owyn will explain later, Allie." She stepped closer and kissed his cheek. "Thank you for trying to protect me. Even after I was so awful."

Owyn swallowed. "You... you weren't awful. You were ignorant."

"I'm not sure that's any better, Owyn," Alanar said. He stepped closer, and his arm brushed against Aria's wing. He turned toward her. "I'm sorry."

"It's fine," Aria said. "I imagine that I take up a little more room than you'd expect from my voice." She touched his hand, and smiled as Alanar took hers. Then she looked back at Owyn. "Owyn, you've confused us all. Explain?"

Owyn scrubbed his hand over his face. He knew what he meant, but putting it into words was hard on as little sleep as he'd had. "It's just... Treesi told us that she'd been taught all this, right? From her books and from people she trusted to teach her. So why shouldn't she trust what they had to say? They told her the wrong thing, but she had no reason not to believe them. Now she knows better."

Alanar nodded, looking thoughtful. "You make a good point. This is what new healers are being taught, and by those that we trust. The older books have been largely taken and archived. Or destroyed. I'm not sure which. But Treesi and I are the oldest of the trainees, and I still have the older books, because I have my father's books. We know — we should know, anyway. We know the difference." He grinned. "I could wish that you'd actually believed it a little sooner, Tree. Because regardless of what the books say, I'm right here." He held his free arm out to the side. "My wings might be gone, but I'm still Air."

Treesi looked down. "Allie, I'm sorry!"

"I know," Alanar said. "And I forgive you. Because Owyn's right."

"About a lot of things," Treesi added. She squeezed Owyn's arm. "Now, we need to stop fussing. Aven's going to wake up, and if tempers are high when he wakes, he'll get upset." She looked around. "This is my fault. I'm sorry."

"Apology accepted," Aria said. She stepped in front of Treesi again. "I want you to know something. Rhexa used your same logic to make the point that it will help to have me here, in this place.

That people will see me as the Heir, and realize that the Mother doesn't make mistakes. Does she, Owyn?"

Owyn grinned, remembering their earlier conversation. "No, she doesn't."

"So I will be here, helping others to see what you see," Aria continued. "We'll help them to see the truth. That we're all the children of the Mother's dreams, no matter what we look like. It will help. And I will need your help. They know you here. They don't know me. Not yet."

Treesi looked up at her, her eyes wide. "You want my help?" she asked. "Even after... everything?"

"You mean, even after you helped save my Water, welcomed me to your home, and have done your best to try and apologize for believing what you've been taught?" Aria asked. "Yes."

Treesi breathed out what almost sounded like a sob. She let go of Owyn's arm and stepped closer to Aria. "I asked you yesterday if it was permitted to hug the Heir—"

"Yes," Aria answered.

The shocked look on Aria's face when Treesi threw herself into her arms made Owyn grin. He looked around, seeing a flame colored ball of fur on the blanket next to Aven's hand. He smiled, and went over to pick Trinket up. She chittered at him, then scaled his arm and perched on his shoulder.

"It wasn't my idea," he told the fire mouse. "You go scold the guards. It's all their fault." He turned, seeing Memfis coming toward him. "Mem?"

"We need to talk," Memfis said, his voice quiet. "Just you and me."

Owyn turned so that his back was to Aria, Treesi and Alanar, and lowered his voice to a bare whisper. "Fa?"

Memfis looked startled, then smiled. He put his hand on Owyn's shoulder. "You're not in trouble, Mouse. I just... no, this can't wait. You remember the list that Meris told you about?"

Owyn frowned. "List... of who I might be? That list?"

"Yeah. I have it. And Jaxis, son of Dyneh and Huris was one of the possibilities." He looked across the room at the others, then back at Owyn. "Huris was a Smoke Dancer. That might be where you get it from."

Owyn nodded. "If he was a Smoke Dancer, does that mean you knew him?"

Memfis shrugged. "It's possible. I can't bring him to mind, but depending on when he started his training, I might have already left Forge. And by the time I came back, he'd have finished his training." He sighed. "And there's always the chance I might not have been sober if I had met him after I got back."

"So you might not remember," Owyn said. "Fa—"

"Can we stay with Mem?" Memfis asked. "I'm used to it. I know what you mean when you say it. Fa is... too new. I might not remember to answer to it."

Owyn smiled. "Yes, Mem," he said. "Does it matter, though? What that list says? I mean, I don't know them. I don't remember them." He reached out and poked Memfis in the chest. "You're my father."

Memfis closed his eyes. Then he caught Owyn's arm and tugged him into an embrace. "My Mouse. I love you, son. I never seem to remember to tell you that."

Owyn squirmed a little. Twice in one day? That was a new record. "I love you, too. Fa." He pulled back and grinned. "Memfa. That's what I'm going to call you from now on. Memfa."

Memfis burst out laughing. "You wouldn't!"

Owyn grinned, then spun as he heard a voice that he hadn't realized he'd been waiting for. Aven's voice

"Aria? Owyn?"

AVEN COULD HEAR VOICES nearby. He wasn't quite awake enough to make out what they were saying, and there were too many voices, all jumbled together. But he heard familiar voices in the mix. Memfis. Owyn. One was missing.

"Aria?" he called. He opened his eyes, frowning at an unfamiliar ceiling. Where was he? He blinked, remembering the frantic night ride. And... "Owyn?"

"Hey, look who's awake," Owyn said, sounding relieved. He sat down on the edge of the bed, making the mattress tip a little under his weight. He rested his hand on Aven's chest. "How do you feel?"

Aven blinked again, trying to think around a head stuffed with sea-foam. "Was I in a healing trance?" he asked.

"You were hurt," Aria said, sitting down on the other side of the bed. "You're fine now. We're safe now."

"Well, almost fine." Owyn reached across Aven and gently tapped his right shoulder. "Broke your collarbone. It'll be fine... how long, Treesi?"

Aven smiled as Treesi came up behind Aria. "I'll want to see what Risha says, but I think you'll be in a sling for a few days. Just to be on the safe side."

Aven closed his eyes. "Sounds right," he mumbled. "Same when I broke my arm."

The bed shifted, and he felt warmth covering him, the brush of hair against his skin, the brush of lips against his as Aria kissed him. He smiled and opened his eyes again as she sat back up.

"My turn?" Owyn asked. Aven turned toward him, and Owyn leaned over, propping himself up on one arm and catching Aven's free arm between them as he cupped Aven's cheek with his other hand and kissed him. It wasn't a gentle brush of the lips, the way

Aria had kissed him. This was deep, tinged with passion and fear, and it told Aven without words just how badly Owyn had been shaken. When Owyn finally broke the kiss, he stayed where he was, his forehead pressed against Aven's, their noses touching. Their breath mingled, and Aven shivered. It had to be an unconscious gesture. There was no way that Owyn could know...

His words confirmed it. "You scared the shit out of me, Fishie," Owyn whispered. "I thought you were dead."

"What happened?" Aven asked as Owyn straightened up. "I remember the ride. I remember that insane plan of mine. It didn't work?"

Owyn sighed. "It sort of worked. They had tangle ropes." He hesitated, then shook his head. "Cloud is dead, Aven. She broke her neck when they took her down. You were thrown—"

"And Owyn saved you," Aria interrupted. "He got you to a safe place, and held off the guards until we reached you. He was magnificent, Aven."

Aven smiled. "I knew he would be," he murmured. He fumbled with his free hand, taking Owyn's hand in his. "Love you, Mouse," he said. Then he turned and looked at Aria. "Love you, too. Just don't have another hand right now."

Aria giggled and leaned down, kissing him again. This time, she lingered as Owyn had, breathing with him. He closed his eyes, basking in the warmth of her breath on his skin. He'd have to explain to her, and to Owyn. What this meant to someone from the Water tribe, what it meant to him especially. She kissed him again, and sat up, and he smiled and looked around. Memfis stood at the foot of the bed, and to Aven's eyes, he looked tired and worried.

"Can we not do that again, Aven?" he asked.

"I wasn't planning on doing it the first time," Aven answered. "Can I sit up? And eat something? I'm hungry."

"You should drink, too," Owyn said. "Treesi—"

"Do we need a normal diet, or the suggested diet for Waterborn?"

"The Waterborn diet," Aria answered immediately.

"Salt water, no milk," Owyn added.

Treesi chuckled. "That's the suggested diet. I'll go, and I'll get Risha while I'm going. She should take a better look at you."

"Thank you, Treesi," Aven said as the healer left. It was only then that Aven realized there was a stranger in the room, a man sitting quietly on the other side of the room. "Ah... will someone introduce me?"

The man smiled and rose, bowing from the waist, his long hair falling forward around him. "I didn't want to intrude. I'm Alanar."

"Alanar is Treesi's training partner," Aria said. "He's a new friend. Now, you wanted to sit up?"

It took a minute of rearranging pillows and shifting things around before Aven was sitting upright. He blinked as it made his head spin, and saw Alanar frown.

"What's wrong?"

"Just a bit dizzy all of a sudden," Aven answered. "I... how did you know?"

Alanar came closer, stopping just out of arm's reach of the bed. He smiled, then shook his head. "How close am I? The last time I was in this room, the bed was on the other wall."

Aria rose. "You're very close. May I help?"

In answer, he held his hand out. She took it, and guided him to the bed. Aven glanced at Owyn as Alanar sat down. Owyn just nodded. He rested his hand on Aven's thigh.

"Now," Alanar said, holding out his hand. "May I touch you? I'm not sure you should be feeling dizzy at all."

Aven took Alanar's hand, and felt warmth spreading up his arm. He closed his eyes, and let the other healer work. Only to hear Alanar chuckle.

"Owyn, move your hand?"

"Sorry," Owyn answered, and the warmth on Aven's thigh went away.

"Thank you. I was reading you and... what have you got with you?"

"I'll introduce you later," Owyn said. "How's Aven?"

Alanar frowned slightly. "I don't feel any remaining damage to the skull or the brain, and there's no bleeding. It might be bruising left over. Aven, do you have a headache at all?"

"No," Aven answered. "How badly was I hurt?"

"I'll let Risha give you the details," Alanar said. "She's the official healer of record. I'm just a trainee."

There was a knock on the door, and a woman dressed all in white came in. Behind her was Treesi, who was carrying a tray.

"Put that down over there, Treesi," the woman said. "He can eat once I examine him. Alanar, you'll need to move." She paused. "Was something wrong?"

"He was dizzy, Senior Healer," Alanar answered. "I can't feel any remaining damage, and there's no bleeding. I suspect residual bruising."

"A fair assessment. Let me see." She looked around. "There are too many people in this room. But I understand that no one wants to leave right now."

Alanar got up and moved to the foot of the bed, while Aria moved to join Owyn on the far side of the bed. The woman took Alanar's place, but didn't sit. She met Aven's eyes.

"My name is Risha," she said. "And I'm the Senior Healer. And I know you're Aven, Jhansri's son. You've quite the legacy to live up to, young man." She held her hand out. "Let's have a look at you."

Aven took her hand. Her healing power flowed through him, almost too warm and too sharp for comfort, and he tried not to flinch. She arched a brow.

"Dizzy when you sat up?" she asked.

"Yes, Senior Healer," he answered.

"Alanar, that was very good. It's some residual bruising in the brain. We'll monitor it, but the healing is already underway. So it should pass in a day or so. Your collarbone is healing well. A sling for a few days should suffice there." She let Aven's hand go, and folded her arms over her chest. "I'm told you're a healer?"

"Yes, Senior Healer," Aven answered. "My father trained me."

She nodded. "If you want, I can evaluate you while you're here. See what other training you'll need, fill in any gaps your father might have left. I spoke to Chieftess Rhexa, and she says you'll be staying?"

"Chieftess?" Aven looked at Aria. That wasn't right.

"We'll explain later, Aven," Aria said. "But we will be spending at least the winter here, I think."

"Then yes, please," Aven said, turning back to Risha. "I'd like to formalize my training, if I can."

"Very good," Risha said. She smiled for the first time. "Then once I clear you as healthy, I'll test what you know, and we'll set up a course of study for you. Treesi, Alanar, you're in a three bed suite. I'll be putting him in with you once he's released from care."

"What?" Aven gasped. "Wait. You're going too fast."

Risha nodded. "Healers-in-training live here, in the healing complex. I doubt you'll be here long, though."

"I..." Aven looked at Aria and Owyn. They both looked as distressed as he felt. "I won't be living with my Heir?"

"We'll give it a week or two," Risha said. "Until you're done with your evaluation and we've gotten things set up. Perhaps we'll be able to make a special exception for you. But for now, and until I say otherwise, if you're a student of mine, you're here in the residential wing."

"It won't be for long," Owyn said. He rested his hand on Aven's leg. "And... well, you'll be busy. The time will fly by. You'll see."

Aven swallowed, met his eyes, then looked up at Aria. "My Heir?" he said.

She closed her eyes, then took a deep breath and nodded. "Finish your training," she said softly. Aven wasn't sure if he heard the quaver in her voice, or if he'd only imagined it. Then Owyn took Aria's hand, and he knew he hadn't imagined it. "It won't be for long, and I will be busy as well. I'll be working with Rhexa, to learn about governance."

Aven swallowed. Then he turned back to Risha. "For now, what do I do?"

Risha smiled. "For now? You eat, and you rest. Tomorrow, we'll see how you're feeling."

CHAPTER SIXTEEN

"SHOULD THAT HAVE HAPPENED?" Owyn asked as they walked out of the healing complex. He glanced back over his shoulder. Aven had been alert and laughing, seemingly normal until he'd finished his meal. Then he'd fallen asleep, almost between one word and the next. Risha had shooed them all out, telling them that Aven needed to rest. But it had happened so fast! "There wasn't anything in his food, was there?"

"You're asking if he was given a sleeping potion?" Alanar asked. "No. This is perfectly normal. He's still healing, and his body is using a lot of energy to do it. He'll eat and sleep quite a lot over the next few days, until the healing process is done. Treesi, where are they?"

"Fourteen Southwest," Treesi answered. "Honestly, Owyn, he'll probably sleep until tomorrow. It's best to let him rest."

"It's odd, seeing him asleep in a bed," Aria said.

"Why?" Alanar asked. "How does he usually sleep?"

"In a hammock," Owyn answered. "Since he can't sleep underwater."

Alanar nodded. He walked in silence for a few minutes, then turned to Treesi, who had her arm linked with his. "Can we rig up a hammock in his room, do you think?"

"I don't know," she answered. "I wouldn't know how to do it. And where would we get one?"

"You're serious?" Owyn asked.

"Of course," Alanar said. "He'll be our training partner. We want him to be comfortable."

Owyn looked at Memfis. "Do you think there's a smith here that would let us use his forge?" Memfis didn't answer, and Owyn poked his arm. "Mem? Did you hear me?"

Memfis jerked, then turned his attention to Owyn. "What? No, Mouse. I'm sorry. I didn't."

"Do you think there's a smith that would let us use his forge to make the hardware for a hammock?" Owyn repeated.

Memfis looked thoughtful. Then he nodded slowly. "We can ask Rhexa tomorrow. Or we can find a woodworker. There has to be someone here that knows how to make a hammock. We're close enough to the blended villages, after all. And if not, well, it'll be good to get back to a forge."

"He may not need it, by the time he recovers," Aria said. "He may have had the time to grow accustomed to the bed."

"Three nights without the hammock while we were on the road didn't do it," Owyn pointed out. "I'm not sure two nights in a bed will. We'll ask him tomorrow what he wants."

"That will be best, yes." Aria looked back the way they'd come. "It will be strange, not having him with us. With me."

"I know," Owyn murmured. He reached for her hand, and she squeezed his fingers. "He's supposed to be with us."

"It won't be for long," Treesi said. "Just until he's done training. And you'll see him... well, around rounds, and when he has free time—"

"We have free time?" Alanar interrupted. "Tree, don't fluff at them. You know we *never* have free time. We're going to have to rush back for rounds as it is!"

Treesi turned pink. "But they're upset!"

"And they'll be more upset when they find out that you weren't telling them true." Alanar sighed. "He'll be busy from dawn to nightfall. He might be able to get some time with you around rounds and lectures, but healers-in-training have more work than hours to do it, so I wouldn't count on it." He smiled. "But you'll be busy, too, Aria. With Rhexa."

"Which leaves me doing... what?" Owyn asked.

"You will be training with me," Aria answered. "You'll need to learn this, too, my Fire."

Owyn nodded. "All right," he said. "As long as she calls me by my name and not who she thinks I am."

"Why wouldn't she call you by name?" Alanar asked. Then he laughed. "Oh, has she decided that you're her missing nephew?"

"She's done that before?" Memfis asked.

"Well, no," Treesi said. "But she talks about him, and about her sister and her husband. She has drawings of them in her office. She misses them. She used to say that she was going to go to Forge to find them, or find out what happened to them. Back before things turned bad. Before the purge." She stopped walking, pulling Alanar to a stop. "I've been talking and not paying attention. I missed the marker. Ah... there it is. See?"

She pointed, and Owyn saw a stone marker set at an intersection. On one side was the number one, and on the other were the words Southwest.

"We're at ring One Southwest. Ring One is closest to the center, and Southwest is... well, it's the southwest spoke in the wheel." Treesi pointed. "Fourteen Southwest is that way, between rings five and six."

"So if I wanted to come back to the healing complex, I'd follow the houses so that the numbers got smaller?" Owyn asked. "Up to ring one?"

"That's right," Treesi answered. She smiled. "You said it was like Forge. So this must be very familiar to you. Or is it not the same there?"

"The streets have names there, not numbers. But they're the same layout. I think we'll be all right," Memfis answered. "Now, you said you'd have to rush back. Go on. We can find the house on our own."

"Are you sure?" Alanar asked. "It's no trouble for us to walk you down—"

"We'll be fine, Alanar," Memfis said. "Go back before you end up working all night."

"That won't be anything new," Treesi said. She tugged on Alanar's arm. "Come on. We have that reading to review—"

The two hurried back the way they'd come, and Memfis led Owyn and Aria down the road toward number Fourteen, walking between them.

"You sent them away," Aria said softly. "Why?"

"Because I wanted to talk to you both without other ears," Memfis answered. "We're alone now, and someone would need a hawk's ears to hear us—"

"Hawks do not have ears," Aria interrupted. "But I know what you mean. Go on."

"I'm not liking this at all," Memfis said. He looked at Aria, then at Owyn. "There's something wrong here. I can feel it. I just... I don't know."

"It's weird. Rhexa tells us about weeding out the hate of the other tribes, then Alanar says it came from her," Owyn said. "Which is it?"

"Does it have to be one or the other? It could be both. Or it could be a third, something we haven't seen yet," Aria said. "We don't know. We won't know, really, until we're here longer. I honestly don't see that we have much of a choice."

"I don't like not being able to see where things lie," Memfis grumbled. "And now I'm having to face that I've been focused on phantoms and ignoring what's actually been going on around me for years, instead of doing something about it."

"What could you have done?" Aria asked, a moment before Owyn asked the same question.

"She's got a point, Mem," he added. "What could you have done, without us? I mean, even five years ago? Aria was up in the mountains somewhere, Aven was out on the ocean, and I was a street whore. We weren't done growing yet. We weren't ready to be... whatever it is that the Mother needs us to be now." He stopped and scratched his head. "We're still not there yet, are we?" he asked. "We're still growing. We'll get there, but we have to get through this first. Whatever this is." He looked up to see Memfis studying him, an appraisingly look on his face. "What?"

"You're right," Memfis said. "You're right, the both of you. I can dislike it all I want, but the fact is that no matter what I saw, there was nothing that could be done until it was time to do it. I just wish I knew the next step."

"That's a funny thing for a Smoke Dancer to say," Aria teased gently. Memfis smiled.

"It is, isn't it?" he said. "Owyn, I have that list—"

"And I don't need to see it," Owyn answered. "I told you, it doesn't matter. Not to me." He looked up at the sky, then started walking again. "And really, she had how long to come find me, if I'm really her kin? And she didn't."

"Could she have?" Aria asked. "I thought the tribes were cut off from each other, after Mannon took control."

"Well, yes and no," Memfis answered. "There had to be some levels of trade, at the very least. Mannon learned that the hard way — part of the reason that rebellion took root so easily in Forge was because we were starving. So there was trade, but it was very regulated. They can't regulate gossip, though. Or illicit goods." He pointed. "There's Fourteen."

"Mem, should I unpack Aven's things?" Owyn asked. "I mean, not that he has much, other than his bag, but should I bring them to the healing complex?"

"No," Aria answered. "Unpack them here. This is our home, for now. This is his home, for now. He's staying at the healing complex while he trains, but his place is with us."

"He'll be back with us once he's finished his training," Memfis said. "So we'll leave his clothes and things here for now. If there's anything he wants, we can bring it to him. We can ask tomorrow what he'll need."

"I'll need to find hooks or something," Owyn said. "For Aven's swords, and for the smoke blades."

"We'll get something," Memfis said. He led them into the house, looked around the front room, and sighed. "It's not the forge, but it'll do. We need some food. Rhexa said something about a dispensary. I don't think she meant shops." He sighed. "Go and try to settle in. We'll figure things out as they come."

Owyn followed Aria down the corridor to the bedrooms. He stepped into the room with two beds and looked around. The bundle of blanket that contained his blades and Aven's swords was on the bed with Aven's carry-bag, and Owyn went and opened the bag to check the contents: The Diadem, Aven's water-gem and the two unclaimed ones, a container that Owyn knew usually contained salt. He didn't see the pearl, but he was sure it was in there. He set the bag down and unwrapped the blades, then laughed out loud.

Bundled in with the swords and his smoke blades was his ruined shirt... and the manacles that Treesi had saved for him.

"She's off her head, she is," he muttered. He took the ruined shirt out, looked around, then stashed it in the topmost drawer of a dresser. He laid the swords and the smoke blades on top of the dresser, then started unwrapping other bundles.

He was just finishing when he heard Memfis' voice. "Owyn, you have a visitor."

"I have a what now?" Owyn called back. He left the bedroom and headed to the front, and saw a familiar face. It took him a moment to remember the name that went with that face. "Teva?"

"Yes," Teva said with a smile. "I came to see how you were settling in, if you needed anything." He looked around. "This is one of the nicer houses. They picked well for you all."

"Teva, Rhexa said something about a dispensary?" Memfis asked. "But I'm not sure what she meant."

"Oh, yeah." Teva nodded. "Well, we used to have merchants who sold things to the healing centers, but when things got bad, they would price stuff really high, and a lot of people were going hungry and there weren't enough supplies. So Pirit changed it to be that everything that came into the healing centers as trade goods belonged to the entire center, and we can all go and draw out what we need. Clothes, or food, or anything. And we work for the center to pay for it. It's a good system, and Rhexa kept it up when we came here." He looked around. "You all need just about everything. So I can take you to the dispensary, if you want?"

"That would be a big help, Teva," Memfis said. He smiled. Then he said, "I'll be back." He disappeared down the corridor.

Owyn smiled. "Thanks, Teva," he said. "For coming and checking on us. I appreciate that."

"Well, I wasn't just making conversation," Teva answered. "I was really hoping we might be able to get a drink. Maybe get to know each other a little better? A lot better?"

Owyn swallowed. "That's a bit too fast. Can you give me a day or two? Just to get used to everything? There's been a lot happening the past couple of days."

Teva frowned. Then his eyes widened. "Oh. Oh, yeah. I can see that. Sure. Look, I'll take you to the dispensary, and help you get settled. Then once you're settled in, maybe I can show you around? We can start slow." He stepped closer. "Unless... you don't like boys? I saw you with your Air girl and I wouldn't blame you a bit if she's all you wanted." He grinned. "She looks like a handful."

Owyn shifted from foot to foot. He wasn't sure how to take that, so he shook his head. "She's the Heir, Teva. And I'm her Fire. So... yeah. But it's not that. I like boys just fine. But today has been a fucklong of a month, and I need to get my head around it."

Teva burst out laughing. "Fucklong of a month? I like that. I'll have to remember that. And yeah, I understand. I'm sorry if I pushed, and made you uncomfortable." He glanced at the corridor. "She's really the Heir? I heard rumors, but you know how things spread. She's really it? She's really the Heir?"

Owyn grinned. "Yeah, she's really the Heir." He cocked his head to one side. 'Why?"

"Because I always thought that the next Heir was going to be a man, and not Air," Teva admitted. He laughed. "Figured, the last Heir was an Air girl, and she went down easy. Next one... well, they needed to be stronger. Which is all kind of messed up, and if Treesi heard me say it, she'd kick my arse from here to Forge and back. Because there's no reason why a woman can't be as strong as a man."

Owyn grinned. "Don't let Aria hear you say that, because she'll help Treesi kick your arse." He shook his head. "Nah, Aria's got a spine of the finest steel. She'll do all right."

"She needs to do more than all right, Owyn," Teva said. He frowned. "She... she can't hear me, can she?"

"I can, actually," Aria called. She came down the corridor and into the front room. When Teva turned pale, she smiled. "And I don't mind. I agree. I have to do much better than all right. I'll need everyone behind me, though." She stepped closer. "Are you behind me, Teva?"

Teva swallowed hard enough that Owyn heard him. "My Heir, I'm where ever you want to put me," he said, his voice firm. He looked at Owyn, then back at Aria. "Do you have your Earth yet?"

Aria shook her head. "Not as yet, no."

Teva nodded. Then he grinned. "Are you holding auditions? Interviews?" His grin grew broader. "I'm a very cunning linguist."

Owyn gasped and stared at him. "You did not just say that!" Teva began to giggle, and Owyn shook his head. "You're terrible. That was a horrible, horrible pun."

"And you wish you'd thought of it?" Teva laughed.

"Well, yes." Owyn turned to Aria, who was looking at him quizzically. He could see the question. "I'll explain it later," he said quickly. "For now, Teva is going to show me where to find the food."

TEVA TOOK OWYN AROUND the town, showing him the library and archives, the farming terraces and the areas that were under special jurisdiction of the healers.

"Everything over the entry terrace is off limits," Teva said. He pointed. "See up there? The buildings painted green? You don't want to go up there."

"Why? What's up there?" Owyn asked.

"Those are the incurables," Teva answered. "The ones who've gone insane, and who can't be helped. They're kept under guard up there, and Risha sees to them herself. They're comfortable, I'm told. It's not my area — I work mostly with animals."

Owyn nodded. "That's a whole lot better than what they do with the insane in Forge," he said.

"What do they do there?" Teva steered Owyn into one of the little parks that seemed to be scattered all over the town. There were benches set in shaded arbors, and they sat down on one.

Owyn leaned back, breathing in the scent of the fragrant flowering vines that surrounded them

"This is nice," he said. "What happens in Forge... isn't. You know we're right on the Smoking Mountain, right?"

Teva nodded. "Yes."

"Well, there are caves all through the mountain. And... well, if someone is deemed to be out of their mind, and incurable, then they're taken down into the caves and left there."

Teva swore. "That's horrible!"

"I know. It's something else that needs to be changed." Owyn rested his elbows on his knees. "I'm glad you like Aria."

"I'm guessing that if I didn't, there'd be no hope for a second date?" Teva asked. Owyn laughed.

"Who said this was a first date?" he asked. Teva smiled and took his hand.

"It's a getting-to-know-you date," he said. "Taking it slow. And taking you home now, by way of the dispensary." He got up and tugged Owyn to his feet. "Sound good?"

Owyn smiled, lacing his fingers into Teva's. "Yeah, that sounds good."

They walked to the dispensary, which was a large building on the entry terrace. As they walked in, they were greeted by an older woman wearing a blue tunic.

"Good morning, Teva," she said. "What may I help you with today?"

Teva glanced at Owyn. "May I?"

"I wouldn't know where to start. Please."

Teva grinned and turned back. "Katrin, this is Owyn. He's just arrived today, and he and his housemates need the new resident setup."

Katrin turned and smiled at Owyn. "A pleasure to meet you. If you'll come this way?" She led him over to a podium, and uncorked a bottle of ink. She dipped a pen and looked at him. "How many in your house, and which house?"

"Ah... Fourteen Southwest," Owyn answered. "And I'm not sure if it's three or four. One will be a healer-in-training."

Katrin nodded and started writing. "Three for now, then. Four once he completes his training. Very good. Names?"

"Owyn, son of Memfis. Memfis, son of Trezi. Aria, daughter of Milon," Owyn answered.

Katrin copied it down, then stopped. "Daughter of... Milon?" she repeated. "Milon, the Heir to Firstborn Tirine?"

Owyn nodded. "Yes."

Katrin put her pen down. "I'd heard rumors. I'd heard that the new Heir to the Firstborn was here in Terraces. Is she..." She stopped and frowned. "Or are you?"

Owyn laughed. "No, not me!" he said. "She's the Heir. I'm her Fire. Aven, son of Jehan is her Water and he's the healer-in-training."

Katrin's brows furrowed. "Water... and healer. And... Jehan? Do you mean Jhansri?"

"Yeah, that's it." Owyn said with a nod. "He's half Earth, half Water. His mother's name is—"

"Aleia," Katrin filled in. "I remember her." She wrote for a moment, then looked up. "All right. Any food sensitivities?"

"I don't think so. At least, not until Aven finishes his training and comes to live with us again."

Katrin made a note. "He needs the Water diet?"

"If you mean extra salt and nothing from milk, then yes."

Katrin smiled. "Yes. And we have some fermented seaweed from up the coast in stores. I'll add some of that to your allotment. It doesn't go off quickly, and it's a delicacy among the Water folk. Also it's good for them. Helps with scale production, I think." She wrinkled her nose, dipping her pen once again. "It's an acquired taste, though."

"I tried it. I've no wish to further acquire that taste." Teva made a gagging noise. "I tasted it for three days, Owyn."

"Oh, that sounds vile," Owyn answered. "We'll try it, though. Aven might like it. Do we take this with us?"

"I'll put together something for you to take, so that you can have midday and evening meals. The rest will be delivered later today. For clothing, each of you should stop in for measurements."

"Do you have clothes for someone with wings?" Owyn asked. "Women's clothes?"

Katrin's pen stopped. "Aria is Airborn?" she asked. "I... am not certain we have anything. I'll check. We might have to tailor to fit. We can do it, but it will mean waiting."

"I don't think she'll mind," Owyn said. "Is there anything else you need to know?"

"Not at the moment," Katrin answered. "I'll send for your day's allotment. Now, you'll come here in the morning for your daily needs or anything perishable, and weekly for staples. If you can make things last, you need not come once a week — some make do with every other week. Don't waste anything. If you get more than you need, share it."

"Except for the seaweed," Teva murmured. "No one wants that."

"Hush," Katrin scolded. "Now, it'll be a moment. You can have a seat while you wait."

"All right," Owyn said. He turned toward a bench, then stopped. "Hey, you wouldn't happen to have a hammock somewhere, would you?"

"A hammock?" She frowned. "I'll look. That's a luxury item, though. It would require more hours—"

"If it's being used in place of a bed, would it be a luxury item?" Owyn interrupted. "Aven has trouble sleeping in a bed, and we lost his hammock in the fight."

She smiled. "In that case, I'll see what we can find and make sure it's in place in the student hall. Now, go have a seat. And welcome to Terraces, Owyn."

CHAPTER SEVENTEEN

OWYN SHIFTED HIS HEAVY basket from one hip to the other and grimaced. It hadn't seemed like that long of a walk when Teva was taking him to the dispensary, even with all the meandering they had done. But the walk back, carrying one of a pair of heavy baskets? Seemed to be taking twice as long.

"I thought smiths were strong," Teva teased.

"This is a different kind of lifting," Owyn grumbled. "It's not the same as working in the forge. And I don't have to carry the anvil for a mile."

Teva burst out laughing. "It hasn't been a mile!" He shifted his own basket, then gestured with his chin. "Looks like they were waiting for you."

Owyn looked, and saw Memfis standing in front of the doorway of number Fourteen, looking up the street toward them. Owyn grinned and raised his voice.

"Hey, Mem!" he called. "I've got supplies!"

"Did you have to go back to Forge for them?" Memfis asked as he came closer. He took the basket from Teva, then laughed. "And you brought back the small anvil?"

"I didn't think it was that heavy!" Teva protested. "What can I do to help?"

"Go on and get the door?" Memfis suggested. Teva trotted on ahead, and Memfis fell in next to Owyn. "I was starting to wonder where you'd gotten to," he said as they walked. "You've been gone a long time."

"Teva showed me around a little before we went to the dispensary. There are some areas that are off limits," Owyn answered. He looked up at the sky. "I didn't think I was gone that long."

"It's been a few hours, Mouse," Memfis said. "We were starting to wonder about supper."

"Ah, fuck, Mem, I'm sorry," Owyn groaned. "I'll apologize to Aria, too. She inside?"

"I think she's taking a nap, actually." Memfis stepped in front of Owyn and entered the house; Owyn followed him in and down the corridor to the kitchen, setting the basket on the worktable next to the one Memfis had put down. He turned to see Teva lingering in the doorway.

"You've got unpacking to do," he said. "And I've got to go make my rounds with the farrier. So I'll see you tomorrow, maybe?"

"Sure," Owyn said. "I want to introduce you to Aven. When he's awake, I mean."

Teva laughed. "I'd like that. Right. I'll look you up tomorrow." He nodded his farewell to Memfis, then headed out. Owyn turned toward the baskets.

"They've got all kinds of rules about the dispensary. We go in once a week, or once every other week, for our allotment of things that will keep," he said as he started unloading cloth wrapped bundles and jars. "If we want fresh meat, or fresh milk, or anything that might go off, we go in the morning. Teva says that in the summer, most folks eat their meat at midday, because it won't keep otherwise. Oh, and you and Aria need to go in to be measured for clothes. They said they might not have for her, but they can tailor things, and... what?" Owyn turned and saw the expression on Memfis' face.

"You were gone a very long time," Memfis repeated. "What were you doing?"

"I told you," Owyn said. "Teva showed me around. He showed me where things were. We walked, and then we went to the dispensary. I didn't realize how long we'd been. I'm sorry. I should have been back sooner." He looked at Memfis, then frowned. "That's not what you're really asking me, is it?" he asked slowly. "When you asked what I was doing?" He stopped, a sudden, sick feeling in his chest. "You want to know if the real reason we took so long is because I let him fuck me, don't you? That's what you're really asking?" He put the jar he was holding down hard on the table, hard enough that he heard the pottery break. He didn't care.

"Owyn—"

"That *is* what you're asking," Owyn breathed. He swallowed, his throat tight. "That... that's not fair, Mem!" he stammered. "It's not fair and you know it! Just because I used to be a whore doesn't mean you get to assume that I'm going to turn arse up for anyone who smiles at me!" He pushed away from the table and dragged his fingers through his hair. "For the record, no. I didn't. And I haven't. I haven't had anyone in my bed since Trey."

Memfis arched a brow, and Owyn stared at him. "Really?" he murmured. "Really, that's what you think of me? Now you think I'm lying? Three *years*, and you think I'm lying about this?" He clasped his hands into fists to keep from grabbing something and throwing it.

"I didn't say that."

"You were thinking it," Owyn countered. "You know you wear all your thoughts on your face, don't you? Granna Meris used to yell at you about it. Karse did, too. He said you were a shitty card player because of it."

"Karse said that?" Memfis asked. "When did he tell you that?"

"Not the point," Owyn snapped. "You think I'm lying to you about this. And apparently, you think I've been sleeping around behind your back. You think after all this time, I'm still a whore." He swallowed. "I'm not. I haven't even had Aven yet. I love him, and we both want it, but we haven't had the chance. So, going back to you, and your fuckheaded ideas. No, I didn't go off and let Teva fuck me. Furthermore, I have no intentions of fucking or being fucked by Teva, for all that he's a nice guy. And, for the record, fuck you for even thinking it. I thought you trusted me. I thought I could trust you." He walked out of the kitchen. He heard Memfis' voice behind him, then Aria's. He didn't turn or stop. He walked out of the house, turned, and left them behind.

ARIA STARED AT OWYN'S back as he walked away, then went into the kitchen.

"I heard shouting," she said. "What happened?"

Memfis didn't look at her at first. He was staring at a broken jar on the table. The contents were thick, and were slowly seeping out of the cracks and spreading out over the table's surface. "I... I ruined it, Aria."

Aria blinked, still not quite awake. "Ruined... the jar?"

"Ruined... everything." Memfis gave a wet-sounding laugh and looked at her. "He's right. I assumed... and I was wrong. I... I made an assumption about him, then thought he was lying to me about it." He looked at the door. "And now he's gone, and I don't know if he's coming back. I ruined... everything. I drove him away."

"What?" Aria looked over her shoulder, in the direction Owyn had gone. "Explain. All of it. Now."

Memfis swallowed. He closed his eyes. "Owyn was gone so long. I assumed...I mean, Teva is a nice looking young man. And Owyn is... Owyn."

"And Owyn has been very uncomfortable with the number of people asking him if he was interested in sex with them," Aria said. "Did he not tell you that?"

Memfis nodded. "He did. And we talked about it. I thanked him, for trusting me to ask. And then I went and assumed he was late because he'd been off having sex with Teva. And when he told me that he hadn't, I didn't believe him. And he called me on it."

"Memfis!"

"I know!" Memfis moaned. "I should have trusted him, and I didn't. And now... I don't know if he'll come back." He looked at Aria. "He will come back?"

"If you're asking me, I think he will," Aria answered. She glanced at the jar, then glared at Memfis. "But I do not think it will be because he's coming back to you," she added, her anger clear in her voice. How dare he?

Memfis flinched. Then he nodded. "He'll be coming back to you. For you. I... do you want me to leave?"

"That is not my decision. That is a question you will have to ask Owyn, when he returns," Aria said. "And whatever he says, you will abide by. Now, if you'll excuse me, I'm going to see if I can find him." She stalked out of the kitchen, following Owyn's path out the door and into the street. She couldn't tell which direction he'd taken. Not from the ground, anyway. She walked to the middle of the street, looked around, then launched herself into the air. Once she was over the height of the houses, she could see people on the road, in the gardens. Some of them were pointing at her, but since none of them were Owyn, she ignored them.

Where would he have gone? Aria circled, taking wider and wider turns each time. There were more terraces below the one where their house rested, more terraces above. A great deal of green space.

And no signs of Owyn. He didn't know this city — not the way he knew Forge. Where could he go?

The healing complex? He might go to be with Aven, even though Aven was asleep. It was worth looking. She banked, flying toward the cliff face and the healing complex.

OWYN WATCHED AS ARIA flew away. Only when he was certain that she wasn't turning back did he move out from the shelter of the arbor. He glanced back once more, then hurried out of the park and down to a lower terrace. He wasn't ready to be found yet. He had too many things to think about, and most of them were making his stomach churn to the point that he was certain he was going to puke.

Memfis had bought Owyn off the block, given him a home and a life, but only because of a vision in smoke. He'd finally adopted Owyn, but only when he'd had no choice. It had been adopt Owyn or have the Council hunt him down as a runaway slave — the laws were clear. He couldn't go more than a mile past the wall of Forge, not even with his owner. Adopting Owyn had been the easiest way to get around that. But just calling Owyn his son didn't make it so — He'd all but admitted it when Owyn had confided in him about how uncomfortable Treesi and Teva's advances had made him. He'd never expected to be a father. He hadn't wanted to be a father. He'd been forced into it. Which meant... what?

He ducked his head and swallowed bile. He knew what it meant. It meant that the last three years were a lie. It meant that the family he thought he had was a lie. Memfis didn't love him, no matter what he said today. He couldn't, not and think Owyn was still sleeping with anything that moved and then lying about it. Memfis thought he was still a whore. The man he'd come to love as a father thought he was still a whore. Possibly thought he'd never been anything but a whore.

Owyn stopped at the top of another set of stairs leading down to a lower terrace. This one looked to be entirely green — either one big park, or farmland. Teva had said there were small farms on some of the terraces, but he hadn't shown Owyn where they were. Owyn turned and studied the skies, but there was no sign of Aria. Where had she gone? He thought about it for a moment, then smiled. She'd gone to see if he'd gone to Aven. Where else would he go?

And there was the problem. Where else could he go? His place was with Aria and Aven. But then he'd have to face Memfis again, and he wasn't ready to do that. He looked around and started walking. This wasn't a farm, and he wasn't sure it was a park, either. It seemed too wild. But that was good — it gave him more places to hide. And no one seemed to be on this terrace at all. It seemed deserted. He kept wandering, heading further down the overgrown road, until he reached a wall and realized that this was the lowest terrace, and looked out over the sea. He rested his hands gingerly on the wall, and when it didn't crumble under his touch, he leaned a little more heavily against it. The water was far below him, not anywhere near as close as it had been when they'd camped on the beach, but it still made him nervous. Somewhere out there was his end.

And right here was his now. He needed to get his head on straight.

"No," he said aloud. "My head is on straight. I didn't do anything wrong. I haven't done anything wrong. It's not me that's the problem. It's not my fault. Memfis knew what I was when he took me in. And it's on him that he can't see past it." He turned and looked around, seeing another of the benches hidden beneath an overgrown arbor. He went and sat down, pulling his knees up to his chest. Once he was settled, he patted his shirt pocket. "You good in there? Want to come out?"

Trinket squirmed a little, but didn't appear. She must have been asleep. Owyn didn't blame her. It had been a long night. He leaned back and looked up at the leaves.

"How could he say that?" he said softly. "He told me I was his son. He told me he loved me. And... he thinks I'm a whore. He thinks I'm lying to him. So just what else does he really think about me?" He ducked his head, talking to his pocket and the sleeping fire-mouse. "He told Granna Meris he was proud of me. I don't think I can believe that anymore. I don't think I can believe anything he told me." He rubbed one hand over his face, grimacing at the feel of stubble against his skin. He needed to shave. He needed a bath, and a solid meal. He needed...

"Damn it, Mem," he whispered, hearing his voice crack. For nearly three years, once he'd really understood that Memfis hadn't considered him a slave, Owyn had thought he'd been lucky enough finally find the one thing he'd always wanted — a family. For nearly three years, he'd had a home, and someone he'd thought of as a father. He'd had someone who loved him, and who he loved with the fierce intensity that came with the knowledge of just how easy it was to lose such things.

And it had all been a lie. Everything that Owyn had built his new life on was a lie.

And he had no idea where to go from here. For a moment, he desperately wanted Aria. He wanted Aven. They knew who he was. Who he had been. They loved him anyway.

Didn't they?

Didn't they?

The cold doubt that wrapped around him threatened to drown him, as bitter as the salt water he still tasted in his dreams. As bitter as the tears that finally broke through his crumbling reserve, and he curled in on himself and wept.

ARIA WASHED HER HANDS at the basin, smiling at the attendant. "I've only been here once," she said. "Which way to number nineteen?"

The woman pointed, giving Aria instructions on where to turn. The halls were quiet, but not empty — men and women in white or gray walked up and down, and some of them stared openly at her. She smiled at all of them, and tried to ignore just how out of place she felt. Then she saw a familiar figure in gray ahead of her.

"Alanar?" she called. He turned and smiled.

"Aria," he said. "I wasn't expecting to hear your voice again tonight. Is anything wrong? You sound... off."

"I was looking for Owyn," she said as she walked up to the tall healer. "Have you..." she stopped, biting her tongue to stop herself from asking the question. He laughed.

"I don't think he's here, but it's been a while since I was last to nineteen. I'm supposed to meet Treesi and Risha there after the last stop in my rounds. So I'll walk with you." He offered her his arm. She took it, and they started walking again.

"I apologize—"

"Oh, don't," Alanar interrupted. He smiled. "You'd be surprised how many everyday phrases revolve around sight. No one realizes until they're faced with a blind man. Then they get all awkward about it. I don't mind, really." He grinned. "Do you like children?"

Aria blinked. "I... yes. Why?"

"How are you with loud noises?" Alanar asked.

"I... if I know they're going to happen, I'll be all right. I don't like to be startled."

Alanar nodded. "We none of us do, the Airborn. Be prepared for loud." He paused, then turned down a corridor toward a set of double doors.

"You know exactly where you are, the same way we do when we're in the air," Aria said as Alanar reached for the doors. He nodded, and she smiled. "Then when you brushed up against me, in Aven's room? That was deliberate?"

"Well, yes." Alanar admitted. His cheeks turned ever so slightly red. "I hope you don't mind? Touch is important."

"Oh, I don't mind."

"I should have known you'd understand. There are still people who think I have some sort of magic. They don't understand."

"Considering that there are some who think we're not human? I'd say so," Aria said.

Alanar sniffed. "It didn't used to be this bad. And no one will say it to your face. Or at least, not to mine. Not that I've noticed, anyway, but they all know me. I grew up with most of the people here as foster parents." He shook his head. "All right. Brace yourself." He pushed the door open, and a cacophony of music and laughter and children's voices poured out. Aria gasped, her grip on Alanar's arm tightening.

"Are you all right?" he asked.

"Yes. You did warn me, but... what is this?"

He grinned. "The children's wing. Come inside." He led her into what turned out to be a large room, lined on both sides with narrow cots for most of the length. At the far end, there was an open space that was filled with cushions, carpets, and shelves overflowing with books and toys. Most of the children in the room were there, along with several adults who seemed to be their caretakers. One of them — an older man — looked up and smiled as they came in.

"Well, Healer Alanar is here!" he called over the din. "Children, go back to your beds, it's time for rounds. We can go back to playing when he's done."

The children all scattered, heading toward their beds. Some of them walked slowly, and there were two on crutches. Several stopped and stared at Aria until they were shooed on their way.

"Sorry about that," the man said as he came to meet them. "Some of the littler ones, they've never seen Airborn before. At least, not with wings. You're new here?" He held his hand out to Aria. "I'm Beryn."

"It's nice to meet you, Beryn," Aria replied, taking his name. "My name is Aria. I've only just arrived."

"Beryn, spread the word, would you?" Alanar said in a low voice. "The Heir is in the Terraces, with her Fire and her Water. Her Water will be a healer-in-training with us, once he recovers from his injuries."

"I heard there was a Waterborn being tended to," Beryn murmured. "And... the Heir? Really?" He looked at Aria and his eyes widened. "You?"

She laughed. "Yes."

He bowed over her hand. "My Heir, it's an honor. How may I serve?"

Aria nodded and looked around. "Help me stay out of the way while Alanar works?"

"I don't think you're in the way," Alanar protested.

"The children aren't certain of me," she said. "Their discomfort will be what gets in the way. Go do your duty, Healer Alanar. I'll stay here with Beryn." She touched Alanar's arm. He smiled and bowed, then turned and walked to the closest bed. The child who occupied it ran out to meet him, taking his hand.

"They're fond of him," Beryn said. "He'll make someone a good husband someday. And an excellent father." He turned to face Aria fully. "Now, shall I show you the children's wing?"

"Please?" Aria asked. "I've never seen a healing center before today, and I've only seen the entryway, the corridors, an office and room nineteen."

"Well, this is where we take care of our children," Beryn said. "If the child is not contagious, that is. If they have something like spotted fever or cheekslap, there are special rooms for them until they're past the contagious period. Then we bring them in here. It's better for them, to be happy."

Aria chuckled. "I had cheekslap when I was very small. I still remember how badly I itched."

"Oh, you had the itchy part?" Beryn grimaced. "Not all children get that. It's wretched when it happens."

"My mother made me wear gloves, and tied them at the wrist so I couldn't take them off and scratch myself bloody."

Beryn shook his head. "Smart woman. I've seen children who were allowed to scratch, and who have scars now. Now, the adults here are healing assistants. We trained as healers, but we don't have the healing ability. We can care for the children and make them comfortable when the healers are taking care of other patients. We're part healer, part teacher, part nursemaid."

Aria nodded. "It sounds like a very important position, Beryn." She saw his brow raise, and smiled. "I'm serious. Healers aren't common, I'm told?"

"Not as much as we'd wish," he answered.

"And if healers in general are anything like my Aven, they'll work themselves to the bone to take care of their charges," Aria continued. "Yes?"

"Which one is your Aven?" Beryn asked. "Because Alanar said you had your Water and your Fire, but not Earth."

Aria nodded. "Aven is my Water. He's part Earth, and he is a healer."

"Ah, I see. Go on," Beryn urged.

"If all healers are like my Aven, then someone has to take care of them, so they can continue to care for others," Aria finished. "That's you, isn't it? And the others? You take care of the healers, so they can continue to care for everyone."

Beryn looked startled, then thoughtful. As Aria watched, he smiled and straightened a little.

"I had never considered that," he murmured. "Now, shall I take you around the room and introduce you to the other assistants?"

"Please?" Aria answered. "So long as we're not in the way, that is." Beryn nodded and offered her his arm, and they toured the room. As he introduced her to the other assistants, she watched Alanar work. He moved from bed to bed, examining each child, sitting with them, listening to them. More than one, the bedside visits ended with close hugs and laughter, and each child seemed better once Alanar had moved on. The children who had been tended to went back toward their play area, but Aria could see some of them watching her.

"Would you like to meet the children?" one of the female assistants asked.

"If you think it won't disturb them," Aria answered. She thought quickly, then smiled. "Malani, correct?"

"Yes," Malani said with a smile. "You're very good."

"It's only the six of you," Aria protested. Beryn snorted.

"Malani is right. There are healers who've been here their whole lives who don't call us by name. We're all 'assistant'—"

"If we're not 'hey, you!'" a young man added. He grinned. "And I'm—"

"Nexim," Aria supplied, and he laughed.

"You are good," he said. "Come on. You can read the children a story, and they'll love you forever for it."

CHAPTER EIGHTEEN

"WHY WAS IT FUNNY WHEN I read that book?" Aria asked as Alanar led her from the children's wing.

"Because that book in particular is a favorite among the children, and every healing assistant in there has read it often enough that they can recite it from memory," Alanar answered. He smiled. "I can recite it from memory, but that's because when I was small, it was my favorite, too."

Aria laughed. "I've never heard the story before. It's charming."

Alanar nodded. "It seems to be unique to Terraces. It's based on a song that's so old no one knows who first wrote it." He turned, guiding Aria down the corridor. "Now, nineteen should be on our left."

"Yes, here it is," Aria said. She opened the door and entered, seeing Treesi first, then Risha. Then Aven, who was sitting up and eating, and who lit up like a candle when he saw her.

There was no sign of Owyn.

"Aria!" Aven called. "I wasn't expecting to see you before morning! How did you know I was awake?"

"I didn't," Aria said. "I came looking for Owyn. Has he been here?"

Aven blinked and looked at Treesi. "I haven't been awake long. Was he here before I woke up?"

"No," Treesi said. "I haven't seen him since we left you all at the crossing. Why?"

Aria bit her lip and looked around. This was not a discussion she wanted to have in company. Risha smiled sympathetically.

"We'll leave you two alone," she said, and shooed Treesi toward the door. "We'll be in the corridor. Call if you need anything."

The door closed behind them, and Aria went to perch on the edge of Aven's bed. He frowned.

"What's wrong?" he asked softly. "You look worried."

"Because I am," she answered. "Because Owyn and Memfis... well, they didn't fight exactly. But Memfis was horrible to Owyn, and now Owyn's gone off and I can't find him. I thought he would come here, because he doesn't know this city. But he clearly didn't, and I don't know where he's gone. I was certain he would be here, so I didn't rush. But I should have come straight here, because now he could be anywhere."

"Wait," Aven said. "Memfis? Was horrible to *Owyn*? What did he do?"

"Owyn went off with a young man who was with us when we brought you here. And who had been admiring Owyn quite openly. They were gone for a long time. Long enough that I fell asleep. I woke up with Owyn shouting at Memfis. He walked away as I came out, and he left. Memfis told me what happened — that he'd accused Owyn of taking so long because he'd been having sex with Teva. And when Owyn told him no, Memfis accused him of lying."

For a moment, Aven didn't say anything. The shock on his face faded slowly, and was replaced with anger. He swallowed, and his voice was very quiet when he finally spoke. "Aria, would you ask Risha to step back in?"

Aria got up and went to the door. She opened it to find Risha, Treesi and Alanar standing just across. "Aven wants you, Risha," she said. She turned back, and gasped. "What are you doing?"

Aven grimaced as he stood up, the blankets falling away to reveal that he was completely naked. He swayed slightly on his feet, but steadied himself quickly. "I'm coming with you to find Owyn."

"No, you most certainly are not!" Risha said. "Sit down before you fall down."

Aven blinked, shook his head, then swayed again. "He needs me. Needs us."

"And what about what you need?" Risha countered. "You need to rest. The healing isn't finished yet. The head wound isn't completely healed yet. Are you trying to cripple yourself?"

Aven set his jaw and narrowed his eyes, and for a moment looked so much like his mother that Aria gasped at the resemblance. Then she shook her head and walked over to him, resting her hand on his bare chest, right over the bandages that kept his arm in place.

"My Water, you are going back to bed," she said softly. "You are not allowed to damage yourself."

"Aria—"

"That's an order, my Water, my love," she said. She met his eyes, then reached up to cup his cheek. "I'll find him. And I'll bring him here so you can see that he's well. But you are not in any condition to help me search." She ran her hand down his neck, letting her fingers linger over his collarbone. There was a bump there, and a scar. Neither had been there before. And the hollow of his throat looked oddly naked without the Water gem. She'd have to bring it to him. "Aven, I need you to be safe and whole. I need you here."

"I'll go," Treesi said. "I can help. And we can get others to help. We'll find him." She bit her lip and looked at Risha. "If that's all right, Senior Healer?"

Risha nodded. "Go on. Alanar, I'll want you to examine Aven. Then you can sit with him and tell him what to expect from his training. I'll take the rest of the evening rounds."

"The assistants aren't going to let Aria back in after sunset," Alanar said.

"I'll tell them to make an exception," Risha said. She turned to Aria. "When you find him, when you bring him back, if it's after sunset, you'll need to be completely quiet when you come through the halls."

"I understand," Aria said. She turned back to Aven, who looked back at her, clearly miserable. She understood completely — she'd felt much the same way when she'd been waiting to learn if he and Owyn had been found after they had been kidnapped in Forge.

Treesi touched Aria's arm. "Let's go. I'll need to arrange runners, and a search team."

"Will that take a long time?" Aria asked.

Treesi shook her head. "Not too long. We'll know soon enough if he tried to leave — the guides at the tunnels would have alerted Rhexa if someone tried to leave alone, and you can't get through the tunnels without passing them. Because people would get lost in there. That's why we have procedures for search teams. But Owyn is still in Terraces somewhere, so it'll be easy to find him. Easier."

"Tunnels?" Aven repeated. "I... I thought that was a dream."

"No, you scared the whole lot of us," Treesi said with a grin. "But that's all right. We forgive you. Now go sit down before you fall down and undo all our work."

Aven blinked. Then he sat down on the bed. He must have just only just realized that he wasn't wearing anything, because he dragged a fold of the blankets over his lap. Aria bit her lip — how much had she changed over the past few months? Aven's nudity had seemed completely natural and comfortable, until he'd covered himself.

"Don't scare him, Allie," Treesi said. She touched Aria's arm again. "Ready to go?"

Aria nodded. But first, she went to the bed and leaned down to kiss Aven. He tipped his head back and smiled up at her as she straightened.

"I have to explain something to you. Later. It can wait," he said. "It can wait until you find Owyn. I need to tell you both." His smile faltered. "Find him? And... even if I'm asleep, I need to know he's safe. So wake me, if I'm asleep when you get back."

"Of course," Aria murmured. "We'll be back as soon as we can." She followed Treesi out of the room and through the halls until they were outside. Treesi looked around, then grumbled.

"Of course. When I want a runner, there's no one around. Come on. It's faster to go around the building than through. At least for this." She set off at a brisk pace, and Aria hurried after her.

"What are we doing?" Aria asked.

"We need runners, and a search team," Treesi said. "And I want to talk to Teva. See what he knows. We'll probably want Marik, too. We can't be everywhere, and he talks to birds—"

"He what?"

"Talks to birds," Treesi repeated. "He's got the earth sense, and it's very strong. Birds listen to him, do what he wants them to do. So he has eyes everywhere. Come on, we're going to the administration building. Then maybe the stables."

The administration building was a small stone structure on the far side of the healing complex. Treesi pointed at a window in the healing complex as they passed, then a door. "That's Rhexa's office," she said. "She should be in the AB — the administration building. But since she works with Risha so much, it made more sense to have her there, and put a door in near her office so she can get here. There's a lot of back and forth between the two. That's why we have runners." She stopped, looked at Aria, and made a face. "Would you mind waiting outside? It's a little close in there, and it won't be comfortable for you." When Aria nodded, Treesi hurried into the small building. A few minutes later, she came back. "Right. Let's go."

"What did you do? And the stables now?"

"No, one of the runners is going to fetch Teva for us. We're to meet the search team in front of Fourteen Southwest. Since that's where he started from, it's the best place for us to start."

They walked side by side down the street, back toward the house. Treesi finally broke the silence. "What happened, Aria?"

"Owyn and Memfis..." Aria paused. "It's very complicated."

"Does it have anything to do with Owyn's scars? Because I saw them, and I know what the crosshatching on his shoulder means," Treesi said. "I don't know if Teva does. But the healers, we all know. We used to get runaways, from the Fire tribes. Not so much anymore."

Aria gnawed on her lip, then lowered her voice. "Owyn was gone a long time. Memfis accused him of being so long because he'd had sex with Teva, and didn't believe Owyn when he denied it."

Treesi coughed. "And Memfis is his father?" she demanded. Then she stopped. "Wait—"

"Memfis adopted Owyn," Aria said.

"I should have put that together," Treesi said with a nod. "Because of Rhexa thinking Owyn was her nephew, and because of the scars." She frowned slightly. "It doesn't bother me. Earth is different. But Air is different, too. Does it bother you, knowing what he was?" She paused. "Knowing that I'm the same? Every other tribe thinks that Healers are whores, don't they?"

Aria stopped and looked at Treesi. "No, they don't. And no, it doesn't bother me. Why should it?" she asked. "Owyn's past made him the man that I need at my side as my Fire." She met Treesi's eyes and decided. Her men would forgive her. "And your past has made you the woman I need at my side as my Earth."

Treesi opened her mouth. Closed it again. Opened it again. And closed it again. She blinked rapidly three times. Then she frowned. "That's not funny."

"I wasn't trying to be. I'll give your gem to you when we get to the house." Aria took Treesi's hand. "I knew from the moment Aven brought you to the camp that you were mine. He told me he knew from the moment he saw you. Owyn knew as well. We all recognized you."

Treesi looked stunned. "I... I just thought I'd met wonderful new people who I wanted to know a lot better. I didn't... I didn't think it was different! It just happens with me. A lot!" She bit her lip, then blurted out. "You should take Alanar. Not me."

"It's not my choice, Treesi," Aria said. "It's the Mother's choice. And She says that you are the one to wear the gem." She paused, then asked, "Why would someone think that being clever with language would make them a good choice?"

"What?" Treesi asked. She started walking again, but didn't let go of Aria's hand.

"Teva. He asked if I was taking interviews for my Earth. He said he was clever with language."

"Clever with... wait," Treesi giggled. "Tell me exactly what he said."

"He said he was a cunning linguist," Aria answered, then stared as Treesi whooped with laughter. "That means something else, doesn't it?"

Treesi nodded, looking mischievous. "He's bragging on being clever with his tongue, certainly. But there won't be much speaking involved. Moaning, maybe. Probably. Teva is very good. And you have no idea what I'm talking about." She giggled. "You really don't. Owyn hasn't shown you? Or Aven?"

Aria looked around, then lowered her voice. "I haven't yet. With either of them. Aven doesn't know what to do so that I won't get pregnant, and... well, he's never had sex before either. Owyn says he'll teach the both of us. And he's played with Aven, but I won't until I'm sure I won't come away with a baby. I'm not ready for one, and I have work to do."

Treesi nodded. "I understand. And... well, there are teas. But if you want a more lasting solution, talk to Risha. She'll do it. She did it for me." She shrugged. "I'd offer, but I only just learned how, and I don't want to make a mistake. Not on you. Because you're right. So talk to Risha."

Aria smiled. "I will. Because I'm tired of waiting. There's the house."

They entered together, and Aria raised her voice. "Memfis?" There was no answer. She frowned and headed down the corridor, checking the kitchen and the bedrooms. The broken jar was still on the table, the other supplies still in their baskets. Memfis was nowhere to be found.

"Is he in there?" Treesi called.

"No," Aria answered. "The house is empty. Perhaps he went looking for Owyn himself?" She looked through the bedrooms again, then went into the room that Owyn would share with Aven, taking the Water gem and the Earth gem from Aven's carry-bag. She'd bring Aven's gem to him in the healing complex — it wasn't right that he should be without it. Then she joined Treesi in the front room.

"The search team will be here soon," Treesi said. "So we should... oh, that's pretty!" She looked closer at the two gems hanging from Aria's hand. "Is the blue one Aven's Water gem?"

"Yes. I'm going to bring it to him after we find Owyn. And this one is yours." Aria held up the brown and gold gem. "If you'll have it. If you'll have me. Will you stand with me, Treesi?"

"Is that even a question?" Treesi asked in response. "I mean, does anyone ever say no?" She grinned. "Yes. I'll be yours. And you'll be mine. And... oh, that means that the men are ours, too?" She giggled. "Do I have to wait? I mean... do you get to have them first?"

Aria's face warmed, making the skin almost tingle. "I have an understanding with Aven. He will be my first. I will be his first woman. Owyn agreed to that. "

"Then I'll have my fun with Owyn, once he's ready," Treesi said. "When do you want your first woman? Because I mean... I'm it, right?"

"I... don't have the first idea what that would be like," Aria admitted.

"That's fine," Treesi said. She took Aria's free hand and kissed her palm. "I can teach you. Now, let's go wait for the search team."

"First, let me put this on you," Aria said. She held up the Earth gem. Treesi looked thoughtful, then shook her head.

"I want to wait until we're all together. So let's go find Owyn first. I want them there for it."

Aria nodded and slipped the gems into her jacket pocket. Then Treesi led Aria back out into the street, looked back the way they'd come, and waved. "Teva!"

"Hey, Tree. What's wrong?" He stopped as he reached them. "My Heir, what's going on? They said someone was missing."

"Owyn had words with Memfis, and went off. We don't know where he's gone," Aria said. "And I'm worried. He was very upset."

"He was fine when I left!" Teva protested. "What happened? Was it something I did?"

"It was..." Aria paused. "It was a misunderstanding, I think. Between Owyn and Memfis. Once we find Owyn, we'll be able to make some sense of it. But we need to find him first."

Teva nodded. "How long has he been gone?"

Aria frowned. "I think it was not long after you left."

Teva's eyes widened. "That's hours now!"

"I thought he would go to the healing complex, to be with Aven," Aria admitted. "So I did not hurry after him as I should have. I spent some time with the children in the healing complex."

"Did they make you read *The Stars Dance*?" Teva asked with a grin. Aria laughed.

"Yes. It was very sweet," she answered. "But now... Owyn never went there. And I do not know where Memfis has gone."

"Maybe out looking," Teva dragged his fingers through his hair, then pulled a cord from his pocket and tied it back into a short tail. "Right. Tree, you called for a search team?"

"They're meeting us here," Treesi answered. "And I sent runners to see if they can find Marik."

"Oh, good idea!" Teva said. "And Aria, you can search from the air, right?"

"I did," Aria said. "But I didn't see him. I circled. Then I flew to the healing complex."

"Which kind of says he didn't go that way," Teva said slowly. "And that he knew you would go up, so he stayed out of sight." He frowned. Then he groaned. "I showed him the arbors in the parks. They're covered, so if he went into a park and sat down, you wouldn't see him from the air!"

Aria blinked. "Where is the closest park?"

Teva pointed. "That way. Not far. I'll go check. Maybe he sat down and fell asleep? He said it had been... what did he say? Oh, today had been a fucklong of a month. I thought that was funny." He sighed. "Look, it's a little park. Barely more than a green spot and a couple of benches. Let me go see if he's there. I'll be right back. Don't leave without me."

CHAPTER NINETEEN

BY THE TIME TEVA RETURNED, there were several small groups milling around in front of Fourteen Southwest. He looked at Aria, shook his head, then went to speak to one of the groups.

"He wasn't in the park," Aria murmured to Treesi.

"We'll keep looking. There's a lot of ground to cover, and a lot of places where someone could go if they didn't want to be found." Treesi stood on her toes. "You met Marik. You rode with him when we came to Terraces. Do you see him?"

Aria turned and looked, searching the street. "No, I don't see him yet."

"He can be kind of hard to find. He spends more time with animals than people. But I told the runner who went after him to tell him that it was Owyn. He might very well go off looking on his own. Which might make things complicated."

"If he finds Owyn before we do?"

Treesi nodded. "Exactly. I'm more worried about what might happen if Memfis finds Owyn first. If Memfis was as wrong as you said he was, I'm worried what he might say if he finds Owyn before we do." She looked around again. "He's Owyn's father. This has to be tearing Owyn up all kinds of ways."

Aria closed her eyes and tried to fight the urge to take off and fly until she found Owyn. "Treesi, we have to find him."

"We will," Treesi said gently. "We'll find him. I'll— Marik!" She waved, then grabbed Aria by the hand and dragged her in the direction of the lone man coming down the street.

"Got your message," he said. "I spoke to the birds, but it's late for the songbirds, and too early for the night singers and the owls. Did hear something interesting from the sea eagles, though. Makes me think he's in the low terrace."

Treesi groaned. "That's overgrown, and huge!"

"So we take it slow," Marik said. "We go down each spoke, and we fan out from there. Leave watchers on the stairs, and work from the seawall back to the stairs." He smiled at Aria. "We'll find him. If it gets dark, the owls will find him."

"So long as they do not find Trinket first," Aria said. Marik arched a brow, and she added, "Owyn's pet. A fire-mouse."

"Then he's definitely in the low terrace," Marik said. "That's what the sea eagles told me. There was a new something down there, and they weren't sure if it was edible or not. It was brightly colored."

"Trinket!" Aria gasped. "They left her alone?"

Marik nodded. "Things that are brightly colored are usually bad to eat. They left her alone. But she was down in the low terrace. They're not all that good with giving me directions, though. There's only so much you can expect from something with a brain the size of a piece of cheese. A small piece of cheese." He turned and whistled, and the chattering around them fell silent.

"He's in the low terrace," Marik announced. "The eagles say so. So fan out, go down each spoke, then spread out. Someone stay on the stairs to watch, and we work our way back from the wall to the stairs. We don't have a lot of time before it gets dark." He started assembling groups, telling them where to go and what to do. Aria arched a brow at Treesi.

"No, it's all right," Treesi assured her. "I was expecting that. Marik is good at this. He's really good at organizing things. People. Whatever. He just can't stay around people too much. He's too sensitive."

"Right. I've sent groups out to West and Northwest. Teva is taking South. We'll take Southwest, and North isn't passable. Rockfall from the last tremor closed the stairs down to the low terrace," Marik said as he came back to them. "And I've left sentries here, so that if Owyn or Memfis come back, we'll know. One of them will come for me." He nodded toward the house, and Aria turned to see three hawks sitting on the roof. She smiled.

"Marik, is there a way to repay them for their kindness in helping us?" she asked. He looked startled.

"I don't think anyone has ever asked me that before," he said. "Ah...you hunt, don't you? I saw you with the javelins, when we went against Mannon's men."

"I do hunt."

"The next time there's a hunting party, go with them. Bring a few birds back for them, or the offal, and that will square things with the hawks." He gestured. "Let's go."

They started walking, and Aria looked back over her shoulder at the three figures on the roof. "You really do speak to them?"

"It's not so much speak as understand, but yes," Marik answered. "I've got what the healers say is the strongest animal sense they've ever seen. It makes things... uncomfortable, sometimes."

"Aven has the animal sense, a little," Aria said.

"Your Owyn has it, too," Marik said. "Or so Teva says."

Aria frowned. "Owyn is Fire, he thinks. Rhexa says she thinks he may be her nephew."

"Huh," Marik grunted. He walked in silence for a moment until they reached stairs leading down to the next terrace. "There might be something to that. He doesn't think so?"

"He doesn't know," Aria answered. "He doesn't remember his parents."

Marik nodded. Then he looked at Treesi. "Isn't there a way for healers to tell if people are related?"

"Level five are supposed to be able to do that," Treesi answered. "So not anymore, no."

"There are no level five healers?" Aria asked. "But I thought those were the teachers? Memfis said that level five healers weren't usually allowed to leave—" she paused, realizing what that must have meant. "Did they all die, when the healing centers fell?"

Treesi grimaced. "You're too quick. Yes."

"First time in our history that we've had a Senior Healer who isn't," Marik added.

"Aven's father was a level five healer," Aria said. "Aven may be that strong."

Marik chuckled. "Then you might have the next Senior Healer at your right hand, my Heir," he said. Then he paused. "He's part Water, and his father was level five. His father is Healer Jhansri?"

"Yes," Aria answered.

Marik nodded. "I'll have to come meet him when he's awake and outside."

"Marik objects to roofs," Treesi teased.

"I don't need a roof," Marik retorted. "I like to see the sky, and I'm not made of spun sugar, to melt when it rains."

"Does it not get cold here?" Aria asked.

"There are caves," Marik answered. "For some reason, caves are easier for me than houses. Doesn't make sense, but then, neither do I." He pointed. "That's the last stair. The lowest terrace is overgrown

— we don't have the manpower to keep it tidy. So it's a little wild down there."

"Good place to hide," Treesi added. Aria glared at her, and she blinked. "What? It's true!"

"True, but it didn't need to be said, Tree," Marik said. "Aria, what I've been telling the birds is to fly out over the water, then fly back in. Most of the arbors face out, so if Owyn is there, he'll be visible from that direction long before we reach him."

Aria nodded and took to the air. She circled over the stairs for a moment, getting her bearings, then headed toward the wall and the sea. She could smell the salt, see the water far below... and the Palace, in the distance off to her right. She circled again, studying Terraces. It was plainly obvious that there were people living here. And there was nothing blocking the view of the town from the sea, and she knew full well that Mannon had ships that sailed these waters. How had no one noticed them?

She flew back in slowly, gliding on an updraft as long as she could, studying the green space. What had Owyn been wearing? Was his shirt blue, or white? She thought it was blue, but was she thinking of the other one, the one that he'd been wearing yesterday, that had gotten ruined? She beat her wings and rose higher, seeing a flash of something light colored through the green. No, that was someone else, someone searching. They waved at her as she flew overhead, circling and flying back out over the water once more.

She flew back and forth, back and forth, and up and down the length of Terraces until heavy clouds had gathered, and the light had faded to a gray twilight that smelled of rain and lightning. Tired, her wings and back sore, she flew back to the stairs at Southwest and landed, then sat down on the stairs and folded her arms over her knees. She rested her forehead on her arms. Where was he?

"Aria?"

She raised her head at the sound of Treesi's voice. The healer's gray clothes were covered in leaves and dirt, and there was a smudge on one cheek. "Are you all right?"

"Very tired," Aria said. "Has anyone found him?"

"Marik is checking with the others, but not that I know of," Treesi yawned. "I can't imagine where he's gotten to! We've been over every bit of this terrace!"

"He either is very good at evasion, or he slipped back into the town before we got here," Marik said. "I can't say which. But he didn't go back to Fourteen."

"Are the hawks still there?" Aria asked.

Marik shook his head. "It's owls now. The hawks flew off to hunt, and I asked owls to take the watch. They say no one has come." He frowned. "Which means that Memfis did not go back to the house either."

"Wonderful," Aria groaned. "Now they're both missing!" She rested her head on her arms again, trying not to cry. She felt lost, and alone, even more than when she'd first been taken by Mannon's men. A warm arm encircled her shoulders, and she leaned against Treesi and bit her lip. "I don't know what to do," she whispered.

"Sleep," Treesi said. "And eat something. Have you eaten?"

Aria frowned. "I don't remember."

"Treesi, take her back to Fourteen," Marik said. "I'll keep hunting, until the rain starts. We'll find him, Aria."

OWYN JERKED, HEARING someone calling his name. He scrubbed one hand over his face and frowned, trying to think, trying to wake up. Who was looking for him? And why? He looked around, then crawled out from underneath the overgrown bench where he'd been sleeping. He heard the voice and barely recognized it as familiar. He couldn't think of the name. Just...

"No," he whispered. If he was caught with whoever that was, he'd get in trouble. He couldn't get caught. If he got caught, the guards would hurt him. He needed a better hiding place. He needed to get away from the people, get low, get back into Forge and get onto the roofs. He could hide on the roofs. He ducked into the underbrush and started moving, away from the voices, going slowly and deliberately so he couldn't give himself away. When the voices got too close, he froze, waiting for them to pass, then started moving once more, threading his way through overgrown brush and poorly maintained paths. Where was he?

He'd reached what looked like fairly fresh rockfall before his half-awake panic finally faded, and he finally remembered that he wasn't in Forge anymore. That he was in Terraces, that he was free, and that no one was going to hurt him anymore. He stopped, hearing the distant rumble of thunder as he turned and looked through the growing darkness. He couldn't hear anyone calling him anymore. Had they stopped looking? Maybe. It was getting dark, and it was going to storm. The people searching were probably smart enough to get out of the rain, even if he wasn't.

Where could he go? Back to Fourteen, and hope that Memfis would leave him alone? Or he could go to the healing complex, and sleep on Aven's floor. It wouldn't be the first time he'd slept on the floor. No. Aven needed to heal. If Owyn went there, Aven would fuss and try to take care of him, and not take care of himself. Had Aria told Aven that Owyn was missing? Mother, he hoped not.

For a moment, he considered going and finding Teva. That had been who had been calling for him, he was fairly sure. If he went and found Teva, he'd have someplace else to go, and probably something better than a floor to sleep on. But what would he have to do, to get that?

No. He had given up paying for a bed and meal with *that* coin years ago. He wasn't going back to it, no matter what Memfis thought of him. He looked up at the sky, then at the rockfall. No way up that way, and he started to retrace his steps. Before he reached another set of stairs leading up to the next terrace, the rain had started, fat, cold raindrops that hit his skin hard enough to sting. He hunched over slightly and cupped his hand over his pocket to try and protect Trinket. By the time he reached the top of the stairs, he was soaked to the skin, and the rain was coming down hard enough that he could barely see. He was wet, cold and hungry, for the first time in years. And he wasn't liking it one bit. He started running, splashing through puddles until he couldn't see for the water in his eyes.

It was the cold that finally decided it for him. He needed to go back to the house, if only to get Trinket out of the cold rain. He frowned, trying to see where he was. He wasn't sure if he was on the right street, or what number house he was passing. Was he in the right place? He didn't see a marker. Where was he? Only one way to find out. He turned to the left and went to the closest house; as he approached the door, it opened.

"Are you lost?" the woman inside asked.

"I..." Owyn stammered. "Yeah. I'm not sure... I'm trying to get to Fourteen Southwest."

"You're on Northwest, and you're in the first ring. You need to go... Owyn?" She stepped out into the rain, and Owyn realized that it was Rhexa.

"I... I don't want to be a bother—"

"You're no bother. Come inside and get dry," Rhexa said. "You've had a lot of people very worried."

"That's why I was trying to go back," Owyn said. "I should go back." Then he sneezed, and Rhexa's brows rose.

"You're going to catch your death," she said. "Come inside."

Owyn swallowed, weighing his choices. Not that he had many. If he went back, he'd have to deal with Memfis. If he stayed...

maybe there might be answers. He followed Rhexa into the house, stopping just inside as she closed the door behind him.

The layout of Rhexa's house was identical to Fourteen — the large sitting room to one side, the dining area to the other, and the corridor directly in front of him. But her house looked lived in — there were comfortable looking cushions and blankets on the couches and chairs, shabby rugs on the floors, and bookshelves crammed full of books and papers. There were pictures on the walls, clutter on every horizontal surface, and a fire burning in the fireplace. Owyn found himself grinning — everything was warm and welcoming. It felt like a home.

"I like your house," he said.

"Thank you," Rhexa answered, sounding amused. "Go stand by the fire and get warm." She went to the closest chair and picked up a blanket, bringing it back and draping it over Owyn's shoulders. "I don't think I have anything you could wear. But take this."

"I'll get everything wet!" Owyn protested.

"So?" Rhexa asked. She patted his shoulder and shook her head. "Go warm up. I'll get us something to drink."

Owyn touched his pocket. "Do you have any nuts? Seeds? Something like that?"

Rhexa looked puzzled. "I have tear-nuts. Will that do?" She stepped closer. "You have something in your pocket?"

"A fire-mouse. And she's cold and hungry."

"Oh, of course. Put her in the fireplace, and I'll see what I have that she can eat. Does she eat fruit?"

"She shouldn't. So not too much," Owyn answered. She headed down the corridor toward the kitchen, and he took Trinket out of his picket and crouched next to the fire. "Here you go," he told the fire-mouse, setting her down on the hearth. "You go get warm."

Trinket sat still for a moment, then darted into the flames. Owyn smiled and sat down right where he was, pulling the blanket more tightly around himself. He could hear Rhexa working in the kitchen, crockery rattling and cabinets opening and closing. She was singing, something that sounded vaguely familiar. Then he heard the words, and staggered back to his feet.

"*The sun is sinking in the west, the moon will soon be high. The stars have come to dance, the midnight festival is nigh.*"

He walked slowly down the corridor, and nearly bumped into her as she came out of the kitchen. She was carrying two mugs, and handed one to him.

"Here you are. A bit of mulled cider, to take the chill off. There's tea steeping, and soup heating up. And you look like you've seen the Mother's winged chariot riding right through my front room. What is it?"

"You were singing," Owyn said. "I know that song. What is it? Where did you learn it? Are there more verses than just the one? And what's the last line of that first verse?"

Rhexa blinked. "In order, it's *The Stars Dance*, and as far as I know, it's only ever been sung here in Terraces. All the children learn it. There are nine verses in this version—"

"In *this* version?" Owyn gasped.

"There are three versions, all slightly different," Rhexa said. "Owyn, come and sit. You know *The Stars Dance*?"

Owyn let her lead him back to the front room, but refused to sit on the chairs, settling back down on the floor near the fireplace. Rhexa dragged a chair over to sit with him.

"I know that song," Owyn said. "I've known that song my whole life. I knew that song when I didn't know my own name! But I only knew the first verse, and not all of it. No one in Forge ever knew the rest."

"I doubt anyone outside of Terraces would," Rhexa said. "The song was written here, I think. And it's been sung here for generations. Oral tradition, first. Which is why there are three versions — there's one that was sung mostly by the Air tribe who lived here. There was one that was sung by the Fire tribe, and there was one that was sung by Healers. That seems to be the most popular version. It's the one that was put down in writing."

"There's a *book*?" Owyn demanded. "You have a copy? Can I see it?"

She smiled. "I'll get it. Just a minute." She set down her mug and left the room, coming back a moment later with a large book that she handed to Owyn. He opened it, and felt a shiver of recognition.

"I've seen this before," he whispered, turning the pages. "I've seen these pictures."

"Look inside the cover," Rhexa said. Owyn looked up, then turned back to the book, opening the front cover. The title was there, and underneath, a name: Jaxia, daughter of Mara. Below that, in faded handwriting, was an inscription: *For my dearest Rhexa. I love you.*

"Is Jaxia who wrote it?" he asked, looking up.

"Jaxia was the artist who did the woodblocks for that book. It took her the better part of two years to do all of them, and we still have them in the archives. We still print books from the original woodblocks." Rhexa smiled. "She was my mother."

"And... if I'm..."

"Jaxis was named for his grandmother," Rhexa said. "She died... oh, Jaxis was only a month or two old. I think it's part of the reason Dyneh took the position in Forge. To get away from the memories."

"And no one outside Terraces knows this story? No one ever took this book to other places?" He frowned and looked down at it. "No, wait. Of course there might be copies of the book out there. But no one else would know the song, would they?"

Rhexa shook her head. "As far as I know, it's only sung here."

"But I know it," Owyn said. He looked up at Rhexa. "And I shouldn't. Not unless someone taught me. Or sang it to me." He frowned. "Did she? Dyneh? Did she sing it to me? Or... or him? Jaxis?"

Rhexa swallowed. "Every night. She sang it as a lullaby every night from the day he was born until the day they left for Forge. I have no reason to think that she didn't keep on."

CHAPTER TWENTY

OWYN CLOSED THE BOOK and set it aside. looked into the fire, seeing Trinket playing in the coals. "You never came for her? For him?" he asked. He didn't look up. He couldn't. He couldn't look at her.

"Of course I did. I made the trip to Forge four times, and met with the Council twice," Rhexa said. "I paid smugglers to get me in, and get me out. The last time, we were almost caught, and Pirit told me I couldn't risk myself for smoke dreams anymore. But I was going to go back. I had all my plans made... and the purges started." She sighed. "The last time was... oh, ten years ago?"

"Ten years ago, I was on the streets," Owyn said. He rubbed the back of his neck, feeling the top of one of his scars. "I was a thief. And I was learning that I was an awful thief."

"Owyn—"

"I might not be him, you know," Owyn said. This time, he did turn. "A song is a really thin chain to hang a hope on."

Rhexa smiled slightly. She got up from her chair and came to sit on the floor with him. "But it's a good chain," she said. She rested her hand on his, then let out a breath. "Now, will you introduce me to your friend?"

"Who? Oh, you mean Trinket? Sure." He held one hand out, flat against the floor. "She might not come out. It's warm in there."

"Maybe she'll come out for these?" Rhexa poured some tear-shaped nuts into Owyn's palm. A moment later, Owyn had a handful of warm, flame-colored mouse. He grinned and shifted back, bringing her closer.

"Does she talk to you?" Rhexa asked.

"What, with words?" Owyn shook his head. "Nah. She just likes me. She used to live in our forge. And when I told her I was leaving, she crawled into my pocket and wouldn't get out. So I brought her with me."

Rhexa reached out and stroked Trinket with one finger. "She's lovely. And you're a good friend to her." She sat back up. "Owyn, what happened? Why did you run off?"

Owyn swallowed. "I... I needed to think. I needed to be away from Memfis. He..." He took a deep breath. Let it out. "He lied to me. He called me his son. He told me he loved me. And he lied to me." He shook his head again. "I don't want to pour this out on your shoulders—"

"They're plenty strong enough," Rhexa said. "Go ahead."

"It's just..." He saw sympathy in her eyes. "I was a lousy thief. I was a better whore. But I was caught and sold. Memfis bought me. Memfis knew what I was when he took me in. He took me in because of a vision. Because the Mother told him he had to take me in. And he adopted me because you can't take a slave out of Forge. He told me he never planned on being a father. He did it because he had no choice. And... today he told me he still thinks of me as a whore."

Rhexa's jaw dropped. "Owyn!"

"I went off with Teva to the dispensary. We took a while, because Teva showed me around. And when we got back, Memfis told me that he thought I'd been so long because I'd been off having sex with Teva. Even though I'd already told him I wasn't comfortable with how easy you lot are about sex. And when I told him I hadn't, he thought I was lying to him. He thought I was lying about not having anybody for over two years. I haven't even had sex with my Heir yet. Or my Water."

Rhexa let out a long sigh that became words. "Oh, Owyn. That was cruel. And so hurtful. I understand now." She glanced away. "The rain has stopped. I'll walk back with you, if you like. And I'll be having some words with His Self-Righteousness Mastersmith Memfis."

Owyn blinked. "You don't have to do that."

"Right now? I'd like to do a lot more. Like kicking him over the seawall and seeing how big of a splash he makes. You don't treat people like that!"

Owyn shivered. "Don't make jokes like that. About throwing people in the sea."

"That bothers you?"

"The sea bothers me," Owyn said. "And...yeah, not talking about it."

"It bothers you a great deal, then," Rhexa said. She got up. "So I won't ask you more. I want you to hear me say this, and know that I mean it. You're welcome here, Owyn. And not just because I think you might be Jaxis. You're welcome here because I like you. I don't care about your past. I like you. I hope you'll be comfortable spending some time with me over the winter?"

Owyn grinned. "Aria wants me to learn from you. Whatever she's studying."

"Does she?" Rhexa looked pleased. "Good. Now, finish your cider. I'll get the soup. Then I'll walk you home."

"THE RAIN IS TAPERING off," Treesi said. "We could go back out, if you wanted."

Aria looked up from the plate that Treesi had set in front of her. She hadn't eaten much of it, had been pushing things around to make it look as if she had. "And where would we look?"

"We could go back to the healing complex," Treesi suggested. "Or we could go to the dispensary. We could see if Teva has found anything. We could—" She turned as someone knocked on the door. "Maybe that's news?" She hurried over and opened the door. "Rhexa? Owyn!"

Aria jumped to her feet as Owyn came inside. He looked rumpled and bedraggled, and his clothes were wet. And the expression on his face spoke volumes — he looked terrified. Of what, Aria wasn't sure. She didn't care. She ran to him and threw her arms around him.

"I'm sorry," he mumbled into her hair. "I'm sorry I scared you."

"Where were you?" Treesi asked. "We hunted everywhere!"

"I went all the way down," Owyn answered. "There are plenty of places to hide down there. And... yeah, I needed to think. I needed to... to not be here." He pulled back slightly and looked past Aria. Then he swallowed. "Where is he?"

"Memfis was gone by the time I came back from the healing complex," Aria said. "I have not seen him since."

"Gone?" Owyn repeated. "Gone where?"

"He might be looking for you," Rhexa said. "Or he might be at the healing complex."

"Where we need to go," Aria said. "I went there first, because I was sure you'd have gone to Aven. He was awake when I got there, and I had to order him back to bed. He wanted me to bring you to him the minute I found you, so that he knows you're safe."

Owyn groaned. "He tried to come out after me?"

"Did you think he wouldn't?" Aria shook her head. "He loves you, Owyn." She touched his cheek. "I love you. You are ours, and nothing else matters." She looked past him, grinned, then met his eyes again. "We should go."

Owyn frowned slightly, puzzled. He looked behind him, saw Treesi's answering grin, and realized what it mean. But he might be wrong, so he turned back to Aria and arched a brow. She giggled.

"Yes, I told her," Aria admitted. "And when we're all together, I will give her the Earth gem."

"Treesi is your Earth?" Rhexa asked. "Oh, that's wonderful."

"You really think so?" Treesi asked. "I thought you didn't like me!"

Rhexa looked puzzled. "Now why would you think that? You're a sweet child, and a good healer. You have your faults, but who doesn't? You're young. You'll learn. And, if the Mother chose you to stand with the Heir, to stand with *this* Heir? Your virtues far outweigh your faults." She smiled. "You'll do just fine, Healer Treesi. So long as you think about things before you act. And forget that nonsense about any of the Mother's children being less."

Treesi turned pink. "Yes, Chieftess. Thank you." She glanced at Aria. "I'd already realized that it was wrong."

"Good," Rhexa said. She looked at Aria. "I can walk with you to the healing complex, if you like? And I can have the search parties start looking for Memfis."

"Wait a minute," Owyn said. "Before you do that, let me see something. And get dry." He kissed Aria's cheek, then disappeared down the corridor. When he returned, he had changed his trousers. He was barefoot and naked from the waist up, and carrying a fresh shirt. "Mem's smoke blades are gone. He's gone off hunting visions."

"Oh?" Rhexa said. "And where would he go?"

"Smoke Dancers usually dance in the caves under the Smoking Mountain, so he might have gone looking for a cave, to get as close as he can," Owyn said. He tugged the shirt on over his head, and his voice was muffled as he continued, "He might be gone for a day or so. He's done this before."

"He left you alone? In Forge? With Fandor about?"

Owyn shook his head. "No, when he was going off looking for visions, I would go stay with Granna Meris." He smoothed his shirt. "All right, I'm ready."

"Where is Trinket?" Aria asked.

"Under my bed," Owyn said. "She'll be fine here, won't she? No cats or anything?"

"Not unless you let them in," Rhexa answered. "Let's go set your Aven's mind at ease, then you can all get a good rest. Treesi, you have rounds in the morning? And lessons?"

"Yes, Chieftess," Treesi answered. "I'll need to stay up to finish my reading." She grimaced. "I hope Alanar found someone to read to him, or we'll both be behind."

"YOU SAID TREESI REVERSES her letters?" Aven said, looking up from the book he'd been reading aloud. "How does she read to you?"

"Her books are printed differently, to help with that. The printers have special type, just for this. I'm told it's a little harder for others to read, but she does all right with it. When she comes back, ask her to show you." Alanar smiled. "You can go to sleep. I can hear you trying not to yawn."

Aven bit his lip. He'd been doing exactly that. "I need to stay awake," he answered.

Alanar chuckled. "Thank you, for not lying to me and telling me I'm imagining things. I'll wake you when they come back." He paused. "They will come back."

Aven swallowed and looked out the window at the darkness. The storm had been equal parts fascinating to watch, and terrifying because Owyn was out in it somewhere. Because he had no idea what was happening. Because all he could do was wait.

"Will this be something I'll have to read?" he asked, turning back to the book balanced on his legs. "Because this is all stuff I know."

"The first thing Risha will do is test you," Alanar said. "Oral and practical exams. Once she knows what level you are now, then she'll assign readings and rounds." He smiled. "Aria came with me on my afternoon rounds today. Because she thought Owyn was here, you understand. She's very good with children."

"Is she?" Aven smiled. "That's good to know."

Alanar chuckled. "For future reference?"

Aven was suddenly glad Alanar couldn't see him. He couldn't see Aven blush. "Eventually. We're going to be busy for a while."

"Truth," Alanar leaned back in his chair and closed his eyes. He grimaced slightly.

"Are you all right?" Aven asked. Alanar shook his head.

"Headaches," he answered. "They're normal for me. It's the muscles around my eyes spasming, because of the damage from the fire. They come and go. Treesi can usually get it to stop, but—"

"I can try, if you want," Aven offered. "And what fire?"

"Oh, you were still asleep when I told Aria and Owyn," Alanar said. He got up and came over to sit on the edge of the bed, moving much more confidently than Aven expected from him. "I'm mixed blood, too — Earth and Air. I was born with wings, and I lost my wings and my sight in a fire when I was ten."

"Mother of us all!" Aven gasped. "Alanar, I didn't know. I'm sorry."

"It's all right. As I told Aria, I'm used to it." He grimaced again. "Except for the headaches. Those, I hate."

Aven chuckled. "Let me see what I can do," he said, and reached out toward Alanar, the tips of his fingers just barely touching the other man's cheek. He closed his eyes, and winced as another muscle spasm started. He soothed it gently, then looked deeper, the way he'd been taught.

"There's a crooked nerve here," he murmured. "It's firing wrong. That might be the root cause of the spasms."

"You can tell that?"

Aven jumped and opened his eyes, turning toward Risha. "I'm sorry, I didn't hear the door open," he stammered. "And, yes. Shouldn't I?"

"Not many can. You've got a sensitive touch," Risha said, coming into the room and closing the door behind her. "What were you doing?"

"I had one of my headaches," Alanar answered. "He offered to help. And yes, he's got a good touch. I barely felt him, and you know I always feel Treesi."

"And me," Risha said. "You told me you always feel me." She looked at Aven. "How are you feeling, Aven-I-shouldn't-be-healing-with-an-uncleared-head-wound? Did I need to say that explicitly?"

Aven bit his lip, then nodded. "Probably. Yes. I didn't know I shouldn't."

"The price of a piecemeal education," Risha said with a sigh. "You know what you know in your bones. And you have no idea what you don't know. Testing you is going to be all kinds of fun. Have you heard anything yet?"

"Nothing yet," Aven answered, glancing at the window.

"But I think that's about to change," Alanar added. He got up. "There are people in the corridor."

The door opened again, and Aria came in, smiling when she saw Aven. Behind her was Rhexa, Treesi, and...

"Owyn!" Aven cried. He started to throw the blankets back so he could get up, and stopped when Aria raised her brows at him.

"Stay there," she said, her voice firm. "He can come to you."

"Then he needs to hurry up," Aven replied, making her laugh. Then Owyn was there. He smiled, but he still looked nervous. Aven met his eyes, wondered why he was hesitating.

"Mouse?" he said softly.

"I worried you," Owyn said softly. "I'm sorry."

"You can make it up to me by coming closer," Aven said. Owyn crept closer and perched on the edge of the bed. Close enough — Aven reached out with his good arm and dragged Owyn into a one-armed embrace. Owyn hesitated, then put his arms around Aven and hugged him back.

"If you're upset, Mouse, come to me," Aven whispered in his ear. "Let me help."

"You're hurt. And you were asleep. You needed to sleep. I..." Aven felt Owyn shudder, and he rested his forehead on Aven's shoulder. "I don't know why he did that. Mem. Why he said that. I... I don't know."

"Have you asked him?" Aven asked, rubbing Owyn's back. "I want to know, too. Where is he? He didn't come with you?" He looked up at Aria, who shook her head.

"He was gone when we got back to the house," she said. "He has not come back."

"I think he's gone off to hunt visions," Owyn added. "His smoke blades were gone when I looked for them." He straightened and stood up, walking around the bed so that he could sit down on Aven's good side. Aven grinned and put his arm around Owyn's shoulders; Owyn pressed close against his side and sighed. "I'm sorry I worried you all."

"You were upset and angry," Aria said. "I understand." She smiled, and took something out of her coat pocket. Aven saw blue flashing in the light.

"Is that my gem?" he asked. She showed it to him, and he grinned. "Thank you. I was missing that. I felt naked without it." He sat very still as she hung the gem back around his neck where it belonged. He sighed as she touched his cheek.

"You are, you know," Owyn murmured. "Naked." He rested his head on Aven's shoulder. "It looks good on you."

"Naked?"

"And wearing only your gem," Owyn said, and grinned. Aven laughed.

"You're feeling better."

"I'm with you and Aria," Owyn said. "How could I not feel better?" He looked up at Aria. "Well?"

"Now?"

"Yes, please!" Treesi giggled. "Now!"

"What's going on?" Risha asked. Her eyes widened as Aria took something else from her coat.

"She knows?" Aven asked. Owyn nodded.

"Aria told her. But Treesi asked to wait for this until we were all together."

Aria smiled and walked over to Treesi, holding the brown and gold gem in the palm of one hand. "Healer Treesi, this is yours. If you'll have it. Have us. Stand with us. It won't be an easy road."

"You'll be on it," Treesi said softly. "You, and Aven, and Owyn. That's the road I want to share." She reached out and touched the gem, then stopped. "It's really mine?" She giggled again, then looked over her shoulder at Alanar. "I still think Alanar would have been a better choice," she said.

"Oh, fuck no!" Alanar yelped. "Not me!"

Aria laughed. She took the cord in her hands and fastened it around Treesi's neck, letting the gem rest against her skin. "The Earth gem is yours. Really yours. You are my choice. The Mother's choice. The only choice. Welcome, my Earth."

CHAPTER
TWENTY-ONE

SEATS WERE FOUND FOR everyone — Aria and Treesi joined Aven and Owyn on the bed, while Risha and Rhexa brought in chairs to sit with Alanar.

"I thought of something," Rhexa said. "Risha, I'm not a healer, but I've lived with Pirit for a good number of years. So I know a little. Check me on this?"

"You usually have good ideas," Risha said. "Tell me."

Rhexa folded her arms over her chest. "Did Memfis tell you that he was an addict?"

Risha's eyes widened. "No!"

"Alcohol, he said. And he pulled himself out on his own," Rhexa said with a nod. "Owyn, will you confirm? Back in Forge, he had people to support him? And who kept him sober?"

"Besides me?" Owyn asked. "Yeah. There was Meris, and Karse. They both kept him honest. And I made sure there was nothing to drink in the house ever, once I understood."

Rhexa nodded. "Now, he's out of his safe area. He has no control over anything, and he knows it. He has no one to whom to turn—"

"He has us," Aria interrupted. Rhexa shook her head.

"He doesn't see you as his peers, Aria. He sees you as his responsibility," she said.

"He said he never planned on being a father," Owyn said. "And now he's got us. And he's got Mannon breathing down all our necks." He paused, then sighed. "Right. So are there taverns in Terraces? Are we going to need to go comb through them and drag Mem out of a bottle again?"

Risha shook her head. "Not the way you have them in Forge, no. Not with the way the dispensary works. Although it wouldn't be hard for him to find something — there are a lot of little distilleries, and there's a brewery on North." She sniffed. "We're going to want to restrict their names in the dispensary."

"I'll take care of it." Rhexa took a small book from one of her pockets, and a stump of a pencil. She wrote something down, then put her tools away.

"He took his smoke blades," Owyn said. "If he's gone hunting visions, he won't be drinking. I hope." He shook his head. "That doesn't explain everything."

"How much do you know of addictive behavior, Owyn?" Risha asked.

Owyn frowned. "I knew addicts," he said slowly. "Alcohol, narcotics, anything you could get on the streets. I tried them, too. Didn't like how they made me feel. But... yeah, once you were hooked, you'd do anything to keep on getting it. That's why some of the street whores were there to begin with. They had nothing left to sell but themselves."

"So you know a bit," Rhexa agreed. "Now, here's what I think, and you can tell me how wrong I am. I'm thinking that Memfis is overwhelmed by the danger you're all in, and by the responsibilities that he's taken on. He's feeling that he's going to relapse. And, given that he knows he's in danger of relapsing, he's expecting the people around him to be feeling the same thing."

Aven felt Owyn shift uncomfortably. "Relapse. That means that he's worried that he's going to crawl back into the bottle, because everything is going wrong and he can't handle it. And because he wants to do that, he thinks I'm feeling the same way, and I'm going to crawl under the first man who smiles at me?" He looked at Aven. "That... sort of makes sense? I think?"

"Risha?" Rhexa said. "What do you think?"

"I think it's hard to say," Risha answered. "But it does sound plausible. What we need to do is have him sit down with someone and unburden himself. Someone for whom he's not responsible."

"You, or me?"

"I think you'll have more access, since you're mentoring his son and the Heir," Risha said. "Now, Alanar, Treesi and Aven. How much of that did you follow?"

Aven spoke first. "Not a lot, actually. We don't have much of an issue with alcohol or narcotics out in the deep."

"I can understand why," Alanar said. "Water doesn't mess with those sorts of things. Virrik said something about that. Trees, do you remember?"

"Oh, Virrik. I remember. I just haven't thought of that in a while," Treesi murmured. "Yes. He said you didn't dabble with things that dulled your senses when you were out in a canoe."

"Who is Virrik?" Aria asked. "I thought I'd met most of the healers today."

"He's not," Treesi answered. "Well, not anymore. He was a healer-in-training, our last training partner. But he left. He didn't leave a note or anything. He just left one night. He was like Aven, Water and Earth. Umm... Allie? What canoe?"

"He was from Tersera's canoe," Alanar said, and Aven shivered.

"You're sure it was Tersera's canoe?" he asked.

"Aven?" Aria asked. She turned to stare at him. Then her eyes widened. "Oh."

"What?" Owyn sat up, frowning. He looked at Aria, then Aven. Then he coughed, "Oh, fuck."

"What is it?" Rhexa asked. "What's wrong?"

Aven licked his lips and looked at Aria. "Should I tell it?"

"If you would," Aria answered. Aven nodded.

"On our way here, we stopped for the night in a cove, south of here," he started. "There was a cave. It looked like it had flooded. Owyn said there was a big storm about two months ago, so we think it flooded then. We found a body. He was Water, and his family tattoo was from Tersera's canoe."

"Mother!" Alanar gasped, sitting up. "No!"

Risha leaned forward. "What else do you know?"

Aven shook his head. "Not much. He'd been there for a while. The body was..." He glanced at Alanar, who looked stricken. Treesi had started to cry, and Aria put her arms around her. She looked at Aven and shook her head, but he didn't need to be told to stop. He'd tell Risha about the damage later. "He'd been there for a while," he repeated. "I... did what was needed for him. I took him to the deep and gave him back to the Mother."

"Mother hold him." Rhexa murmured. "He was a good boy, a good healer. I'd wondered why he left so abruptly. And how. None of the guides ever admitted to taking him through the tunnels."

"He might have found a way down through the seawall," Risha said. "We probably won't know. And we're getting off topic. Alanar, Treesi, I know I've covered addiction with you. Does what Rhexa proposes sound like it makes sense?"

Aven felt Owyn shift. "I... I don't think now is a good time—" he started to say.

"They're my healers-in-training, the both of them," Risha interrupted. "They can have off times on their own time. Which is not when I'm teaching. Well?"

Alanar cleared his throat. "I... ah," he stammered, looking completely flustered. He closed his eyes, swallowed, and winced. "I..." He winced again and folded forward in his chair, holding his head as he started to cry. Treesi jumped to her feet and dashed to his side, holding him.

"Enough, Risha," Rhexa said. "He's in pain. They're both in pain. Let them be."

"I don't tell you how to run this town—"

"Oh, horse-shit," Rhexa snapped. "You complain about my administration every damn day. Now let them mourn and leave them alone. Lessons can wait."

Risha scowled. Then she got up and left, slamming the door behind her. Rhexa sighed, closed her eyes and took a deep breath. Her lips were moving slowly, and Aven realized that she was counting. She'd reached thirty before she turned the rest of the way toward them, letting out another long breath.

"Treesi, why don't you take Alanar back to your room?" she said, her voice almost calm. "You have rounds in the morning, and you need to sleep."

Treesi sniffled. "I'm not sure I can sleep," she said in a quavering voice. "Virrik—"

"I know, sweetheart. I know," Rhexa said. She moved over to Treesi and touched the younger woman's shoulder. "It's hard. We'll mourn him. At least now we know. And we know he's gone back to the Mother."

Treesi nodded. She sniffed again, then looked at the bed where Aven, Owyn and Aria sat. She touched the gem at her throat. "Shouldn't I—"

Aria shook her head. "You should do as Rhexa says. You have your responsibilities, Treesi. Being my Earth doesn't change that. Go take care of yourself, and Alanar. We'll see you tomorrow." She looked at Rhexa. "How much longer can we stay?"

"I wouldn't stay too much later," Rhexa answered. "Given how well he's doing, I think Risha may intend to test Aven tomorrow.

Regardless, he needs to sleep, too. And you should go back to Fourteen, in case Memfis comes back early."

"If he's off hunting visions, I wouldn't expect him back before tomorrow midday," Owyn said. "And if he's like he usually is, he'll record his visions, eat like he's never seen food before, then sleep the day around." He leaned against Aven. "I really don't want to leave right now," he added. Aven chuckled, and kissed the top of Owyn's head.

"Aven needs to go to sleep," Alanar croaked. His voice was thick. "He was keeping himself awake by reading to me. He needs to sleep."

"We will stay until he sleeps," Aria said. "Cousin, go to bed. Treesi—"

"I'll take him," Treesi said. She took Alanar's arm. "Come on, Allie. I'll put you to bed." She paused. Frowned. Then shook her head. "I owe all of you kisses. Tomorrow."

"Don't worry about us," Aven said. "Tomorrow you'll give us each two."

Treesi smiled slightly. "I like that. All right. Come on, Allie." She led Alanar out of the room, closing the door gently behind them. Once they were gone, Rhexa sat down and rubbed her forehead.

"Is there anything else you need?" she asked. "Any information I can provide?" She smiled. "Anything you want to add?"

Aven glanced at Aria, then looked down at Owyn. "The body... Rhexa, he was dead when he hit the water. He wasn't changed — he still had legs. And his legs were shattered. The bones were destroyed completely. His hips were torn apart. I've never seen anything like it."

Rhexa paled. "Oh, thank you for not telling that to Alanar and Treesi. Tell Risha tomorrow. She might have some ideas. I was thinking he might have jumped from the lowest terrace. But hearing that... no. I don't know." She grimaced. "I'll check with the tunnel guides, see if any of them have seen Memfis. Aria, Owyn, I'll be in my office tomorrow morning. No need to rush, though. I spend most of my mornings doing very boring paperwork."

"We will see you there," Aria answered. "We will need to learn the boring parts as well, will we not?"

"We've had enough exciting," Owyn added. "Boring looks really attractive right now."

Rhexa laughed. "You're going to regret saying that. I can give you a great deal of boring." She smiled at them and left. Once the door closed, Owyn sighed.

"I really am sorry I worried you both," he said. He shook his head, leaning more heavily against Aven's side. "What Rhexa said made sense. I just... I suppose. If he ignored every single thing I'd said about being uncomfortable, then yeah. Maybe."

"When he comes back, we'll all talk. All of us," Aria said. "And he will make it right."

"How?" Aven asked. "How do you fix something like this? How can you repair trust?"

Aria shrugged. "He will have to find a way," she said. She poked Owyn's leg. "You like Rhexa all of a sudden?"

Owyn scratched his nails over his trousers. Then he nodded. "I... I think she might be right, Aria."

"Right about what?" Aven asked.

"She thinks I might be related to her. That I might be her sister's son," Owyn answered. "The idea... it kinda scared me, when she told me before. When she first saw me, she said I looked like her sister. That's when I went and got lost and met Alanar. But, there's something else. There's... Aven, when we were still out there, were you ever awake enough that you heard me singing?"

Aven frowned. Then he shook his head. "Not that I remember. I've heard you hum, but not sing. Not yet."

"I haven't heard you yet, either," Aria said.

"It's just... there's one song," Owyn said. "Not even a whole song, really. It's just part of a verse. And I've known it forever. No one else ever knew it, anywhere in Forge." Owyn took a deep breath. "When I was trying to get out of the rain, Rhexa found me. She sat me down in front of her fireplace, and went to get something for me to eat. And she was singing, while she worked in the kitchen. It was the same song. The same song that I've known my whole life, and that no one else ever knew. She knew it. The whole thing, even the parts I didn't. She said it's something specific to Terraces. And she said that her sister used to sing it to her son, as a lullaby, before they went to Forge." He looked startled. "I might have been born here!"

"There are ways to find out, you know," Aven said. "Healers know—"

"Aven," Aria interrupted. "Treesi says there are no level five healers left."

Aven's jaw dropped. "None?" he croaked. "But—"

"There is a great deal we need to tell you," she said. "Things we've learned while you slept. First among them is that this is the only healing center left. According to Rhexa and Risha, there were purges—"

"Treesi said something about that, didn't she?" Aven interrupted. "Before we had to run? That Mannon had burned all the healing centers?"

"Yes. And apparently, many of the healers died." She paused. "The Senior Healer died. Your grandmother, Aven."

Aven's brows rose. "Pirit? Was Senior Healer?" He shook his head. "I didn't know that. I never met her, and Fa didn't talk about her much. I think they fought before he left."

"It's a good thing he did leave," Owyn said. "He might be the last level five healer left."

Aven swallowed. "If he's still alive," he said softly.

"He is still alive," Aria insisted. "And we will find him. And when we do, then we will have an answer for Owyn." She dusted her hands together. "Now, Aven must sleep, and I want to sleep. And I am hungry. Treesi tried to make me eat, but I didn't eat much."

Aven nodded. "All right. Owyn, you both go back to... where are you staying?"

"They gave us a house," Owyn answered. "Fourteen Southwest. You have a bed there, when you're done with learning stuff." He grinned. "We're sharing a room, you and me."

"And I have my own bed?" Aven asked, and laughed as Owyn poked him. He closed his eyes. "I miss you," he murmured. "I don't like being alone here."

"It's one more night," Aria said. "Tomorrow, you'll be in the student housing, with Treesi and Alanar."

"And they're going to set up a hammock for you," Owyn added.

"They are?" Aven smiled. "That's nice of them." He closed his eyes for a moment, then hugged Owyn more tightly to his side. "I should have been there for you. And... did I ever thank you, Mouse?"

"Thank me? For what?" Owyn frowned. Then he chuckled. "Oh. For that. The whole saving your life thing. You did the same for me."

"He killed six guards," Aria said. "To keep you safe."

Aven turned and stared at Owyn. "You did that? For me?"

"For us," Owyn answered. "For all of us. Because we're not doing this without you. We love you, Fishie." He twisted, knelt on the bed, and kissed Aven. Then he got up. "And now, we need to let you sleep. And I need to go feed our Heir before she wastes away to nothing."

"She's not leaving without kissing me," Aven said. Aria smiled, and to Aven's shock, she got onto the bed, crawling up over him until they were nose to nose. Then she kissed him, and he closed his eyes, reaching up with his free hand to touch her cheek, tasting her lips, breathing in her scent.

Breathing.

The kiss was eternal, and not nearly long enough. When she pulled back, he stopped her and said, "There's something I need to ask you." He looked at Owyn. "The both of you. You both did something, when I was awake earlier. Did you mean to breathe with me? Do you know what that means?"

Aria sat back on her heels, glanced at Owyn. Then she shook her head. "No."

Aven blinked. "You both did it. Ah... Owyn, come here?" He waited until Owyn was standing at the head of the bed, then took Owyn's hand and tugged on it until Owyn bent. Once Owyn was close enough, Aven pressed his forehead to Owyn's, their noses touching, and they breathed together for a moment before Owyn straightened.

"Yeah, I remember doing that," Owyn said. "That means something?"

Aven nodded. "It's... it's tradition, among Water. It goes back to Abin and Axia. They say that she would wait at the edge of the water for him to surface, and they would rest like that while he changed, so that the first breath he took would be the air from her lungs. Now, it's something special. It's not a casual greeting. It's... it's something you only do to family, and to close family at that. It's how you show that someone is truly part of your family. You share breath."

Owyn's eyes were huge. "I didn't know that! I had no idea!"

"Nor did I," Aria said. She looked thoughtful. "And... you've never had anyone do that to you before, have you? Except your parents?"

"Except my mother," Aven said. "Fa wouldn't. He said he didn't have the right to, since he wasn't part of the tribe."

"I told you, we need our own mark," Owyn said. "A tattoo, to show that we're our own tribe." He looked at Aria. "Tell him!"

She smiled. Then she yawned, and her face turned pink.

"Tomorrow," Aven said. "Kiss me goodnight now, and convince me tomorrow."

WHEN ARIA AND OWYN reached the house, it was dark, and still empty.

"He'll be back tomorrow sometime," Owyn said, lighting a lamp. "Now, let's see what we've got to eat." He led the way into the kitchen, looked around, and let out a long sigh. "Once I put this all away."

"I'll help," Aria said. "I wasn't sure where anything was supposed to go, so I didn't know what to tell Treesi. And she didn't want to put things away where they wouldn't be found."

"No, that's fine. Here, hand me that jar."

They spent the next hour organizing the kitchen, putting away all of the supplies, then putting together a light dinner. In the dining area, they found the remains of the meal that Treesi had made, and finished that off as well. By the time they were done, he could see Aria was nodding.

"Do you want a bath?" he asked. "There's a bath in the back. There's probably a cistern on the roof, and there's a boiler." He frowned. "I'm not sure if the boiler was lit, though."

"I'll fall asleep in a bath," Aria said. "I'll bathe in the morning." She got up and picked up a stack of plates and bowls.

"Leave that," Owyn said. "I'll take care of it. Go to bed." He got up and came around the table. "Look, you've worn yourself to nothing worrying over me and Aven. We're both fine now. Go to bed. Let me take care of this. And of you."

She smiled and nodded, setting the stack back down. She came to him and kissed his cheek. "My dear Owyn," she murmured. "I do love you. Thank you."

He hugged her, then stepped back. "I love you, too. Go to bed."

Once she was gone, he cleaned up and washed dishes, putting things away. He studied the layout of the kitchen as he worked. It wasn't too different from the kitchen in Forge. He could work here. He wondered if the dispensary had the right kind of flour and if anyone had a bread starter they could share. Making bread would be a good way to get used to the oven, and he enjoyed doing it. They'd be here for the winter, maybe he'd have time to make a starter of his own. He could teach Aven how to make bread. That might be fun. He banked the fire in the front room, and thought about setting a lamp burning on a low flame, in case Memfis came back in the night. No. Not safe. Memfis wouldn't come back in the dark anyway.

He yawned and went down the corridor to the bath — his skin itched, and he couldn't remember the last time he'd had a real bath. Before they'd left Forge, maybe.

By the time he came out of the bath room, he had already almost fallen asleep twice. He stumbled down to his bedroom, dropping his dirty clothes in a pile in a corner. He'd need to find out how to do laundry here. He crawled into bed and shifted around until he was comfortable, then closed his eyes and sighed. Real sleep. A real bed.

A floorboard squeaked, and he sat up, startled out of a half-sleep. "What?" he croaked. "Aria? Mem? Who's there?"

"I... I woke you," Aria's voice came out of the darkness. "I'm sorry. I—"

"What's wrong?" he asked, rubbing a hand over his face. "Is Memfis back?"

"No," she answered. She sounded almost nervous. "It's just... I can't sleep. I was going to go sit—"

"You can't sit up all night," he said. He frowned. What would Aven do? "I... you can come share with me, if you want?" he stammered. "I... I won't... won't do anything."

"Are you sure?" she asked. She sounded relieved. "I don't want to make you uncomfortable."

"I wouldn't have offered if it did," he answered. "Do you need a light?"

"No," she answered. A moment later, she was slipping into the bed next to him. He settled back down, and she curled up against him, her body warm on his, her head pillowed on his shoulder. "Thank you."

He smiled and slipped one arm around her, then kissed her forehead. "Goodnight, Aria."

MEMFIS TRUDGED THROUGH the tunnels, disgusted with himself. All the visions had told him was something that he already knew — that he'd been wrong. He'd been wrong in so many ways, both over the years and over the past few hours. But at least now he had an idea of how he could mend things. He just hoped he could mend things with Owyn. That was the most important part.

Keep to the left, the guide had told him. On the way back out, keep to the left. But this tunnel seemed to be slanting downward. Had he missed a turn? He stopped, turning around. Maybe he should go back? He started back the way he'd come, and was surprised to hear echoing footsteps. Maybe someone had come looking for him. He saw a flicker of torchlight, and a moment later, realized that someone *had* come looking.

The wrong someone. The men facing him wore the uniforms of Mannon's guards.

"There is he," one of them said. "Take him."

CHAPTER
TWENTY-TWO

OWYN WOKE UP ALONE, with the sun filtering through curtains and creating dappled patterns on the blankets. He heard crockery rattling, and smelled something breakfasty, and lay there for a moment, savoring the peace and quiet. But he'd gotten too much in the habit of getting up early and taking care of breakfast, so he got out of bed and pulled on his trousers from the day before. Shirtless, he wandered out to the kitchen. There was a pot on the stove, and Aria was stirring whatever was inside. A pan next to the pot contained something that looked like flat bread.

"Good morning," she called over her shoulder.

"Good morning." Owyn came up behind her, avoiding her wings as he slipped his arms around her and hugged her. "It smells wonderful, whatever it is."

She turned her head and kissed his nose. "Foods from home. Flatbread, and porridge. One of the jars I put in the cupboard last night was labeled with the right kind of flour."

"It was?" Owyn looked into the pot. "I'd missed it. I was thinking last night about flour, and making bread. I need to see if anyone has a starter they can share. So what kind of flour is this?"

"Barley." She looked over her shoulder at him again. "You need to move. Because I need to move."

Owyn stepped back, and Aria picked up a towel and wrapped it around the pot, carrying it off the stove. She turned the bread, then added it to a plate that contained several other similar loaves.

"We have no butter," she said. "But we do have honey, so it will suffice."

"Perishables we have to go fetch the day we need them," Owyn said. He went rummaging through cupboards until he found bowls.

"That does us no good if we want buttered tea with breakfast." Aria picked up a ladle and took one of the bowls from Owyn. She filled it with porridge, then gave it back to him and took the other. "The honey is on the table in the dining area. There's also a teapot. I'll bring the bread."

Owyn was taking a seat at the table before he realized that something Aria had said made no sense. "What's buttered tea?" he asked as she came to the table.

"Exactly what it sounds like," she answered. "It's very good. When we have butter, I'll make it for you. You can have it. Aven cannot."

Owyn winced. "Yeah, that would probably not agree with him." He poured some honey over his porridge, then took a bite. It was nutty — she'd done something to the flour before cooking it. He'd have to ask her what.

"You didn't have to cook," he said, taking a piece of the bread. "That's usually mine to do."

She shook her head. "I enjoy cooking, and I have not been able to do it in ages. It's calming." She smiled. "You were talking about making bread?"

"Yeah, I like it," Owyn said around a mouthful of warm bread. There was no tang to the bread like he was used to, but an oddly bitter aftertaste. "How did you make this?"

She shrugged. "Flour, water, and pearlash."

"Pearlash?"

She grinned. "It's what you have left over after you make soap."

Owyn stopped eating and looked at the bread. Then he looked at Aria. "I know you're not making fun of me, because you wouldn't. But really? Which Air genius decided that eating the soap leftovers was a good idea?"

She giggled. "Do you like the bread?"

"Well, yeah. It's bitter, but it's good."

"Then it was a good idea." She took a bite of her porridge, then picked up the teapot. "Tea?"

"Yes, please."

She poured, and they ate in silence for most of Owyn's bowl, and two pieces of the bread.

"What were you talking about last night," Aria asked as she sipped her tea. "Tattoos?"

"Oh, that. It was something I suggested to Aven, since his grandmother won't let him have his family tattoos. I told him that we could have our own, since we're a family," Owyn answered. That talk on the beach suddenly felt as if it had been years before. "I can do it. I know how."

"And you could design it, too?" Aria asked. When Owyn nodded, she looked thoughtfully at him over the rim of her teacup. Then she nodded. "Do that, please. I want to see your designs. Then I'll decide."

"What? Really?" Owyn gasped. He grinned. "I'm going to need to think about this. It'll have to be something that means something."

"Take your time," Aria said. "I'd rather wait for a good design than see a rushed one tomorrow."

Own nodded, his mind already racing. Something for each tribe, definitely. A flame for Fire. Waves for Water? Maybe. What for Earth, or Air?

Wait. He already knew what he needed. He already had all the right symbols — he just needed to put them together. He had to get his book—

A knock at the door dragged him out of his reverie so abruptly that he jumped. Aria looked startled, but raised her voice anyway. "Come in!"

The front door opened, and Teva came in. "Good morning," he said, and smiled when he saw Owyn. "I heard you were back."

Owyn shifted in his seat. "Teva. Uh... sorry. I'm sorry about that. Yesterday, I mean. I'm—"

"Sorry," Teva finished. "I... me, too. I'm sorry. I'd never have kept you out so long if I'd known you'd get in trouble for it."

"Have you eaten?" Aria asked. She got up from her place at the table. "Sit. I will get something for you. And I will refresh the teapot." She picked up the pot and left, going down the corridor to the kitchen.

Teva came closer to the table, but didn't sit. "She's trying so hard not to be obvious that she's leaving us in private that it's really obvious she's doing it."

Owyn laughed. "Yeah. Especially since the teapot is mostly full. It's not your fault, Teva. But thanks for apologizing. I didn't mean to scare the whole town." He gestured to a chair. "Sit."

Teva sat down. He folded his hand on the table top, took a deep breath, then looked at Owyn.

"The answer is no, isn't it?" he asked softly.

"I'm not sure I know what the question is," Owyn answered. "If the question is 'are we going to fuck?' then yeah, that's a no. If the question is 'can we be friends?' then that, I hope, is a yes?" He looked down at his bowl. "I think I want a friend more than I want someone new in my bed. And I like you. I just don't... you know... like you like you. Not like that." He frowned. "Did that make sense?"

"Yes," Teva answered. "It did. And yes, we can be friends. I'd like that." He grinned. "You're more Earth than Fire, aren't you?"

"Not sure," Owyn answered. "Not anymore. Why?"

"Just feels that way," Teva answered. He shrugged. "So, why did Memfis get mad? Or do you not want to talk about that?"

"He didn't get mad," Owyn said. "He..." he paused. How did normal people handle something like this? Teva was a friend. A new friend. Did he get to know everything at this point? Did Owyn trust Teva that much? Well, perhaps. He trusted Teva enough to tell him part of the truth. He took a deep breath. "Teva, before Mem adopted me, he owned me. I was a slave. And before I was a slave, I was a thief and a street whore in Forge."

Teva's face paled. "I... I was wrong, then. I saw your back, and figured you just liked it rougher than I usually go. Some people do. I just didn't realize... fuck, Owyn. And... he what? He thought you'd started up again?"

Owyn nodded. He picked up his tea, drained it, then set the cup down and laid his hands flat on the table. "Yeah," he said quietly. "And when I told him that I hadn't, he didn't believe me. So... I got mad, and I yelled at him, and I left. And I went all the way down to the last terrace. I hid, and I—" He stopped. If it had been Aven sitting across from him, he could say that he'd cried himself to sleep like a child. But he couldn't stay that to Teva. Not yet. "I fell asleep, and when I woke up, I didn't really. I forgot I wasn't back in Forge, and I thought I needed to get hidden before I got caught and whipped again. I didn't really wake up until it started raining on me."

Teva's eyebrows were raised so high that they were disappearing into his hair. "That... Owyn. I'm sorry! I never meant for you to get into trouble like that! I didn't know—" He pressed his palms together in front of his face, resting his fingertips on his forehead.

"I'm sorry," he repeated, shaking his head. "Look, what can I do to help make things right? Is there anything?"

Owyn shrugged. "Fuck if I know," he said. "I'm still learning how normal people deal with this sort of thing. I've only really been people for about three years now."

"What?" Teva looked puzzled. "You're people now? What were you before?"

"Pretty much an animal," Owyn answered. "So you tell me, how do normal people deal with stuff like this?"

"Normal people, or healers?" Teva asked.

Owyn laughed. "You're saying that healers aren't normal?"

"No!" Teva laughed with him. "At least, not where Risha can hear me. No, I'm saying that healer normal isn't the same as regular people normal. And regular people normal, for me, is Earth. Which might not be the same as Fire normal." He shrugged. "I know how we'd handle it."

Owyn nodded. "All right. Tell me that."

Teva smiled. "All right. How old are you?"

Owyn blinked. "Twenty-two, we think."

"Close enough. Anything over twenty is good. At twenty, you're an adult, under Earth tribe law," Teva said. "So there's nothing that says you have to stay with him. Lots of people tell their parents they want out when they're legally old enough. Here, you go to the dispensary and tell them you're setting up housekeeping for yourself. They'll assign you a place and get you set up, the same way they did here." He looked around. "Although, you might want to tell him to move out. This place is assigned to the Heir, not to Memfis."

The idea was startling — tell Memfis to move out? Owyn shook his head. "No, I can't do that."

"Sure, you can," Teva said. "Or you can ask Aria to do it. It's technically her house. I saw it in the notes at the dispensary." He tipped his head back, then raised his voice without turning around. "Did you know that?"

"That this house is mine? I did not," Aria answered, coming out of the corridor. She set a full bowl down in front of him, then poured a cup of tea. "How did you know I was there?"

"Something was rustling. I think it might be that you fidget." He smiled up at her. "Are we friends, too?"

She returned the smile and went back to her chair. "We were already friends, Teva. And Owyn is right. We can't ask Memfis to leave. It's complicated, but we need him."

Teva nodded. "So do you have a plan? About what to do when he comes back?"

Owyn shrugged. "No idea. I'm thinking that when he comes back, the very first thing he'll do once he wakes up is apologize." When Teva looks confused, he grinned. "He took his smoke blades. He went off looking for visions. Which means when he comes back, he's going to eat and sleep, in that order. Possibly eat, sleep and eat again. Then he'll apologize. And we'll talk."

"He went looking for visions?" Teva repeated. "Where? I don't think you can find those in the dispensary."

Aria giggled. "That would be very convenient."

"He'd go looking for caves," Owyn answered, throwing his napkin at Aria. She caught it and tossed it back, and he laughed.

"So, he'd go into the tunnels?" Teva asked. He nodded. "Then that's a thing I can do. I can make sure you have warning for when he's coming back. One of the tunnel guides is a friend of mine."

"Teva, you don't have to—"

"I want to," Teva said. "I want to make it up to you." He looked down at his bowl. "What am I eating here, Owyn?"

"Owyn did not cook. I did. And this is barley porridge," Aria answered. "There is honey here."

Teva dolloped some honey into his bowl, then took a bite. He took a bigger bite and grinned. "This is good. Thank you. You both have plans for the day?"

"We're meeting Rhexa," Aria answered. "I am to start learning from her."

"And I need to take Aria to the dispensary to be measured for clothes. We both need to go, actually." He glanced at Aria. "And we need to see Aven."

"I should come and meet him properly. Not when he's unconscious or screaming his head off." Teva took another bite of porridge. "You sure you don't need another man around the house?" he asked. "You can feed me this any morning. You're a good cook, Aria."

"Thank you. And I'll need all the help I can get. But not yet." Aria reached out and picked up the teapot, freshening her cup and Owyn's. "Owyn, do you want anything else to eat?"

Owyn looked at the plate of flatbread, tried to judge how full he was. "Split a loaf with me?"

"If she doesn't, I will," Teva mumbled around a mouthful.

"Go ahead," Aria said. "I will go and clean up, and we can go and start our day."

AVEN JERKED AWAKE WHEN someone knocked on the door. Before he could collect himself to say anything, the door opened and Treesi came in. She was carrying a tray, and she sounded unnaturally merry as she called out, "It's time to start the day!"

Aven blinked, and looked at Alanar, who came in behind Treesi. "Is she always this happy in the morning?" he asked, his voice scratchy.

"She's almost always this happy," Alanar answered. "You learn to live with it."

"I have your breakfast," Treesi added. "Sit up and eat. Alanar has your uniform."

"Can I have my arm back?" Aven asked, shifting around to sit on the edge of the bed. He yawned, and looked at the tray. "And is there tea?"

"You didn't sleep well, did you?" Alanar asked.

"Not really," Aven answered. "I'm getting used to it, but I'm still not really sleeping until I pass out."

"We'll work on that hammock," Alanar said. "Ah... no, I'll ask you later."

"What?" Treesi set the tray down on the bed and looked up. "What are you asking... oh. Oh!" She giggled. "Allie!"

"What?" Aven looked from Alanar to Treesi, then grinned. "It's something to do with sex, isn't it?"

Both Treesi and Alanar burst into laughter. "You're learning," Alanar wheezed. "And yes. What's sex in a hammock like?"

"I've no idea," Aven admitted. He thought about it, then chuckled. "I'd end up on the floor, I think."

"That's what I was wondering. You've never tried it?"

Aven bit his lip, and saw Treesi's eyes widen. "Oh," she murmured. "Oh, that's right."

Alanar frowned and turned toward Treesi. "What's right? What didn't you tell me?"

"I'm surprised Aria told her," Aven murmured. Then he paused and thought about it. He shook his head. "Actually, no. I'm not surprised. You're her Earth. You should know. Alanar, I promised Aria that she would be my first woman. And Owyn... well, there's been no time."

Alanar's brows rose. "You're a virgin? And you're how old?"

Aven snorted. Aven snorted. "I'm not. Not entirely. Ah... it's complicated, Alanar. And I'm twenty-five."

"Complicated. I understand that." Alanar nodded slowly. "You can explain later. Or not. I don't mean to pry." He held up the bundle of cloth he was still carrying. "These are for you. Treesi guessed at your shirt size, but she's pretty good at that."

"Let me get your arm, first," Treesi said. She moved to Aven's right side and started untying bandages. "You might be sore at first. That's just from the healed muscles. Move slowly—"

"And it will pass. I know," Aven finished. "My father taught me that." The last bandage fell away, and Aven gingerly moved his right arm, testing the range of movement, stretching out, then up. The muscles were tight and sore, just as he'd expected. But there were no unusual aches, and he said so.

"Good!" Treesi beamed at him. "Now, eat your breakfast. Then you can bathe and dress."

"Yes, Healer," Aven replied, and laughed when Treesi poked him in the ribs. He turned to the tray and started uncovering bowls. The second one stopped him.

"Is this... this can't be fermented sea oak?" He looked up. "I haven't seen this in ages! Sea oak doesn't grow out in the deep water where we lived, so I only ever saw it when we were with the family canoes. Where did you get it?"

"There's a village up the coast a few miles. They make it there, and we used to trade for it, back when there were more Water tribe living here. There are jars and jars of it in the dispensary," Alanar answered. He set the bundle of clothes down on the bed, then dragged one of the chairs over to sit with them. "There aren't many left who like it. So enjoy it. There's plenty where that came from."

Aven stopped in the middle of mixing some into a bowl of oat porridge. "Not many left? Where did they go?"

Alanar shook his head. "I don't know. No one does. The Water folks just started leaving. Not a word to anyone. There was a passage down to the sea caves, and we think they went that way.

Can't really be sure, because the tunnel there collapsed about a year ago—"

"Allie!" Treesi sounded almost shrill. For a moment, Aven wondered what had upset her. Then he realized she was looking at him.

Aven swallowed. "That wasn't a dream?"

"No, it wasn't," she answered gently. "You were so scared. Owyn got you calmed down, and I put you back into trance. He explained after we'd gotten you settled."

"That's probably for the best," Alanar said. He leaned forward and rested his hand on Aven's knee. "We'll make sure that Risha knows, so she doesn't assign you anything in the tunnels."

Aven nodded. He took a bite of his porridge and smiled at the taste of the seaweed. A taste of home. "Would either of you like some?" he asked after he'd swallowed. "There's plenty."

"There's a reason there's plenty where that came from," Alanar answered. "No one else likes it. Well, Marik likes it. But he's... what? Quarter Water?"

"I think so," Treesi said. She sat down next to Aven on the bed. "Once you're done, you can take a bath. Then you can get dressed."

"Alanar said you guessed at shirt size. What about trousers?" Aven asked. Treesi frowned.

"You want trousers?" She looked past him at the bundle. "We brought a kilt, but if you want trousers—"

"You brought a kilt?" Aven gasped. He turned to look at Treesi. "I can wear one here?"

"If that's what you want to wear," she answered. She looked confused. "You couldn't in Forge?"

"I'd have stood out like a beached whale in Forge if I'd worn a kilt," Aven answered. He took another bite of his breakfast, then picked up a cup of tea and took a sip. It was salted, but also heavily sweetened with honey, and he shuddered.

"Too sweet?" Treesi asked. "Allie, I told you. Not everyone likes tea with their honey."

"It'll help wake you up," Alanar said with a shrug. "The sugars will help perk you up."

"And then I'll fall over when they burn off." Aven sipped the tea again. The second sip was more palatable, and he finished his oatmeal and seaweed concoction, as well as the small loaf of bread. He ignored the accompanying small bowl of honey. There was something that looked like the red fruit that Owyn had given to him back in Forge, but this one was green. "Is this an apple? It's not red."

"It's a different variety," Alanar said. "This one isn't as sweet as the red ones."

Aven nodded. "I'll save it. I'm full. Where's the bath?"

Treesi pointed, and got up. "I'll show you. If you've never used a sluice boiler before, you might burn yourself. And I just finished putting you back together."

Aven chuckled. "You sound like my Fa."

"Careful," Alanar called as Aven got up and followed Treesi to a door on the far wall. "You'll turn her head with compliments like that!"

"Compliments?" Aven stopped and turned around. "Saying she sounds like my father is a compliment?"

"Comparing me to Healer Jhansri?" Treesi said, turning in the open door. "That's the highest compliment." She stopped, and wrinkled her nose. "You don't know. His books are required reading for healers-in-training. You'll get copies of them. Or you can use ours."

"Books," Aven repeated, following her into the bath. "My father wrote books. I... he never told me."

"He might not have known that they became part of the healers' canon," Alanar said. He got up from his chair and followed

Aven to the bath. "If I remember properly, he finished the second one right before he left."

"What are they about?" Aven asked.

"First, bath," Treesi said. She showed the tub to him, and pointed to the levers. "The blue one is the cistern. The red one is the boiler. You can either fill the tub part way with hot water and cool it down, or fill it part way with cold water and warm it up. But be careful with the boiler lever. It's hot."

Aven played with the water controls, and learned quickly that he needed to test the water temperature at the far end of the tub, not where the water mixed. He swirled one hand in the water to mix it, then looked up. "So, the books?"

"A treatise on mountain fever. That one is required reading," Alanar answered. "And a treatise on anatomical differences between the tribes."

Aven blinked. Then he laughed. "Well, I suppose he'd know," he said. He slipped into the bath and relaxed in the warm water. "He only lived with members of the other tribes for five years. If anyone knew the differences, it would be my Fa." He looked around. "Is there soap?"

Treesi reached across him and handed him a block of something. When he just looked at it, she laughed. "You've never seen soap before?"

"Not like this. The soap in Forge is like sand."

She handed him a rough cloth. "Get the soap wet, and rub it with this."

"And it'll start doing soap things?" Aven asked, only to have the others burst into laughter.

"Hey, what's so funny?" a familiar voice called from outside the bath. Owyn peered in through the open door. "You're having far too much fun without us, you know. Aria, he's got both arms!"

"And we should let him bathe and get dressed," Treesi said. She escorted Alanar out of the bath, and came back carrying the bundle of clothes. "If you need anything, shout. Otherwise, take your time."

CHAPTER
TWENTY-THREE

BY THE TIME AVEN WAS bathed and dressed, and had come back out into the bedroom, the room had gotten very crowded. Aria and Treesi were sitting side by side on Aven's bed, and Owyn was sitting on the floor at Aria's feet, his head resting on her knee. Alanar had taken one of the two chairs and was talking with Risha, who was seated in the other chair. There was a stranger leaning against the wall near the bed talking with Aria. He was the first to see Aven enter the room, and he grinned.

"He cleans up nice, your Water," he said to Aria. Aria smiled and touched Owyn on the shoulder. He shifted and she got up and came to Aven. He pulled her close, feeling her arms around his neck, breathing in her scent.

"I missed you," Aria whispered in his ear. He nodded, her hair brushing against his cheek, and started to let her go. She moved back only far enough to shift and kiss him, sliding her fingers into his hair as she pulled his head down to hers. He tasted honey and tea on her lips, and tightened his arms around her. He never wanted to let go.

But he had to. He couldn't stay kissing her for the rest of the day, no matter how much he wanted to do just that. He pulled back, but she didn't let go, touching his forehead with hers, breathing with him. He smiled, and loosened his arms.

"I missed you too," he whispered to her. She smiled and stepped back. Her smile widened.

"It's good to see you in a kilt again," she said. "You look much more yourself."

"It looks good on him," Owyn called from the floor. He got up and came closer. "She's right. You're more comfortable like this. Your shoulders are down."

Aven blinked. "What?"

"Something I noticed," Owyn said. "After we got you wearing trousers back in Forge, your shoulders started creeping up to your ears. It never really went away, even when you were relaxed. Now it's gone." He grinned. "Is there a kiss in there for me?"

"You even need to ask?" Aven said with a laugh. He reached for Owyn, tugged him close, and bent down to kiss him. There was something tentative about the kiss — none of Owyn's usual enthusiasm. Was something wrong? Aven closed his eyes, shifted, and tipped his head to get a better angle to kiss Owyn, taking it a little deeper; Owyn sighed and relaxed against him. Better.

Owyn finally pulled back, but not before he repeated Aria's gesture — breathing with Aven for a few breaths before moving away. "I like that," he said softly. "Breathing with you. It's like kissing, but it's more." He grinned. "Not that I don't like kissing."

Aven laughed and pulled Owyn to him, turning the other man so that his back was against Aven's chest. He wrapped his arms around Owyn's shoulders and just held him. "Are you all right?" he asked softly. "You seem off."

"Still not all right in my head from yesterday," Owyn answered, leaning back into Aven and holding on to Aven's forearms. "I'll be all right."

Aven kissed the top of Owyn's head, and looked around. Treesi had moved to Aria's side, and had taken her hand. She smiled at Aven, seeming to be happy with that much. And there was still the stranger, who Aven had forgotten. "Who is our new friend?" he asked.

"Oh, right," Owyn said. He laughed and pulled gently from Aven's arms, moving to stand next to him. "This is Teva. Teva, this is Aven."

Teva pushed off the wall and came over to them, holding his hand out. "Nice to actually meet you when you're awake," he said. He clasped Aven's wrist, the way someone from the Water tribe would. Then he laughed. "Yes, I know how Water says hello."

"Because there were Water here?" Aven asked. "And we met when I wasn't awake?"

"I was in the rescue team. And a good friend of mine is part Water. His family is from up the coast a bit, and I spent time with them back before things got tightened down here."

Aven frowned. "Tightened down?" He looked at Owyn. "What does that mean?"

"After the last round of purges, when we moved the main healing center here, we made changes to make sure that we were safe," Risha answered. "We keep a close watch on who leaves through the tunnels, and the only ones who know the way through are the tunnel guides."

The idea of going back out through tunnels made Aven's skin crawl. "So no one comes in, and no one goes out," he said.

"Not that draconian," Risha said with a smile. "We keep track of who comes and goes, since the tunnels are the only way in or out of Terraces. And, since I know you have trouble with tunnels, I won't be sending you through them without putting you out first."

The words may have been meant to comfort, but they didn't make Aven feel any better. If the only way in or out was through tunnels, then he was trapped here.

"Aven?" Owyn said softly. "What is it?" He stood in front of Aven, looking up. Then he reached up and put his hands on Aven's shoulders. "Your shoulders are up again. Tunnels?"

"Yes," Aven answered. "I... tunnels." He looked down. "It's a little embarrassing."

"It's nothing to be ashamed of," Risha said. She got to her feet. "Now, as charming as this reunion is, we have work to do. Aven, you're with me this morning. Alanar and Treesi, you have rounds. And I'm not certain where I should be telling the rest of you to go."

"We're off to work with Rhexa today," Aria said. "And Teva, you said you'd talk to the tunnel guides?"

"Sure," Teva answered. "I'll come find you around midday. We can have something to eat." He looked over at Risha. "Can we steal Aven for the midday meal, or are you going to work him to a nub on his first day?"

"He has testing," Risha said simply. "Don't expect to see him before the evening meal."

Aven's eyes widened. "How much testing is there?"

"You'll see."

Aria took Aven's other hand. "You'll be busy. So will we. We'll see you tonight, and you can tell us about your day."

"And we can tell you about what you're going to need to learn next," Owyn added. Aven stared at him, and he laughed. "Well, it's true! We're learning to govern. You're going to be part of that, so you need to learn it, too. But you have to do this, first. Priorities."

"Exactly. And right now, his priorities belong to me," Risha said. "Come along, Aven."

Aven swallowed. He leaned down and kissed Aria, then Owyn. Then he walked over to Treesi and held his hand out to her. "You said something about two kisses today? You haven't even given me one yet."

"I didn't want to presume," Treesi said, taking his hand and standing up. "I've already made Owyn uncomfortable. I'm learning. Really, I am."

Aven smiled. "I appreciate that." He tugged her close and hugged her, then leaned down and kissed her on the lips, then on the nose. She giggled. Then he let her go and followed Risha out of the room.

THE DOOR OPENED, AND Treesi peered inside. Aven was sitting with his head tipped back against the wall. She knew that look — he'd been put through the examination wringer. "The Senior Healer said I should come see to you," she said. "That you weren't sure where you were supposed to go."

"More like I couldn't find my way out of a room with only one wall," Aven answered. He straightened and looked at her. "My brains feel like bleached coral."

"Is that a good thing or a bad thing?" Treesi asked. "And this way. I'll show you to our rooms."

"It's a bad thing," Aven answered as he got up and followed her out of the testing room. "Bleached coral is dead."

"Oh," Treesi murmured. "I didn't know coral was alive to begin with. It's hard... wait, is it like a bug? The skeleton is on the outside?"

Aven grinned. "Yes. And they live in colonies, all together. They're very brightly colored when they're alive—"

"And they turn white when they die? The piece I have is white. Marik gave it to me."

Aven blinked. "Have I met Marik?"

"Not yet," Treesi answered. "I don't think. He was there when we rescued you and Owyn. And he helped us when we were looking for Owyn. He's Earth and Water, but he doesn't change. And he talks to birds."

"I think I'd remember that," Aven said. "Where are we going?"

"The residential wing. You can tell by the colors. In the healing wing, the tiles are blue." She pointed to the floor. "In the residential wing, they're yellow. Now, when we make the turn here, we'll be in the wheel. And we want three corridors over on my writing side."

"On what?" Aven looked at her. "Which is your writing side?"

"This hand." She held her hand up. "Did Alanar tell you that I have trouble with directions?"

"Yes."

"It's all sorts of directions, too. I get things backwards, and I mix up letters. So, third corridor on this side." She wiggled her fingers, and turned into the wheel. They turned down the third corridor, which had yellow tiles, then made another turn. She checked the door closest to them. It was marked no entry, and she nodded. "Right place. Come on. We're in room double-M."

"The rooms on this hall are lettered?" Aven looked around. "To make it clear that they're not healing rooms?"

"Exactly," Treesi answered. "And we're in double-M because m's look the same forwards and backwards." She stopped outside a door marked with two brass m's. "You have your own room, and Alanar went and told the dispensary that we'd need a hammock for you. They had one waiting for us, and someone was going to come put it up. I don't know if it's set up yet, though. And you can use Alanar's books until we get copies for you."

Aven looked blankly at her. "Risha said that she'd send copies of the texts that I'd need."

"You don't want the new versions. They're wrong," Treesi blurted. "They changed your father's book. Someone did, anyway. Memfis said that there isn't any way that your father wrote what it says in our books." She looked up and down the corridor. "Come inside."

They entered the sitting room of the suite. She'd always liked this suite, and the sitting room in particular. There were two comfortable chairs and a battered couch, along with a round table and three wooden chairs. There were three doors on the far wall, and one to the right. Treesi closed the door, locking it.

"Changed my father's book?" Aven asked as she turned from the door. "How?"

Treesi looked down. "I made Owyn yell at me," she murmured.

"What?" Aven said. She felt his hands on her shoulders, and looked up to see his confused expression. "Treesi, you're jumping around and I can't follow. Start at the beginning?"

Treesi rested her hands on Aven's forearms. Then she looked at them — his sleeves were rolled up to the elbow. "You have no tattoos," she said. "Funny. I've seen you all over, and I just noticed."

"Long story, Treesi," Aven said. "Book?"

Treesi shook her head. "Right. I made Owyn yell, because I repeated what it says in your father's book. But it's not what he wrote in his book when he wrote it. It's what they changed it to. But I don't know who changed it. It's not in the copies Alanar has. Those are his father's copies. But it was in the copies that were printed for me when I got here. And it was in Virrik's copy."

Aven squeezed his eyes shut. Then he opened them again and took a breath. "What does it say in the original book? The one Alanar has?"

"It says that the Water tribe and the Air tribe are extrahuman," Treesi answered.

Aven nodded. "I remember Fa using that word, yes. And... in your books?"

Treesi's stomach whirled like leaves in an eddy. "It says subhuman," she answered in a small voice. "My teacher...well...

Risha, she says subhuman, too. And when I said it, Owyn yelled at me."

Aven looked startled. "My father? Use the word subhuman? Impossible!"

"I understand that now," Treesi insisted. "But I didn't before. I believed what they told me, even though—"

"Even though you lived with an Air and a Water for how long?" Aven demanded.

"Long enough that I should have known better," Treesi admitted. "And...well, it was seeing Aria that really convinced me I was wrong. She's the Heir! And she's Air. The Mother wouldn't make someone Heir if they weren't people. And if Aria is people, then so are you."

"I'm honored you think so," Aven answered, his voice tart. "Who changed the book? And when?"

"I... I don't know," Treesi answered. "I didn't bring the old books with me when I came here, because they were my brother's and he needed them. So when I came here, they gave me all new books. I hadn't gotten to the comparative anatomy book yet, so I don't know if it was changed in my brother's book. But Virrik was here when I got here, and his books said the same thing."

"But Alanar's books are different, because Alanar's books are older." Aven walked away, his arms folded over his chest. He was frowning, and Treesi clasped her hands behind her back, wondering what he was thinking. He sighed, and shook his head. "I don't know," he said at last. "But... Treesi, you said that Risha uses the term subhuman. Have any of your other teachers?"

"No. Just since I got here."

Aven's frown deepened. "And she's going to be teaching me," Aven said. He turned away and ran his fingers through his hair. "Fuck."

"Aven!" Treesi gasped. She'd heard people swearing before — Healers tended to be very sweary. But she never expected it from Aven! She wouldn't even have expected him to know the words! He looked at her and grinned.

"Sorry. I picked it up from Owyn."

"I was just surprised," she admitted.

He nodded. "Treesi, is she going to give me a fair chance?" he asked. "If she doesn't think I'm human—"

"You're a healer. So is Alanar. According to the way I was taught, only humans can be healers. So that means that the books are wrong about Water and Air not being human." She grimaced. "I never got my brain around that one. Not until Owyn yelled at me. Alanar used to explain it until his face turned red. But apparently I needed a bigger hammer."

Aven frowned. "Bigger hammer?"

She giggled. "How you fix something stubborn. Use a bigger hammer."

"That sounds like how you break something stubborn," Aven said slowly.

Treesi shrugged. "Sometimes you have to break something for it to heal straight. You know that, right?"

Aven nodded. He smiled. Then he gestured at the doors. "Which one is mine?"

"The one on the end, by the bathing room." She led him to the door and opened it, looking inside. "Oh, they set up the hammock!" She stepped out of the way. "It's not a big room, but it's comfortable. You have your own desk and space for your books in here. And... oh, the new books are already here. We'll tell you which ones are good and which are a problem."

Aven nodded and walked around the small room. The bed had been taken out to make room for the hammock, but otherwise it was identical to Treesi's own room — small nightstand, a dresser, a desk and chair. There were shelves over the desk, and a small window that let in just enough light.

"You can decorate however you like," Treesi added. "Or... well, you probably don't like. You're going to be moving out to Fourteen Southwest as soon as you can."

"That doesn't mean I might not want to break up the vast expanse of white walls," Aven replied. He grinned. "It's boring."

"You can do anything but paint," Treesi said. "Nothing permanent."

Aven looked around. Then he looked thoughtful. "Was this Virrik's room?" he asked. "Since he was your training partner?"

Treesi swallowed. "Yes. It's been empty for months. You don't mind, do you? I mean... some people might, I don't know. It might bother them that this room belonged to someone who's dead."

Aven glanced at her, then took her hands. "Does it bother you?" he asked gently. "That I'm taking his room?"

'Bother me?" Treesi repeated, trying to make sense of the question. "Why would it... oh!" She giggled. "Oh, no. Virrik and I weren't lovers. Not at all. He was a good friend, but he didn't sleep with girls. It might be a little odd for Alanar, though. They were lovers, and they were really close."

Aven nodded and looked around. When he met Treesi's eyes again, he looked troubled. "Treesi, I don't want to hurt him by being here."

Treesi squeezed his hands. "I think you'll help him, actually," she said. "Allie was hurt when Virrik left without telling him. He's been brooding over it, thinking it was something that he did."

"Something Alanar did?" Aven shook his head. "I don't know him well enough to really say, but I have a hard time thinking of Alanar doing anything hurtful enough to make someone want to leave like that."

"That's what I told him," Treesi agreed. "They were so sweet together it would make your teeth itch. They never fought, they never disagreed about anything. They would finish each other's sentences. So when Virrik left... Aven, how did he die?"

Aven shook his head. "You don't want to know. And I'm not telling you."

Treesi winced. "That bad? Oh, Mother. Poor Virrik." She shook her head and let go of Aven's hands. "Look, let me let you explore in here and get settled. Then we'll go get something to eat. I'm betting you're starving."

Aven smiled. "I could eat. A lot. All right. There's not much exploring to do here. And I don't have much of my own at the house with the others."

"We'll go to the dispensary and get your uniforms and anything you might need," Treesi said. "We'll go before we eat."

"All right," Aven agreed. He looked over at the hammock. "I want to try out the hammock and see if it's been put up right. Then I'll come out and we can go."

Treesi nodded and went out to the main room. She washed up, then went into her own room and changed out of her uniform. When she came back out into the main room, there was still no sign of Aven, so she went and tapped on his door.

"Aven?" she called, and looked inside. The hammock was swinging gently... and Aven was sound asleep. Treesi stepped inside, walking carefully to keep from waking him. He must have fallen asleep the minute he was in the hammock — she hadn't realized he was so tired! Gently, she brushed his hair back from his face, then leaned down and kissed his cheek. He didn't even move.

She went back to her room to get a piece of paper and a graphite stick. In careful, block letters, she scrawled a note, just in case Aven woke up to find her gone.

Gone to meet the others. If you wake up before I come back, meet us at Fourteen Southwest. -T.

She carefully left the note on his chest, where he wouldn't miss it. Then she left the room and hurried to meet Alanar. He was waiting outside the healing complex with Aria and Owyn. Aria smiled when she saw Treesi. Then she looked past her, and frowned.

"You're alone?" she asked. "Where is Aven?"

"Testing his new hammock," Treesi answered, and Owyn laughed.

"He's asleep, isn't he?" He looked past her at the healing complex, then shook his head. "He hasn't been sleeping well."

"He hasn't," Alanar agreed. "He said this morning that he hasn't been sleeping so much as passing out from exhaustion."

"And he was completely wrecked from his testing. He looked like a limp rag when I went and fetched him," Treesi added. "So we'll let him sleep. We can bring something back for him to eat when he wakes up." She went and took Aria's hand. "Where are we going to eat?"

"I was going to cook," Owyn said.

Alanar chuckled. "Should we be worried?"

"No, you should not be worried!" Owyn retorted with a laugh. "I'll show you!"

Laughing, they walked away from the healing complex.

"AVEN?"

There was a light tapping, then someone called his name again. "Aven? You have to wake up. You'll be late."

Aven blinked and looked up. White ceiling. White walls. Where was he... oh, right. His room in the student hall. He shook his head and looked around, seeing sunlight streaming through the window.

"Treesi?" he croaked. "How long did I sleep?"

The door opened, and she came inside. "It's tomorrow morning, Aven. So I suppose that means the hammock works?"

"Tomorrow?" Aven cleared his throat and looked at the window, then saw the covered bowls on his desk. "What's that?"

"Last night's supper. Owyn is a very good cook." Treesi came closer. "I went to the dispensary for you. There are uniforms and supplies out in the main room. You have time to eat and clean up before we start rounds, but only if you hurry."

Aven nodded. He blinked and shook his head, then looked at the bowls. "Were they angry, Treesi?"

Treesi smiled and stood right in front of him, tipping her head back to look up at him. "No, Aven. They weren't angry. They were both very glad you were getting a good rest. And we'll see them tonight."

Aven smiled. Then, on impulse, he leaned down and kissed Treesi lightly on the lips. "Thank you, Treesi."

She giggled. Then she hugged him. "All right. Hurry up. You don't want to be late on your first day!"

CHAPTER
TWENTY-FOUR

"SO WHAT LEVEL ARE YOU?" Owyn asked. He sat on a blanket with his legs folded under him, his thigh pressed against Aven's leg. "Treesi and Alanar won't tell us. They said it's personal — that one healer can't talk about another's training."

"They're right," Aven answered. He was lying on his back, his head resting on Aria's thigh. She smiled down at him, then went back to reading the treatise that Rhexa had assigned to her. They were all supposed to be working through their meal. But there wasn't a lot of working happening — the picnic had been an excuse so that they could spend time together for the first time in nearly a week. Owyn had arranged the picnic in the lowest terrace, so that they were secluded, and had made enough food to feed a small army. But despite the stated "working meal" that they'd told Risha and Rhexa, the only one actually working was Aria. Aven's textbook lay face-down on his chest, and Owyn hadn't even touched his paperwork.

He poked Aven in the leg. "So? Are you going to tell us?"

Aven smiled. "Risha says I'm starting as a four. A low four, with potential."

"That's very good," Aria murmured without looking away from her reading. She started combing her fingers through Aven's hair, and he sighed and closed his eyes.

"I've missed you," he said. "It's like an ache I can't do anything about. I'm so busy I shouldn't notice, but I do." He opened his eyes and propped himself up on his elbows. "Still no sign of Memfis?"

Owyn swallowed, suddenly glad that he'd eaten already. He'd never have been able to swallow around the anvil in his throat. "No," he said. "It wouldn't be the first time that it took a Smoke Dancer time to find the visions, especially if he wasn't all right in his own head, the way Mem might be. But...yeah, it's too long. A week is far too long. And Teva says that the tunnel guides never saw him. They're supposed to be searching, but nothing yet."

Aven blinked. "Doesn't that mean that he didn't go into the tunnels?" he asked. "Are there other caves?"

"Teva says no," Owyn answered. He scratched the back of his neck. "But Marik says yes, and he's been looking. Just in case Memfis got turned around." He looked down at his legs, then shook his head. "I don't know. I don't know where he's gone and it's been a week."

"Have you looked?" Aven sat up. "Have you danced?"

Owyn gaped at him for a moment, then realized that Aven wasn't joking. "I... no. No, I haven't. I..." He stopped and closed his eyes. "I... I should, shouldn't I? I don't know what's happening, I need to go and look." He looked past Aven to Aria, who had laid aside her reading. "Aria?"

"Now? Or later?" she asked. "We can do it now. It's quiet enough here. You can go back and get your blades."

Owyn frowned. Then he shook his head. "Later. We can come back once the sun goes down." He looked over at Aven. "And I'll come find you first thing tomorrow and tell you what I see. All right?"

Aven nodded. "You know best what needs to be done, and how. Tell me tomorrow." He swung around, folding his legs so that he matched Owyn. "I asked Treesi to join us," he said. "I thought it might be a good idea, so she can start getting used to us. So we can get used to her. But she's testing today — Risha is pushing her really hard."

"She is a low two, she said," Aria said. "Is she capable?"

"I think so," Aven answered. "She's good. I think she'll be a better healer than she thinks she can be, given the right support."

Owyn laughed. "And you've decided that you're it?" he asked. "Because that's you all over. You can't not support us."

Aven blushed slightly. "Well, now that you mention it... I was showing her some of the ways my Fa taught me when I was younger."

"That will not get you in trouble, will it?" Aria asked.

"I don't think so," Aven answered. "I don't know. I can't see how it would — the way Alanar says it's supposed to work here is that advanced students are supposed to teach the others. And I'm more advanced than either of them. Even Risha says so." He shook his head and pushed his hair back. "Enough of my work. What are you working on? I know you're doing something with Rhexa, but not really what."

"At the moment? Learning the history of the tribes, which Owyn knows far better than I do," Aria answered. "And learning the tribal laws."

"Which includes stuff that I've never heard of," Owyn added. "And I've kind of gotten a pet project." He reached out and picked up the book he'd brought and ignored. He flipped it open and held it out to Aven, who took it and studied the sketches inside.

"Maps?" Aven asked.

"Part of the problem we had on our way was that we didn't have enough information," Owyn said. "We didn't know what was where, or which towns were gone. So we need better maps, and more information. And we need to know where people are, so we can make sure they have what they need. Rhexa liked the idea —

she says Aria is going to need that kind of information. So she's got me starting with Terraces. Complete maps of each level, and a census of who lives where." He took the book back and flipped through the pages. "I've got to work with the dispensary, so they can keep their records accurate, too. I've only been at this for a couple of days, and I've already found a lot of inaccurate records. People who weren't where they were supposed to be. Houses empty that should have had people living in them."

Aven frowned. "You've found people missing?"

Owyn shook his head. "They're still drawing their allotments from the dispensary. But they didn't tell the dispensary that they'd changed their residences. So once I find out where they are now—"

"Does that happen a lot?" Aven interrupted. "People move houses with no warning? What does Rhexa say?"

Owyn looked down at his book. "She hasn't seen my list yet. But it does seem like they do. Why?"

Aven rested his elbows on his knees. "Just... something isn't right. There are a lot of children in the healing complex. Aria, you met them. Which reminds me, they want you to come back and read to them again."

Aria laughed. "I'll find the time. What about them?"

"Malani told me that more than half of them were abandoned," Aven answered. "They came into the hospital for one reason or another, and their families never came back for them." He laced his fingers together. "And all of the abandoned children are mixed blood, either Water or Air. There are three sisters in there who are going to be sent to their mother's family up the coast, because no one knows what happened to their mother."

Owyn stared at Aven. "I'd say you were joking, but I know you wouldn't joke about something like this," he said. "Aven, how is that possible?"

Aven shook his head. "No idea. But... cross reference your list of people who have moved residences with the list of people who've left Terraces. I'm willing to bet that none of them left, and that none of them moved. They vanished. Like Virrik."

Aria coughed. "Does... does that mean that they are dead? Like Virrik?"

Aven shook his head again. "I don't know. I'd be interested in what Rhexa has to say." He tipped his head back and studied the sky. "And I need to get back. I have rounds this afternoon."

"And we have a meeting," Aria said. They cleaned up the picnic, packing everything into the basket they'd used to carry it. Owyn put his book into the basket and hefted it, and they started back up the Southwest spoke to Fourteen. Aven looked around curiously as they entered the house.

"This is ours?" he asked. "Show me around?"

Owyn chuckled. "Not much to see, really. Come on." He led the way down the corridor to the kitchen, leaving the basket on the worktable. "We take turns cooking," he said. "Aria is a good cook."

"You are?" Aven asked, smiling at Aria. "I didn't know that."

"When did I ever have the chance to cook for you?" she asked in reply. He laughed, and Owyn led them out of the room and back toward the bedrooms.

"This one is ours," he said, opening the door. Aven walked inside and looked around, his smile broadening when he saw his swords hanging from hooks on the wall.

"Thank you," he said, pointing to them.

"Is there anything you want to take with you?" Aria asked. Aven looked thoughtful, then shook his head.

"No. I can't wear my vest when I'm working, and my swords are better here. I'll be sleeping here soon enough, I think." He turned around, holding his hands out. Aria moved in closer, taking his left hand, and Owyn took his right; Aven pulled them in close to his sides, putting his arms around them.

"I'm going to sneak out one night, and come spend the night with you both," he said. "I've gotten used to having you with me."

"Have you learned what you need to know?" Aria asked. Aven shook his head.

"Not yet. I've read the recipes for the teas, but they're not nearly as reliable as having a healer block fertility. Which hasn't been part of my lessons yet. Alanar says he was never taught it, and Treesi doesn't know it well enough to show me. I'll ask Risha to show me tonight after I finish rounds." He hugged them both more tightly, then sighed. "I need to go. I'll be late for rounds."

"We'll walk back with you," Owyn said. Aven nodded and let them go, and Owyn felt cold where Aven's arm had been. He reached out and grabbed Aven's hand, holding on tightly.

"I've missed you, too," he said. "We both have."

Aria nodded agreement. "I didn't think it needed saying, but yes. I wish you could be here with me. Both of you. It's odd to have my Earth and yet not have her here. You both should be here, so we can grow together."

"I know," Aven said. "Having Treesi with me helps, but it's not the same as all of us being together." He sighed. "It's not for long. I keep telling myself that."

They walked out of the house and started up the street. Aven walked between Aria and Owyn, holding their hands in his. Owyn turned toward him, started to say something, and saw movement up the street. Someone running...

He reacted before he had a chance to think about why he was reacting, twisting to put himself between the running figure and his Heir and Water. Something hit him in the left shoulder, making him grunt. A second missile hit him in the lower back, hard enough that his knees buckled. He heard a shout, but couldn't make out what was said. He felt Aven's arms around him, catching him as he fell.

"Aria! Get in the air! Get out of range!" Aven snapped. Owyn heard the beating of wings, and felt the rush of air as Aria took flight. Then Aven scooped him up like a child, as if he weighed nothing at all.

"Put me down!" Owyn protested. "I'm fine!"

"You're hurt," Aven growled. He ran back toward Fourteen, and Owyn heard a heavy thump, and Aven's breath catch. Then they were inside, and Aven slammed the door. He leaned against it, breathing hard.

"Rocks," he panted. "They were throwing rocks."

"Put me down," Owyn repeated. "Let me see you. They got you, didn't they?"

Aven nodded, and set Owyn onto his feet. "I don't think they broke the skin," he said. "I'll bruise, but I've got more padding than you do. You're bleeding. Turn around. Let me see."

It was only then that Owyn noticed the warmth trickling down his back. And there was blood on Aven's sleeve. He was about to turn around when something hit the door, hard enough that it bounced partly open. Aven slammed it closed again and leaned against it.

"Weapons," he hissed. "Now."

Owyn nodded and ran down the corridor to the bedroom, grabbing the pouch with his whip chain, his smoke blades and Aven's swords. He carried them back to the front room, then realized the problem.

"There's no room to use these in here," he whispered as he handed the swords to Aven.

"No, but there is outside." Aven replied.

"Oh, no, you don't," Owyn snapped. "The last time you took the fight to them, it damn near killed you!"

Aven grinned. "Love you, too, Mouse." He cocked his head toward the door and frowned. "Misborn freaks."

"What?" Owyn gasped.

"Misborn freaks. That's what he shouted. The one who threw the rocks."

"I didn't hear him," Owyn breathed. "Rhexa said we were safe here!"

"Apparently, she was wrong," Aven answered. "Take a peek? Be careful."

Owyn nodded and slipped along the wall to peer out the window. There were four men in the street, all of them wearing hoods to hide their features. He moved out of sight before they saw him.

"Four of them."

Aven scowled. "There were more than four. They came out of the other houses when you went down. Owyn, is there another way inside?"

Owyn blinked, then shook his head. "No. Not like the forge, no. There's no back door."

Aven nodded. Then he winced as a rock crashed through the window in the dining area. Another thumped hard against the door. "Isn't there anyone around here? In any of the other houses? Someone to notice what's happening?"

"I don't know," Owyn admitted. He winced as something hit the door, and moved in close to lend his weight to Aven's. "I haven't gotten to this street yet. I'm guessing either no, or they're all off doing whatever it is they do during the day." He looked up at Aven. "What do we do?"

Aven grimaced. "Hope that Aria got away safely," he said. "And that she found someone to help. They were waiting for us. Who knew we'd be down here?"

"Rhexa knew. I'm assuming you told Risha? Treesi and Alanar." Owyn frowned. "I don't know who else. Katrin, at the dispensary, maybe. I told her we were doing a picnic, but I don't think I told her when." Owyn shook his head. "It wasn't you they were after, Fishie. Or me. They wanted Aria. And she lives here. All they had to do is wait."

Aven growled softly. Then he nodded. "If we don't go out, they'll break out the windows and come in. Do you have your whip chain?"

"Yeah."

Aven nodded toward the window. "Take another look. Tell me what you see."

Owyn went and peered out, then jumped backward to avoid a shower of shattered glass. "Five now," he said. "And they're coming."

"Then we're going," Aven said. He moved away from the door, faced it, and smiled at Owyn. "When I say so, open the door. Stay behind it. I'll get them clear. You follow."

"Aven—"

"Do you have a better idea?" Aven asked.

"I'm starting to think the better idea is knocking you over the head to save your fucking life!" Owyn blurted, and Aven laughed.

"Just follow me, Mouse. And you can hurt them, but try not to kill them. I want to know why." He looked at the door, licked his lips, then nodded. "Now."

Owyn swallowed, and pulled the door open; Aven burst out the door as if he'd been fired out of a cannon, screaming like a madman. Owyn swore and followed, and saw that Aven was already in the midst of the attackers, his swords flashing in the sunlight. Owyn reached for his whip chain, then stopped. If he used it, he'd risk hitting Aven. He couldn't do that. He hefted his smoke blades and dove into the fray.

It didn't take him long to realize that the men who had attacked them weren't fighters. Not the way Aven was, or the way he'd been trained. No, these were bullies — street thugs who relied on size and threats to get their way. He'd known more than his share of them in Forge where he learned that his size made him a target. He'd learned to stay away from them. Now... he didn't have to be afraid of them anymore. He dodged another flung missile, but the man who threw it wasn't as lucky. Or as fast — Owyn connected hard with his left hand blade, and the man went down. He turned, hearing the scream of a hawk from above. Another scream, this one from a man, one who was waving his arms wildly as a hawk flew at him, slashing at his head with its talons. Another swooped in as he watched, then a third. Aven backed away from them, lowering his swords.

"Friends of yours?" he panted. "Or... is this something I didn't know Aria could do?"

Owyn blinked, then realized that they were friends. Sort of. "Marik. Aria must have found Marik!" For a moment, he couldn't remember if Aven knew who Marik was. It didn't matter — he could see Marik running toward them, with two other men right behind him. Aven saw him, too, and stepped forward with his swords raised.

"Aven, no," Owyn said. "That's Marik. The birds are his."

"You said he's a friend?"

"Yeah, he's a friend."

"What the fuck is going on here?" Marik called as he came to a stop. "The hawks said there was fighting."

"They attacked us," Owyn answered. "Throwing rocks."

"Right," Marik nodded. He turned, and the hawks all flew off. "We'll take care of them," he said. Then he nodded to Aven. "You're the Water healer. Nice to meet you. Are you all right?"

"Bruised," Aven answered. He looked up. "Bruised and late."

Marik winced. "The late part is worse than the bruise," he said. "Owyn, you?"

"Banged up," Owyn said. "But I'm fine. Marik, they were after Aria."

Marik's eyes widened, and he swore softly. "Where is she? Is she safe?"

Owyn went cold. "I... oh, fuck. Oh, fuck. Oh—"

"She's on the roof," Aven said. He pointed with one sword. "Owyn, she's behind you."

Owyn whirled, and saw Aria crouched behind the chimney. As the guards picked up the injured and herded the other men up the street and away from the house, she flew down. Without a word, she walked back into the house. Aven glanced at Owyn, who shook his head. What was she... oh.

Aria came back out strapping on her crossbow.

"I should never have taken it off," she said. "I should never have taken her word that we were safe." She looked from Aven to Owyn, then went to Owyn first. She studied him, turned him around so she could see his back, then turned him back to face her. "You knew. You knew they were attacking. How?"

Owyn frowned, trying to answer the question. Then he shook his head. "Spent too many years on the streets. You see someone running at you, you get the fuck out of the way."

"Or put yourself in the way," Aven added. "Let me see your back."

"What's happening here?"

Owyn looked up to see Rhexa coming toward them at a run, her hair flying wildly around her head. She stumbled to a stop, and her eyes widened. "Owyn's bleeding. Why is Owyn bleeding? Marik, why did you send for me? I saw the grooms and those men. Who were they? They're saying they didn't do anything? So what happened?"

"You said we'd be safe here," Aria said, her voice cold. "They attacked us. They were waiting for us, and they attacked us. Misborn freaks, they called us."

CHAPTER TWENTY-FIVE

RHEXA'S FACE PALED. Then she exploded, spouting forth a fountain of profanity the likes of which Owyn had never heard before, not in all his years on the street. It went on for nearly a full minute, when she finally stopped to breathe. Then, to Owyn's surprise, she turned on Marik.

"You told me that you'd be keeping watch over them!"

Marik's brows rose. "I have been. But hawks can't judge motive, and I was all the way on the other side of Terraces when they called me. Then I had to raise some help on the way. I told the hawks what to do as soon as I could see what was happening." He pointed. "I was just past the second ring."

"You've been watching us?" Aria asked.

"Guarding," Marik said. "Hawks during the day, owls at night."

"I asked him to," Rhexa added. "Because I did promise that you would be safe here. And I asked him to let me know if anything happened, which is why I'm here now." She glanced at Marik. "Although I wasn't expecting to have a jay screaming outside my office window."

Marik grinned. "Got your attention, didn't it?"

Rhexa made a face at him, then looked at Owyn. "You're bleeding—"

"He stepped between a rock and Aria," Aven said. "I'll see to him before I go." He looked up and scowled. "What's the penalty for being late to rounds? No one has told me yet."

"I'll go with you," Rhexa said. "It's not your fault. I'll make sure Risha knows it. Who were they, Marik?"

Marik shook his head. "Rhexa, I didn't know them. At all. I've never seen them before."

Rhexa's jaw dropped. "That's... that's not possible." She licked her lips and looked around. "And no one was home? None of the neighbors came out to help?"

Aria frowned. She looked at Owyn, then back at Rhexa. "We've seen no one in any of the surrounding houses since we came here. I'd assumed they didn't want to know us. But... Owyn, your findings?"

"Yeah," Owyn murmured. "Rhexa, you've got a bigger problem. Let me get my book, and I'll show you."

"Go put your weapons away," Aria said. She touched Owyn's shoulder, met his eyes, then looked down. He frowned slightly, then realized where her gaze had gone — the pouch with his whip chain. He nodded.

"Right. And I'll grab my book." Owyn headed into the house, hearing Aven behind him. He went back to the bedroom and put his blades back on their hooks. He turned to see Aven cleaning his swords; the towel he was using was streaked with red.

"You should check your blades," he said without looking up. "You hit that one pretty hard."

"I... did I?" Owyn turned and looked at his left-hand blade, and saw a clot of blood and hair. "I... may I have that when you're done?" He swallowed bile, remembering a thread of conversation that now seemed so long ago.

"I'll be using my smoke blades to fight. I've never done that before. I know it's been done. It's part of the history I had to learn in my

training. Smoke Dancers used to fight, too. But I've never done it. I don't know if I can. I mean, I've never fought like that before. I don't know if I can kill someone."

It hadn't been that long ago that he'd been standing in Meris' house, saying those words to Aria and Aven. Now... how many people had he killed now? He'd killed Fandor. He'd killed those guards, too. How many? Shouldn't he know that?

"Aven?" he said, his voice sounding strangled. Whatever he was going to say, he didn't finish. Before he could turn around, Aven was there, his arms wrapping around Owyn, holding him tight as he shook.

"I've got you, Mouse," Aven murmured. "I'm not letting you go."

Owyn nodded, grabbing fistfuls of his Aven's shirt and clinging to him. He wanted to cry, to scream...

He wanted Memfis. As angry as he still was, it didn't seem to matter anymore. He wanted his father.

Aven's grip tightened just before Owyn heard Aria's voice. "Aven? Is everything... oh."

"—'m all right," Owyn stammered. He tried to pull out of Aven's arms. "I'm fine."

"You are not," Aria answered. She joined them, pressing against Owyn's back, wrapping her arms around him and Aven. "Oh, Owyn. My warrior."

"I am not," Owyn protested. "I'm not."

"You are," Aven said. "You've protected us both. You've saved the both of us."

"I..." Owyn stopped. He looked up at Aven. "I'm not a warrior."

"You do a very good impression of one," Aria murmured. She leaned over his shoulder and kissed his cheek. "And you have others believing it. That's the important part."

"You shouldn't lean on me," Owyn said, turning so that his nose brushed Aria's. "You'll get blood on you."

"I already took care of the cuts," Aven said. "But you should change your shirt."

"Then you need to let me go."

Aven laughed. "Never letting you go, Mouse. You're ours." He opened his arms and stepped back, letting Owyn go to the dresser and take out a fresh shirt.

"I go through more shirts," Owyn grumbled, pulling the bloody shirt off over his head. Aria smiled and perched on the edge of Owyn's bed.

"Maybe you should go without?" she suggested. "I won't object."

Aven chuckled. "I wouldn't, either. I don't think Treesi would mind."

Owyn looked at them, then grinned. "When we're alone, maybe? Not when I have to go out in public." He pulled his shirt on and rolled his shoulders, hearing the muscles pop. "All right. Rhexa is waiting. Let's go."

TO AVEN'S SHOCK, RISHA was waiting by the fountain in the entry hall. Treesi and Alanar were there, too, standing off to one side. Treesi looked nervous, Alanar stone-faced. Neither said anything.

"Nice of you to finally join us," Risha snapped as they came through the door. "You're late."

"For a very good reason," Rhexa said, moving to stand in front of the group. "Senior Healer, your student, the Heir and her Fire were attacked."

"What?" Alanar gasped. Treesi stepped forward, her freckles standing out against her pallor. She stopped when Risha glared at her.

"Attacked?" She looked Aven up and down. "He looks hale to me. They all do. Attacked how?"

"Yes," Aven answered. "On our way here. Men throwing rocks, calling us misborn freaks." He rested his hand on Owyn's shoulder. "Aria got away unhurt, but Owyn was hit twice, and I've probably got a bruise the size of a plate."

Risha blinked and stepped forward. "Turn around."

Aven did, and felt her hand on his back, the rough touch of her healing power working under his skin. He winced as she probed the deep bruise.

"Rocks, you said? You're lucky that didn't break the skin. Or the bone. Benefits of the Water anatomy," she murmured. "And who was it?"

"Marik says he couldn't identify them," Rhexa said. "And I didn't get a good look before the grooms who were helping him took them away. You'll probably be sent for — at least two of them were hurt. Marik went off to see if he can find out who they are."

"Couldn't— Really, Rhexa?" Risha stepped away from Aven and shook her head. "You had me believing you up to there. So now you can tell me what really happened. Well, Student-Healer Aven?"

"Well, what?" Aven asked, incredulous. "You've had the truth of it from us and from Rhexa. We were attacked. I didn't know any of them, but I wouldn't. Marik says he doesn't know any of them. If you want to see who they are, you can check with the grooms. I don't know where they'd have taken them, though. There were six of them, and they ambushed us right outside Fourteen Southwest." He looked at Aria, then at Owyn. "Owyn stepped in front of the attack, and was injured. I already healed him, but I can't work on myself. And you saw what's on my back."

"And you got away how?" Risha asked. "Six against two?"

"And we were right outside our own house, where our weapons are," Owyn snapped. "Aria got away, and we got inside. They started breaking windows, if you want to go check that, too." He glared at Risha, then looked over at Rhexa. "Auntie, when you question that lot, I want to be there."

"And I," Aria added. Aven turned to see the shocked look on Rhexa's face, and the poorly concealed smile.

"I'll make sure you're both there," Rhexa said. "Now, Senior Healer, I came with them to be sure that you knew the truth of it. So if you're going to call all of us liars, kindly get it over with so I can drag you over to Fourteen Southwest and show you the truth of what I say?"

Risha's eyes widened. "You wouldn't dare!"

Rhexa sighed. "Risha, do you really want to have this fight? Now? In front of your students and mine?"

Risha's eyes narrowed, and she turned back to Aven. "You're late for rounds," she said. "You'll have to stay later to finish. And I have special lessons planned for you tonight."

Aven blinked. Special lessons? He frowned, then looked back at Owyn. His Mouse seemed a little more calm, but Aven could see that there was still a hint of something in his eyes. "Senior Healer, can I do those lessons tomorrow?" he asked. "I need to attend to my Heir tonight."

Risha folded her arms over her chest. "Your duties as a healer-in-training—"

"Do not supplant my responsibilities to my Heir," Aven interrupted. "Whatever these lessons are, they can wait."

"Aven!" Treesi blurted out. She brushed past Risha and came to stand in front of Aven. "You don't want these lessons. Not yet."

"Healer-in-training Treesi!" Risha snapped. "Have you lost your mind?"

"If she has, then so have I," Alanar said. He crossed to stand with Aria. "I told you already that I objected."

Risha turned red. "I could have all three of you restricted to the student residences for insubordination."

"And if you tried, I'd leave," Aven answered, his voice sounding much calmer than he was actually feeling. It was as if Melody were swimming tight circles in his stomach, and he wanted to throw up. But he wasn't going to be pushed, or let his friends be pushed. "I don't need to be recognized by you to be a healer. I was one before I got here. I'll still be one if I turn my back on you. So don't threaten me, Risha. You won't like the way it turns out."

"And no, I haven't lost my mind," Treesi added. She straightened and looked at Aria. "I found my Heir. And my spine. Aven, these lessons have to wait. You made a promise. And I won't be part of them." She swallowed. "Not yet."

Aven blinked. "Lessons... in sex?" he demanded. "Without warning me or asking if I consented?" He glared at Risha. "Is that the way the Earth tribe works under your rule? Bullying and coercion?"

"Not under mine," Rhexa said, sounding furious. She rested her hand on Aven's arm. "Senior Healer, you're perilously close to exceeding your authority. You cannot compel your students to have sex — that's a complete violation of the healers' canon. Pirit would never have allowed it!"

"Pirit is not the Senior Healer anymore," Risha said. "He needs to be introduced to the physical aspects of what we do, and to the healing potential. He's mastered almost everything else in the canon, but he's still a virgin—"

"Is not," Owyn muttered, just loud enough that everyone heard him. Aven felt his face grow warmer and glanced to his side as Owyn took his hand. "Look, I don't know where you got that idea, but he isn't. And it can't really be all that important, or you'd make it part of the testing." He squeezed Aven's hand, then let go.

Aven looked at Risha. "I have no objections to training with Treesi and Alanar, or to having them in my bed—"

"You don't have a bed," Treesi whispered. Aven bit down on a laugh.

"Or being in their beds," he amended. "But I made a promise to my Heir."

"And that promise is... what?" Risha asked. "That she be the first woman in your bed? Well then, what's keeping you?"

A cold hand slipped into Aven's, and Aria spoke, "I cannot come away with a child. Not yet. It's not yet safe for us to think of children."

Risha's jaw dropped. "Your father taught you nothing about contraception?" she gasped.

Aven swallowed. "It wasn't necessary. I wasn't exactly considered the best choice as a husband in my family canoe."

Risha sniffed. "Just shows that they're idiots. And so are you. If you'd told me what you needed..." Her voice trailed off. She sighed. Then she looked at Aria. "Come with me. Let's get this taken care of."

Aria's hand in Aven's shook. "I... what?"

"I'll do it," Risha answered. "Since you make the very true point that right now pregnancy would be a disaster for you, I'll set the contraceptive block. I'll show Aven how to do it later."

For a moment, Aven couldn't think. It couldn't be that simple. Could it? He stole a look at Aria, to find her looking at him.

"This is still what you want, is it not?" she asked softly.

He licked his lips. "Yes. And... and you?"

She smiled and stretched up to kiss him gently on the lips. "With all my heart. I'll be back shortly." Then she let go of his hand and followed Risha out of the entry hall. Aven swallowed, then pulled Owyn to his side and draped his arm over the smaller man's shoulders.

"Are you all right with this?" he asked softly. "I don't want to leave you out. Not after everything."

Owyn smiled, but Aven could see it didn't reach his haunted eyes. "I'm fine," he said. Too quickly. "You two have been wanting this for a long time. So now you get to have it—"

"And Owyn can spend the night with me and Allie," Treesi said. She hugged Owyn's arm. "It doesn't have to be for sex. Just friendly. Is that all right?"

This time, Owyn's smile was real. "Sex can be pretty friendly," he said, and Treesi laughed.

"If it isn't, you're doing it wrong," Alanar said. He rested his hand on Owyn's shoulder, then frowned. "You're very tense. Are you feeling all right?"

"I'll be fine," Owyn said.

"That was unpleasant," Rhexa said as she joined them. "And I'm going to be doing some deep thinking about how this tribe will continue. Because that's so far past acceptable behavior that it might as well be on the moon." She shook her head. "That's a problem for tomorrow. For now... I don't understand why no one came to help you," she said. "There should have been people around, even at that hour."

"I... ah... Auntie—" Owyn started. Rhexa turned slightly pink.

"When did you decide that?" she asked. "To call me that?"

Owyn looked sheepish. "It just happened?" he offered. "I opened my mouth, and it fell out."

"The same way you called Mother Meris Granna?" Aven asked. Owyn nodded.

"Yeah, just like that. Sometimes, I don't know I've decided something until I say it out loud." His eyes widened. "You... you don't mind, do you? I mean, it's not like we really know. I could be wrong. I mean, I'm probably wrong. I—"

"Owyn," Rhexa silenced him with a single word, then kissed him on the forehead. "I don't mind. And sometimes, our families are the ones we make, not the ones we're born to. If you want to call me Auntie, I'd be honored."

Owyn's cheeks turned very slightly pink. He looked down, then back up. He smiled. "Thank you. And... ah, we need to talk. About why no one came to help us. Auntie, I don't think there's anyone in those houses. And there are people missing. I'll show you."

"People missing?" Rhexa repeated. "Oh, I definitely need to see this. All right. Once we get to my office. And Aven, you still have rounds. Do try to pay attention to what you're doing?"

Aven grinned. "I'll pay attention. I have work to do."

"And make sure you do it well. Don't give her any excuses to issue punishment details. She's going to make us pay for that bit of insubordination as it is," Alanar murmured.

"Pay?" Rhexa repeated. "Pay how?"

Alanar grimaced. "Best to forget that I said that."

Rhexa looked shocked, and there was steel in her voice when she said, "Alanar—"

"No." Alanar's voice was firm. "We're in enough trouble. And don't interfere, Chieftess. We'll take our punishment, and it'll be over."

"Punishment?" Owyn repeated. "For standing up to her? And you put up with that?"

Alanar frowned. "She's my teacher. She's the only one who can certify me as a healer. What else am I supposed to do?"

"You shouldn't have to put up with abuse," Rhexa said. "Alanar, I want to know what she's doing. If I know, I can put a stop to it."

Alanar cocked his head to the side. "And then what?" he asked. "She's Senior Healer. She's the highest ranking fully trained healer left."

"Until one of you finishes your training," Rhexa said. "Think on that, Healer Alanar."

"He has nightmares about that," Treesi said softly. "Alanar doesn't want to be in charge of anything."

"I'm a healer, not a leader," Alanar said, wrapping his arms around himself. "I don't want to do anything but heal. And besides, who'd follow me?"

"I would," Treesi said. "And so would most of the healing assistants here. Because you're very good at what you do, Alanar."

"And what I do is healing, not leading," Alanar said. "So, no. And it can't be Aven, because he's spoken for." He sighed. "There's no one else, Rhexa. Anyone else who looked to be even remotely qualified left rather than deal with her. Virrik wasn't the first healer-in-training to leave before they finished training. He won't be the last. So we've got no choice. Damn Mannon for it."

"I do. Regularly," Rhexa said. She glanced to the side, in the direction where Risha had taken Aria. "In any case, it's a futile discussion, and one that we need to stop having where anyone can hear us."

CHAPTER
TWENTY-SIX

ALMOST REFLEXIVELY, Aven looked around. There was no one else in the entry hall, which was surprising. Shouldn't there be a healing assistant here? Had Risha sent them away?

He turned back to the others. "You didn't have to fight her. Not on my account," he said softly. Alanar smiled.

"Treesi will tell you I usually don't fight her. But this... I couldn't betray your trust like that." He rested his hand on Aven's arm, his fingers warm through the sleeve of Aven's shirt. "If you're ever in my bed, it'll be because you want to be there. Not because you were told to be there." He hesitated. Then he shook his head. "And I'm not sure I'd ever feel right asking you. You're too much like him. Like Virrik. It would feel like I was trying to replace him."

Aven winced and covered Alanar's hand with his own. "You're my friend, Alanar. That's important to me. Too important for me to want to risk hurting you."

"And besides," Alanar said with a laugh. "You've got more than enough to keep you busy." He cocked his head to the side. "They're coming. We'll talk later, when we're doing reports. I'll have some advice for you."

"Advice?" Aven realized what Alanar meant even as he said the word. "Oh," he stammered. "I... I'd appreciate that."

Alanar chuckled and tugged his hand out from underneath Aven's. "Friends, right?"

"Absolutely," Aven said. He turned to see Risha and Aria coming into the entry hall. Aria looked paler, and somehow uncomfortable. Aven's mouth went dry.

"Aria?" he said. She looked up at him and smiled.

"It's done," she said. "I'm fine." She looked back at Risha. "This will pass, you said?"

"An hour, perhaps less," Risha answered. "Now, my students have rounds, and they're already late. If you want him to join you tonight, I need him now."

Aria nodded. "I have work, too. So we'll go."

Aven tugged her close, wrapping his arms around her and holding her. She melted against him, and as she did, he sent his power flowing through her, trying to understand why she was so pale.

"Stop that," she whispered. "I can feel you."

"You can?" Aven whispered back.

"When you heal, it feels warm. And this is nothing." She hugged him a little tighter. "Cramps," she added. "It will pass. She said some women react to the block this way."

"Ah," Aven murmured. He buried his nose in her hair, breathing in her scent of wind and sunshine. "I don't like seeing you hurting."

"I am fine. And you have to go to work." She tipped her head back, then kissed him. "Go to work, Aven. I will see you later." She stepped back, out of his arms, and turned toward Owyn. "Let's go. We have so much to do!"

Owyn grinned and nodded. He led Treesi over to Aven. "We'll all meet up for the evening meal?" he asked.

"We might be late," Treesi warned. "Since we're starting late."

"So we'll eat late," Owyn answered. He kissed Treesi on the cheek, then slipped his arm free from hers. He grinned up at Aven. "I'm not a warrior."

"Oh, yes, you are," Aven replied. He laughed and leaned down to kiss Owyn. Then he nodded to Rhexa, and followed Risha out of the entry hall.

OWYN LAID HIS BOOK down on Rhexa's desk. "The map isn't nearly finished, but when I compare it to the dispensary records, there are some big problems," he said. "The houses I've marked? Those are empty. But the dispensary records say they're not. And someone is still drawing those allotments." He frowned. "Aven suggested that I check my list against the list of people who have vanished. But if they've left, wouldn't the dispensary know?"

"Unless they didn't officially vanish," Rhexa said. She went into her desk and took out a book that she paged through, glancing between the writing there and the pages of Owyn's notes. Then she pressed her hands together and touched her fingers to her lips.

"Who have you told?" she asked in a soft voice. Owyn frowned. "No one. Well, Aria and Aven. But no one else."

Rhexa nodded. She ran her finger down the list in Owyn's book. "Some of these..." She stopped. She stood up, went to her window and closed it, locking it and closing the curtains. Then she walked around to the door, looked out into the hall, then closed the door and locked it. She returned to her desk and sat down. She licked her lips and folded her hands.

"What I am about to say goes no further than this desk," she said in that same soft voice. "Several of the names on this list are people who I personally helped leave Terraces. I know where they are. I am not telling you that information. But they are alive and safe." She frowned. "And they're not the ones whose allotments are still being accessed. Those... I had no idea they were missing." She glanced up. "The first two rings of Terraces are usually reserved for healers, healing assistants, and their families. So they can be closest to the healing complex. I'd wondered why Risha's students always seemed to be so busy. They shouldn't be — it's horrible for their learning to be always on the run. But I just thought it was because we were so short on healers. I didn't realize it was because so many of the healers and the assistants had gone missing."

"Why are they going missing? And why did you help people leave?" Aria asked, keeping her voice low. Rhexa met her eyes.

"Do you remember what Alanar said, about healers leaving rather than putting up with Risha?" she asked. "He doesn't have it quite right."

"Oh, fuck," Owyn breathed. "She's doing something to her competition, isn't she?"

"I have no proof," Rhexa said. "I have nothing but worries and suspicions, and a way out of Terraces that Risha doesn't know about." She looked down. "You know the North spoke in the wheel? How the stairs to the lowest terrace are blocked?"

"Yes," Aria answered. "Marik said it was a rockfall?"

Rhexa nodded. "They're not as impassable as we've let people think. And there's a way down to the low tunnels, and out of Terraces." She reached into her desk, took out a folded piece of paper and a bottle. "I've been holding this, just in case. I think you need it."

"What is it?" Owyn took the paper and unfolded it. "This... this is a map. A good map." He arched a brow. "Why am I making maps if you have one this good?"

"Partly because this one is marked with things I don't want anyone to know," Rhexa answered. "Like the way to the low tunnels." She tapped the spot. "There. It's rough, but you can reach it. Marik is completely trustworthy, and he knows the way. If you need to take that route, he'll take you. That's the other reason he's watching you, by the by. In case you need to run, he'll meet you at the north stairs.

"And the bottle?"

"Is a sleeping potion." Rhexa touched the top of the bottle with one finger and tipped it. "Just in case."

"In case we need to get Aven out of here in a hurry," Owyn said softly. "That's what you're saying."

Rhexa nodded slowly. "I thought he'd be safe. He's your Water. He's a Companion. He cannot be Senior Healer. There's no way he can be a threat to Risha. Then I saw his testing results." She looked at them. "What did he tell you? I assume that he told you what his results were?"

"That he was a low four with potential," Aria answered. Rhexa nodded.

"He's not," she said. "And I think that Risha is undermining her students. Treesi and Alanar should both be ranked much higher than they are. Alanar especially — he's a high four, possibly even a five, or I'll eat this desk." She paused. "If you have to use the tunnels, take him with you. I know you'll take Treesi. Take Alanar, too. Get him out of here before it's too late."

Aria picked up the bottle. "Rhexa, what do you think is happening?" she asked.

"And what level is Aven?" Owyn added.

"I wasn't sure about what might be happening. I had suspicions, but I didn't know anything," Rhexa answered. "Not until you told me about Virrik." She smiled slightly. "Alanar is right. Aven is very like Virrik. Right down to the healing ability. Virrik was a natural five. I think Aven is, too. Thinking about his bloodline, and comparing his testing results to Virrik's, I'm almost certain. For a natural five, healing is like breathing." Rhexa leaned back in her chair. "Virrik didn't believe me when I told him that I thought he was in danger. I showed him the list of names of healers who have vanished, and he told me that he was certain I was wrong. That he wasn't going to leave when he was so close to finishing his training. It was the last conversation we had. I thought that perhaps he'd changed his mind. But he wouldn't have left Alanar." She let out a long breath. "And I've been worried that Memfis has gone the same way."

"No," Owyn protested. "He couldn't have..." Then he stopped. "I mean, could he? Auntie, you don't think someone hurt him, do you?"

"I don't know," Rhexa answered. "I wish I did. Marik has been searching the tunnels, and he's found nothing. At least, nothing he's told me."

"So, you think Risha has been getting rid of anyone who could challenge her." Aria picked up the bottle and slipped it into her coat. "Why? She's a healer herself. Why would she..." Her voice trailed off, and she reached for the book and turned it. "Rhexa, how many of these healers who have vanished were of mixed blood? Treesi told us that when she started training here is when she first heard her teacher use the word subhuman. Her teacher is Risha. So how many of the healers who have vanished would Risha have called subhuman?"

"And don't say that it can't be her," Owyn added. "There's no one else who can reach that many healers. Except you, and we know it's not you." He paused. "Well, we're pretty sure it's not you."

"I'm humbled by your faith in me," Rhexa said dryly.

Owyn turned red. "Oh, Auntie—"

"No," Rhexa said with a wave of her hand. "Please, keep questioning. Keep being skeptical. It might save your lives someday. You're right. Risha is the only one with the influence to change so many minds about the other tribes. I can't imagine why—"

"Is it Mannon's doing?" Aria asked. "Do you think?"

Rhexa shook her head. "In this? I think not. No, I'm fairly certain it is not. He would be biting his own tail." She looked at Aria, then at Owyn. "Neither of you know?"

"Mannon is Fire, I thought," Owyn said slowly.

"The son of Firstborn Elcam, yes," Rhexa agreed. "And his mother was Elcam's Air. If I remember correctly, her name was Falla." She shook her head. "No. As much as I'd like to blame everything ill in the world on that man, including my sore feet, in this I think the source is somewhere else. And perhaps it lies no further than our own healing complex."

"But why?" Owyn slumped in his seat. "We're all the Mother's children. It's at the heart of every tribal law and all the stories we tell. How can any of us be less?"

Rhexa shook her head. "I don't know. I don't understand it. I don't understand how anyone can hate so much, and for such silly reasons." She sighed. "All right. Let's reconcile your list with the dispensary rolls, see if we can't figure out where those supplies are actually going."

AVEN SAT FACING ALANAR at the long table in the healer's common room, writing up his reports as he listened to the clicking of beads from across the table. It had fascinated him, the first few days, to see Alanar do his own reporting. The blind healer used a series of knotted cords, each tipped by a bead with a different texture — a different bead for each patient. There was a matching bead on that patient's door, or in the case of the children's ward, on the foot of the bed. Alanar had tried to teach his system to Aven, but it had ended in hilarity — Aven tried it, only to somehow manage to tangle the knots in such a way that Alanar told him that the imaginary patient they were charting for was a ninety-year-old male who was pregnant with their sixteenth child. Once Aven stopped laughing and could breathe again, he went back to using a record book and a pen. He wrote the notes on his final patient of the day, a young woman who had been kicked by a horse, then set his book into the basket where they left their reports for Risha to review. He capped his inkwell, wiped his pen, then leaned back in his chair and rolled his shoulders, hearing the muscles crackle and pop.

"So how are you not entirely a virgin?" Alanar asked in a soft voice.

"Can you talk and do your charting at the same time?" Aven asked in response.

"I'm done," Alanar said as he laid aside his final cord. "So, explain?"

Aven smiled. "Owyn called it playing. But there wasn't any penetration, so I'm sort of yes, and sort of no. There was never any time for more after that once."

Alanar snorted. "That makes more sense. Have you read any of the pillow books? Treesi said she was going to leave them where you could find them."

"Oh, is that where those came from?" Aven laughed. The small, extremely explicit manuals had seemed to appear overnight throughout the suite. "Yes. I'm wondering if those are a little bit advanced, though."

"A bit," Alanar agreed with a nod. "The most important thing you need to know tonight is that Air folks are not comfortable lying on their backs. So let her ride you."

Aven swallowed, suddenly warm as he remembered the night on the beach, and Aria pinning him to the sand. "Good to know," he stammered. "Anything else?"

Alanar paused, then laughed. "I've just turned your brains off, haven't I? Your heart is racing."

"Alanar, what level are you?" Aven asked. "Because I can't tell what your heart rate is doing from across the table, not without touching you first."

"I'm more sensitive, for some reason. Treesi thinks it's because I can't see." Alanar shrugged. "And somewhere between three and five, I think. It doesn't matter to me. Not really. I'll be serving here until I fall over."

Aven blinked. "You could teach—"

"Aven, who'd listen to me?" Alanar asked. He spread his hands wide. "I spend most of my time in the children's ward, because most adults can't see past my scars. They're more blind than I am."

"But you're a good teacher!" Aven protested. "And you're an excellent healer!"

"And I'm blind and crippled," Alanar said. "And people will always see me as less because of it. And I've learned to live with that. I thought... well, it doesn't matter what I thought. Treesi will go with you when you leave, and I'll stay here. I'll serve in the children's ward. I don't aspire to more than that."

"You deserve more than that," Aven grumbled. To his surprise, Alanar laughed.

"Mother, you do sound like him!" he said. "Do you know how many times Virrik told me the same thing?" He shook his head. "Enough. It's not me you should be worrying about. Tonight, it's all about you. You read the pillow books. You have the basic training, I assume? In theory, at least?"

"Yes," Aven said. He rolled his shoulders again. They felt unusually tight. It took him a moment to realize why.

He was nervous.

"When do we go over?" he asked. Alanar smiled.

"You're finished with your reports?" he asked. "If you are, we can go now. Let's go find Tree."

IT FELT ODD, KNOCKING on the door of the house that was supposed to be his own. Aven opened the door and looked inside at the empty front room. "We're here!" he called, and walked in. Treesi and Alanar followed him, and Alanar took a deep breath.

"That smells good, whatever it is," he said. "I hope there's a lot of it."

"There is," Owyn said as he came out of the corridor. "And a lot of other things, too." He waved at the table. "We'll be out in a minute. There's wine—"

"There's what?" Alanar asked. "You got wine? I thought you didn't keep it in the house."

"I didn't get it. Rhexa sent it." Owyn grinned. "And if Mem chooses this moment to walk through that door, I'll pour the whole bottle out myself."

"Then I'd better pour a glass first," Alanar said. Treesi laughed and rested her hand on his arm.

"I'll do it. You're a horrible judge of a pour," she said. She filled three cups and brought them back, handing one to Aven. He sniffed it, feeling the alcohol tickle his nose.

"Have you ever had wine before?" Treesi asked.

"No," Aven answered. "I know what it is, but we don't have things like this out on the water. Nothing that muddles your head. I had kawa, once. It's for ritual, and it's only served at the Winter Solstice festivals. My cousin and I sneaked into the stores and we each had a sip. Grandmother tanned us both for it. But it's not like this." He took another sniff. "I had fireberry mead once. Mannon gave it to me. I didn't like it."

"Mead is too sweet for me," Alanar agreed. He sipped his wine, and his brows rose. "This is nice."

"Is it?" Aven asked. He took a tentative sip. The liquid was warm, and tasted a little sharp. "This is nice?"

"It's a good vintage," Alanar answered, taking another sip. "Smooth. I taste... oak. Cherries. And..." He stopped and took a sniff. "Pears?"

"Pears," Treesi agreed. "There's definitely pears. Aven, you don't have to drink it."

"I don't even taste any of those things," Aven said. "It's sharp—"

"That's the oak," Alanar offered. "Take a sip, then breathe in through your mouth, and out through your nose. Without swallowing."

Aven blinked. Then he did as Alanar instructed, only to cough and hand his cup back to Treesi. "Not tasting anything but sharp. It makes my nose itch."

Alanar smiled. "Wine is a learning experience."

"I'll be ignorant, thanks," Aven answered, and Alanar burst out laughing.

"What's so funny?"

Aven turned to see Aria coming into the front room; he met her halfway without even noticing that he was in motion. She moved into his arms and into his kiss, and time seemed to stop.

Unless Owyn cleared his throat and said, "I thought that was for after we ate?"

Aria burst into giggles, which made Aven laugh. He let Aria go and looked around. "Well... no, I'm not saying anything. Not a word. Is there anything I can do to help?"

"That was an awful lot of words for not saying a word," Owyn teased. "Come help carry."

Aven laughed and followed Owyn back to the kitchen. There were a number of plates and bowls and platters, and the table in the dining area was well laden when they all sat down. Alanar took a deep, appreciative sniff.

"Someone knows how to properly season their food," he murmured. "What am I smelling? It's familiar, but I can't place it."

"Have you ever had momo?" Aria asked. Alanar gaped at her.

"Not since I was small! I loved them, and no one else knew how to make them after my mother died!" He picked up his plate and held it out. "Please?"

The meal was a joyous one — full of laughter and talking, and when the first bottle of wine was empty, Owyn opened a second. When the plates were all empty and the glasses drained, Owyn leaned back in his chair and smiled.

"We did good, Aria," he said. "That was good."

"That was excellent," Alanar said. "Aria, will you share your recipe for momo? So I can find someone to make it?"

"You're welcome to come with us when we leave," Aria said. "You've become a part of our family, Alanar. I would like to have you as part of my court."

Alanar's jaw dropped. "Me? But—"

"If you're about to say something about how you do not deserve to serve the Firstborn because you cannot see, then you can stop right now," Aria interrupted. "You are a good man, and a wonderful healer. You are wise, and I couldn't find a truer counselor if I searched the whole world. You are not my Air, to my regret. But you are my friend."

Treesi reached out and rested her hand on Alanar's arm. "This is where I get to say I told you so, isn't it?"

"No, you don't," Alanar said. He covered Treesi's hand with his own. "I have been thinking what it would be like when you left. When you took Treesi with you and went off to challenge Mannon. And I'd resolved myself to being alone for the rest of my life."

"Allie!"

Alanar turned toward Treesi. "It's true, you know. Even though you're here with me, you're not *for* me. Does that make sense?" He picked up his wine cup, took a sip, then gestured with it. "You're for Aria, and for Owyn and Aven. The only one for me was Virrik." He frowned. Then he set his cup down. "I think I've had too much."

Treesi reached out and took the cup, moving it away. "You need to stop, or you'll be no use to Owyn later."

"Assuming he wants me to be of use to him?" Alanar asked. He tipped his head to one side. "Owyn? You don't have to do anything you don't want to. And we can discuss it back in the suite."

"And I think that's our signal to clean up," Owyn said. He stood up and started stacking plates. "Then I'll put together some stuff for tonight."

"Can I help with anything?" Treesi asked. "Carrying or packing?"

Owyn smiled and nodded, and he and Treesi carried stacks of plates out of the dining area.

Aven picked up his cup of salted water and drained it, then glanced at Aria before reaching over to take Alanar's hand. "You're not alone, you know," he said gently. "You're one of us now."

Alanar smiled. "Thank you. It's not quite the same thing." He squeezed Aven's fingers. "But it helps."

OWYN LED TREESI INTO the bedroom. "This is mine. Mine and Aven's, but for now, just mine."

Treesi looked around. "We could stay here, if you wanted," she said. "The bed is big enough."

Owyn snorted. "Nah," he answered. "It'd be weird. They need their privacy for the first time. We don't want them getting all shy, you know?" He gestured to the dresser. "I'll get a basket. If you'll grab a shirt and some trousers for me?"

He turned to root under the bed, and heard a drawer slide open. And the clanking of heavy metal. He looked up to see that Treesi had found the manacles. She held them up and arched a brow. He shivered.

Did he trust them?

Yes.

"And those, yeah," he answered. "The keys are in there, too."

CHAPTER TWENTY-SEVEN

THE OTHERS LEFT, AND Aven helped Aria in the kitchen, washing up, drying dishes, and following her directions on where to put things. They didn't talk, other than questions and answers about where things went. It was a comfortable silence, albeit one layered over nerves stretched as tight as sailcloth in a high wind.

"I enjoyed the... what did you call them again? Momo?"

"Yes," Aria answered. She put the last bowl away in a cupboard, then turned to face him. "I worried they might be too heavily seasoned for you."

"No, they were good." Aven leaned back against the table, folding his arms over his chest. "Different from anything I've had before, but I liked them. Will you make them again?"

She smiled and moved closer, stopping so close to him that he could feel her warmth. "If you like them, then I will make them for you."

"Not just for me," Aven protested. "Alanar liked them, too."

She rested her hands on his chest. "I will make them for you," she repeated, and leaned against him. "I'll wake you with them tomorrow," she said, and ran her hands up over his shoulders, up his throat, twining her fingers into his hair as she pulled his face down to hers. He slid his hands down her sides, wrapping them around her and pulling her tightly to him, kissing her as fervently as she kissed him. She let go of his hair, and started unfastening the buttons on his shirt, and Aven had a brief moment of clarity, a memory of sitting on the floor in the kitchen of Memfis' house, and of Memfis' amused instructions.

Not on the kitchen floor.

In one movement, he scooped Aria up in his arms and headed for the door. He had to pass sideways to not hit her wings, and he stopped in the corridor, unable to remember which room was hers. It had a larger bed than the ones that were in the room he would share with Owyn. He remembered that much, but he couldn't remember which room was which!

"The room on the left," she whispered against his lips. Aven laughed, and headed for the door.

Inside, he set Aria down on her feet and met her eyes. "I love you," he said softly. "I want to be certain that this is what you want."

She licked her top lip, the barest hint of the tip of her tongue peeking out between her lips. "It's what I've wanted since I first woke up on the island. Since I saw you for the very first time. I am not changing my mind." She frowned slightly. "Are you?"

"No," Aven said. "I just want to be sure."

She rested her hands on his waist. "I'm sure. I want this. I love you." She tugged on the waistband of his kilt. "We're both wearing too many clothes."

Aven chuckled. "Then we should undress." He moved to step back, but stopped when Aria tugged on his kilt.

"Where are you going?" she asked.

He blinked. "To undress?"

She tugged him closer and started to undo the fastenings at his waist. "Now where," she asked, "is the fun in that?"

OWYN LOST TRACK OF where he was in the healing complex almost immediately. Not because he was lost, but because he wasn't really paying attention to the turns. His mind was racing. He wasn't sure just what he was feeling for Treesi. It wasn't as intense a feeling as he had for Aria or Aven, but then, he'd spent barely any time with the red-haired healer. He liked her. A lot. And he liked Alanar. A lot.

All right, he admitted to himself as he shifted the basket on his hip. He was in love with her. Maybe with both of them.

And neither of them knew the truth about him. Treesi knew a little, and she'd seen his shoulder and his back. But neither of them knew all of it.

Aven and Aria had accepted him. Would Treesi? Probably. She was a Companion, after all. She sort of had to. But what about Alanar?

Treesi had been walking on Alanar's other side. She abruptly stopped, dropping behind them, and came up to take Owyn's free hand.

"You're awfully quiet," she said. "Second thoughts?"

"Second thoughts are for amateurs," Owyn answered. "I'm into the double digits."

She squeezed his fingers. "We won't bite, Owyn." She paused. "Unless you want one of us to bite?"

"No, I never really got into biting. Never liked it when someone left marks," Owyn answered. He saw Alanar's brows rise, and felt his face grow hot. "I... I need to be straight with you both, before we do anything."

"About..." Treesi's voice trailed off, and she let go of his hand and rested her hand on the small of his back. He nodded.

"Yeah, about that." He glanced at her and smiled. "You didn't tell Alanar?"

"No," Treesi answered. "It's not mine to tell, and I wouldn't betray a trust like that."

"It's something we're trained to do, actually," Alanar added. "Keep our mouths shut. Healers aren't allowed to discuss patients with anyone but their families."

"Not even another healer?"

"That's what charts are for," Treesi said. "This is our door."

They led Owyn into a sitting room that looked comfortable and well lived in. He set the basket down inside the door and stepped out of the way, looking around.

"Sit," Alanar said. "The couch is lumpy but comfortable. Then you can tell me why your heart rate is so high. You're not nervous, are you?" He took one of the chairs. "Owyn, you can always say no. You don't have to share either of our beds. There's always Aven's hammock—"

"I fell out," Owyn blurted. "Aven had me try one, and I fell out. When we were still on our way here. I don't know how he sleeps in that without breaking his neck." He moved over to the couch and sat down, slumping back in it. It was lumpy, and had clearly seen better days, but Alanar was right. It was comfortable. Treesi sat next to him, taking his hand again.

"Do you want to tell us the whole story?" she asked. He rubbed his thumb over her knuckles.

"Yeah, I'll start at the beginning," he answered. He swallowed, then started. He told them about his years on the streets, about learning to steal. About turning from stealing to whoring. About Fandor, and being betrayed. About Memfis buying him. About learning to be a smith, and a Smoke Dancer. Learning to be a person.

About going out to the coast road that morning, and finding Aven and Aria. About Memfis adopting him. About starting on the journey as a Companion and a free man.

He rubbed his hands on his trouser legs. "So, that's it. That's me. And... yeah." He looked at Treesi, then back at Alanar. Alanar had leaned forward, his elbows on his knees, his fingers laced together. There was something intense about him, a heaviness that Owyn knew hadn't been there before.

Then he sat up. "Owyn," he said. "May I touch your back?"

Owyn swallowed. Then he took a deep breath and nodded. Treesi snorted.

"You nodded, didn't you?" Alanar asked. He grinned. "Love that reflex. If the answer is yes, will you take off your shirt?"

"Right. Of course," Owyn answered. He got up and stripped his shirt off over his head. Then he went to stand in front of Alanar, considered it for a moment, then knelt in front of the healer, facing away from him. He felt Alanar's hand on his shoulder, and the warmth of his healing power as it spread under the skin. It felt different from when Aven did it. No, not felt. Tasted. It tasted different.

"Can you taste healing?" he asked, closing his eyes as Alanar's hand moved down his spine. "Because your power tastes different from Aven's."

"Taste? On your tongue?" Treesi asked.

"Is there another way to do it?" Owyn asked in response. He didn't open his eyes — Alanar's hands felt good.

Alanar laughed. "In a way. For the very sensitive, different healers can feel different. And some people interpret that as taste. Or as a note of music."

Owyn nodded, letting his head loll forward. The warmth under his skin was doing a lot to relax his tattered nerves.

"You had a lot of deep damage here," Alanar murmured. "Not properly treated. Impressive scarring—"

"There's nothing impressive about scars," Owyn grumbled. Alanar ran his finger down the length of one.

"There's nothing shameful about scars, either," he said. "I have them, too. We can compare. Yours are rougher than mine, though."

"I didn't see a real healer until Memfis claimed me," Owyn told him. "And it wasn't an Earth healer. He used potions and bandages and gut. Before him, though, it was make-do, and hope for the best."

"Barbaric," Alanar murmured. His hand swept the length of Owyn's spine, then across his shoulders, lingering over the cross-hatched brand. "We'll do our best to make sure that you don't end up aching in cold weather like some of the old men do."

Owyn opened his eyes and turned his head. "We? That means you decided? You're coming with us?"

Alanar smiled, resting his hand on the back of Owyn's neck. "I've known what it was like to be part of something more. And then I lost it. I didn't understand why he left me. I still don't. And knowing that he's dead, that I'm never going to have an answer? That's hard." He paused, frowned slightly, and the fingers resting on Owyn's neck flexed slightly. "I thought I was going to be alone for the rest of my life," he said softly. "But you and Aria and Aven, you're offering me more. I'd be a fool not to grab it with both hands." He started stroking Owyn's neck, his shoulders, and Owyn shivered slightly. "What do you want, Owyn?" he asked. "Both of us? Just one? Neither?"

Owyn swallowed, trying not to think about the conversation that he and Aria had had with Rhexa. About how she suspected that Virrik hadn't left of his own volition. He couldn't tell Alanar that. Not without some kind of proof. So he forced his mind back to the question. "I... it's been a long time," he said slowly. "Three years. So... I'm not even sure. And everything I did before... it was different. I just... did what they wanted. Whatever they were paying me for. And Trey—"

"Who's Trey?" Treesi asked.

Owyn turned to look at her. "I didn't tell you about Trey? He was another one of Fandor's boys. He was in one of Fandor's brothels, him and his brother. And he got out when Fandor killed his brother. He helped me out when he could. Hid me in his room when I was sick from being on the street or from a whipping. And when we were both out from under Fandor's thumb, we fucked. Because that was what we knew. Now, we're friends because we know we can be without the fucking part. He's in the guard now. But he's the last person I fucked, so it's been about three years."

Alanar nodded slowly. "So... you don't know what you like," he said. "What did you not like? What would you never do again, given a choice?"

"No piss," Owyn said immediately, and Alanar coughed.

"People do that?" he sputtered. "But... that's degrading."

Owyn shrugged. "It's not like they saw me as a person, Alanar. For most of them, I was a thing. And for Fandor, I was a possession."

Alanar growled softly. "Barbaric," he repeated. He started kneading the muscles in Owyn's shoulders, coaxing the tension out. "There's a difference, you know," he said. "Between fucking and loving."

Owyn let his head fall forward again, thinking about Alanar's words. He'd suspected as much. Was almost sure of it, given how he felt for Aven and for Aria. How he was starting to feel for Treesi and Alanar. "I... I don't know the difference," he said slowly. "But I want to."

"I think we can show you," Alanar crooned. "And we can show you things you might like."

"He liked these," Treesi said, and Owyn heard metal clinking. He hadn't heard her get up and go to the basket, but when he looked up, she had the manacles. "We can try them."

Alanar's hands went still. "Metal... chains?" he asked. "Were those chains?"

"I... um... yeah," Owyn stammered. He couldn't bring himself to look at Treesi. "I... they used them on me, chained my hands behind my back. Then... well, then you lot came and saved us, and Aria flew down and she kissed me and... umm... yeah."

Alanar started stroking the back of his neck, and the caress was somehow different from the massage. "And you liked that?" he asked. Owyn shivered — he could practically taste Alanar's lust.

"I..." Owyn swallowed. "I'm not sure if it was the chains or if it was Aria."

Alanar chuckled. "It could be person-specific, yes," he agreed. "Do you want to find out?"

"You like that?" Owyn asked. "Chaining people up?"

"Tying, actually," Alanar answered. "Virrik and I never used chains. He was always afraid I'd lose the key if we used chains. But ropes? Yes, I like that. Really, how else am I ever going to have the upper hand?" He snorted. "And this isn't about what I like. It's about what you like."

"Well, you said you were going to show me things I might like," Owyn countered, and Alanar's hand fell still.

"I did," he said softly. "I did. May I?"

Owyn turned on his knees to face Alanar. "I want to know," he said. Alanar's smile lit up his face.

"Treesi, would you help me, please?"

Following Alanar's directions, Owyn got to his feet and let Treesi chain his wrists behind him. As the second manacle clicked closed, he shivered.

"Are you all right?" she asked, resting her hand on the small of his back.

"I... maybe?" Owyn answered. He forced a laugh. "I... it's not the first time. For sex, I mean. But the last one... that was Fandor."

"Oh, fuck, Owyn!" Alanar gasped. "And you didn't tell me that why?" He reached out, resting his hand on Owyn's waist. "Is this something you still want to try?"

Owyn closed his eyes for a moment, rolling his shoulders as much as he could. Treesi's hand was warm, and Alanar's hand was scorching. He wanted that heat, needed it.

"I want this," he said. "I want to see the difference. With both of you."

Alanar smiled, and reached out with his other hand to tug Owyn to him, giving him gentle instructions and steadying him until Owyn was kneeling astride his legs on the chair. He reached behind Owyn and took the chain in one hand.

"There now," Alanar said, his voice suddenly deeper. "Now what are you going to do, hm?"

Owyn shivered and pressed closer to Alanar. "I... not much, I don't think," he answered.

Alanar's deep laugh washed over Owyn like warm velvet. "Oh, I can think of one thing," he murmured. "You're going to scream for me."

AVEN WOKE SLOWLY, WITH Aria's scent in his nose and her weight on his chest. It was dark in the room, the tiny flame in the oil lamp trimmed sleeping-low, casting barely enough light to see. What had awakened him? Aria mumbled something in her sleep and cuddled closer, and Aven closed his eyes to try and go back to sleep when he heard it again.

Someone was moving around in the corridor.

Aven blinked and started to shift out from beneath Aria. She gasped, and grabbed for him.

"Aven?" she whispered. "I... what is it?"

"I heard something," he answered. "I think Owyn might be back."

"Oh? Oh, dear," Aria murmured. She let him go and sat up. "Go and see?"

"I was going to. I didn't mean to wake you up." He sat up and reached for her, kissing her gently. "Let me go see if he's all right. If he's back here, he might not be." He slipped out of the bed and turned up the flame in the lamp so that he could better see. Aria was sitting up in the bed, the sheets puddled around her hips, her hair wild around her face. He leaned in and kissed her again, then headed for the door.

"Owyn?" he called as he opened the door. "Is that you? Is something wrong?"

There was a figure in the corridor outside the door, and Aven had just enough time to see that it was a man, that he was too tall to be Owyn, and that he was wearing a mask over his mouth and nose. Then he raised something and sprayed a fine mist into Aven's face. Aven gasped, stepping backward, tasting the liquid on his tongue, smelling it. It was familiar...

Dreamflower!

He spat and blew out hard through his nose, trying to clear the dreamflower from his head, but he could already feel the effects. Everything seemed to be slowing down, seemed to be blurring. The figure came into the room, the container raised, doing something with his hands. Pumping, Aven realized. He was using one of the aerosol bottles that they used in the healing complex, to spray medication on wounds. He was building pressure to spray the mist again. He had to stop them, before they used it on Aria. He lurched forward; the attacker stepped back and raised the container again, then swore as something crashed into the wall next to him. Shards of glass flew everywhere, and the attacker staggered to the side. He didn't drop the container, though — he raised it, spraying wildly, catching Aven in the face as Aven attacked.

Aven fell, hearing Aria shouting as the world spun and darkened around him. He had to get up. He had to protect her.

"Time for a nap, Fish."

Warm, stinking mist splattered into his face, and he realized as the world faded away that he *knew* that voice.

CHAPTER TWENTY-EIGHT

THE WATER SMELLED WRONG.

It was the first thing that Aven noticed as he woke up — he was wet, but the water smelled *wrong*. No, not wrong. Sick. The water smelled sick. He blinked, blinked again, groaning at the pain in his head. It was from the dreamflower, more than likely. Between the pain and the stench, he felt his gorge rising. He swallowed, pushing himself up on his hands. It was then he noticed the manacles around his wrists, the weight on his ankles. He stared at his hands for a moment, then looked around.

He was alone. Stone walls rose over his head, dark and crusted with salt. There was a ladder, and a lantern hung from a chain high above. It cast enough light for him to see the chain hanging from the ceiling. It led to the ring that connected the manacles on his wrists. And when he tried to stand, he found that the chains on his ankles were attached to rings set into the stone floor. Where was he?

And where was Aria?

He looked around again, and the last of the dreamflower haze burned off with a sudden, panicked realization.

He was *underground*. He had to be, in order for there to be water creeping in. He was underground, and he was trapped.

"Can anyone hear me?" he shouted. "Is anyone there?" His voice echoed off the stones, and he pushed himself up to his knees, then managed to get to his feet. The chains kept his feet shoulder-width apart, and he tugged against the rings on the floor for another futile moment before raising his voice again. "Can anyone hear me?"

Above his head, he heard a metallic screeching, and voices.

"He's awake. That was faster than I'd expected." Risha appeared at the top of the ladder, looking down at him. "We've hours yet before we can properly begin." She shook her head. "I'd put him out again, but I can't guarantee I'd be done with her before the tide came in."

"Just let him stay, then." Aven's heart lurched as the second figure moved into view. He'd recognized his attacker's voice, he thought. Now he knew for certain. Teva joined Risha near the ladder. "It's not like he's going anywhere."

"Risha, what is this?" Aven called. He was shivering. The tide, she said. The tide was coming in. This room... he glanced up at the walls. At the salt-crusted walls. This room would *flood*.

"An experiment," Risha answered. "I've been trying so hard over the years, to save you poor beasts. To deliver all of you from your misery and make you human. I've had such success with the bird-folk. But the fish... oh, you've given me so much trouble!"

"Deliver us... Risha, we *are* human!" Aven protested.

Teva snorted. "Why are you explaining it to him? He can't understand. He's a fish!"

"He's half-human," Risha said. "He's Pirit's grandson. He has the potential to be human. If he survives the process."

"What process?" Aven demanded. "What are you doing to me?"

Risha smiled. "I've tried many things over the years, you know. Removing the gills, for example. The surgery is very intricate, but it never really worked properly."

Aven swallowed, raising his hands and touching his throat, the ridges that marked his gills. "You... you can't—"

"Perhaps someone with more skill might be able to do it," Risha continued. "Then I thought, perhaps if we can break the cycle of the change? Hence, this experiment. We've come close, but I think perhaps my specimens weren't the best. The closest I've come was the last one."

Aven moaned softly. He knew what was going to happen now, and there was nothing he could do to stop it. This was what had happened to Virrik. This was what had destroyed Virrik's legs.

"You murdered Virrik," he croaked. "You're going to murder me." He looked around. "Where is Aria? What have you done with her?"

"Oh, don't worry about her. She'll be fine. I've perfected the techniques to save the bird-folk," Risha answered. "She's lovely. She'll be perfect, once we remove those abominable wings." She shook her head. "Now, we've hours left. I need to prepare her. So we'll leave you here. I'll come back later." She glanced up. "Teva, darling, we need to finish setting up the experiment."

"Yes, Risha," Teva answered. He moved out of sight, and Aven heard more metallic screeching; the chain that dangled from the ceiling slowly started to rise.

"Risha," Aven called, tugging against the chain as it rose higher, pulling his arms up over his head. "Risha, don't! Please! You'll kill us!"

Risha just laughed as the machine finally stopped, leaving Aven dangling, his feet barely on the wet stones.

"There. Now the experiment is set, even if I'm not here to see it start." She looked up again. "You have trouble with the dark. I remember. I'll leave you the light. Teva, come along."

THE THUNDERCLAP THAT woke Owyn was so loud, and went on for so long, that it felt as if it was shaking the bed. He jerked, tugging against the chains that still bound his wrists. The evening had been educational in many ways. Alanar had indeed made him scream, and more than once. Then Treesi had joined in, and they'd passed Owyn back and forth between them like a favorite toy, teaching him things about sex and pleasure and his body that he'd never learned on the streets. They'd fallen asleep curled around each other like a nest of fire-mice. And, apparently, they'd all fallen asleep at roughly the same time, and no one had been awake long enough to remember to let him loose. Alanar was sprawled face-down on his wide bed, with Owyn half on top of him, half underneath Treesi.

Owyn blinked in the gloom, looking at the dark window. It looked like it was still hours until dawn, so he settled back down, repositioning his head on Alanar's shoulder, and closed his eyes, relaxing against the other man's warmth, feeling under his cheek the top of the ridge of scar that was all that was left of Alanar's left wing. The long scars ran from Alanar's shoulder blades to the small of his back, perfectly straight converging lines that were horrifying in their significance. Owyn rubbed his cheek against it, feeling Treesi shift where she was curled up against his back. Until the thunder rolled again; another deep, booming rumble that Owyn felt in his chest. He heard Treesi gasp behind him, and her nails dug into his thigh; he hissed in protest, which woke Alanar.

"Was that thunder?" Alanar mumbled. He scrubbed one hand over his face. "Is it morning?"

"I don't know," Treesi answered. "It's dark out." Alanar's bed shifted as she untangled herself from them and got up, leaving the room. Alanar shifted out from underneath Owyn and rolled onto his side, pulling Owyn closer and running his hand down Owyn's arm. His brows rose.

"We never unlocked you?" he asked. "Are you uncomfortable?"

"I'm fine," Owyn answered. He was very aware of Alanar's body pressed against his, the warm length of him comforting and arousing all at once. Then Alanar moved closer still and kissed Owyn, reaching behind him and grabbing the chain in one hand. Owyn whimpered, but Alanar broke the kiss as Treesi came back into the bedroom.

"Allie, is the water clock broken?" she asked.

"I don't think so," Alanar answered. "Why?"

"Rounds started half an hour ago."

Alanar let go of Owyn and sat up. "What?" he gasped. "It can't be that late!"

"It's so dark out, I thought it was wrong." Treesi came into the room, grabbing the keys off the desk. "We need to wash up and get going. I don't know why there's not someone pounding on our door!" She hurried around the bed, sitting down and reaching over to unlock the manacles. "I'll put these in your basket, Owyn."

"You two should hurry up and get where you need to go," Owyn said, sitting up and stretching. "I can find my own way out." He frowned. "Shouldn't Aven be here by now, if rounds have started? Wouldn't he be the one banging the door down?"

Treesi stopped and stared at him. "He's late, too? Oh, and after yesterday... Risha will have his head on a plate!"

"Right," Alanar grumbled. "New plan. Trees, you and Owyn go find him. He's probably still asleep. I'll get out to rounds and stall Risha. If one of us gets started, then she won't be as mad."

"You hope?" Treesi asked.

"I hope." Alanar scrubbed his hand over his face and swung his legs over the edge of the bed. "Hurry."

They rushed through washing up and dressing, and headed out into the healing complex. The corridors were quiet, but it didn't feel like the usual quiet. Owyn stopped as they came out of the wheel.

"Something's wrong," he murmured.

"You feel it, too?" Alanar asked. "Something is off. I don't know—"

"Healer Alanar!" A young woman in healer whites appeared at the end of the corridor and rushed toward them. "There you are. We've been looking for you. Do you know where the Senior Healer is?"

Alanar blanched. "She's not here? Malani, what's going on?"

"I don't know," Malani answered. "There's a terrible storm coming in off the ocean, and Rhexa's ordered us to prepare for the worst, but I can't find the Senior Healer."

"That's why it's so dark," Treesi murmured. Alanar nodded, dragging his fingers through his hair.

"Right. All right. All right. Malani, you know the procedures for storm preparedness. Get Beryn and bring the patients to the lower levels and see them comfortable." He continued giving orders, and sent Malani off at a run. "We'll join you as soon as we can!" he shouted after her. Then he turned toward Treesi and Owyn. "Owyn, did anyone tell you what to do in a storm?"

"No," Owyn answered. "Why?"

"Because Terraces gets hit hard with summer and fall storms, and if Rhexa is telling the healers to prepare, then this looks to be a bad one. Everyone has their storm shelter, but if you haven't been told where to go to evacuate, Aven and Aria won't know where to go either. And we need Aven here. All healers shelter in the healing complex." Alanar turned. "Treesi, let's go."

"You're both going with me?" Owyn said. "But rounds—"

"Rounds are suspended in an emergency," Alanar answered. "No way you could know that, since no one told you about storms. We need to get Aven and Aria to safety. So let's go."

Walking out of the healing complex was like walking into a whirlwind. Owyn was blown back several steps before he recovered from the shock.

"It was never this bad in Forge!" he shouted over the screaming wind.

"This is worse than any I can remember," Alanar shouted back. "We need to hurry!"

They pushed through the streets, passing people rushing to wherever they were supposed to shelter. Treesi kept hold of Alanar's hand, and as they made the turn on to Southwest, Owyn took Alanar's other hand. He could see the storm clouds seething in the distance, flickering bright with lightning.

"It smells close," Alanar said. "Treesi, how much time do we have?"

"None," Treesi answered without hesitation. "We have no time. Owyn, go on ahead. Run. We'll catch you up. Or you'll meet us."

"Right. Be careful," Owyn said. He squeezed Alanar's hand and took off running, trying hard not to stare out at the storm. He'd never seen one like it, and it was fascinating and terrifying at the same time. He burst through the door into Fourteen, and immediately knew something was wrong.

"Aven!" he shouted. "Aria! We need to go!"

There was no answer. He headed down the corridor, peering into the kitchen, seeing Trinket in the middle of the floor. He darted in and scooped her up. "Hey, Trinket," he murmured. "Not safe for you here, either. Come on. Where is everyone?" He headed back out into the corridor, going back to the bedrooms.

They were empty. Aria's bedroom was completely wrecked, blankets and pillows on the floor, broken glass near the door. Owyn stood there for a moment, blinking. Then he turned and looked into the room he would be sharing with Aven. Nothing out of place. Nothing moved. Nothing changed.

"Owyn?" Treesi called. "Owyn, where are you?"

"They... they're gone!" Owyn called back. He looked around the bedroom, seeing the smoke blades and swords on their hooks, and Aven's battered carry-bag on his bed. "Treesi, they're gone, but they're not gone where it's safe. Something's happened!" He backed out of the bedroom, turning to see Treesi and Alanar in the corridor. "They're not here. The room is all broken up, and Aven's carrybag is here and he wouldn't have left it. They're gone. They're gone and—" His entire world wobbled, and he grabbed the doorframe. "They were took. Someone took them. Marik... his birds... where the fuck were Marik's birds?"

"Owyn, slow down," Alanar said. He brushed past Treesi and came to stand with Owyn, resting his hands on Owyn's shoulders. "How do you know they didn't go willingly? Someone could have come and taken them to shelter. Marik could have come and gotten them."

Owyn swallowed, looked back into the bedroom. "My blades. Aven's swords. Aven's bag. They wouldn't have left those behind. And..." He tugged away from Alanar, went and picked up the bag. He reached in, feeling the Diadem, the unclaimed gem. Aven's salt jar. And...

"The pearl is still here," he said. "Aven wouldn't have left this behind. Not today."

Alanar gulped audibly. "All right. What now? We need to get to shelter."

Owyn closed his eyes, trying to think. Trying not to panic. They were gone. They'd been taken.

He had to find them.

Which meant...

"We need to get out of here," he said, opening his eyes. "We need to get away." He went to his dresser, taking his book from on top and shoving it into his bag. He opened the map that Rhexa had given him and studied it for a moment, then nodded and put it into the bag as well. Then he slung the bag over his shoulder and started picking up other things. His whip chain. His smoke blades. "Alanar, do you mind wearing something on your back?" he asked.

"What?"

"Aven's swords. He wears them on a harness on his back. Can you wear them? I can't carry them and my blades, and Treesi's the wrong size for the harness."

"All right," Alanar said slowly. "And then what?"

"Treesi, go look in Aria's room for her crossbows," Owyn said. He grabbed the harness for Aven's swords and brought it to Alanar. "And there should be javelins, too."

"Right. Anything else?" Treesi asked. "And what should I put them in?"

"Take Aven's bag," Owyn answered without looking away from Alanar. He strapped the harness on to the healer, then sheathed the swords. By the time he was done, Treesi was back, Aven's bag bulging with her burden.

"Now what?" she asked.

"Now, we have to go to the lowest level," Owyn answered. "And I need you to trust me." He looked at Treesi, then up at Alanar. "All our lives might count on this. But especially Aven and Aria's. Alanar... I think what's happening with them is what happened to Virrik. And to a lot of other healers here. I think they've been taken."

Alanar went pale. "You think Virrik was *taken*? Taken by who?" He shook his head. "That's impossible. Who would do something like that?"

"I think he was," Owyn said. "And I don't know. Not for sure. I was trying to help Rhexa prove it. I didn't..." He paused. "I didn't want to say anything until I knew. But there's no time left. We have to go. Now."

"Where are we going?" Alanar asked as they headed out into the wind. Owyn took his hand, looked up and down the empty street, then started toward the lower terraces.

"Someplace safe," he answered. He didn't voice the last words — *I hope*. If he had, he'd have unleashed the panic that went with them.

They were supposed to have been safe here. Memfis had told them that. But he'd been wrong.

Rhexa had tried to keep them safe. She'd failed.

Now it was up to him. He needed to get Alanar and Treesi to safety. Then he would find Aria and Aven.

Then... he wasn't quite certain what would happen once his Heir and his Water were safe. But there was one thing he knew in his bones.

He was going to be adding another tally-mark to his kill list.

"WHERE ARE WE GOING?" Treesi demanded. She stopped, digging her heels in when Owyn would have kept moving forward. Alanar stopped walking. Then Owyn stopped, looking back at her. "No. Not another step until you tell me where we're going. We can't go any farther. North is blocked—"

"It isn't," Owyn interrupted. He glanced nervously at the seawall, then looked back at her. "There's a way down. I have a map. And Marik... well, we'll worry about him when he catches up with us." He looked at the seawall again. "But we need to go now, Treesi. We can't wait."

"Where are we going?" Alanar repeated Treesi's question.

Owyn scowled, then nodded. "There are tunnels, ones that Risha thinks are blocked. But there's a way out of Terraces down there. A safe way out. Rhexa has been taking people out that way.

She was going to take Virrik out that way, but he wouldn't go. He wouldn't leave. He thought she was wrong."

Alanar frowned. "Stop that," he said, his voice barely audible over the wind. "Stop using his name to goad me along."

"I'm not!" Owyn protested. "I'm telling you the truth!" He looked at Treesi, and she suddenly realized just how frightened he was. She rested her hand on his arm, shivering when she felt his racing heartbeat. How could Alanar not notice?

"We don't have time to argue about this," Owyn continued. "We need to get out of the storm. We need to get to safety—"

"Then we should go to the healing complex," Alanar said. "It's safe there—"

"No, it isn't!" Owyn snapped. "Look. I said I didn't know who was doing this. But I think it's Risha. I think Risha is behind this. She's behind all of this. She's been getting rid of stronger healers, and she's been doing something to the mixed bloods. Making them disappear. Killing them, maybe. And we need to go this way before she finds us and kills us, too." He looked around. "Alanar, I promised Rhexa I'd get you to safety if we had to run. I *promised*. I'm not leaving you here to die. I can't." His heart-rate spiked, and Treesi could feel how close he was to panic before he added, "You're all I have left!"

"Alanar, we have to go with him," Treesi said. She turned to look up at Alanar, and saw movement past him, on the stairs coming down from the higher terraces. Guards, four of them, pointing and shouting.

Mannon's guards.

Owyn saw them, too. He dropped his smoke blades and pulled free of Alanar's hand, tugging a length of chain from the pouch at his belt as he raced to meet the guards.

"What's happening?" Alanar demanded.

"Guards!" Treesi answered, grabbing his arm. "Mannon's guards. Alanar, he's right! He's right and you know it! So stop arguing with him and listen!"

"Guards?" Alanar repeated. "But... where's Owyn?"

"He's..." She turned to look, saw Owyn whip his arm around, saw one of the guards fall in a shower of blood. "Mother of us all!"

"What?" Alanar turned. "Treesi, what is it? What's happening?"

Treesi clung to Alanar's arm, watching as Owyn danced among the guards, the chain slicing through air and flesh with equal ease. "I've never seen anyone move like that," she said.

"Treesi!" Alanar growled. "What is *happening*?"

"He... he's fighting them off. He's killed two—" She stopped as a third guard fell. "Three of them. Alanar, he said he wasn't a warrior—"

The last guard fell, and Owyn stood for a moment, slowly letting the chain stop moving, then gathering it up. He came back toward them, breathing heavily. His clothes were splattered with blood. He bent and picked up his smoke blades, then met Treesi's eyes.

"Right," he snapped. "Mannon's guards are in Terraces. Do you believe me *now*?"

Alanar nodded. "Which way are we going?"

CHAPTER
TWENTY-NINE

IT TOOK BOTH OWYN AND Treesi to get Alanar over the rough ground and the fallen rocks to more level ground. By the time they had found some shelter from the wind, Alanar was shaking.

"That... can we not do that again?" he asked, laughing. "I mean... I know where I am, usually. But I also usually stay where the ground is level." He rested his hand on Owyn's shoulder. "Where are we?"

"Let me check the map," Owyn answered. He tugged the folded page out of his bag and opened it, holding it so that Treesi could see. "We were here, see? We came over the rockfall here, and around. That means we're in this cave, and we need to get around that way." He traced a line with his finger, then folded the map and put it away. "I'm not sure how rough it will be, and I don't know how much time we have before that storm hits. We need to hurry."

"Leave me here."

Owyn blinked, then stared at Alanar. "I'm sorry? Did you just say to leave you here?"

"Allie, stop being stupid," Treesi added. "We're not leaving you."

"I'm only going to slow you down," Alanar said. "Leave me here. I'm sheltered, and you can come back for me later."

"What?" Owyn gasped. "No! No, we're not leaving you behind."

Alanar turned toward him and smiled. "Owyn, you can't afford to be sentimental. I'll be safe here. No one knows I'm here. And I don't know where you're going, so even if someone does find me, I can't tell them anything. Leave me here. Come back for me later."

"Stop that," Owyn snapped. "I am not leaving you behind." He got to his feet and looked around. "Treesi, help me with this idiot, will you? We need to move."

Treesi got up and took Alanar by one arm, and Owyn took the other. It took both of them to get Alanar to his feet, but he still protested, and finally shook them off.

"Stop it, the both of you!" he snapped. "I'm not going to be of any use to you! I'll only slow you down. So leave me here."

Owyn glanced at Treesi, then looked back at Alanar. "No," he said firmly. "I'm not leaving you here. If they find you, they'll kill you. You're coming with me if I have to knock you over the head and drag you by the hair." He scowled, then reached out, grabbed the front of Alanar's shirt, and pulled him down, kissing him hard on the lips. "I love you, you fuckheaded idiot. Now move."

Alanar looked startled. "I... you *what*? Owyn, now who's being stupid?"

"Still you, last I checked," Owyn answered. He took Alanar's arm again and pulled him forward. "Come on. I'm not leaving you, and I really don't want to drag you. I like your hair the way it is."

"Treesi, has he gone insane?" Alanar asked.

Treesi looked at Owyn, then took Alanar's other arm. "I think he's the sanest one of us. Sanest? Most sane? Which is right?"

"Doesn't matter," Owyn said. "Let's go."

He tugged Alanar after him out of the cave and back into the wind. As they came around the cave wall, he stopped walking. He could see out over the water, where columns were rising up out of the sea.

"What is that?" he gasped, pointing with his smoke blades. "Those things. What the fuck are those?"

"Water spouts," Treesi shouted. "Tornadoes over water. As long as they stay out there, we're fine."

"But the Water tribe isn't," Owyn shouted back.

"They go deep when there are storms like this," Alanar shouted over the wind. "Virrik told me. They're safe. We're not. Where are we going?"

Owyn tore his gaze from the undulating towers of wind and water and led them the way that the map had directed him, carefully guiding Alanar over rocky areas, winding their way through the rockfall until they reached a cave half hidden by rocks and a fallen tree. He led them inside, and realized immediately that they had a problem.

The inside of the cave was as dark as pitch, and he had no torch.

"Owyn, where do we go from here?" Treesi asked. Owyn nodded toward the darkness.

"That way. But... I don't know how we're not going to get lost." He tugged the map out and shook his head. "There's no instructions from this point. Rhexa said Marik would lead us, but we can't wait for him. But... we also can't go without him."

"What's wrong?" Alanar asked.

Owyn shoved the map back into his bag. "No directions from here, and no light—" His voice trailed off as Alanar laughed. "What?"

"You don't need a light," Alanar said. "I can lead from here."

"Allie?" Treesi said. "How? You've never been here. I know you've never been here."

"But I always know where I am," Alanar answered, his smile bright in the dim light. He laughed again. "And here I thought that I was useless."

"The only one who ever said you were useless was you," Treesi replied. "You won't walk into any walls, but how are you going to know which way to turn?"

"I'll know," Alanar said. He sounded so confident that Owyn believed him. Almost. But they didn't really have a choice — another thunderclap, loud enough that Treesi squeaked in surprise and grabbed Owyn's arm.

"We can't just stand here," Owyn said. "Alanar, you're in charge."

Alanar held his hands out. "Don't let go," he said. Once he had Owyn and Treesi's hands, he started walking, leading them into the darkness.

Owyn had never liked the dark. He'd learned young that things happened in the dark. There were threats hiding in the dark, and a smart boy, not to mention one who wanted to survive the night, avoided areas of total darkness. He wasn't as bad as Aven. He knew that. But he couldn't imagine ever getting Aven down into these tunnels while the Waterborn was awake. If it wasn't for Alanar's hand in his, and the soft weight of Trinket in his pocket, Owyn would wonder if he really existed.

"These tunnels are remarkably level," Alanar said softly. "I haven't stubbed my toes or tripped on anything since we started."

"Can we talk, while we walk?" Owyn asked. "Or would it distract you?"

"Are you all right?" Treesi asked. "Owyn, you don't sound all right."

"I'm not," Owyn admitted. Alanar squeezed his fingers. "I... I don't like the dark."

"We can go back," Alanar offered. "We can go and wait for Marik."

"No," Owyn answered. "No, we need to keep going. We don't know if Marik is coming."

"He's right," Treesi said. "Allie, which way?"

Alanar stopped walking. He didn't answer, and they stood silent in the dark for a long moment. Then he tugged on Owyn's hand. "There's a left branch up ahead. That's our way."

As they walked, the ground underneath their feet sloped downward sharply, and Owyn slipped. He tried to hold on to Alanar's hand, but it slipped from his grasp as he tumbled into the darkness. He lost his smoke blades almost immediately, and curled up to try and protect his head and Trinket. The long, dizzying tumble ended abruptly, as he slammed into a wall, hard enough that the pain nearly made him pass out. It was hard to tell if the world went dark when the world was already dark. He moaned, unable to move, hearing shouting through the rushing in his ears. He was still awake, then.

"Owyn!" Alanar shouted. "Owyn, can you hear me?"

It took Owyn a moment to draw in enough of a breath that he could answer. "I hear you," he croaked. Then he whimpered, as the weight of the darkness settled over him. "I don't know where I am!"

"I'm coming, Owyn!" Alanar called back. "We're both coming. We have to go slow. Talk to me. Are you hurt?"

"I hurt," Owyn said. "But I'm not sure how much I'm hurt."

"That doesn't make any sense!"

Alanar sounded far away, and worried, and Owyn tried to sit up. Pain shot through him, and he gave up. How badly *was* he hurt?

Badly enough that he was seeing things, he decided.

"Alanar, I'm hurt enough that I'm seeing things!" he called. "There's a light—"

"You're not seeing things," Treesi sounded excited. "I see it too!"

"Don't move, Owyn. We're coming," Alanar added. "Keep talking."

"Is Trinket all right?" Treesi asked.

Owyn touched his pocket, felt the fire mouse shifting around. "Yeah," he answered. "Better than me, I think." He blinked, peering into the not-quite as inky darkness. "The light is getting bigger."

"Who's there?" Alanar shouted. "Can you hear us? We need help!"

"We're coming!" a woman called back, her voice a faint echo through the tunnels.

"Owyn, keep talking," Treesi urged. "We know you're here, but if you don't talk, we can't find you."

"No, no, no," Owyn sputtered. "You need to find me. You can't leave me alone in the dark. Come find me. I don't want to be lost down here all alone. Well, all alone except for Trinket but she doesn't talk back when you talk to her and you need to find me right fucking now." He shifted, and yelped as pain lanced up and down his legs. "Shit. I did something. I hurt my back. Alanar, I hurt my back. I can't move. It hurts."

"I'm coming, Owyn," Alanar said, sounding much closer. "I'm coming."

Owyn heard a pebble skitter past him, then the scrape of a footstep on the rock. "Treesi?" he gasped. "Alanar?"

"Allie, I've got him," Treesi said. He heard her as she knelt down next to him, and her hand was warm on his face as she found his cheek. "We've got you, Owyn."

More hands touched him, as Alanar settled next to him. "We've got you," he echoed. His hand shifted to the back of Owyn's neck, and Owyn felt warm. "You'll be fine," Alanar said gently. "You didn't break anything."

"I can't move—"

"You wrenched the muscles pretty badly when you hit, it looks like," Alanar said. He started to stroke Owyn's neck. "You'll be fine. I'll need to put you under to work on it. Once whoever is coming gets here." He raised his voice. "I hope you have a litter! Our friend shouldn't move."

"We have one," the woman called back. "We'll be there shortly."

Owyn relaxed slowly as Alanar petted him, touching his pocket once more to check on Trinket. "My blades," he murmured. "I lost them when I fell."

"The woman, she has a torch. And apparently, friends," Treesi said. "We'll find the blades." She ran her hand down Owyn's leg. "Where did you learn to fight like that? With a chain?"

"Memfis taught me," Owyn answered. "It's a traditional Fire weapon. And it's a bit like smoke dancing, so I wasn't learning two different things."

"I wish I could see you dance," Alanar said softly. "You must be amazing to watch."

Owyn fumbled in the dark and rested his hand on Alanar's leg. "I wish you could see, too. I need to, you know. I need to go hunting visions. See if that can help me with finding Aven and Aria."

"Once we're safe and you're not hurting anymore," Treesi said.

Owyn turned his head, seeing the distant light. It was definitely larger, large enough that he could see that it was more than one light. They came closer, separating until there were four separate beacons of light coming closer. Until he could clearly see the torch-bearers and their companions — there were eight people in all, and all of them wore healer white. There were five men, and three women. One of the women was at the front of the group, holding one of the torches.

"That... no, that can't be!" Treesi gasped as they came closer.

Alanar's hand tensed on Owyn's neck. "What? Treesi, what is it?"

Treesi didn't have a chance to answer before the woman reached them. She passed her torch to the woman standing next to her, and knelt next to Owyn. This close, he could see that she was older — perhaps halfway between Rhexa and Meris in age. Her white hair was pulled back tightly, and the angles of her face looked familiar. She smiled, and he almost had it....

"Well, you've done yourself a world of hurt, haven't you?" she said. She rested her hand on his chest, then arched a brow. "Fire mouse in your pocket?"

"You can tell?" Owyn asked, feeling warmth filling him, and pain receding. "Yeah. I'm—"

"Owyn. Yes, I know. Rhexa described you quite well. My name is Pirit—"

"What?" Alanar yelped. "But, you *died*!"

She smiled, and Owyn saw the resemblance again. "Clearly, I didn't. You've grown, Alanar. And Treesi. I've had glowing reports about both of you. Where's Marik?"

"He never caught up with us," Owyn answered. "We did the best we could—"

"Which is what led you down the left hand path?" Pirit asked. "The right hand is less direct, but more even. Marik would have known that. How you even found your way without a torch—"

"What does a blind man need with a torch?" Alanar asked. Pirit glanced at him, then smiled.

"You used your Air sense? Very clever," she said. She looked back at Owyn, then her eyes narrowed. "Where are the Heir and my grandson?"

"Taken," Owyn answered, blinking. The warmth was making it hard for him to think. "Risha took them. Think it was Risha. Need to find them. Need to find my smoke blades. I dropped them when I fell."

"We'll find them," Pirit said. She patted his chest and slowly got to her feet. "He'll be asleep in a moment. Get him onto the litter and back to the lair. Dumfry, see if you can find his blades. Aristi, go with him."

Owyn wanted to protest, wanted to say that he didn't want to sleep. Not yet! But the weight of the warmth in his bones said otherwise.

TREESI FELT OWYN SLIP into the healing trance, and looked up at Pirit. "You were supposed to be dead," she said as she got to her feet. "You were supposed to have died when the healing center was attacked."

Pirit didn't answer until Owyn had been gently moved onto a litter, and had been picked up. Then she held her hand out to Treesi. "Walk with me, children. I'll show you the way through the tunnels."

"We're neither of us children anymore," Alanar said. He joined Treesi, and arched a brow when Pirit took his hand.

"I forgot you were so tall, Alanar," Pirit said, starting to walk. "And no, you're not children. You're wearing gray — she hasn't named you a full healer *yet*?"

"I'm not ready—" Alanar started to answer. Pirit snorted.

"You were almost ready four years ago. I can't imagine you haven't advanced since then. If you continued the way I'd have expected, you should have been a full healer three years ago. And Treesi?"

"Not yet," Treesi admitted. "I'm slow. You know about me and reading."

"I remember. But you should still have advanced by now." Pirit frowned slightly. "How many healers has she named since I went into hiding?"

Treesi frowned, thinking. "Ah... three? And they all left... but no. They didn't really leave, did they?"

Pirit sighed. "One did. He's here. The other two? No, they didn't. What do you know?"

"Not much," Alanar answered. "Just... Owyn says that he thinks Risha is behind the disappearances. That Risha is the one who took my Virrik away."

Pirit sighed. "She is. She's in Mannon's pocket, and has been the whole time. She's remarkable at hiding her true loyalties. I never saw what she was really was until it was too late. And Virrik — Rhexa tried to get him out. She told me she was worried that he would be next. He was too good a healer, and too vocal in his opinions—"

Alanar chuckled. "He was that."

"He'd have been able to challenge Risha, and win. When he vanished, I hoped that he'd gotten away on his own."

"He's dead," Alanar said, his voice clipped.

Pirit stopped. "What?"

"Aven and Owyn and Aria. They told us," Treesi said. "They found his body in a cove south of here. He'd been there for a while, Aven said. He said he brought Virrik back to the deep."

"Mother of us all," Pirit breathed. "Alanar, I'm so sorry."

"Why?" Alanar asked softly. "Why do this? Why kill him? Or anyone? She's a healer—"

"That doesn't make her a good person," Pirit said. "No matter how much we want to think she is. Or how hard we wanted her to change." Pirit was silent for a moment as they walked. "She came to me half-trained. She was pure Earth, from a long line of pure Earth healers. Her mother line traces all the way back to the first Earth

Healer, or so they claim." She sniffed. "I didn't realize what else they were teaching her until she met her first Waterborn healing instructor. She refused to learn from him. She told me that the animal tribes were an affront to the Mother. I should have sent her home that day. Instead, I tried to bring her out of her ignorance." She stopped, turned around. "There's someone coming. Garrity!"

The closest man came trotting back to them, his torch flame snapping as he ran. "Senior Healer?"

"There's someone coming," Pirit said.

"I'll check." He turned and whistled, and another man came and joined them. Garrity looked back at them and smiled at Treesi. "Healer, may I give you my torch?"

"I'm not a healer yet, but yes, please," Treesi said. Garrity nodded and handed the torch to her, then he and the other man headed off back the way they'd come. Pirit watched them go, then started walking again.

"I thought I could reach her," she continued. "I tried to be gentle with her. I pointed out that all of the tribes were born from the dreams of the Mother, and that we were all Her children. I reminded her of Liara, and of Abin, and that Alaine, the Firstborn of Firstborn Axia was a daughter of Water. I should have known better. There are some people you just can't teach. She didn't learn anything from it, except how to hide her bigotry and her hatred." She sighed. "Do you know why the Purges came?"

Treesi frowned, looked at Alanar to see the same expression on his face.

"If you're asking that question," he said slowly. "Then the answer isn't the reason we've been taught, about the purges being because of the rebellion."

Pirit laughed. "You learned too well from me," she answered. "No, the reason wasn't because of the rebellion. It was because I discovered what Risha was doing." She hesitated, and Treesi saw her glance toward Alanar. "I think you may have planted the seeds, Alanar. All unknowing."

"Me?" Alanar sputtered. "Why? What did I do?"

"She was the attending healer after the fire. She was the one who saved your life."

Alanar looked startled. "I didn't know that," he said. Then his jaw dropped. "That means—"

"She's the one who took your wings," Pirit finished. "You were, I think, the first. And the only one whom there was legitimate cause to do so. When I finally discovered what she'd been doing, there were dozens more just like you. She orchestrated the destruction of the healing centers because I was going to have her arrested and sent to Mannon to be tried for her crimes against Air and Water."

Treesi swallowed, suddenly cold. "Senior Healer, she has Aria and Aven. She's going to take Aria's wings. What will she do to Aven?"

Pirit was silent for a moment, then shook her head. "I don't know. We've never found any of her Water victims. We don't know what she's done to them."

"Owyn knows," Alanar said.

"Then when he wakes, I will ask Owyn. For now—" she stopped, turning as someone behind them called her name.

"Garrity?"

"We need you, Pirit!" he shouted. "It's Marik!"

CHAPTER THIRTY

OWYN JERKED AWAKE, looking around. He was lying on a narrow cot in a small room, and Alanar dozed in a chair at the foot of the bed. Treesi was nowhere to be seen.

Owyn sat up, wincing slightly as his muscles protested. It wasn't nearly as bad as it had been — now it was closer to the pain he'd have felt the day after he had lifted too much weight at the forge. He'd be able to dance... if someone had found his blades. He shifted down to the edge of the bed and poked Alanar in the arm. "Hey, wake up."

Alanar jumped, and Owyn saw Trinket dart into the front of Alanar's shirt. "What?" Alanar sputtered. "Wh... Owyn?"

"Yeah," Owyn answered. "Sorry. I didn't mean to scare you." He looked around. "Where are we? And... was I dreaming? Was that really Aven's grandmother?"

Alanar nodded. Then, surprisingly, he burst out laughing. "Hey, stop that!" he said, and reached into his shirt. Owyn chuckled.

"Didn't realize that you were ticklish." He walked over to stand in front of Alanar, so close their knees touched. "Trinket, stop tickling. He doesn't like it. Come on out. It's just me."

The fire mouse poked her nose out of Alanar's shirt, her whiskers twitching at Owyn. He laughed. "I'm sorry! Look, I'll find a... well, I don't know what sort of treat I can find for you. But I'll find you one. Deal?"

The mouse jumped out of Alanar's shirt and ran out his leg, standing up on her hind feet and chittering at Owyn. He grinned and picked her up, letting her climb back into his shirt pocket.

"Do you understand her, or is it just fancy?" Alanar asked.

"I think we understand each other," Owyn answered. He moved a little closer. "Mind if I kiss you?"

Alanar smiled, tipping his head back. "I was wondering if you were going to ask."

Owyn leaned down and took Alanar's face between his hands, kissing him gently. Alanar hummed softly as Owyn let him go.

"Maybe next time, I'll let you top me. I want to see what you can come up with," he murmured.

"Let's make sure we have a chance for a safe next time, hm?" Owyn answered. "What have I missed?"

Alanar took a deep breath. "Sit down."

Owyn sat, and Alanar took another deep breath. "After Pirit put you under, she heard something, and sent men back along our trail. And they found Marik."

"He followed us?"

"Escaped is more like it. He was half dead, Owyn. He'd been beaten, pretty badly," Alanar paused, then shook his head. "He told us it was Teva. Teva had invited him over for the night, and... you know Teva liked tying people? Like I do?"

"Yeah, he mentioned it to me," Owyn said slowly.

"Once he had Marik secure, he beat the shit out of him and left him. Then he left, and Marik says he thinks that Teva went and shot the owls watching the house. He isn't sure, but he felt them die."

Owyn closed his eyes. His stomach was churning. "Teva... he wanted me in his bed. He... he was our *friend*. He wanted to be a Companion!"

"Somehow, I think Marik would disagree with Teva being your friend. He's pretty upset — they'd been on-again, off-again lovers since the both of them were old enough. He's wondering how he never saw the truth about how Teva really felt about him."

Owyn sighed. "It's not his fault."

"I know. And you know. But he's pretty raw right now," Alanar said. He rolled his shoulders, then dragged his fingers through his hair. "Treesi is with Pirit, who's raising her army—"

"Her what now?" Owyn sat up. "She has a what?"

"An army. She's been building it since before Risha betrayed the tribe. And it's time to strike now, while there's still a chance of saving Aria and Aven." He grimaced. "But we're not sure where Risha would have hidden them."

"Then it's my turn to contribute something," Owyn said. He got up and stretched, feeling the pull and ache of his sore muscles. "Did they find my smoke blades?"

"Pirit said that they were still looking, but if they can't find yours, they have another set."

Owyn frowned. "Where would they have gotten another set of smoke blades?" he asked. Then he coughed. "Oh, fuck. Where are they?"

"The blades? Or Pirit and the others?"

"Both."

Alanar got to his feet and led Owyn out of the room, which turned out to be one of several cell-like dormitories in a long, narrow building. Outside, the walkways were lit by torches, and Owyn wondered when it had gotten so dark. When the storm had blown over? He couldn't have been asleep that long. He looked up and realized that they were inside an enormous bubble cave.

"Fuck me," he breathed.

"I thought you wanted to wait?" Alanar murmured, and Owyn burst out laughing.

"We're still underground. This is incredible!" Owyn said, tipping his head back. He couldn't see the top of the cave at all. It

was larger than the Heart of the Tribe underneath Forge. Which...
"Aren't caves like this only around volcanoes?" he asked. "I mean,
we have them under Forge. The Council meets in one. But we're
right on the Smoking Mountain. We're nowhere near a volcano
right now, are we?"

"Maybe there was one underwater?" Alanar suggested. "But I
don't know. Not for certain. And it doesn't matter right now. Pirit
said anyone we saw would be able to take us to her workroom. See
anyone?"

Owyn looked around, and saw a familiar face. "Treesi!"

Treesi turned when she heard her name, squealed, "Owyn!"
and ran to them, throwing her arms around Owyn's neck and
kissing him deeply enough that time seemed to stop. When she
finally broke the kiss, she didn't let him go, drawing back only far
enough that she could talk.

"I was worried about you. When they brought us to see you
and you were so quiet... and then I couldn't stay and wait for you to
wake up."

"He's fine, Tree," Alanar said.

"Although, if I said I wasn't, would you kiss me like that again?"
Owyn added. Treesi laughed.

"I'll kiss you like that again if you don't get hurt, all right?" she
said. She unwound her arms from his neck and slipped her hand
into his. "Come with me. Pirit has questions before she starts giving
orders. And Rhexa is here."

"She is?" Owyn immediately looked around.

"She's with Pirit. But worried about you." Treesi bit her lip.
"Owyn, Pirit has questions. Uncomfortable ones."

Owyn blinked. "About what?"

"About the cove, and what you found there." Treesi started
walking, and pointed with her free hand at another long, narrow
building. "There. She already said that we don't have to stay—"

"I want to," Alanar said. "I want to know."

Owyn looked up at Alanar. "Are you sure?"

Alanar nodded. "I'm sure. I deserve to know, I think."

Owyn took a deep breath. "All right."

They walked in silence to the building, and Treesi knocked on the door. It opened and Pirit smiled at them from inside.

"They're here," she said, and stepped out of the way. Treesi led them inside, and Owyn heard his name.

"Owyn!" Rhexa cried, and rushed over to hug him. She stepped back, studied him for a moment, then hugged him again. "You're all right. I was so worried!"

"I'm fine. We got out," he said. "Aria and Aven didn't. They're taken. And I need my smoke blades." He turned to face Pirit. "Treesi said you were looking for mine, but that you have another set. Where did you get them?"

"They were found in the caves."

Owyn nodded. "I thought you were going to say that. Can I see them? I mean... may I? May I see them?"

Pirit gestured toward a long shelf set into the wall. Owyn saw the blades sitting there, and knew them immediately. He still made himself walk across the room. Pick up the blades that he knew as well as he knew his own hands.

"These are Memfis' blades," he said softly. "Did you know?"

"I suspected," Rhexa said. "Pirit showed them to me when I got here, and asked if I knew where they'd come from. It was all I could think of."

"He's been taken, too, then," Owyn said. He turned to look at her, and a weak laugh bubbled out of him. "That's a relief, actually."

"A relief?" Pirit asked. "Why?"

"Because the other alternative was that he abandoned me," Owyn answered. "That he gave up on me."

"Oh, Owyn," Rhexa breathed. "We'll find him."

Owyn nodded, swallowed around the lump in his throat. "I can dance with these, but they're really too heavy for me. Do you think they'll find mine?"

"I'll see what's been found. For now, would you tell us what you found in the cove?" Pirit waved Owyn toward a chair. "Sit, please. I know this will be unpleasant—"

"It won't be as specific as you might want it to be," Owyn said as he sat down. "I didn't really look. I just know what Aven told me. What he told us later. Auntie, he told you, didn't he?"

"Yes," Rhexa said. She took the chair next to Owyn. Then she looked up, smiled, and rose, moving around the table to sit facing him. Alanar took her empty chair, and Treesi sat in the chair on Owyn's other side. Owyn glanced at Alanar, then reached out and covered his hand.

"We were looking to see if the tidal pool in the cave was deep enough for Aven to sleep underwater. We... we smelled him before we saw him. And... then we saw it. Saw him." He looked at Alanar again, then looked away and closed his eyes. "There were parts of his skull visible. That's how we saw him. He'd been there for a while, and the animals... well, best not to finish that. Aven recognized his family tattoos. That's how we knew his canoe. We're not sure how he died, but he was dead when he hit the water, Aven said. Because he wasn't changed. He had legs." He shifted his grip on Alanar's shaking hand. "Something had broken his bones. Torn his legs up from the inside. Aven said his hips were completely destroyed. And that he'd never walk again. He didn't have any idea what would have done something like that."

Next to him, he heard a moan. He turned and saw the tears streaming down Alanar's face, and was up and out of his chair in a heartbeat. He wrapped his arms around Alanar and held him. "I'm sorry," he whispered into Alanar's hair. "I'm sorry."

"Thank you, Owyn," Pirit said, her voice quiet and somewhat heavy. "I... we'll stop her. We'll stop this." She sighed, and Owyn saw her rub her finger down the bridge of her nose, and he realized that what he'd just described was what was going to happen to Aven if they didn't find him soon.

Or was it too late?

Only one way to know. He kissed the top of Alanar's head, then straightened. "I need my smoke blades," he said, his voice oddly firm for as shaky as he felt. "I need to see what I can see."

Pirit got to her feet. "Let's go see if they've found anything." She spoke quietly to Rhexa for a moment, then came around the table and gestured for Owyn to go with her. They were almost to the door before he realized that no one was following them, and he looked back to see Rhexa and Treesi were seeing to Alanar.

"We can stay, if you like," Pirit said softly. Owyn considered it for a moment, then shook his head.

"No," he answered. "I can't help him right now. And we need to find Aven before the same thing happens to him." He looked up at Pirit. "Where are we going?"

"To see if they've found your blades," Pirit answered. "What will you need, other than that?"

"A place to dance," Owyn answered. "Big, flat, maybe ten feet by ten feet?"

"Larger will work? We have a practice field."

"That will be perfect," Owyn said. He looked up. "And I'll need something to eat after—"

"To ground. I did know that," Pirit said. "One of my partners was a Smoke Dancer. Probably before you were born, though. Regardless, I do remember the care and feeding of Dancers. I'll make certain that you have what you need after. But all Dancers are different on what they want before."

"I just need a space," Owyn said. "And my blades. I'm not fussy." He looked around as a cool, damp draft tickled the back of his neck. "There's a breeze, but we're inside. How?"

Pirit chuckled. "There are chimneys in the roof of the cave. With the storm outside, there are areas where the caves sound like flutes."

Owyn stared at her. "I'd like to see that. Hear that. When we're done and everyone is safe." He looked around. "We need to hurry. I'm not sure how long Risha's had them." He frowned. How long was too long?

"And she's had more than enough practice in amputating wings," Pirit muttered.

"She's *what*?" Owyn had never heard himself go quite that shrill before. "No! Nononono. She can't take Aria's wings!" He sputtered for a moment, near incoherent. Then he met Pirit's eyes. "She's a Smoke Dancer. Like her father. Like me. She's had her waking vision. But she doesn't dance with blades. She dances on air. We can't let Risha take her wings!"

Pirit paled. "I didn't know," she whispered. "No one told me!" She looked around. "Evarra, tell me you found the smoke blades!"

"I was just coming to find you," the young woman answered. "I came on ahead. We have them."

"Bring them to the practice field. We'll meet you there."

The woman nodded and sprinted back off the way she'd come. Pirit looked at Owyn and sighed.

"This way."

THE PRACTICE FIELD was large, enclosed by a rail fence. The ground was level, raked sand, and it was about four times what Owyn needed. He walked around inside while they waited for his blades, then nodded and joined Pirit at the fence and started taking off his boots.

"I'll need something to write things down with," he said, looking up. "To record the visions."

"I'll send someone for paper and a pen and ink. How long will you dance?"

"Charcoal would be better." He set his boots side by side next to the fence post and stood up. "And I'll dance until I have an answer." He turned, seeing Evarra coming back toward them, his smoke blades cradled in her arms.

"Sorry I took so long," she said as she reached them. "I was afraid that if I dropped them, they'd break. They're beautiful."

Owyn smiled and reached out to take the blades from her. "Thank you," he said. "For finding them."

She smiled, then bit her lip. "May I watch?"

"You might have a bit of an audience, Owyn," Pirit added. Owyn shrugged.

"As long as they don't get in my way or try to distract me, I'll be fine." He walked out to the center of the field, feeling the sand under his feet. Remembering the last time he'd danced on sand, on the beach. He stopped, closed his eyes. Took his first breath. His second breath. He could feel the stillness creeping in around the edges. But there was an urgency to it that had never been there before.

The third breath, and he started to flow into the dance, his blades moving in patterns that were older than time. And just like on the beach, the visions rose to meet him.

Memfis. Alive, but in chains, staring out the window of a room that reminded Owyn of one of the sitting rooms in Meris' house in Forge. There was a tray of food on the table behind him... and a half-empty bottle next to it.

A bearded man that he didn't know, sitting on a cot in a tiny, dirty room. Another prisoner. Someone important, but who?

The beautiful blond whom Aven had called Del. He was bundled up against the storm, and was walking behind a taller, heavy man. Through the rain, Owyn recognized the streets as they walked toward the healing complex.

Aria! She was lying face down on a table in what looked like a surgical room in the healing complex. There were straps holding her in place. She wasn't moving, and her eyes were closed. Her wings were intact.

Finally, finally, he saw Aven, and almost fell out of the vision. Aven, chained with his wrists above his head, in water that was almost to his chin. There were blood streaks down his arms, and he wasn't moving — he must have been chained in place below the water. He was... singing? His voice sounded rough. No, no, he was chanting, and Owyn remembered Aven saying that the Water tribe had honor chants for the dead. Who had died? Then Aven stopped, in the middle of a word. His eyes closed, and his face went deathly pale. He opened his mouth to scream... and no sound came out.

Owyn opened his eyes to find himself kneeling in the middle of the sandy yard. He swallowed and pushed himself up to his feet, only to find Pirit already standing there, holding out an apple. Owyn grabbed it, took a bite, and almost choked as he tried to swallow it whole.

"What did you see?" Pirit asked.

Owyn swallowed, then met her eyes. "I know what they did to Virrik. And it's killing Aven. We need to find him. Right now."

AVEN'S THROAT WAS SORE. He'd tried screaming for help, but no one had come. Now, he focused on the discomfort, trying to use it as a shield against growing panic. He looked up at his hands again, at the blood drying on his forearms. He'd tried to force his hands through the manacles, but all he'd managed was savaging his wrists on the sharp metal. He wasn't sure what he'd have done if he had gotten his hands free — how would he have freed his ankles?

It didn't matter anymore. Not now. Even if he freed his hands, it was too late. The cold salt water had risen far more quickly than he'd expected, and was lapping at the base of his throat. He couldn't reach the chains on his ankles without submerging himself and starting the change. There was no way to stop this. No way to save himself.

And no one was coming to save him. Not this time.

Was this where he died? He wondered if he'd have seen this room, if he'd been gifted with Owyn's visions instead of the change?

No. If he'd been a Smoke Dancer, he wouldn't be here. Because Risha thought that the Fire tribe were human.

How many others were there, like Virrik? Like him? How many of his tribe had she murdered?

He swallowed. No one was going to sing the honor chants in his name, to tell the Mother to watch for him. No one was going to take him to the deep. He was going to die here, and be forgotten by the Mother.

He felt the water splash against the sides of this throat, and closed his eyes. Then he started to sing his own honor chant.

Perhaps the Mother would hear him.

CHAPTER THIRTY-ONE

PIRIT TOOK OWYN'S ARM and led him to the fence, then left him there before striding off and giving orders. Owyn leaned on the rails and cradled his right hand blade against his left arm, rubbing his face. He needed more food, and to think about what he'd seen. He needed....

"Fuck," he breathed, and turned. "Pirit!" She turned when he shouted her name. "Mannon. Mannon's in Terraces!"

She came back to the fence. "Are you sure?"

Owyn nodded. "He's got a slave. Del. Del is in Terraces—"

"Which means Mannon is in Terraces," Pirit finished. "Probably to collect the Heir." She turned, raising her voice as she walked away.

"I want the first assault team ready to move in five minutes! We rise now!"

Owyn closed his eyes, listening to her voice fade into the distance. Maybe there was still time to get to them. Maybe—

"Owyn?"

The voice was familiar, and Owyn looked up at Marik — his face still showed pale yellow bruises, and there was a bandage over his left eye. "Hey," Owyn said. "You don't look all that good. How do you feel?"

"Like shit," Marik answered. "Gran said you needed to eat. Come on. I've got food waiting, and the paper and charcoal you wanted. And Treesi and Alanar are waiting."

"Food is good. I need food," Owyn agreed. "And I need to record the visions." He staggered a little as he walked out of the field, feeling as if his legs were two different lengths. Marik took his arm to steady him, and started steering him toward the building where Owyn had left Alanar and Treesi.

"Do all Smoke Dancers act like they're drunk when they're done dancing?" Marik asked. "It's the first time I've seen it."

"Yeah, it's hard to get your head back in the real world," Owyn answered. "That's why we need to eat. Who's Gran? I haven't met anyone named Gran."

Marik laughed. "My grandmother, Owyn. Pirit."

Owyn turned, nearly knocking himself off his feet. "Pirit is your grandmother? Like Aven? That means you and Aven are cousins?"

"Yes and yes," Marik answered. "When I told Gran that the Heir was here and that Aven was with her, she told me to keep an eye on him, and not to say anything." He snorted. "I got one part right, at least."

"It wasn't your fault, Marik," Owyn said. "I mean, Teva was... was nice. I liked him. I might have fucked him. Maybe, once I knew him better."

"I don't think any of us knew Teva," Marik said, his voice low. Owyn heard the hurt in him as clear as a bell. "I never did."

"And that's all on him," Owyn insisted. "It's not your fault. You're not the first man to trust the wrong person." He snorted. "Believe me. I know that for a fact."

Marik nodded, and they walked in silence to the long building. Treesi met them at the door. Her clothes, Owyn noticed, were rumpled in a way they hadn't been before.

"Alanar is asleep," she said quietly. "Did you learn anything?"

"Things I'm not telling him," Owyn answered. "And things that might save Aria and Aven. Ah... Mannon's in Terraces. And Memfis is alive."

Treesi let out a long breath. "Oh, thank the Mother for small favors. We'll find them. Come inside and eat." She stepped out of the door and let them pass. On the table, Owyn saw a stack of paper, a bundle of charcoal sticks, and a lot of food.

"Sit down," Marik said. "You need to record the visions? You write, I'll put food in front of you."

"Good plan," Owyn agreed. He sat down and looked around. There was no one else in the room, but there was a door on the far side that he hadn't noticed before. Alanar must be in there. He nodded, then picked up a charcoal stick and went to work.

The drawings came quickly, and in order. Memfis, by the window. The stranger in the little room. Del, the hood of his cloak framing his face. Aria, on the table. And Aven, his face contorted. He drew, added details, noticed things that he'd missed when he danced the images the first time. And as he worked, food was put into his free hand. Bread smeared with soft cheese. A roll stuffed with meat. Another apple, cored and sliced. A cup of watered wine, which he refused, and which was replaced by a cup of sweet tea.

Finally, he sat up, putting down the charcoal and rubbing his hands over his face. His head felt hollow, and he had a pounding headache.

"Drink this."

Owyn looked up to see Pirit holding a cup out to him. He took it and sipped the contents, then made a face.

"What is that? Piss?"

"It's pickle brine," she answered, and sat down. "It's very good to help with dehydration. Which, if I'm remembering correctly, is something that can happen after an extended vision?" She cocked her head to the side. "Headache?"

"Yes. How long was I out there?"

"About three quarters of an hour." Pirit smiled. "Drink the piss, Owyn," she said. "The first and second assault teams are gone. The third wave will be leaving in five minutes. I'll be going with the last wave, but I wanted to see what else you've seen. May I?"

Owyn took another sip of the pickle brine and grimaced. "Go ahead."

"I thought you'd be writing things down," Pirit said as she picked up the closest drawing. "That's what Tivi did. My Smoke Dancer. I still have his journals. I didn't know that you'd be drawing them out. You're very good." She frowned over the picture of Aria. "Treesi, do you recognize this theater?"

"I haven't looked yet," Treesi said. She came over to stand behind Pirit. "Oh. I... Owyn, that's incredible. And no, I don't know that place."

"Neither do I," Pirit said. "We'll ask Rhexa. But I don't think this is one of the theaters in the healing complex." She frowned, then shook her head. "No, it can't have been. Not with the emergency sweeps they did for the storm evacuations. Someone would have found Aria. Which means that Risha has set herself up a workplace somewhere else." She picked up the drawing of the stranger, and her eyes widened. "Owyn, do you know who this is?"

Owyn shook his head, then winced and drained the cup of brine. "I've never seen him before. Do you know him?"

"I know him," Pirit said. She laid the picture down. "It's been a long time since I last saw him, but he hasn't changed all that much. This is my son Jhansri."

"That's Aven's fa?" Owyn craned his neck to look closer at the picture. "Yeah, I can see that. All right. Where is he?"

"Pirit, that looks like one of the solitary cells up in the green levels," Treesi said slowly.

Pirit looked up at her, then back down at the picture. She nodded. "We'll search there. And... I wonder if that's where this theater is, as well?" She touched the picture of Aria.

"Makes sense," Owyn said. "Where better to hide something you don't want people to find?"

"Someplace where you've made sure that no one else is allowed to go," Treesi answered. "What about this?" She touched the picture of Aven with one finger. "This is horrible."

"The room floods. Salt water. It triggers the change," Pirit said, her voice quiet. She glanced at the closed door. "His legs must be anchored, or he'd float. Mother of us all, no wonder we never found any of her victims. They'd be submerged for six hours, at least. They must have died in agony, all of them."

"We need to find him," Owyn said. He was impressed that his voice didn't shake. He looked around, saw Marik standing near the wall. "Marik, what are the tides like? When was this?"

Marik came over and looked at the picture. His visible eye widened. "That... shit. With the storms, we can't count on having a regular tidal flow. It'll come in faster, be deeper. This... this was probably almost high tide," he said. He pointed at the shading on the wall. "If this is what I think it is, that's the high water mark. So this happened hours ago. The tide is going out right now. It has been for a few hours."

Owyn's jaw dropped. "How... fuck. They must have taken Aven and Aria hours ago! This... how long does it take before the tide comes all the way in and goes all the way out?"

"What are you thinking?" Pirit asked.

"I see where he's going. They can't have gotten him into that position with water in the room," Marik murmured. "So they had to have brought him in when the tide was out. And that was last night... just after moonrise."

"So that's when they hit the house," Owyn said. "Because they had to have the timing right. And you said the tide is going out now. How long before that room is empty again?"

Marik frowned. He sat down in the chair across from Pirit. "Ah... two hours? Maybe?"

Pirit stood up. "All right. I'm taking the last wave up. And we'll sweep the green levels. Marik, where would that room be?"

"Down below," Marik answered. "The low caves, the ones that the Water tribe used for canoe storage and their fishery. That's probably what that room was — part of the fishery."

"Then you take a squad down into the caves and find him." Pirit turned toward the door. Owyn looked at Marik. Thought a moment. Then he got to his feet. "I'm coming with you," he called.

Pirit looked over her shoulder. "With me?"

"Aria called me her warrior. She's right." Owyn touched his belt, and the pouch that held his whip-chain. "I'm coming with you."

Pirit nodded. "Then come with me."

INSIDE THE HEALING complex, Del tossed his hood off and shook his head, wiping away the water running down his face. He wasn't entirely certain why they had been sent for, what was so important that they had come out in this storm. It had taken them twice as long as it should have to get here — the roads had been awash. Mannon had told him he could stay in the Palace, that he'd be safe. But Del knew that being alone was never safe. Riding all night through the storm was safer. Even though it meant having to see *her*.

She was waiting by the fountain in the lobby, her color high. Del knew that she'd been entertaining a fantasy for years that someday, Mannon would finally admit that he had been mistaken all these years. That he'd finally admit that he'd been desperately in love with her, and that no other woman had ever mattered to him.

He also knew that Mannon despised her. Only tolerated her because he would never have won the Earth tribe lands without her.

"There had better be a good reason for you to send for me in this weather, Risha," Mannon growled. "I've never seen a storm like this."

"It will pass," Risha said, waving one hand dismissively. She ignored Del. "I have her."

"Her?" Mannon repeated. "You have the Heir?"

"Tucked away, waiting for you," Risha said with a smile. "I've been busy with the storm. Rhexa's vanished, the bitch. I'm doing her job and mine, so I'm not quite ready to hand the Heir over, but it won't be long."

"Not ready?" Mannon repeated. His eyes widened. "You bitch. You were going to take her wings! And after I told you I wanted her unharmed!" He glanced back at Del, then turned on Risha. "What about her Water? Where's Aven?"

"Unimportant," Risha said. "And honestly, it won't hurt her. I've perfected the technique. There will barely be a scar—" Her voice choked off as Mannon grabbed her by the throat, moving so fast that Del was caught off guard.

"I told you unharmed. Don't try and tell me that taking her wings won't hurt her. I told you years ago that you were not to go forward with these experiments, Risha. If you're saying you perfected the technique, that means you disobeyed a direct order." He shoved Risha away, and she gasped and panted for a moment.

"I did as I thought best!" she wheezed

"You're a monster," Mannon snapped. "I want her intact, Risha. Now. And I want Aven. Intact. Now."

"You can't have him," she answered. "I'm so close—"

"You really think you can tell me no? Woman, you are going to take me to my nephew now." Mannon's voice was low, quiet, and Del instinctively took a step back. Mannon saw him move, looked at him, and shook his head. Del swallowed, nodded, and moved behind Mannon. He could feel Risha watching him. But she said nothing. Instead, she drew herself up and walked away.

"She lied to me. She told me that she'd never hurt anyone else, and she still kept at her experiments," Mannon murmured. He looked at Del, who arched a brow and raised his hands.

"*You expected her to listen?*" he signed. He'd never asked how Mannon had convinced his tutor to teach him Water signs. Maybe the old man had just felt sorry for the mute. crippled child.

"Given the way we both know she's obsessed with me? I thought she would, yes." Mannon shook his head. "I'm an old fool is what I am. I should have never trusted her. Not when I know full well what she's capable of. How many more lives is the Mother going to hold against me, hm?" He tousled Del's hair. "Still want to go with me?"

Del's answer was emphatic, his movements crisp and sharp. "*I'm not staying alone.*"

Mannon nodded. "Then stay close." He turned and followed Risha, and Del saw his hand move to the hilt of his sword.

To Del's surprise, they left the healing complex and walked through the downpour and wind to a higher terrace. Risha led them into the tunnels, stopping just inside to light lanterns. They walked downward for a long time, finally passing into caves that felt damp and cold. He could hear dripping, and wondered just how far down they actually were.

"Where are we going, Risha?" Mannon demanded.

"You wanted Aven. I'm giving him to you," he answered, her voice clipped. "He's down below, in the old fishery. I thought it was the best place to keep a fish—"

"Woman, that's my nephew and heir you're talking about."

Risha stopped and turned, her eyes wide. "Excuse me?"

"No, I won't excuse you. I told you who he was and why I wanted him," Mannon replied. "He is Elcam's grandson, and my nephew. And he's bonded to the girl already. I intend to bring them both out with me. They are my future, Risha. You are not. And if you've harmed him at all, the Mother herself won't be able to save you from me. Now where is he?"

Risha paled. She spun and started walking again, her back straight. Mannon scowled and followed her. Del started after him, and stopped when he heard footsteps behind him. When he saw who it was, he turned and hurried to catch up with Mannon.

Being left alone was bad. Being left with Teva was... almost as bad.

They finally stopped in front of a heavy wooden door. Risha and Teva both tugged hard on it, and the hinges screamed in protest as the door slowly swung open. Risha gestured, and Mannon scowled. He walked in, and swore violently.

"Risha! What did you *do* to him!"

Horrified, Del pushed past Teva and into the room, and skidded to a stop inches from the edge of the walkway. He might have tipped over the edge if Teva hadn't grabbed his arm and pulled him back. He shook off Teva's hand and stared.

Mannon was already down the ladder, splashing through water up to his knees toward the single figure dangling limply from his wrists in the center of the well. For a moment, Del thought he was dead. Then Mannon reached Aven's side and raised his face; Aven groaned softly.

"He lived?" Risha gasped from behind Del. "It worked? Blesséd Child to come, it worked!"

"What did you do to him?" Mannon demanded. "Risha, *what did you do?*" The last time Del had heard that much anguish in Mannon's voice, it had been the day he'd come back to the Palace to discover what had happened to Del in his absence.

Risha didn't notice. She grabbed Teva's arm and burst into giddy laughter. "It worked!" she crowed. "I broke the cycle of the change!"

"You what?" Mannon roared. He scrambled back up the ladder and grabbed Risha by the shoulders. "What did you do?"

It was Teva who answered. "When removing the gills didn't work, we decided to try to break the cycle of the change by forcing the fish into it under circumstances where they can't finish changing. This room floods—"

Mannon went white, then red. He let Risha go, then stepped back. He glanced at Del, then looked back at Risha. "I want him out of here now. He's mine now, and you had better pray that he survives—"

"None of the others has," Teva volunteered.

"If he dies," Mannon said softly. "Then both of you do, too. What has this done to him?"

Risha cocked her head to the side. "If his injuries are in line with the others, then his hip joints have completely shattered. There is possibly some breakage to the leg bones. I can't really tell until I examine him."

"You're going to put him back together," Mannon ordered. She snorted.

"There's no healer alive who can," she answered. "But he's human now—"

Mannon started to draw his sword, only stopping when Del touched his arm. When Mannon looked at him, Del signed, *"We don't have time. He needs help."*

Mannon scowled. He glanced at Risha, who seemed to have only realized how much trouble she was in. Then he looked back at Del. "Later?"

Del snorted. *"Only if I can watch."*

That got a smile from Mannon, who resheathed his sword and stepped back. "I want him out of here, now," he repeated. "I want him on a litter and into a cart. I'm taking him back to the Palace."

"In this storm?" Risha asked. "We can make him comfortable in the healing complex—"

"I'm taking him to the Palace. I want him as far from you as possible. And I want the girl. Where is she?" He looked down. "No matter. Bring her to me. Unharmed, and with her wings intact. Am I understood?"

"Yes, but—"

"Woman, do not push me." Mannon growled. "I'm going to have a job of work to do to salvage this." He sighed and scrubbed a hand down his face. "Risha, you have developed an unfortunate habit of mutilating my heirs. It stops now." He shook his head and led Del out into the corridor. Del leaned against the damp wall, watching as Teva came out of the room and went sprinting up the tunnel. From inside, they heard machinery, and a loud cry of pain.

"Risha!"

"I have to lower him," she called back. Her voice was distant, and when Del looked inside, he didn't see her at all. She must have been in the well.

"We could leave her in there," he signed. *"It would be fitting. Chain her down the way she did to the others."*

"You're bloodthirsty," Mannon signed back, his motions choppy. *"Do you blame me?"*

Mannon shook his head. "Not at all." He sighed. "Aven will never forgive me. He'll think this was on my orders. He'll never hear me out now."

"I'll tell him otherwise. He'll believe me."

Mannon looked quizzically at Del. "You never did tell me what happened that night. Fandor said that he was secure, in a locked room. And the bastard left you alone for... what, ten minutes? Fifteen? Normally, that long being alone would have you in a state where it would take me hours to calm you down. Instead, I came back to find you completely fine, and him gone."

Del smiled. *"Maybe I'm getting better?"*

"Maybe you had something to do with him getting away?" Mannon countered. Del laughed, and Mannon snorted and reached out to ruffle his hair again. "If you went up to where he was being held, you weren't alone. And the guards said he couldn't have been gone for very long when I got back. So I repeat, you never did tell me what happened that night."

"I can't tell *you anything."* Del emphasized the gesture for 'tell' and Mannon laughed.

"Don't sass me, Del," he said. Then he looked up the tunnel and his face went serious. Del followed his gaze, and saw Teva running back, followed by several men. One of them was carrying what looked to be a rolled up litter, and Teva was carrying a crossbow.

"We have a problem," Teva panted as he reached them. "Terraces is under attack."

CHAPTER THIRTY-TWO

"FAN OUT!" PIRIT ORDERED. "Search everywhere! I don't want to see a speck of dust that hasn't been examined!"

Owyn took off running. He heard shouting behind him, but he didn't stop. The others, he knew, would be searching for prisoners. The cells, Pirit had told him, were in a wing off to his left. So he went to the right. He needed to find that theater. He tore open the closest door, and went in.

The room was wide, and he could hear screaming and crying coming from ahead of him. Another door, this one barred, and when he looked through, he saw two rows of doors facing each other across the corridor. More cells? Probably. And these, it sounded like, held the insane. So he kept going, heading for a door that led off to his right. He heard nothing coming from that direction, so he started walking, letting his whip-chain dangle from his hand. There wasn't enough room to really swing it, but even a short length of chain would do some damage at close range. The door wasn't locked, and he walked through and into the corridor.

Having the door being unlocked probably meant these weren't cells. He hoped. He wasn't prepared to have to defend himself against an innocent who was seeing things that weren't there. He peered through the window grating on the first door, saw an empty room. They were cells. But it was so quiet.

Maybe? He raised his voice, "Aria! Can you hear me? I'm coming!"

He didn't expect an answer. The surgical theaters in the healing complex weren't on the same corridor as patient rooms, and these rooms all seemed to be empty. But to his shock, he heard a voice answering him. A man's voice.

"Aria? Is Aria out there? Who's out there?"

"Where are you?" Owyn called back. He had a good idea who he was talking to, but it didn't hurt to be careful. "Bang on your door. I'm coming!"

A rhythmic thumping started, leading Owyn to the very end of the hall, and the last door on the right. He found himself looking at an older man. The bearded man he'd seen in his vision.

"I know who you are," he said. "Let me get this door open."

"That makes one of us," Jehan called back. "Who are you? Other than Aria's Fireborn."

"My name is Owyn," Owyn answered. "I know you're Jhansri. Jehan. And you're Aven's fa." He studied the lock for a moment. Keys. He needed the blasted keys.

"Is my boy with you?" Jehan asked. He grabbed onto the grating with both hands. "That bitch Risha wouldn't tell me anything when I woke up here, and no one comes unless I'm asleep. I haven't seen or talked to anyone in I don't know how long. Where's my son? Is his mother with you, too?"

Owyn had crouched to look more closely at the lock, and looked up at the question. "I... look. Aria is in trouble. Aven is in more trouble. We don't know what happened to his mother. I need to get you out of there, so where the fuck did they hide the keys?"

Jehan laughed. "Behind you. There's a hook. I can see them, but there's no way I can reach them."

Owyn stood up and turned around, and saw the ring hanging directly across from Jehan's door. "She's something, that Risha. I'm not sure what, but it's something," he muttered as he went and got them. The door unlocked easily, and Jehan stepped out into the corridor. He looked wild — ragged beard and unkempt hair, and a Waterborn kilt that had seen better years. The clothes he had been wearing when he was brought in, Owyn realized.

Without thinking, Owyn snorted. "You're going to frighten your ma, looking like that."

Jehan's eyes widened. "My mother? She's dead. They told me she was dead."

"She's leading this attack," Owyn said. "She's in another part of the building, looking for Aria. We think she's here — Risha was going to amputate her wings. She's in a surgical theater. Do you know where those are?"

Jehan nodded slowly. "I can find them. Who are you again?"

"Owyn, son of Memfis," Owyn answered. "Adopted son of Memfis," he added, when he saw Jehan's brows rise. "And he's missing, too. I don't think he's here, though. The vision showed him in too posh a place."

"You're a Smoke Dancer. And Memfis's son." Jehan shook his head. "I have so many questions."

"And we have no time for me to answer them," Owyn answered. "Which way to the theaters?"

AVEN WAS UNCONSCIOUS when they brought him out and laid him on the litter. Risha ordered him strapped down.

"Where are we going? And who would be attacking Terraces? I thought you said there were no rebels left? You told me you dealt with them all," Mannon asked.

"We're going out the long way, and I have no idea," Risha snapped. "I wasn't up there. Teva, what did you see?"

Teva shook his head. "No one I knew."

"Then how do you know that you're being attacked?" Mannon asked.

"I got shot at," Teva answered. He turned to face Mannon, and pointed to a tear in his sleeve, then tugged it open to reveal the graze beneath it. "It's windy, or I'd have been hurt."

Mannon nodded. "My men were waiting in caves at the northern tunnel mouth."

"We'll go by way of the stables," Risha said. "The stable passage feeds into the northern tunnels, and there are carts there. If we go quickly, we can be away—"

"We?" Mannon interrupted. "You're not coming with me, Risha. You're staying and fixing this disaster."

"I... you heard Teva! We're under attack!"

"And you assured me that you'd done away with all the rebels," Mannon said. "Which means that you should have no trouble putting down this little insurgence. I'll even leave you a squadron to help."

Risha's mouth opened and closed several times, making her look like a fish. Then she turned and snapped at the men. "Is he secure? Then let's go. The stables."

They started walking. Del stayed a step behind Mannon for a moment, then slipped on ahead and fell in next to the litter. Aven was quiet and still. He shouldn't have been quiet or still. He was too vital to be so quiet. There had been something compelling about him, even when they'd brought him into the house unconscious. Whatever it was, it had drawn Del out of his terror of being left alone. It had pulled him out of the kitchen where Fandor had left him. It had made him give in to temptation, and defy Mannon's orders. And regret not leaving when Aven asked him to go. Del hadn't seen Aven smile that night in Forge. He'd wondered ever since what it would look like. Would it reach his eyes? Would there be laugh lines?

He touched Aven's hand. They'd left him chained, and Del could see where the edges of the manacles had carved deep gouges into Aven's olive skin.

"Del?" Mannon called. "Come away."

Del looked back over his shoulder. He looked down, hesitated, then went back to Mannon's side.

Mannon tapped him on the shoulder, then signed. *"What is it?"*

"He shouldn't be so quiet."

"Mother of us all... Boy, did you go and fall in love with him? In one night?"

Del snorted. *"Me? Of course not."* He looked back at the litter. *"He was nice to me. He asked me to run away with him. He promised to come back for me. He thought I was a prisoner, too."*

"So you did have something to do with him escaping," Mannon said softly. "You scamp. I told you I wanted him."

Del's face grew warm. He looked down, then jumped when Mannon's arm closed around his shoulders. "I'm not angry," Mannon said, his voice still quiet. "As a matter of fact, I'm actually pleased."

"Why?" Del asked.

"Because you have never defied me before. You've been so afraid, and for so long, that you've never dared to do something that bold before. You did it for him, and I'm grateful." Mannon hugged Del to his side, then let go. "I'll tell him that myself, when he wakes."

Del swallowed. *"If he wakes?"*

Mannon scowled at the question. But he didn't answer Del. Instead, he raised his voice. "Risha, you said you had that brother of mine. Where?"

Risha answered without turning. "In solitary confinement in the green levels. Why?"

"Because I want him," Mannon answered. "We've never agreed on anything, but he's an immensely talented healer. He saved my life, and dozens of other lives, and he wasn't even fully trained. He may be able to undo the damage you've done. Send him to the Palace as soon as this place is secure."

Risha didn't answer, and Mannon's scowl deepened. "Risha, don't make me send men in after him," he said, his quiet voice barely carrying in the tunnels.

She turned, her chin raised. "Really, and what will happen if I disobey? Will you remove me?" she demanded. "What other healer will follow you? What other healer will the Earth tribe follow?"

Mannon smiled. "He's on the litter. You no longer have any bargaining chips, woman. Now take us to the stables."

They walked the rest of the way in silence. Teva moved from rear-guard up to the front, to walk with Risha. Del couldn't hear if they were talking, or what they were talking about. It worried him. The silence only grew more tense when they reached the stables, and Aven was loaded into the back of an open wagon. Del waited with Mannon while their horses were saddled, and while another was hitched to the cart. Risha drew Teva off to the side, then left him and came toward Mannon and Del.

"Teva will drive," she said. "If that meets with your approval?"

Mannon nodded. "So long as all he does is drive," he said. "He's not to pester Del."

"You think far too highly of your boy, Mannon," Risha said with a sniff. She looked at Del with contempt. "Honestly, he's far too insolent. Teva might teach him some proper manners—"

"If Teva touches my Del, Teva is getting thrown bodily from the cliffs," Mannon said. "Now make sure he knows."

"Oh, I hear you," Teva called. "What if he asks for it, though?"

"Teva—"

"Just asking!" Teva shrugged and shifted his crossbow. "I'm driving? Fine. Let's go. It'll be a long, wet trip."

Del touched Mannon's arm, waited until he had Mannon's full attention. *"I'm riding in the cart with Aven,"* he signed.

Mannon looked shocked. *"That puts you in arms reach of Teva."*

"I can fight back," Del replied. *"Aven can't."*

Mannon looked thoughtful. *"You think he's going to try something?"*

"I think we'll reach the Palace to find that Aven died somewhere en route." Del answered. He hesitated, then shook his head. *"No, I'm sure of it. I think you pushed Risha too far by saying he'll take her place."*

Mannon sniffed. *"Maybe. Maybe you're right. And you can fight back. Really. I'm growing more and more grateful to Aven by the second."*

Del swallowed and looked down, hearing Mannon chuckle. He pulled his cloak hood up and walked over to climb into the back of the cart, settling down next to Aven. There was a canvas cover draped over the cart, and Del arranged it to better protect Aven. As he did, a thought occurred to him.

If Teva had been given orders to kill Aven en route, there was nothing that would stop him from trying to kill Del, too. And for all that Del had said that he'd fight back, for all that Mannon had brought in weapons masters and fight instructors, Del knew that if Teva attacked, he wouldn't be able to defend Aven or himself. He looked over at Mannon, saw that Mannon was looking at him. Then, to Del's amazement, Mannon's hands moved.

"Do it. Save his life. You know where the south tunnels are. Look for Rhexa. She'll protect you." Mannon smiled slightly. *"I love you. Go."*

Del swallowed. He nodded once, then moved, clambering over the back of the cart onto the driver's seat and grabbing the waiting reins. He released the brakes, snapped the reins, and the cart lurched forward. No one was close enough to grab the horse, and the sudden escape stunned the grooms and the guards into immobility.

Except for one. Del heard a raised voice, a faint snap. Then something slammed into his right shoulder, hard enough that it nearly knocked him off the cart. If he could have spoken, he'd have howled in pain; instead, he gritted his teeth and kept driving, hearing Mannon's roar of fury behind him as he drove out into the storm.

JEHAN LED OWYN THROUGH corridors that must have led back into the caves — the walls grew rougher, and the floor slanted.

"Where are we going?" Owyn asked.

"Next turning," Jehan answered. He cocked his head to the side. "You hear something? Is that someone following us?"

"Sounds like... Marik?" Owyn raised his voice. "Marik? That you?"

"Owyn!" Marik came running down the corridor, and pulled to a stop when he saw Owyn wasn't alone. His eye widened. "You found him?"

"If by him you mean me, yes," Jehan answered.

"Tell me you found Aven?" Owyn demanded.

"I wish I could," Marik answered. "We found the room, but he was gone. They moved him."

"Fuck," Owyn breathed. "All right. We're still looking for Aria."

"The surgical theaters are this way, I think," Jehan added.

"They are. Gran tried to reach them from the other side, but the tunnel collapsed," Marik said. "I ran ahead to see if I could find you. She'll be glad to see you, Uncle."

"Uncle?" Jehan turned and looked at Marik, his eyes narrowed. "Marik, son of...?"

"Danzi," Marik answered.

Jehan snorted. "So she finally settled down?" He nodded. "Nice to meet you, Marik. Can we go?"

Owyn walked on ahead, and raised his voice again, "Aria! Can you hear me?"

Distantly, he heard a wail, "Owyn! Help me!"

He ran. He heard Jehan and Marik behind him, but they didn't matter. Nothing else mattered but Aria, who was somewhere ahead of him, screaming and crying, calling his name. He found the door, stared for a moment at the shiny lock that was keeping him from his Heir. He needed to open it. He needed the keys. He needed...

He turned, and burst out laughing. The keys were on a hook set into the cave wall opposite the door. He grabbed them, unlocked the door, and tore it open. The room was exactly the way he'd seen it in his vision, except that now Aria was awake. Awake and crying.

"Aria," he breathed, and ran to the table. He touched her shoulder, her face, ran his hand over her hair. "I've got you," he said to her. "It's over. You're safe. It's over." He repeated himself over and over as he fumbled with buckles and straps, aware that Jehan had joined him, was doing the same on the other side of the table. Finally, she was free, and Owyn took her hand and helped her to sit up. "Gently, love, gently," he said. "You're going to be stiff. I've got you." He helped her off the table, and suddenly she was in his arms, clinging to him, sobbing. He wrapped his arms around her and held tight, murmuring nonsense, watching as Jehan moved around the table and started going through cabinets until he found what he was looking for — a sheet. He unfurled it and brought it back.

"Aria," Jehan said gently. "It's over. You're safe now."

At the sound of his voice, she jerked, looking up and turning. Her face lit up. "Jehan! You're alive!" She blinked. "And... hairy."

Jehan grinned. "You're not one to talk about appearances right now, love. You're a little smelly. Here." He held up the sheet. "Let's get you covered, and we'll see if you're hurt."

Aria let go of Owyn. While Jehan helped her, he went to the door. Marik stood outside.

"You keeping watch?" Owyn asked.

"That, and... well, she's Air. Not Earth. I know the difference," Marik answered. "I haven't been invited. Not like you have."

Owyn nodded. "Thank you." He looked back into the room, then stepped out into the tunnel. Aria and Jehan followed him; Aria looked at Marik and gasped.

"Marik! What happened to you?" she asked.

"Teva went through me," Marik answered. "He lured me out of the way, beat the shit out of me, then killed my owls so they couldn't warn you. I'm sorry. I failed you, my Heir."

"Oh, Marik," Aria whispered. "I'm sorry. And you didn't. You were betrayed, too. We all were." She looked around. "Where is Aven? Did you find him?"

"Not yet," Marik answered. "We're still looking."

"Come on," Jehan said. "We need to get out of here. We need to get someplace safe." He looked at Aria and smiled. "And some of us need to get cleaned up."

She took Jehan's hand. "We'll find him. We'll be all right."

Marik led them through the tunnels and back into the corridors. Aria clung to Jehan, and Owyn followed behind them, trying to sort out his feelings. Shouldn't she be clinging to him? He'd found her. He was her Fire. Her warrior. But... Jehan had known her longer. Maybe he was some kind of a father figure? That was it. That had to be it.

But it didn't soothe the ache that worried at him. The gnawing, sinking feeling that he hadn't done enough, and that she'd turned from him. As they walked out into the storm, they heard shouting.

Owyn moved to stand with Marik, looking out over the Terraces. Down below, he saw armed guards leading a cart toward a group of people; he picked Pirit out at the front of the group. Sitting next to a guard in the driver's seat of the cart, his cloak soaked with blood, and his wrists bound before him, was the blond from Owyn's visions.

"Del," Owyn whispered. "That's Del." He turned. "I need to get down there."

"Who?" Aria asked.

"I've seen him in visions twice now. Back on the beach, and today when I was looking for you," Owyn answered. "He's important. I need to go down there. Marik, bring them down?"

"Go," Marik said. "We'll follow."

Owyn nodded. He ran for the stairs, realizing halfway down that Aria had said nothing else. He thought about going back, then decided against it. This was important, and Del was hurt. He raced for the growing crowd and shoved his way through, shouting, "Let me through! Let me pass!"

The crowd parted, and he saw Pirit and Rhexa staring at him. Rhexa met him halfway. "Owyn?"

"We found Aria," he said. "And Healer Jhansri. Marik is bringing them." He pointed. "Let me through."

"He's—" Pirit started to say.

"He's important," Owyn interrupted. "And he's hurt. Are you healers or not?"

Pirit sniffed and let him pass. Owyn drew his knife as he reached the side of the cart. Del looked at him, his face white with fear. Owyn smiled up at him.

"It's all right," he said. "I know you're Del. I'm Owyn. I'm not going to let anyone hurt you." He glared at the guard. "In case you didn't notice, he's got a fucking arrow in his back!"

"And a half-dead Water in the cart," the guard added.

"Aven?" Owyn gasped, and looked at Del. "You brought Aven out? You saved him?"

Del nodded, and Owyn reached up and neatly sliced the ropes binding his wrists. "Right. We'll take it from here. Pirit!"

"I heard," Pirit said, and started snapping orders. The canvas cover was moved, and Owyn saw Aven for the first time.

"Oh, fuck," he breathed.

"We'll do what we can for him," Pirit said softly. "Rhexa, I need Alanar and Treesi! And any other healer above a level three!"

"I'm in."

Jehan led Aria through the crowd. Pirit turned, and her jaw dropped.

"Oh. Oh, Jhansri," she sputtered. "We... you're getting cleaned up before I'm letting you anywhere near the healing complex."

"That goes without saying," Jehan answered. "Mother, I want to see my son."

"Of course," Pirit stepped back, and Jehan walked away from Aria and looked over the side of the cart. His expression went stony.

"Mother, when you find that bitch, she's mine," he growled.

"No, she isn't," Aria said. She came over to stand next to Owyn. "She is mine. For what she did to me, and to my Water, and to all of the Earth tribe, she is mine."

Jehan met her eyes, then nodded. "Yes, my Heir. But I want to help." He gestured to the guards. "We need a healer to work on this young man. But we need to get Aven stable now. Del, is it?" Del nodded. "Can you walk?" Del nodded again, and Jehan looked at Owyn. "Right. Catch us up, then. Owyn, help him down."

Owyn reached up and helped Del to the ground, and the cart started moving, rolling toward the ramp that led down to the healing complex. Aria looked thoughtfully at Del.

"You... I think you may be mine," she said softly. "I'd wondered. When I saw your picture— no, that's not important now. You need to be seen to. Can you walk?"

Del nodded, but stumbled when he started after the cart. Owyn caught him and steadied him.

"You don't weigh anything," Owyn said with a laugh. "You just lean on me."

Treesi was waiting for them in the healing complex doorway, and came running as soon as she saw them, hugging Aria first, then Owyn.

"You did it!" she squealed. "You found them!"

"I had a lot of help, Treesi," Owyn protested. She shook her head, kissed him quickly, then turned to Del.

"I'm Healer-in-training Treesi," she said. "And I'm going to do something about that shoulder. Come inside."

She brought them into the healing complex and into a treatment room right off the main lobby. Inside, she turned to a basin and washed her hands. Then she came back and ran her hands underneath the cloak. "All right. That should be numb now. Del, that looks like a crossbow quarrel. Is it?" Del nodded, and Treesi moved around behind him and examined the hole in the cloak. Then she came back around and smiled at him. "Looks like the hole was made by a square point. That makes this easier. Aria, if you'll stay over there? Thank you. Owyn, you're stronger than I am. Can you pull it out?"

Owyn nodded. "Yeah, I can do that." He moved behind Del and rested his hand on Del's left shoulder. "He's not going to feel this, is he?" he asked.

"I've numbed Del's shoulder. All he's going to feel is pressure," Treesi answered. She took Del's left hand in hers. "It'll be all right, Del."

Del smiled weakly and closed his eyes. Owyn squeezed his shoulder, then pulled the quarrel as hard as he could. There was a moment of resistance, and a sickening pop as it pulled free. Del winced.

"Good," Treesi said. She reached over Del's shoulder and took the bolt, examining the head. "Good. Good clean joining. This is going to be easy to heal. You'll be fine in an hour or two, Del. Now, let's get the cloak and shirt off."

Owyn helped Del strip off his heavy cloak, laying it aside to see if the garment could be saved. The blood could be soaked out, Owyn hoped. The shirt underneath was long sleeved fine linen, and had no buttons.

"I'm going to cut this," Owyn said. "I'm sorry, but I can't see how to get it off you without moving your arm."

Del nodded, and Owyn ran his knife up the center back of the shirt. The cloth parted easily, revealing Del's bare back... and the long, straight scars that ran from his shoulder blades to the small of his back. Aria gasped, and Owyn felt sick.

"You're Air," he stammered. "You... you had wings."

CHAPTER THIRTY-THREE

TREESI CAME AROUND the table and looked closely at the scars. "These are old. You were very young when this happened."

Del nodded, and made a gesture with his left hand. Owyn came around to stand in front of him.

"Do that again?" he asked.

Del repeated the gesture, and Owyn looked at Aria. "Water signs?"

Aria nodded. "It looks very much like what Aven showed to us, yes." She gnawed her on her lip. "Del, we've had no time to learn them. We do not know what you're saying."

Del looked from her to Owyn, his face clearly showing his distress. Owyn looked at Treesi, then blinked. "Wait. Can you write?"

Del grimaced and tapped his right shoulder. He winced, and Owyn laughed. "Sure. You're right handed. Yeah, I know that feeling. Umm... Treesi, how long before he can use that arm?"

"The healing is going very nicely," Treesi answered. She went to a cabinet, came back with a length of cloth that she folded into a sling. "Keep this on, and try to get some sleep. Healing should take two hours, maybe a little less. And in the meantime, try using your other hand, Del. Messy writing is better than locked inside your head." She smiled, reached out to cup his cheek. "You're safe here with us," she said. "And you're one of us." She looked at Aria. "Isn't he? He feels like it."

Aria licked her lips. "I... I think perhaps, but I am not certain. Treesi, where is Aven?"

"In the big surgical theater," Treesi answered. "Pirit told me to come there once I had Del settled. Ah... Owyn, why don't you take them to Alanar and my suite? You can rest and Aria can wash up. I'll see about clothes, but you're welcome to go through my things and see what I have that might fit you. And there are paper and pens there. Maybe we can learn a little more about Del?"

Del smiled. He caught her hand in his and kissed her knuckles, and Treesi laughed. "All right. Owyn, can you find your way?"

"I'm fine. Go. Let us know what's happening when you can," Owyn said. Treesi hugged him again, kissed him just hard enough to slow time, but not hard enough to stop it, then hurried out of the room. Owyn took a deep breath, picked up the blood-stained cloak, then looked at Aria and Del.

"Right. Let's go get lost."

In the end, he only made two wrong turns, and caught them almost immediately. Owyn let the others into the suite with a satisfied flourish. Aria and Del followed him inside, and looked around.

"That's Treesi's room," Owyn said, pointing as he set the cloak down on a chair. "That's Alanar's room. That's Aven's room, and that's the bathroom. Aria, you take as long as you need."

Aria moved slowly around the room, running her fingers over the surface of the table. "I... Owyn, I want Aven." She sounded close to tears.

Owyn swallowed. "I know. So do I. But we have to let the healers work."

She nodded, wrapping her arms around herself. "We thought it was you," she said softly. "In the corridor. We thought something had gone wrong, and you'd come back to the house. But it wasn't you."

"I wish it had been," Owyn said. "I might have been able to stop them."

"Or you might have been killed," Aria replied. "She didn't want you. She wanted me, and she wanted Aven. She wanted to save us, she told me." She hiccupped, then looked past Owyn. "Is that what she told you?"

Owyn turned to see Del standing behind him. Del shook his head, then looked around. He frowned, then mimed writing. Owyn nodded.

"Just a minute," he said, and went into Aven's room. He found a sheaf of paper, ink, and a pen, and carried them out to the table. He uncorked the ink, and handed the pen to Del. In blocky, unsteady letters, Del wrote, "*I was six. She told me I was a mistake.*"

"Mother of us all, why?" Aria breathed. "You and I, we're the same. You're Air and Fire, just like me. I can tell from your eyes. She didn't want to kill me."

Del shrugged his left shoulder, then wrote, "*Was in her way. Wants M. Killed Mother, tried to kill me. No proof except for me, and I couldn't tell for years. Law says M couldn't do anything without proof.*"

"M?" Owyn read. "You mean Mannon?"

Del nodded. "*Not slave,*" he wrote. "*Excuse so I can stay with him. Can't be alone, not ever.*" He gave a wry smile. "*Panic.*"

Owyn snorted. "Oh, I don't know a fucking thing about panic, do I?" he said to Aria. She didn't answer. There was an odd expression on her face.

"Del?" she asked. "Who was your mother?"

Del smiled. Then he wrote, "*Her name was Yana.*"

———— ❧ ————

TREESI HURRIED INTO the large surgical theater and went directly to Alanar's side. "What's happening?" She could see Aven on the table, pale and silent, covered with a sheet from his armpits to his feet. Pirit stood next to the table, her hand hovering over Aven's chest.

"Nothing yet," Alanar answered. "Pirit is stabilizing him, seeing the extent of the damage. I'm feeling a little ill. I've never had to work on someone I was close to before."

"We can't be working on him," Treesi protested. "We're not full healers yet."

The door opened, and Jehan came in. He had washed and changed, and had slicked his hair back. He nodded to Treesi as he came in. "Good, you're both here. We can start."

"Start... what?" Alanar asked. Jehan blinked.

"You're going to mesh your gifts with ours," he answered. "You're both over level three, Mother says."

"I'm fairly certain Treesi is capable, yes," Pirit said absently. "She's come along nicely. She might even be a four by now."

"We can assess later. So, come on."

"Mesh gifts?" Treesi said, feeling strangely out of sorts. "I—"

"She didn't teach you that?" Jehan interrupted. Then he groaned. "Of course she didn't. She's not a strong enough healer to master this skill, so she couldn't teach you. Come here. Crash course in advanced healing."

Treesi took Alanar's arm and led him to the table, then waited for instructions. Standing closer to Aven's battered body did nothing to ease her discomfort — she looked at him and wanted to cry. A hand settled on her shoulder, and she looked up at Jehan. He smiled gently at her.

"I know," he said. "We're going to do the best we can for him. Now, here's how we begin. Treesi, put your hand out. Alanar, put your hand on hers. Mother, are you leading this or am I?"

"I'll lead," Pirit answered. "I'm less... personally involved."

"He's your grandson," Alanar said weakly.

"Who I haven't formally even met yet," Pirit answered. "I've not yet had a chance to grow attached. So I'll have an easier time of hurting him to better heal the damage." She met Treesi's eyes. "Once we begin, your entire gift must be at my disposal. Once you know how to open to me, you must remain so for the duration. Do you understand? And do you have any reservations?"

"I understand," Alanar answered. "And I have no reservations. Drain me dry if necessary."

"Me, too," Treesi added. "Whatever it takes."

Pirit nodded. "Jehan?"

"All right," Jehan said. He laid his hand atop Alanar's. "Focus the way you would on your healing, but do not send the power. Let me take it. Try it now."

Treesi closed her eyes and opened herself to her gift, the way she'd been taught. The way she'd just done to heal Del's shoulder. She'd always thought of her healing as drawing from a pool, and that was the image she focused on — the glowing pool of pure water that she applied in order to heal the sick. She felt a stronger power surround her, and the familiar pull of healing leaving her hands.

"Good," Pirit murmured. "Very good. If you can, you both should monitor what I do. I hope you'll never have to use such knowledge, but it can't hurt to have."

So Treesi watched as the combined healing power of four healers slowly drew together the shattered bones and torn cartilage, knit together muscles and reformed tendons. There was something odd about Aven's left hip...

"What's wrong with his left hip?" Alanar asked. "It doesn't feel right."

Pirit was silent for a moment, and the power surged in response. "I see..." she murmured. "The femoral head is deformed. There's something... oh. Oh, he didn't..."

"Didn't what?" Jehan asked. Then he swore softly. "I told him not to! I told him never—"

"Given how much pain he must have been in, it may have been instinct," Pirit interrupted. "We'll see if we can't undo what he did here. But it may be permanent."

"He tried to heal himself?" Treesi gasped, and almost lost her focus on her healing. Alanar steadied her, and she whimpered. "Will he walk again?"

"Fuck that," Alanar growled. "Will he *change* again? Or did she cripple him?"

Pirit sighed. "I don't know. We won't know until he tries. Let's finish here."

The power surged again, pulling from Treesi, soothing the lacerations in Aven's wrists and hands, seeking out and burning away the beginnings of infection, and setting long-lasting healing spells in place to support the knitting bones. Finally, Pirit laid a healing trance over Aven and sighed. "That's enough," she said. "You can all release."

Treesi felt Pirit slip from the mesh. Then Jehan. When Alanar left her, she swayed, and would have fallen if two sets of hands hadn't caught her.

"Easy," Jehan murmured. "Easy. You've done a lot, Healer Treesi. Now it's time to rest."

She looked up at him. "Healer-in-training."

He smiled. "I meant what I said," he said. "Mother?"

"I quite agree," Pirit said. She leaned on the table, looking worn. "And you're definitely a four, my dear. Well done."

"Me? A level four healer?" Treesi laughed. "That can't be right. I'm backwards. I can't read or tell my right from my left without help!"

"Which doesn't impact your abilities at all," Pirit assured her. "And as for you, Healer Alanar. Well, it's nice to know that the Earth tribe will be in good hands when I'm dust."

Alanar frowned. "You're saying I'm a level five?" he asked. "And... me? Senior Healer? But, who'll follow me?"

"Anyone with a brain in their head," Jehan said dryly. "All right. Go get some rest. We'll move Aven to a room—"

"Use nineteen," Treesi blurted. When Jehan arched a brow, she felt her face grow warm. "He's used to the bed there. A little."

"I... someone will explain that to me later," Jehan said. "But nineteen it is. Someone will come and let you know once he's settled. Mother, have all your people taken shelter? It's still nasty out there."

"They've returned to the lower caves for now. Except for Marik, who will go and bring them up once it's safe. I'd like your opinion on his eye. I'm not happy with the way it's healing. Will you see to him, Jhansri?"

Alanar took Treesi's arm. "We're done here. Come on. Let's go."

"Owyn and Aria and Del are in our room," she said.

"Who?"

"I'll explain while we go."

OWYN PROWLED AROUND the room, unable to sit still for more than a minute. Aria had bathed, then disappeared into Treesi's room; when Owyn had looked in on her, she'd been asleep. Del sat on the couch, his legs folded and a book on his knees, reading. Someone had come with Owyn and Aven's bags, the hook swords and his smoke blades, but that had been the only outside interruption since Treesi had left them here.

There'd been no news on Aven at all.

Something growled, and Owyn jumped. He turned to see Del's face turning red. He laughed.

"Hungry?" he asked. When Del nodded, he sighed. "Me, too. I can go find us some food, if—" Del shook his head sharply, his eyes suddenly wide. "Right. No leaving you alone." Owyn slumped into Alanar's chair. "Aria is in the next room. That doesn't count?" Del glanced at the closed door, frowned, then shook his head, and Owyn nodded. "All right. Hrm…" He felt movement in his pocket, and grinned. "How about a fire mouse?" he asked, and coaxed Trinket out. She sat in his palm and chittered at him, and he laughed. "You could have stayed in Forge, you know," he told the mouse. "Where it was nice and safe and no one was trying to kill us. Well… all right. There was someone trying to kill us, but it wasn't all the time. And you were safe in the oven!" He glanced up at Del, who was staring. "Now, Trinket, this is Del. Del, hold your hand out." Del held out his hand, and Owyn poured the fire mouse into his palm. "Del, this is Trinket. She's a fire mouse. She won't bite you. She eats bugs, fruit and seeds. And she's probably hungry, too. Do you think she can stay with you while I go find us some food?"

Del looked startled. He stared at Owyn for a moment, then down at the fire mouse in his palm. He smiled, and nodded.

"Good!" Owyn said. He got up and came over to run one finger over Trinket's back. "She likes to hide. And she tickles, if she gets into your shirt. I think she likes it when she makes humans squeak." Del arched a brow, and Owyn laughed. "I know. You won't squeak. All right. I'll be back as soon as I can." He turned and headed for the door, opened it, and ducked to avoid being hit by Alanar, who had been about to knock. "Hey!"

Alanar gasped, then laughed. "Did you hear me coming?"

"Not this time, no," Owyn answered, and laughed as Alanar blushed. "No, I was going to go find food. But it can wait a minute. You're here. How's Aven?"

"Inside," Treesi said. She guided Alanar inside. "We're neither of us the attending healer, so we're not supposed to tell you anything, but he'll be fine. Mostly."

"Mostly? What does mostly mean?" Owyn stammered. "How can he be mostly fine? Isn't that like being a little bit pregnant? I mean, you are or you aren't. Fine, I mean."

Alanar chuckled. "Slow down, Owyn. We'll explain." He stopped, cocked his head to the side. "There's someone else here?"

"Del is here. I told you?" Treesi said.

"Right, you did. And he's mute." Alanar waved vaguely. "Hello. I'm Alanar, and we're going to have an interesting time." He passed a hand in front of his face. "Mute man, meet blind man."

Owyn heard a soft series of huffs, and looked to see that Del had tipped his head forward, and his shoulders were shaking. "You made him laugh, Alanar," he said.

"Oh, good. I'm useful," Alanar said. "There are too many people in here. Where's my chair?"

"There's only two more than you're used to," Treesi chided. She led him to his chair, then went and sat down next to Del. "May I check your shoulder?" Del nodded, and Treesi touched his arm. "Alanar, you start explaining."

Alanar nodded and leaned back in his chair. "Pirit and Jehan showed us how to work in concert. I didn't know healers could do that. It took all four of us to undo the damage. And... well, it looks like he might have tried to heal himself."

"He did what?" Owyn gasped. He came and perched on the arm of Alanar's chair. "He told us that healers aren't supposed to do that! That bad things happen."

"And in this case, a bad thing might have happened. What do you know about how hips work?" Alanar asked.

"Not much?" Owyn answered. He looked up as a door opened, and Aria came out of Treesi's room. She was wearing clothes that were both too big and too short.

"I heard voices," she said. "Aven?"

"Will recover," Alanar said. "I'm just not sure in what state. And we won't know until he wakes up." He held up both hands, made one into a fist, and folded his other hand around it. "This is basically what your hip looks like. The long bones of the thigh come together into what's called the femoral head, and it fits into the pelvis like a ball and socket joint. With me so far?"

"Yes," Aria said. She came further into the room and stood with her arms wrapped around herself.

"Healer Pirit thinks that Aven was in enough pain that he acted on instinct, and tried to either block the pain or numb the area. And it didn't work properly. He changed something in the shape of the femoral head, and it's not sitting properly in his pelvis. It doesn't feel to me as if it will keep him from walking, but we won't know for certain until he wakes up." Alanar started to let his hands fall, then reached up, grabbed Owyn, and pulled him down into his lap. Owyn yelped, then laughed.

"What are you doing?" he demanded as Alanar's arms tightened around him.

"Checking on you," Alanar answered. "You've been off doing crazy, dangerous things for hours, and I was worried."

"I'm fine. Hungry, but fine." He shifted, trying to get off Alanar's lap, but the healer held on more tightly.

"Pay a forfeit," Alanar said softly.

"Forfeit? Oh." Owyn laughed and kissed Alanar. "That enough?"

"Maybe," Alanar answered and loosened his arms. "You can owe me the rest. Ah... they've taken Aven to room nineteen."

"He's used to the bed there," Treesi said absently. She sat up. "Your arm is doing very well, Del. You can take the sling off."

"Aven is in nineteen?" Aria repeated. "Can we go and wait there for him to wake?"

"I think that's the plan, but we have to wait for them to get him settled, and most of the healing staff are still in the safe rooms," Treesi answered as she helped Del remove the sling. He stretched, then rolled his shoulder. Then he nodded. "So we can wait here for right now. Del, we need to find you a shirt." She looked up at Aria and giggled. "My clothes don't fit you at all. We need something better. Ah... one of Aven's kilts, maybe? I'm not sure what to do for a shirt." She nodded toward her door. "Let's go into my room, and I see if I can find something better."

Aria nodded and turned, going back into Treesi's room and closing the door. Treesi went into Aven's room, and Alanar tipped his head back against the back of his chair.

"Jehan says we're full healers," he said softly. "Me and Treesi both."

"Congratulations," Owyn said. "You don't sound happy?"

"I'm wondering if I'm ready," Alanar said. "I didn't know about meshing gifts before today. What else did she not teach us, because she couldn't do it herself? What else do I not know that I'll need to save someone's life?"

"Good question." Owyn looked up to see Jehan standing in the partially-open door. "The door wasn't closed," he added. "And that's a very good question. We'll see what you're missing, Alanar. I won't leave you with holes in your education."

Alanar turned. "Thank you. Come in. The rest of the way in."

Jehan stepped inside, closing the door behind him. He nodded as Treesi came out of Aven's room.

"We'll be ready to do whatever you need once I get Aria changed," Treesi said. "My clothes are too big in one dimension and too small in another. We're figuring something else out. Del, try this on. Excuse me?" She handed Del a folded shirt, then hurried past them and tapped on the door of her room, slipping inside. Jehan came over and leaned on the back of the other chair.

"Del, if your arm is up for a long session of sign, I'd like to know your history, please," he said. Del nodded, then looked over at the table and pointed to the paper and pen that still lay there. "Written is better. Go ahead."

Del nodded again. He set Trinket onto his leg and pulled the shirt on over his head. Then he picked Trinket up and stood up. The shirt was too long, and the sleeve cuffs hung down to his knuckles. He shrugged and handed Trinket to Owyn, then went to the table and sat down. For several minutes, the only sound was the scratching of the pen on paper.

"Now what?" Alanar asked. "Risha can't be Senior Healer anymore. Is Pirit taking it back?"

Jehan cleared his throat. "Ah... she won't take it. She says her fight is too important. So... it appears to be me."

"You're Senior Healer?" Owyn asked, sitting up straighter.

"With Rhexa to assist me, the way she used to help Mother," Jehan answered. "So once this storm is over, we'll assess the damage. Then we'll find all of Risha's followers and deal with them. And then..." He snorted. "My brother is not going to know what hit him when I'm done with him."

Owyn blinked. Then he remembered Aven telling him that his father and Mannon were listed as brothers in the Book of Silver. He nodded slowly. Then he closed his eyes. Alanar was warm, his arms strong, and Owyn was tired.

"We need to eat," Alanar murmured. Owyn nodded, not opening his eyes.

"We can bring food into room nineteen while we wait," Jehan said. "It'll be hours yet before Aven wakes up."

"Will he walk again?" Owyn asked. "Or change?"

There was a moment of silence, then Jehan softly growled, "Alanar."

"You really think I wasn't going to tell the people who love him that he'll live?" Alanar asked.

"In this one case, I suppose. The Companions do count as next of kin in a legal setting. But remember your oath. We do not discuss our patients, or patients who are not ours. Not without their express permission."

"Yes, Senior Healer," Alanar answered. He didn't sound at all contrite, and Owyn snorted. He opened his eyes and slowly got out of Alanar's lap, putting Trinket down on his chest. She immediately dove into his shirt, and Alanar yelped.

"Trinket!"

Treesi's door opened, and she came out, followed by Aria. Aria was wearing one of Aven's student gray kilts, and had a brightly colored something wrapped around her chest, covering her breasts.

"The scarf was the best we could do until we get back to Fourteen Southwest," Treesi said. "Can we go now?"

Del looked up and nodded, wiping off the pen and corking the ink. He stacked them, clearly planning on taking them with him when they left.

Jehan got up. "Right. Let's go."

CHAPTER THIRTY-FOUR

ROOM NINETEEN WAS CROWDED once they brought in enough chairs for everyone to sit around the narrow bed. Treesi had given Del a writing board to bring with him, and once they had all eaten, he sat in the corner with his paper and pen and ink. The sound of his pen was the only sound that broke the silence.

"Is he going to wake up screaming?" Treesi asked quietly. The sound of her voice made Owyn jump, and he twisted to look around. The storm seemed to be dying outside the window, but rain still pelted the glass, and it was impossible to tell what time it was.

"Why would he?" Jehan asked.

"He did when he woke up in the tunnels," Treesi answered. Jehan blinked.

"You never did tell me why he was familiar with the bed in this room," he said slowly. "Let's hear it."

Everyone turned to look at Owyn, who mock-scowled.

"Fuck you all. Individually and collectively," he grumbled, and Alanar chuckled.

"Promises, promises. Tell the story, Owyn."

Owyn took a deep breath. "Well, truth of the matter is your son has some really fucking awful ideas. But they're so crazy that they work. Almost..."

AVEN DIDN'T HURT ANYMORE. He wasn't sure why. Everything had hurt, and he'd been certain he was going to die. But now... he was warm, and nothing hurt. He couldn't feel his legs at all. And he was certain that he heard Owyn's voice.

"So that's it. It was a crazy idea, and it almost got him killed. But it worked."

"I'm not sure which impresses me more. The fact that he even thought of something that reckless, or that he actually did it."

He was dreaming. He had to be dreaming. That couldn't be—

"Fa?" His voice sounded broken to his ears. He tried to open his eyes, feeling as if they were full of sand. He blinked, blinked again, and recognized the ceiling. The healing complex. Room nineteen. He must be dreaming. It had all been a dream. He hadn't been tested. He hadn't moved into the student residence. He hadn't finally shared Aria's bed. That had all been a dream, one that had fed into a nightmare. Then a face moved into his view, and he blinked again.

Not a dream. He'd never dreamed a beard onto his father!

"Fa?" he repeated. "You're not dead?"

Jehan grinned. "Neither are you. I'm glad to see you, Ven."

Aven smiled slightly. He blinked more sand from his eyes. Then he frowned. "I can't feel my legs," he said softly. "Fa, I can't feel my legs!" Panic started to rise like the tide. If he hadn't been dreaming, then it had happened. It had really happened. His legs—

"You have a spinal block," Jehan said, his voice firm. "While the healing spells work. I'll remove it if you calm down."

Aven swallowed. "I still have legs?"

In answer, Jehan hauled Aven up to a sitting position, and he saw the outlines of his own legs through the sheet. He relaxed enough to look around... and see Aria standing next to the bed. Owyn stood behind her, with Treesi by his side. And... where had

Del come from? He focused back on Aria, who looked pale and lost.

"Aria?" he said. He held his arm out. "I'm sorry."

She burst into tears and threw herself into his arms, hard enough that Jehan couldn't keep them both upright. Aven fell back on the bed, with Aria on top of him, and he just held her as she cried. Over her shoulder, he could see Owyn, coming closer, going to his knees next to the bed. His hand was warm on Aven's shoulder. Treesi came around the other side of the bed, taking the place that Jehan ceded to her, and ran her fingers through Aven's hair.

"We're all here," she murmured. "We'll be all right. We'll heal. All of us. We'll be all right."

Aven nodded, closing his eyes. They were all here. They were all safe. "We all came through all right?" he asked. He ran his hand down Aria's back, feeling the base of her wings. She still had her wings. Risha had failed.

"For varying values of all right." That came from Alanar. "The important part is that Risha is gone. She's not going to have a chance to hurt you again."

Aven nodded. He rubbed his face against Aria's hair, then closed his eyes. "I want the block off. I want to know how bad it is."

"It isn't," Jehan said. "Except that you might have broken rule one."

The others moved, shifting so that Owyn could help Aven to sit up. "Broken rule one? Healed myself? I didn't!"

"Mother thinks you did it by instinct," Jehan said. "Oh, and yes. Your grandmother Pirit is very eager to get to know you."

Aven blinked. "I thought she was dead?" He looked up at his father. "Where's Ama?"

Jehan took a deep breath. He ran his fingers through his hair. Then he shook his head. "I don't know. I pushed her overboard. I thought she'd follow you. If she didn't, and she's not here, I don't know."

"They're still searching the green levels, aren't they?" Treesi said. "Maybe she is here, and we just don't know yet?"

Aven bit his lip. He looked at Jehan, and knew that the same thought had occurred to his father. Was probably haunting his father. If his mother had been a prisoner in Terraces, Risha wouldn't have taken her to the green levels. She'd have been taken to the room that flooded.

"So, you want that block off?" Owyn asked.

"Please. Fa, what did I do? When I broke rule one?" Aven leaned into Owyn's chest. He looked over his shoulder and smiled. "Thank you, Mouse."

"Any time, Fishie," Owyn answered, and kissed his cheek. "Aven, do you want me to stop calling you that?"

"From you, it's not an insult," Aven said. He looked at his father. "What did I do?"

"You changed the shape of your left femoral head. I'm not sure how it's going to move in the socket, and we won't know until you try to walk." Jehan rested his hand on Aven's knee, a touch that Aven didn't feel. "And I have no idea how it will impact your change. We'll find out."

Aven nodded and closed his eyes. "Do it."

The feeling in his legs came back in pins and needles first, and he winced. As they faded, they were replaced with the little aches and twinges that came with extensive healing. And one sharp pain in his left hip. He winced and shifted.

"It hurts," he said. Jehan frowned, then looked slightly unfocused.

"We'll have to see if we can reform that," he said at length. "Mother said she'd do some research into just how. It'll take a little time, but we have that time. No one is going anywhere until spring."

Aven nodded and shifted again, then looked around. Del had joined Alanar at the foot of the bed. He was wearing a shirt that was far too big for him, one that Aven recognized from his own closet. He had a stack of papers clutched to his chest, and his eyes were wide. He laid the papers down and started to sign, "*Mannon told me to get you away from her. We were going to take you to the Palace, but I thought Teva might try to kill you before we got there. So I... took you.*" He dropped his gaze. "*I've never done anything like that before.*"

Aven's jaw dropped. "Wait. Mannon told you to take me? Wasn't this his idea?"

Del's answer was emphatic, "*No! He was furious! He banned this ages ago, when he found out what Risha had done to me, and to other Airborn. I couldn't tell him until years after she took my wings and left me to die. I was six. I didn't write, and I didn't know signs.*"

"You're Air?" Aven said. "Well, I suppose that answers that." He glanced at Aria. "Did you know he was Air?"

"I knew," Aria said. "He wrote things down for us."

"Wait. Mannon told you to do this. But you're still a slave, and now you're a runaway," Aven said. "That's not going to end well and you know it."

Del laughed. "*Mannon isn't my owner. Mannon is my father!*"

"What?" Jehan gasped. "Did I just read that wrong?"

Aven licked his lips. "Mannon," he repeated slowly, "Is your father?"

Aria jerked in surprise. "What?"

Del nodded. He set the sheaf of papers on the bed in front of Jehan. "*It's all there.*"

"Del's mother is Yana, Aven," Owyn said softly. "The last Heir."

"And now he's our Air," Treesi said. "Isn't he? Aria?"

Aria had been very quiet, ever since Aven had sat up. She lowered her head, staring at her hands. Then she squared her shoulders and stood up.

"No," she said, her voice shaking. "No, he is not."

"Aria!" Aven gasped. "He is! We all feel it!"

"He is not!" Aria insisted. "I refuse him. I will not have him by my side. I will not have one of Mannon's blood by my side or in my bed." She stalked out of the room, slamming the door behind her.

Aven felt her words like a blow. He stared at the door, trying to understand what had just happened. Why it felt as if his entire chest had been ripped open, when there wasn't a single drop of blood on the immaculate white sheet.

"Aven," Owyn whispered. "Fishie, she... she didn't mean it. She's upset. There... there's been a lot happening. She needs to calm down. I... let me go find her. I'll get her calmed down. We'll talk. You'll see. She doesn't mean it." Aven nodded slowly. Owyn kissed him and got up. "Treesi, come help me?" he asked, and the two of them left.

"I... I'll leave you and your father alone," Alanar said. "I should probably check on the rest of the patients. There were no rounds today, and the children are probably frightened. Senior Healer, if you'll excuse me?"

Aven nodded, then looked up. "Did they take my things? From the house?"

"No," Alanar answered. "Owyn kept your bag. It's in our room now. Should I put it on your bed?"

"Yes. Yes, please." Alanar left the room, and something that he'd said registered. Aven turned to look at his father. Jehan had picked up the papers that Del had left on the bed, and was looking at them. He looked up when Aven asked, "Senior Healer?"

Jehan shrugged. "I'm the ranking healer," he said. "And I have no place else to be. So I'm it."

Aven nodded. He closed his eyes, trying to think. "Fa—"

"She didn't mean it, Ven," Jehan said gently. "It's like the pool all over again. Once she calms down, she'll realize she's wrong." He held up the papers. "Mind if I read these?"

"I didn't write it for fun," Del signed. Jehan laughed and stood up.

"I'm going to look in on Mother, and see if I can find Rhexa. You rest, and I'll be back." He tucked the papers under his arm and left. Del came and sat down on the bed, facing Aven.

"What do you need me to do?" he signed.

Aven swallowed. Then he signed back, *"Help me up."*

ARIA HEARD THE DOOR open and close, and heard Owyn's voice. "Aria?"

"I'm here," Aria called back. She stamped her foot into her boot and came out of her room. Owyn was at the end of the corridor, soaking wet and furious.

"That was a new fucking kind of stupid," he thundered at her. "Do you even realize what you've done?"

Aria stared at him for a moment. "I..."

"You told me yourself. You can't refuse the Mother's choice. Del is it, like it or not."

"I won't have him!" Aria insisted.

"And you won't have Aven, either," Owyn snapped back. "Do you realize what you said?"

"I..." Aria stammered. She frowned and closed her eyes, trying to remember exactly what she'd said.

I will not have him by my side. I will not have one of Mannon's blood by my side or in my bed.

Her heart fell into her boots, and she opened her eyes to see Owyn nodding at her. "You got it, didn't you?" he asked. "You just threw Aven away. He risked his fucking life for you how many times? And you threw him away!"

"I.. I didn't!"

"He's Mannon's nephew! He's Mannon's blood, and you knew it!"

"I forgot," Aria whispered. "Mother, I forgot he was."

"You forgot," Owyn scoffed. "Well, everything will be all right now, because you forgot!" He pointed at her. "You are going to haul your ass back to the healing complex. You're going to make this right. I don't know how, but you're going to make it right." He glanced to the side, and Treesi moved into view. She looked unusually serious.

"How?" Aria asked. "How do I fix it?"

"You're going to have to ask Aven," Treesi answered.

They walked back to the healing complex through the rain, and made their way through the halls to room nineteen. Jehan was waiting outside, and turned to glare at them.

"Tell me you've seen Aven," he demanded.

Aria went very still. "He isn't in there?"

"I wouldn't be asking that if he was," Jehan snapped. "I just got back. He's gone, and Del is gone. Where would they go?"

"Our suite?" Treesi offered.

"Fine. Let's go look there."

Between them, Owyn and Treesi got them to the room on the first try. Aria walked in, and knew immediately that the room was empty. She raised her voice anyway. "Aven? Aven, I'm sorry." She brushed past Jehan and went to the room Owyn had told her was Aven's. It was empty, but a flash of blue caught her eye.

On Aven's desk was the Water gem. And nestled next to it was a single, flawless gray pearl.

———— ⟲⟳ ————

PIRIT STUDIED THE TWO young men in front of her. "You want to what?" she asked, not sure she'd heard them correctly.

"Leave," Aven answered. "I need to go." He looked at Del, then back at his grandmother. "Don't ask me why."

"Whatever it is, it's killing you. I can see that. It's not safe for you to leave yet. You're not completely healed," Pirit answered. "And where would you go?"

"Home," Aven answered. "I need to go home. I need a canoe. I need supplies. I need to go. And... I need your help. Grandmother, we only just met, but I have no one else to turn to."

Pirit nodded. "You want to go back to the waves. And Del? I assume you want to go with him?"

Del signed, then shook his head and pointed at her desk, and the papers there. She passed him one, and a pen, and he wrote neatly and quickly, *I'm going with him. We'll figure out the rest later.*

"Very well," Pirit said slowly. "Let me make some arrangements. Aven, what do you want me to tell your father?"

"Nothing," Aven answered. "Not until tomorrow after the tides change."

"Are you sure?"

Aven looked at her, and his eyes held more pain than she thought was possible. "Grandmother, I'm not sure of anything anymore. That's why I need to go. I need to find myself again."

It took several hours, but finally she saw her grandson off, safe in the care of his cousin. Once the cart had rolled out of the stables, she made her way back to the healing complex.

She needed to tell her son something that he wasn't supposed to know, and caution him to act as though he didn't. At least, until after the tides changed tomorrow.

CHAPTER THIRTY-FIVE

AVEN'S AUNT DANZI HAD been amused to learn that she had a new nephew who was a year older than her own son. Marik had brought Aven and Del to his mother's house, and had left them there. He'd assured them that Danzi would see them outfitted, and she had. Now Aven slipped another bag of provisions into the storage compartment and closed the hatch. He got to his feet slowly, feeling the unending ache in his hip. He hadn't tried to change yet. The idea made him slightly nauseous.

And yet, he was going back to the sea.

He could still go back to Terraces. It was an option. He could go and be a healer with his father. Try to make a life that didn't include Aria. Which, wasn't really an option. She was his life. She was his Heir... and she didn't want him. So, he'd go.

"Del, did you get the sweet water casks?" he called over his shoulder.

"If he didn't, I'll get them."

Aven turned and nearly fell. His father stood by the hull float, Owyn by his side. Aven stared at the both of them for a moment, then said the first thing he could think of, "I'm not going back."

"I wasn't expecting you to," Jehan said. "I came to say goodbye. And Owyn figured out that I knew more than I was telling, and came with me."

"You didn't say goodbye," Owyn said softly.

"Because I can't stay, and you can't come with me," Aven answered. "I'm going out to the deep, Owyn. You can't follow me."

"I can go with you so far," Owyn said. He pointed to his waist. "This deep. I've been working myself up for it."

"I..." Aven sputtered for a moment, then realized what Owyn was saying. "You know I haven't changed yet."

"I figured. I thought, if I went with you, it might help?" Owyn smiled, but it looked like brittle, broken glass. He held his hand out. "Come on, Fishie. I want to see you swim."

Aven stepped clumsily down from the canoe and took Owyn's hand, seeing Del go to stand with Jehan. Jehan turned, his hands starting to move, but Aven missed the signs as Owyn led him down to the water.

"Are you sure, Mouse?"

"Are you?" Owyn countered. "About this? About leaving? She's really upset about what she said."

"She really meant it, too. She doesn't want me because of things I can't control." He grimaced. "It sort of makes her no better than Risha."

"Ouch," Owyn winced. "Ah... yeah. I'm not telling her you said that."

"You can tell her, or not." Aven looked out at the water. "Are you ready?"

"Are you?"

Aven snorted. "Fine. Let's go."

They walked slowly out into the water. Ankle deep. Knee deep. Hip deep, and Aven felt Owyn's heart rate spike. "You don't have to keep going," he said.

"I said waist deep. I mean it."

Another few feet, and Owyn was waist deep in the water, shaking like a leaf. Aven turned to face him, then leaned forward and kissed him. "I'm sorry I didn't say goodbye."

"You're coming back, aren't you?"

Aven bit down on an answer, let his legs go out from under him, and slipped under the water.

His chest grew tight, the way it always did when his gills opened. But this time, there was an odd burning sensation that went with it. He stretched out underneath the water, feeling his legs starting to fuse. A hand plunged underneath the surface, and Aven grabbed on to Owyn as his bones reformed and his legs became a tail. As the change finished, he pressed a kiss to the back of Owyn's hand and let go, swimming into deeper waters, feeling the sharp ache as he flipped his tail to gain speed. It hurt, but not as much as walking did. He went deeper and wondered — could he still do it?

Down, down as deep as he could, then flipping his tail and shooting to the surface like an arrow. He shot out of the water and arced through the air, hearing Owyn crowing with delight as he splashed back down. It hadn't been painless... but it wasn't impossible, either.

He could still change. He was still Water.

And Risha, he thought as he swam back to Owyn and escorted him back to the shallows, could go fuck herself.

Changing back was just as uncomfortable, and he winced as his gills closed and burned. By the time he had feet again, Jehan and Del had joined them in the shallows.

"How was it?" Jehan asked. Aven slowly got to his feet.

"It hurt, and my gills burned. I think there might be some damage to them. But it's not terrible. I can still change."

"And do acrobatics," Jehan added. Aven smiled.

"And do acrobatics." He looked out over the water. "The tide is changing. We need to go."

Jehan nodded. "Take your season. Come back in the spring."

Aven swallowed. He held his hand out. "Thank you, Fa."

Jehan stared at his hand. "Really?" He grabbed Aven's hand and pulled him into a tight embrace. "The Mother go with you, Ven. I'll see you in the spring."

"We will see you?" Owyn asked. "No going under to get out of answering. You are coming back?"

Aven took a deep breath. Looked down at the water. "I don't know, Mouse."

AVEN GUIDED THE CANOE alongside the larger one, and held it steady while Del threw a line across. Finding the family canoes had been more trouble than he'd been expecting — they weren't in their usual range, and he'd finally found them in waters that were much closer to shore than he was expecting. Why had his grandmother brought the canoes here?

Well, he'd find out shortly. He took in the sail and made sure the lines on their end were secure, then gingerly made his way across to the larger canoe. He recognized some of the faces, knew that they probably knew him, but there were formalities.

"Aven, son of Aleia, of Arana's canoe, of the line of Abin and Axia," he announced. "My companion is Del, son of Yana, of no canoe. I need to speak to the clan mother."

"We've been expecting you, Aven, Aleia's son," a familiar voice called, and a man stepped forward. Aven grinned.

"Othi," he greeted his cousin. "You're looking good."

"And you look like chum, Ven. We've heard your name on the waves. You're doing the Mother's work." He frowned. "You're limping."

"Doing the Mother's work isn't without risk," Aven answered. He didn't want to answer questions about why he was limping. Not yet. Not when it was more interesting to know that the canoe was talking about him, and in a positive light. "I need to speak to Grandmother. Will she allow it?" He looked up at Othi, and realized that there were two half-healed parallel cuts on Othi's left cheek. Mourning stripes. Two deaths in the family. Two important deaths. "You... mourning stripes? Othi, is Grandmother dead?"

Othi nodded. "The last storm. The Mother's Rage, we've been calling it. It's why we're here, and not in our usual waters. We were hit pretty bad. Took half the family canoes, took Grandmother, and my mother."

"Aunt Jisa, too?" Aven gaped at his cousin, feeling Del's hand warm on his back, offering silent support. "Othi, is Neera clan mother now?"

Othi looked back over his shoulder, then stepped out of the way as his younger sister approached. She had grown since Aven last saw her, and was as tall as he was. She was dressed simply, the only mark of her rank the necklace that the stories said dated back to the first canoe, the first clan mother. Her mourning stripes were on her shoulder, as was appropriate for a woman. She nodded at her brother as she passed, then approached Aven. Before he knew what she was doing, she moved in close, rested her hand on his right shoulder, and pressed her forehead to his. Aven felt her breath, warm on his face, and started to shake.

"Welcome home, cousin," she said as she straightened. Her eyes narrowed. "And that was too much for you, surprising you like that. You can introduce your friend later. Come with me. We have a lot to talk about."

Numbly, Aven followed Neera to the big shelter built beneath the upper deck of the canoe. She led him inside, closed the curtain, then turned and gave him a sheepish smile. "I'm sorry," she said softly. "I shouldn't have surprised you like that."

"You recognized me as family," Aven whispered. "No one—"

"We're going to be fixing a lot of mistakes," Neera interrupted. She moved to sit down, and Aven followed, carefully lowering himself to the ground. His hip protested, and he grimaced and shifted until he was a little more comfortable. Neera watched him, but said nothing until he was settled. Then she smiled. Not at him, but at Del.

"I'm Neera," she said. "Welcome to our canoe."

Del smiled and started to sign, and Neera's brows rose. She glanced at Aven, who chuckled.

"I didn't teach him. He had a tutor."

"Well, you can tell me who later," Neera said. "It's nice to meet you, Del. Be welcome. Now, tell me everything."

"You first," Aven said. "I think yours will be shorter than mine. Clan mother?"

She nodded. "Years and years before I thought I'd ever be ready," she said, her voice full of mingled wonder and pain. "Mother— no, what Mother said and thought isn't important. I wasn't ready. I'm still not ready, and it's terrifying. I spend a lot of time asking myself 'What would Aunt Aleia do?' This should have been hers." She swallowed and looked around, then reached for a pitcher and poured the contents into two cups, one of which she handed to Aven. She used a second pitcher to fill another cup, and handed that one to Del. Aven sipped his sweet and salt fruit juice, then frowned.

"How did you know I'd have someone with me who needed sweet water?" he asked.

"Stories first," Neera answered. "I'll finish mine. I ask myself a lot what Aunt Aleia would do, and the answer is undo the wrongs that Grandmother did. So I announced to the clan that when you returned, we were going to be welcoming you as a full member of the family. You can have your tattoos whenever you like. Since we were already hearing about you, there weren't any objections."

"What were you hearing about me?" Aven asked.

"That Aven Waterborn stands at the right hand of the Heir to the Firstborn, a woman of Air. Not very much else," Neera answered. "So now it's your turn."

Aven swallowed. He set his cup down — his hands were shaking, and he didn't want to end up covered in fruit juice. "It started when we saw a ship from our island," he began.

He talked, and talked, until his throat felt sore and his eyes burned. Neera didn't interrupt. She didn't ask questions. When he recounted what Risha had done to him, and to countless other Waterborn, she paled and covered her mouth with her hand. But she said nothing. Finally, Aven held his hands wide.

"And now she's sent me away," he said. "She says she won't have me by her side because of my bloodline. Because I'm his nephew. I've lost everything." He looked back at Neera, and his voice cracked. "I don't know what I'm supposed to do now!"

Neera was next to him in an instant, holding him as he cried tears that had been a long time coming. Distantly, he heard the susurration of the curtains opening and closing, but it didn't matter to him who saw him. Not anymore. He had nothing left to lose.

He cried until he felt like he was drained dry. When he finally sat up, Neera wiped his face with her thumbs and handed him his juice. "Drink that. I wish I had something stronger."

"I might not come out of the bottle," Aven said with a hiccup. "What do I do now?"

"Now?" Neera cocked her head to the side. "You heal. You've been through so much. You take the time to heal. You're home now. And you have your Del."

Aven nodded. He glanced at Del, who had fallen asleep somewhere during the telling. "I still have him. He followed me onto the waves. I don't know why."

"Maybe because he loves you?"

The voice went through Aven like a spear, and he twisted in his seat to see a figure in the shadows. She stepped forward, and he choked out the word, "Ama!"

Aleia smiled. She looked older. Tired. "Welcome home, Ven."

"Ama... how..." Aven looked at Neera. 'You could have told me!"

"She asked me not to," Neera said.

"How did you get away from them?" Aven asked. "Fa... he doesn't know you're alive! He thinks you're dead. He thinks that Risha tortured you to death the way she almost killed me!"

Aleia's jaw dropped. "I didn't know *he* was alive!" she gasped. "I thought they'd killed him. I knew I'd never be able to find you in Forge without being caught. So I came back. I had just gotten here when the storm hit." She sighed.

Aven nodded, then asked, "Why aren't you clan mother, then?"

"Because I didn't want it," Aleia answered. "No matter that Milon is dead, I'm a Companion. My responsibilities are to the Heir, not just to my tribe."

"Aleia has another role," Neera answered. "One that she is far better suited for."

Aleia smiled. "War leader. The canoes are united, Aven. We rise to fight for the Heir."

Also by Elizabeth Schechter

The Rape of Persephone
Fools Rush In
Her Captive
To Market
Infernal Machine
Chains of Light

Watch for more at elizabethschechterwrites.com.

About the Author

Elizabeth Schechter has been called one of the top erotica and alternative sexuality writers in the world. Her writing credits include the award-winning steampunk erotic romance *House of Sable Locks*, the Celtic fantasy *Princes of Air,* and the dystopian fantasy *Rebel Mage* trilogy. Her shorter work has appeared in anthologies edited by D.L King (*Carnal Machines*), Laura Antoniou (*No Safewords*), and Cecilia Tan (*Jingle Balls*; *Like a Prince*).

With *Written in Water*, the first in the *Heir to the Firstborn* series, Elizabeth is exploring new ground, with her first new adult romance that was written entirely in real time on Patreon.

She was born in New York at some point in the past. She is officially old enough to know better, but refuses to grow up. She lives in Central Florida with her husband and son.

Elizabeth can be found online at http://elizabethschechterwrites.com, or on Facebook at https://www.facebook.com/Elizabeth.A.Schechter. You can also find her on Patreon, at https://www.patreon.com/EASchechter.

Subscribe to Elizabeth's newsletter at https://www.subscribepage.com/k4u7k2

Read more at elizabethschechterwrites.com.